M. Laszlo lives in Bath Township, recluse, rarely seen nor heard. *Anastasius ....* is his third release and second with Alkira Publishing. Rumour holds that Laszlo is a pseudonym inspired by the character of Victor Laszlo in the classic American film *Casablanca*.

ANASTASIA'S MIDNIGHT SONG

M. LASZLO

ALKIRA
PUBLISHING

Anastasia's Midnight Song
M. Laszlo
Copyright © 2024
Published by Alkira Publishing, Australia
ABN: 32736122056
http://www.alkirapublishing.com

ISBN: 978-1-922329-76-9

What songless tongueless ghost of sin crept
through the curtains of the night,
And saw my taper burning bright, and knocked,
and bade you enter in?
—OSCAR WILDE
'The Sphinx'

To R. S.

I.

Saint Petersburg, Russia. 27 August 1917.

At dusk, Anastasia T Grace collected the urn containing her mother's ashes and brought the vessel to Moskovsky Prospekt Railway Station. 'The cremation services went well,' Anastasia whispered, holding the urn close. 'You've been purified by fire, and now I'm taking you to be blessed by water. *Baptised.* Yes, Mama, I'll sprinkle your remains all about the Arkhangelsk shore.'

A memory of their first journey to the White Sea whirled Anastasia back to the past—that time her mother had described Arkhangelsk as a harbour town. And in the days of 1907, that was all it was.

So, why did we travel there? A lady from the House of Fabergé asked Mama to meet a steamship out of Reykjavík. Yes, Mama aimed to collect a consignment of volcanic glass.

The hissing and shunting of the train brought her back to the present. *It's 1917.* Clutching the urn containing Mother's ashes, she pulled herself up into the train. Then she edged along the narrow passage and slid into the sleeping car. She placed the urn beside the bed.

With a rumbling of the wheels and a piercing whistle, the train set off on the long journey to Arkhangelsk.

Late in the night, as the train approached a deserted outpost and clanked over a section of the line lacking proper railway ties, Anastasia jerked awake. Sitting up, she looked to her lap and revisited that first journey, a decade ago, that moment the engineer had jammed on the brake and she'd been shaken awake as she had just now. *What had happened that night?*

The train had shuddered to a halt then, too, but her mother slept on, her gentle breathing soft in the darkness. Turning to the door, Anastasia had sensed an ineffable presence stirring to life outside in the passageway.

I remember it as a scrabbling sound, an uncertain footfall— the rustle of a Tibetan fox struggling onto its hind legs. Did I see it? Did anything happen at all? That was such a long time ago. What a dreamful night, too. When I arose from bed, was I sleepwalking? She fussed with her nightdress, running her hands over the handwoven linen. Powerless to sleep, she stared at the cabin door. *That night, all those years ago, what happened to me?*

Slipping out of bed, she'd gathered all her courage and opened the cabin door, drawing back, startled. Standing before her was a little bald girl bundled up in a sleek fur coat. A silvery brooch—in the shape of a diadem spider—glinted from the lapel.

'Are you a ghost?' the young Anastasia said.

'Yes, I'm Svetlana, and I've come to groom you and make you ready for your secret admirer.' The girl's brooch transformed from silver to the colour of high-tin bronze. 'My,' she said, 'but you're more beautiful than the Grand

Duchess Anastasia.'

'Who are you? What's this all about?' As Mother murmured in her sleep, Anastasia studied the ghost girl's face. 'Who are you? Where did you come from? What's your purpose in appearing before me this way?'

The ghost girl shifted to the side, revealing three piercings in her left ear. 'It's hard for me to say. I work for someone very powerful.' She stole down the passageway, and no matter how awkward her gait, her bare feet made no sound.

'Come back here!' Anastasia called out, her voice wavering. 'Tell me why you knocked on my door.'

'Come along,' Svetlana told her. 'This way.' She trotted off to the very end of the sleeping car.

A moment later, as Svetlana dissolved through the door in the way ghosts do, Anastasia looked to her feet. 'I'm only dreaming,' she told herself. 'Could it be a waking dream?'

Mother stirred in her sleep and whispered something unintelligible. Had she become lost in visions of her own childhood? Anastasia studied her awhile. Mother had fallen asleep with her eyes open. How anguished her expression, too. Had the architecture of her dreams offended her?

With a trembling heart, Anastasia advanced into the passageway. Once she had closed the cabin door, she tiptoed along—until she reached the caboose, where she joined the ghost girl outside on the landing.

What a splendid Arctic summer: the midnight sun bathed the tundra in a soft-orange haze, the wildflowers alive with a scent not unlike that of Belorussian honey cake.

What had happened? She remembered a rosefinch fluttering by, one of the sensual creature's crimson feathers falling onto her shoulder before sailing off on the warm, steady current. *Then what? Did I happen to notice anyone about? There might have been a hunting party off in the distance. No, I was all alone, just me and . . .*

Svetlana reached into her coat pocket and removed a little wooden flute with which she performed a prayerful tune—Mussorgsky's 'Hebrew Song'. When the ghost girl completed the solemn piece, she poked Anastasia's arm. 'Do you know why the train stops here?'

'*No.* Tell me why.'

'Ask the conductor and he'll tell you that we stop here only so that we don't collide with one of the trains out of Finland. But that's not so.'

'No?'

'No, not at all. In truth, we stop here only because the Arctic fox *compels* the engineer to stop here. Yes, for this would be the place where the Arctic fox prefers to climb aboard and prey upon hapless little girls. Just like he preyed upon *me . . . .* last summer.'

Anastasia pointed at the railway tracks then. 'Look around. There's no Arctic fox anywhere. I'm sure we're all alone. It's just you and me.'

'No, he's here. It's just that he's chosen to render himself invisible.' As the train rolled forward, the ghost girl smiled. 'Well, I suppose you'll evade the terrible fox this time around. Still, whatever you do, you shouldn't come back this way.'

'But we *must.* Back at the House of Fabergé, the bookkeeper and everyone else, they're waiting for Mama to bring them a box of volcanic glass. The House of Fabergé; they hope she'll fashion something great with it.'

As Svetlana offered an indifferent shrug, the train's steam trumpet bellowed.

Yes, rather mournfully. Anastasia's thoughts drifted back to the present. This time, she found herself all alone in the carriage. She fell asleep and did not awaken again until the train pulled into Arkhangelsk. Grabbing the urn containing Mother's ashes, she disembarked. Passing the trainmaster's office, she wandered into the quiet harbour town. *To the White Sea, we go. Yes, Mama, I'm off to scatter your ashes upon the waters.*

Anastasia stopped beside a little gooseberry garden. A decade earlier, a minstrel with a barrel organ had stood here, the street performer cranking out the tune to that felicitous number 'Ta-ra-ra Boom-de-ay'.

Mother had motioned to her then. '*Venez, chère,*' she said, before taking her hand and guiding her down to the waterfront.

Later, as Mother paced back and forth before the customhouse door, Anastasia studied the cotton grass growing wild about the shoreline. Had the Arctic fox concealed himself there? Spotting an array of wooden crates stacked by the dockworkers into the shape of a truncated pyramid, she climbed to the top. Her jaw set, she stared at the various merchant vessels and whaling ships but saw nothing unusual.

After a while, the customhouse sergeant happened along. 'Have you come for the hog bristles?' he asked Mother.

'No, I've come for the volcanic glass.'

'*Oui. Je me souviens. La maison Fabergé.*' He unlocked the door and guided Mother into the building.

Smiling at the memory, Anastasia lifted her face to the summer breeze. As the whistle of the soothing current resounded like a well-written coda, she opened the urn containing the ashes and scattered Mother's remains upon the wind and water.

When the urn was empty, Anastasia gazed upon the customhouse. *I remember the very moment Mama showed me the volcanic glass.*

Mother opened the box, and young Anastasia knelt to study the bag of glistening, black shards. At once, she imagined the volcanic glass to be the remains of an Arctic fox—its broken bones.

'*Pourquoi pleures-tu?*' Mama asked the moment Anastasia melted into tears.

'*Pourquoi?*' Anastasia scrambled back to her feet but then bowed, defeated. 'Don't let's travel home by train,' she said. 'Let's climb aboard a ship, and we'll sail somewhere far away, maybe *Alexandria.*'

'What's all this?'

'Listen, Mama. Last night, an airy spirit told me not to journey home the same way we came.'

'You had a nightmare, that's all.' Mother unclasped the braided-wheat chain from which a Huguenot cross and pendant dove dangled. 'Wear this piece,' she said, 'and it will preserve you from any and all wicked spirits and whatever more you dream up. *Je vous promets.*' Three times over then, Mother tapped her beloved pendant dove.

Yes, I remember that. Anastasia fingered the Huguenot cross Mother had clasped around her neck so many years before. Anastasia remembered her ninth birthday, the moment Mother had pointed at the necklace.

'We aren't just any Huguenots,' Mother said. 'No, our matriarchs were always free-thinking Christian mystics, the kind the Chair despised and often burned at the stake. That's why the Holy See never ceased to persecute us, and that's why our kind had no choice but to take refuge in Russia.' Mother had wept then.

In the evening, Anastasia trudged back from the shore in time to catch the very same train just as it pulled out. As she sat in the club car, she again thought back a decade. *In the night, the ghost girl reappeared in the sleeping car. Yes, her eyes shining like sardonyx. That's right.*

Svetlana grabbed Anastasia's arm and sought to pull her into the passageway. 'We've very little time,' she whispered. 'Any moment now, we'll reach that place where the fox wills the train to stop.' The ghost girl drew a deep breath. 'You foolish Huguenots never should've taken refuge here in Russia.'

'But we had no choice,' Anastasia said. 'Back in those days, the seventeenth century, everyone in Paris conspired to destroy us.'

The brakes shrieked, and the train tramped along by degrees.

'So, have we reached the spot?' Anastasia asked her.

'Yes,' the ghost girl answered. Her breathing shallow, she clasped her palms together. 'We've reached that spot where the engineer has no choice but to stop, and should you fail to close the caboose door, the Arctic fox must climb aboard. And he'll speak to you with . . . *une voix superbe, divine, et . . . so seductive and . . .'*

Anastasia followed the ghost girl down the long passageway and onward through the caboose.

Sure enough, the back door stood ajar. Had the conniving fox already commanded it to open?

Outside, the nighttime breeze pulsated with the scent of fresh, wild Arctic willow—and a herd of reindeer galloped off through a field of blinding-white Arctic poppies.

The ghost girl folded her arms across her chest. 'What do you suppose alarmed all those reindeer? A hungry wolverine? Sure, that's all it was.'

Anastasia grabbed hold of the rusty knob and pulled and

strained every muscle in her body—until she could barely breathe. All her efforts proved futile, though, for the hinge screws had plainly come loose: the door sagged so badly that the bottom rail could not clear the landing.

Svetlana cursed the midnight sun hovering within the topaz blue of the Arctic sky, and then she grinned. 'Come aboard,' she said, addressing some unseen entity. 'Leave the barren poppy fields behind. Come, my master. Pillage all that you desire.'

Anastasia hugged herself. 'No! Go away, whoever you are. Go away!'

A presence as of a warm vapour crept up onto the landing, the strange entity swirling all about the brake wheel.

As Anastasia gripped the rusty knob to steady herself, the invisible being bumped up against her left leg—and as the warmth of his pelt radiated through her, she heard the steady, insidious, nonmetrical beat of his heart.

And just what did Svetlana say to me in that moment, or did the heartless ghost girl say nothing at all?

Young Anastasia let go of the knob and reached down to stroke the creature's delicate, invisible back. She took his long pointed muzzle into her hand in an attempt to charm him. At the time, the gesture seemed like a good idea. She removed her hand. 'Please be friendly,' she said. 'Find someone else to be your quarry.'

A sinister noise caught her attention: the Arctic fox slowly, methodically, ground his teeth.

Coming back to the present, Anastasia staggered to her feet and left the club car. *All those years ago, how could I touch and hold and caress something so primitive, so bestial, so wicked?*

8

~

29 August 1917.

The train pulled back into Moskovsky Prospekt at dawn, at which time Anastasia arose from her bed in the sleeping car. She slipped into a ruffled-top gown, packed her overnight bag, and disembarked. Squeezing her eyes shut against the smoke, she thought of the dream fox. *Where could he be these days?* When she was a little girl, the entity had come to dwell somewhere inside her—so now she rubbed her belly. 'Awake.' All those years ago, she had believed the creature could hear. And like a girl with an imaginary pet, she would contrive his response. For a moment, she longed to revert to her girlhood game of make believe. 'Let's talk and quarrel and tease one another, like we did before. *No.* Console me, won't you?'

When the dream fox finally stirred to life, the creature laughed and screamed and yelped the way foxes do.

'Please speak to me.'

'What would you have me say?' The creature's low, smoky, breathy, throaty, husky voice resounded inside her head.

Had she ever heard such a seductive tone? Until that moment, she had expected the creature to sound fatherly, but no. For the longest time, she tapped a section of her overnight bag against her knee. 'Explain yourself. Were you friend or foe? Tell me why I always believed in you. In times bygone, what did we talk about? My growing sexuality?'

'We spoke of this and that. Concentrate. It's already coming to you.'

'Honestly?' She wondered if the fox had a faint Persian accent. 'Tell me more. Did you help me with all my confusion? Do you remember the way I always studied and doubted my

9

body? At times, I couldn't think of anything else.'

'Little girls always brood that way. They wonder if they'll be good enough for a beautiful creature like me. But now you're a woman, and you're comely enough. So, learn to be bold and womanly.'

'Tell me something. What made me so sick? Why did I dream you into being?'

'Maybe the death of your father scarred you. Could it be you loved him so? Plenty of little girls feel that way. Meditate on memories of your father, what you thought of him, the way he made you feel. Remember how you envied your mother, her power over him.'

'Do you know something? I'm bereft of late. Yes, Mama's gone, and I'm all alone. And maybe that's why the hysteria has me in its grips again.'

Deep inside her womb, the dream fox called out in an admixture of Russian and French.

As the thick grey smoke of the railway station swirled all around her, she dropped her hands to her sides. 'Did you know my father was a British diplomat? He even had close family ties to George V, Emperor of India. Talk to me in English, the way my father taught me to do.'

'If that's what you want.'

'Why did my father have to die all those years ago? Do you know? Did you know he died not three weeks before Mama and I travelled to Arkhangelsk? Yes, that must've been what brought about my delusions, my habit of hallucinating you.'

A soft explosion resounded: a passenger train had only just arrived from Moscow, the engine car hissing.

As a third locomotive's steam trumpet reverberated, Anastasia made her way over to the wooden bench. There she sat and contented herself to watch the hot smoke drifting about the platform.

After a long while, as the last thin wreath of exhaust dissolved not three inches from her left foot, she ran the tip of her thumb across her eyebrow. *What shall I do with the rest of my life? Have I any purpose or calling or charge? Why do I exist?*

The hustle and bustle of Moskovsky Prospekt grew steadily more intense—people disembarking, boys and girls darting this way and that, the various porters trundling steamer trunks along the platform.

She felt at the contours of her cheeks and fussed with her gown's ruffled top. Placing her hand on her belly, she hugged herself. 'Why did you have to make so much trouble for me way back then?' She trembled all over, for she knew the answer. *When I was a little girl, my own loneliness made me susceptible to fantasy. And that's why I brought the fox back all these years later. Loneliness. Isolation. Friendlessness.*

Deep inside her womb, the dream fox stirred. 'A creature like me could never harm anyone.'

'No, you sought to manipulate me. And I was so young. Just a little girl.'

'But you were a sensuous girl back then. With golden hair and big blue eyes. Like a noblewoman. Yes, and you conspired to make others adore the little freckles on the tip of your nose. You wanted me to think they're so faint they'd disappear the next time you powder your face with your little wool puff.'

Her nose wrinkled. Anastasia glared at her belly. *If only I had a real friend.* Sneering, she approached a nearby caboose and peered into the window.

What a sad, austere space. The train car happened to be empty but for a cast-iron *cuisinière*, a cracked washtub, and a rusty ladder reaching into the cupola.

She fixed her gaze upon the washtub. Once more, she revisited the past. All throughout the days of 1907, she had bathed herself in the dolly tub in the hope that she could rid herself of the dream fox—its uncanny presence, its indescribable stench. *I'm sure I only ever harboured mixed feelings about him.*

Deep inside her womb now, the fox whistled. 'Are you daydreaming? Does it please you to recall the past? Think back to the night you espied me for the very first time. Did you think my coat looked lovely in the glow of the midnight sun?'

She sneered again. *How do I get free of this confounding creature?* She clenched her fists.

At her back, fragments of conversation resounded: a passenger lamenting the fact that she had lost her daughter's baptismal gown in one of the sleeping cars; another passenger wondering if someone had purloined the item; yet another passenger wondering if the guilty party might be that poetess from Gothenburg, Sweden.

All the intrigue made Anastasia's hands shake. In a world where thieves seize upon little girls' baptismal gowns, who would ever pity someone like her? Looking to her feet, Anastasia departed Moskovsky Prospekt and traipsed along through the streets of Saint Petersburg. *Where do I go now that I'm all alone?* In truth, she had no living relations who might help her. To the best of her knowledge, she had no family other than her godfather—Vadim Dementieva. What good was he, though? He had gone quite mad many years before. As the summer breeze played through her fringe, she tapped her overnight bag against her knee. *What if I'm no less deranged than my tragic patron?*

The summer breeze grew steadily stronger, until the current pushed her forward.

Once more, she fussed with her gown's ruffled top, pulling at one of the fabric strips, until she tore it. *I've got to convince myself that the fox was never anything more than a harmless figment of my imagination, the stuff of hysteria, the feelings that puzzled me as the curves of my body grew.* She continued along through the streets, only to stop before Slobodanka Julian's famed art gallery.

In the window, the director had displayed an oil canvas depicting a company of fallen soldiers from the Cadet Corps— their bodies lying along the bank of the River Dnieper.

Anastasia fixed her gaze upon a lone, leather, Russian Army boot—the kind her father once wore. The art gallery's lights flickering, she studied the canvas a little bit more closely and imagined the locale to be none other than Arkhangelsk—a battle scene from the Crimean War.

Deep inside her womb, the dream fox kicked. 'What are you doing? Are you thinking about the past? The train journey?'

'I think you ought to leave my body.'

'No, how should a dream fox leave you? Am I not a part of you? Yes, I am . . . unless you convince yourself I never existed. Go on, then. Try.'

She looked at the clouds. *I've got to move beyond the past. I'm not a little girl anymore. Already, I'm nineteen years of age.*

The rest of the day dragged on, the fox howling.

Nighttime arrived, and though the Arctic sun proscribed any pall of darkness, the skyglow itself made her shudder. *I am the darkness, the profanity, the terrible thing that has no right to be.*

31 August 1917.

Anastasia strolled back down to Moskovsky Prospekt and loitered there for the better part of the day. At dusk, the Arctic sun shone brightly—but even so, she intuited the presence of evil. *Yes, someone has only just arrived. A stranger. And he's ogling me.* She looked down and rubbed her belly. 'Do *you* feel anything?'

'Yes. Someone approaches, a person with no conscience. And do you know what that means? It's someone who only ever blames others. Never the self. No. The stranger, he insists he should never be responsible for his actions. Even when he slips into his killing trance.'

With nowhere else to go, she raced back to the Huguenot Quarter. As usual, the French-language street names on the signposts made her blush and feel warm. The names reminded her that she was not a proper Russian woman. *No, I'm something alien.* Her body upright and her hands in a relaxed fist, she raced along. Only when she reached her doorstep did she pause to catch her breath.

'Don't go inside,' the fox told her. 'How devastating it should be to enter an empty house. So disagreeable.' The fox scampered about inside her womb. 'Do you even feel strong enough to bear the solitude?'

'But I must go inside.' She studied the townhouse façade's neo-Gothic design and even reached for the pointed arch that crowned the door. When she dropped her arm, she continued inside. In the foyer, she tapped on her belly. 'Keep me company,' she pleaded.

The creature failed to answer. Had the miserable thing

gone lost in fitful slumber? For a moment, the fox made a snoring sound—the kind a little girl sometimes makes.

Anastasia continued down the hallway. In the sitting room, she paused before the wall and studied a watercolour depicting a magnificent, Icelandic fjord—the waters frozen over as if by some mysterious, indomitable, polar vortex. *So, did I elude the stranger? What if he followed me here? Am I alone?*

When she continued upstairs to her mother's room, Anastasia grabbed a memory book from the shelf. She leafed through the pages and studied a photograph of her mother as a dour-looking little girl. *Why did Mama always insist on pouting?* Anastasia knew the answer: Mother had rarely ever grinned due to her high lip line and gummy smile. *Yes, that's right.* Mother had always sought to conceal the alleged imperfection. *No, Mother was no more complicated than that.* Anastasia rolled the tip of her tongue over her gap tooth.

Deep inside her womb, the dream fox hissed. 'Do you think you're something more beautiful than your mother? Yes, you think your gap tooth must be a sign of good fortune, a mark of God's favour. How foolish, though. Yes, we've got to secure this house before the stranger arrives. If he makes his way inside, there would be no escaping him.'

'What do you think he wants?'

'For all we know, he wants to destroy us. And afterward, he'll conceal any and all evidence of his having been here. Yes. Why should the stranger care to preserve the integrity of the crime scene?'

She attempted to ignore all. Once more, she studied the photograph—until the dream fox brushed its tail against the lining of her womb and made her shiver. She tiptoed downstairs and placed her ear against the door. Her hands jerking, she listened for the sound of footsteps. When she thought she heard something, she raced through the house and locked the windows. Finally, she sat before the lone painting in the sewing room—a view of the Sinai Peninsula. *I'm safe now. I'm not even here. I'm there in that lovely desertscape.*

An hour or more passed by, and she tormented herself with all kinds of ideas as to who might wish to trespass upon her that night. Repeatedly, she entertained the notion that a whole skulk of dream foxes schemed to force their way into the house that very night.

Late in the evening, as she wandered the unlit halls, she stopped before the coat closet and thought back to a newspaper report concerning a band of fiends that had climbed in through someone's window. According to the article, the scoundrels committed the most unspeakable crimes against the woman of the house and her children, too.

At nine o'clock, as Anastasia sat on the staircase, the fox grew still. 'The stranger, he's already here. Yes, he's inside the house. Soon, you will perish. Death by blunt trauma.'

'No, you just wish to unnerve me. There's no one about.'

'Maybe he'll take you away from here. Yes. The crime of abduction. Then, after weeks of torture, he'll destroy you and place your body in a shallow grave.'

At bedtime, Anastasia could not sleep. Just as she had done earlier that evening, she wandered the dark passageways. 'Why do you tease me?'

'Would I do that? I'm sure the killer must be here. Perhaps your death should prove to be but the beginning of the stranger's reign of terror. He'll tell everyone so. Yes, he'll write it all down on a leaf of paper and send it to the detectives for no other reason than to taunt them.'

After a while, she heard something outside. *Was it footfalls?*

Her heart pounding, she stopped at the guest-room window and looked out across her mother's garden. In the darkness, it seemed as if someone had toppled the birdbath. *I wonder if the murderous scoundrel has crushed the little rapunzel. Yes, he's probably destroyed that solitary bellflower.*

The dream fox shook his tail. 'Maybe the detectives should solve the caper someday. They'll find the killer's knife. And then they'll study his lip imprints, their distinctive ridges up and down the hilt, just there where he held it in his mouth.'

The nighttime breeze sailed through Mother's garden, but the bellflower barely made any movement at all.

'Someday, one of the poor girls should live just long enough to help the foolish detectives,' the dream fox said. 'Yes, she'll make a dying declaration and name the killer.'

From somewhere outside, a trio of instruments—it was a pump organ, a piano and a flute—played a selection from Goudimel's '*Sonate pour Flûte et Piano*'. The music seemed too loud; discordant, too, and arrhythmic.

Anastasia closed her eyes and imagined a horse dancing to the tune right here in the guest room. *Yes, Mama's childhood pony. The one she named Arkady. He's come back to . . .*

The growl of the pump organ or melodeon or whatever it was droned to a halt, and then the piano changed key before falling silent. A moment later, the flute offered one last tweet.

As the night grew quiet again, Anastasia opened her eyes and returned to the sewing room. For five minutes or more, she studied the desertscape. *What a peaceful place, Sinai.* She let out a remorseful laugh, for she knew perfectly well what a violent place Egypt had become. Time and again, she had read newspaper articles concerning the Egyptian people's bitter struggle to emancipate themselves from the British Empire. *Everyone longs to be free. No, I'm not the only one.* She shook her head and exhaled.

Outside the sewing-room window, something stirred: it might have been the neighbour's dog, but who could say for certain?

As the Arctic fox snickered and squealed and barked, she lay down on the floor and curled up into a ball. *Sleep.* She slipped into unconsciousness and became lost in vivid dreams of Sinai—the barren mountains, the moonlit wastelands, the picturesque villages looking out over the Red Sea.

She awoke to a shriek that sounded like the shattering of mirrors. 'Was that you? Why did you wake me like that?'

'Because I forgot to tell you something,' the dream fox answered. 'I wanted to tell you that in a world as perilous as ours, we do not have the luxury of retreating into puerile fantasies to indulge our emotional scars. No, we must never let our guard down.'

As the fox stretched out in her womb, she lay back down on her side. How soothing was his presence inside her. She wondered if the sensation might be the same as the feeling of sexual congress. Her body growing warm, she kicked her feet and laughed like a mature, experienced, sensuous woman— someone shamelessly overcome with absolute erotic fantasy.

II.

The Village of Al-Hubu, the Wilderness of Sinai.
1 September 1917.

Jack arrived at the seaside village late that afternoon and continued down to the beach to set up his campsite.

The accommodations looked less than impressive. Truly, it was nothing more than an expanse of coarse black sand streaked with a dozen or so pieces of yellow coral. If not for his two steamer trunks standing to the side, who would even recognise the plot of land as someone's home?

The wind whipping into his face, he sat in the sand and winced. By night, the current would be much too cold and much too harsh. He contemplated the Gulf of Suez—and as he did, he sought to think of somewhere better to lodge. *I bloody well got to go somewhere.* He peered in the direction of the Red Sea and decided to stay put. *I got no place to go.*

With the sea breeze whistling across the desolate shore, he debated whether some violent, incomprehensible impulse possessed him. Back home in Bloomsbury, he had already detected the presence. *Maybe it's me fate to descend into madness until I don't know what's real and what's delusion. And then I'll transform into something monstrous.* Now he lay in the sand and contemplated the clouds directly above. *What caused me aberrations? Maybe it was something natural, something like the chemical science of me own psyche.*

At midday, he slouched into the village—a modest jumble of hostels, hotels, Christian chapels, handicraft shops, elaborate villas, storerooms, banks, restaurants, a post office, and an array of gardens filled with medicinal plants. What a beautiful place: the locals had constructed almost every building out of an ethereal pale limestone. No matter the beauty, though, the vast majority of the locals seemed bitter and distraught.

They resent British imperialism. And why wouldn't they? He wandered the crowded marketplace but could not bring himself to engage with others. His loneliness only made him question his sanity that much more. Whenever he did manage to say something, there could be no disguising his glum mood. Time after time, he spoke in hushed tones—or else he mumbled. More often than not, he grew so tongue-tied that the other person eventually pulled a face and walked away.

No matter how odd the locals found him, and for that matter, no matter how much the people rued the British Empire, he had good reason for living in Sinai: if he had not sailed away from England, the War Office would have conscripted him. And how would he have survived the Great War, the trenches? He was nothing like the fit youths of the day. For one thing, he had always had an artistic temperament. As a child, he had lazed about the house. All day long, he would study his little tin soldiers and imagine them lying dead on some battlefield. Lately, he had developed the habit of listening to his gramophone and losing himself in melancholy daydreams.

One afternoon, his father called him into the study. 'I can't let a poor thing like you take part in the Kaiser's War. And you'll not have to do so neither, lad. It all comes down to the fact that I've made some good investments in the motor trade, haven't I? That's why we got options, places for you to take refuge. So, I'm sending you off to Sinai. And when you get there, you'll tell everyone a good fib. Say you're *exempt* from conscription. Make everybody believe you aim to attend divinity school. That's right, you'll tell everyone you aim to take to the pulpit someday, just like the chaplain-general himself.'

A few weeks later, on his eighteenth birthday, Jack brought his things down to the Port of London and boarded a vessel bound for the Red Sea. 'Fare thee well, River Thames.'

During the voyage from England, he did not speak to anyone. On the first few nights, he had contented himself to stand at the gunwale and ponder the stars. The glorious spectacle did nothing to cheer him—even if the various constellations might have filled anyone else with great elation. He registered no such inspiration. *No, I'll rejoice only if I catch a glimpse of something rarefied. Like a nova flare shining alongside the star Rigel, or maybe a few of the Jovian planets falling out of their orbits, or any number of deep-space phenomena, perhaps even some sign of the metagalaxy itself.*

When nothing happened, he cursed his luck. For the rest of the voyage, he sat in a deckchair. All bundled up in his duffle coat, he belted out one of the vulgar songs of the day:

> *Do your balls hang low?*
> *Do they dangle to and fro?*
> *Do they swing in stormy weather?*
> *Do they tickle with a feather?*

Most of the time, he gazed at his deerstalker, where it lay in his lap. As he did, he thought back to his failed audition before the Royal Academy, not six months before. *What a bloody debacle that was.* A bundle of nerves, he had not performed to the best of his abilities that fateful afternoon. And much more than that, he should have played something proper. Instead, he had performed the first piano piece that he had ever composed—'Midwinter Memory', a peculiar, polytonal, overwrought work with far too many ghost notes. Moreover, even if the vulgar, repetitious piece had been good, which it was not, and even if he had played it masterfully well, which he had not, the audience must have missed just about every last one of the quiet parts. *Ghost notes indeed.*

By the time the ship berthed at Port Said, he had grown so exceedingly morose that he had ceased washing himself.

The next day, the second of September, Jack boarded an omnibus bound for the Red Sea shore. All throughout the long desert journey, though, what a frightful, alien landscape it was. Over and over, he played in his mind a series of melodramatic, descending piano chords. *I should've gone into hiding somewhere closer to home. What about the Isle of Wight? Been there on holiday, haven't I? Plenty of places to hide. That's right. What about King's Quay?*

Given how noisy was the crowded marketplace, Jack's thoughts drifted back to the matter at hand. *I wonder if any of them shopkeepers might be able to sell me a ridge tent? That'd be perfect for me encampment.* He found a promising-looking shop but did not go in, for he did not know how to haggle. Talking to himself, he dragged his weary body along.

Down by the post office, he sat with his face buried in his deerstalker and recalled the inappropriate missive he had sent to the Royal Academy not two weeks after he had received the rejection slip. For ten pages, he attempted to defend his peculiar brand of music. On page eight, he had alluded to some of the great experimental operas—including *Tristan und Isolde*. Without a shred of evidence, Jack argued that Wagner had learned to write the notorious, atonal act after having heard Cosima Liszt's pussycat darting across the fortepiano's keyboard one summer afternoon. Suffice it to say, no one from the Royal Academy had even troubled himself to vouchsafe a reply.

When Jack finally looked up from his hat, he watched a few beautiful girls walk by, but did nothing to engage them. Back home, he had never spoken to anyone. If only he looked better, perhaps then some of the girls might have approached *him*—and one day maybe one or two of them might have even offered him a lock of her long fine hair. In truth, though, there was never any danger of some comely girl embarrassing him in such a manner. As it so happened, he did not look good. Indeed, on two separate occasions, two different acquaintances had told him that he resembled a callow, youthful Paganini. As a matter of fact, he did resemble a callow, youthful Paganini. Moreover, just like the celebrated musician, Jack had always been both exceedingly gaunt and bloodless. Even now, he could not have weighed in at more than ten stone.

As Jack departed for the shore, an Englishman stopped him. 'Why you wandering about the Oriental bazaar?' the stranger asked. 'What're you doing here, you gobby blighter? Are you bloody mental? Did you maybe come here in a fugue state?'

Jack made no response. Instead, he raced off down a blind alley. There, standing at the wall, he looked through the refuse in the hope that he might find some kind of canvas with which to fashion a tent. As he looked about, though, he half-convinced himself that he heard the steady approach of footsteps. He looked up to find an elderly chap standing there.

The gentleman removed his high-crowned straw hat, greeted him, and pointed to the peacock-feather lapel pin attached to his raggedy sheepskin coat. 'At ease, young man. If you require assistance, I shall help you with whatever is the matter.'

'Who are you?'

'Call me Mr Beddoes. I've got ties to the consul general. Served on the Dardanelles Commission as well. I'm a friend. Do you want a friend? Don't answer. I know you're not doing well. You look like you carry the weight of the whole world upon your shoulders.'

'*No,*' Jack whispered. He wondered if he ought to speak of his youthful sorrows, but decided against it. *I'm too self-conscious. Better to keep silent.*

The old man tapped Jack's arm. 'I was a glum lad, long ago. Always brooding and directionless and sitting on my bird dog. In the end, my isolation and loneliness had me talking to imaginary friends.'

'Wot? That's bloody mental.'

'No, at first it was nothing more than the stuff of innocent whimsy. But then . . .' The elderly fellow stepped back and went into a mild seizure.

Jack did nothing to help, for he did not know what to do. As the old man sat down amid the refuse, Jack scuttled off. Down by the nickelodeon, he stopped. Looking over his shoulder, he prayed the old man would come along. If so, maybe the two of them would take in a show. When the old man failed to appear, Jack removed his deerstalker and looked to his feet. *Just how long before me growing estrangement*

24

proscribes me from befriending anyone? For that matter, how long before me right-diseased mind resolves to manufacture diabolical figures to keep me company? He gripped his hat tightly and shook his head.

Late afternoon, he exited the marketplace and doubled back to his encampment—where a few locals eyed him warily. He shook his head. From this moment on, he would have to try to act inconspicuously. *Or else I ought to console them good people. Or why not help them in their great struggle against British colonialism?* At last, he approached two Egyptians. 'Don't pother about me none. I'm a friend. Ye ought to love me loads. Tomorrow morning, I mean to donate all me money to one of the local charitable endeavours what look after the poor.'

Neither one of the Egyptians responded. Together with the English expatriates and colonists living in the village, the two locals seemed to realise how maladjusted he was.

At dusk, Jack dragged himself back into the deserted marketplace. *I got to find that old man and check that he's well. Maybe I'll apologise for abandoning him the way I did.* Down by a dustheap, he located the old man. 'Mr Beddoes. There you are.'

'That's right. As lonely as you'd be, you left me. Affrighted by my recurring seizures, no doubt. At ease, friend.' The gentleman fussed with his lapel pin. 'I'll not never forsake you, not for one bleeding instant. That's because I detect something of myself in you. Yes, afflicted by depression, I was. Just like you. Yes, it's a terrible disease what possesses you. When I was your age, the sorrows came over me in the course of a few dismal days, until the oppressive disease came to dominate my unconscious mind, which in turn resolved to pour every nihilistic thought I'd ever had into

. . . hallucinations, imaginary friends, apparitions, visitors. Ah, but the whole time, they were mere projections of my thoughts.'

His face wrinkling, Jack lurched off through the alleyway and stopped before a second dustheap. When the friendly old man followed, Jack looked to his feet. 'Please go away,' he whispered.

'No, I can't do that,' the old man told him. 'With a heavy heart, I wish to tell you that it might be best for me to stay by your side. But you've got nothing to fear. At ease, lad. I'm no tramp. I'm no journeyman. Got ties to the State House, I do. As a matter of fact, I happen to know the principal secretary up there in Cairo.'

'Listen, I'm sorry I left you the way I did. But you affright me, and it's not just your seizures.'

'Just listen to you, so confounded by daydreams of being this or that chap, you can't even speak right. At times you sound Irish and then Cockney, like you don't even know, and that's because you're a hopeless daydreamer, always imagining you're someone else.'

'Perhaps we shouldn't speak to one another anymore.'

'No, I'll not go away, no, not until you know just what binds us and all. And it's a hell of a thing, but we got ourselves the same faulty biochemistry. The same impulse what never gives over tormenting the psyche, that grave impulse what never lets some suffering bastard forget the debasements of his past. I detected it in you, my lad, for it's there in your sad, blue eyes, all those grave chemical reactions what exist inside a youthful chap's noodle for no other reason than to make certain he *never* forgets. Yes, you've got it inside you. The merciless beast, the black dog what exists for no other reason than to gnaw away at you. What a rueful plight.' The

26

gentleman hummed Verdi's '*Chœur des esclaves*', until a second seizure threw him into violent convulsions.

Go on, get away. Jack trailed back to his beachside encampment, where he heard some kind of disturbance at his back. *What's that, then?*

A storm of soft, downy feathers blew about along the pathway winding through the dunes.

Like a spellbound poet, someone inclined to lose himself in random streams of thought and word association, Jack contemplated the feathers and reasoned that the elderly chap had left them there to convince him that a songbird had come along to pluck away each and every last one of its plumes—until both its bloodied mantle and belly looked impossibly grotesque. *But why did the inconsolable thing do that?* Jack sat atop the sea wall and tormented himself with the question. As the strong, frigid, nighttime sea breeze whistled through the breakwater, he revisited his schooldays. *Doughty Street Lyceum.* Back then, his ever-worsening depression estranged him from the other pupils—until the disorder filled him with self-loathing and self-doubt. *What the devil happened to me? Where did the curse come from? Deep inside me psyche, that's where. Me nature.* As the wild sea breeze sailed across the shore, he slumped down beneath a little carob tree and held his head in his hands.

Two angry seagulls screeched, their mewing reminding him of a girl who had lived just down the street from him in London. Day by day, she had played on a baroque cello. What a talent, too: she often slid her hand down toward the scroll, and in so doing, created cello harmonics that sounded just like a pair of lovelorn gulls calling to one another.

The angry seagulls soared off, and no sound remained but the sea breeze rattling the boughs of the carob tree.

Against his will, he revisited a dozen or more awful memories from his schooldays—the endless insults, the schoolyard threats, all those times someone might belittle him. On and on, a jumble of voices resounded all throughout his stream of consciousness.

'You think you'll speak like a Dutch uncle to me, then?' one voice asked.

'Speak like a Dutch uncle to me, and you'll be a bloody Dutchman,' a second voice tormented him. 'Yes, you'll be well in Dutch, you weird bastard, you.'

How to forget such threats of violence, and how to overcome the shame of not fighting back? Over and over, Jack revisited memories of every bully who had ever trespassed against him. As the swaying, wind-blown carob tree rained tree litter against his face, he recalled some of the craven little imps—the ill will by which the sadistic little children sought to compensate for their insecurities. *At least regarding all them, I could've done something. Maybe I should've lowered me shoulder into some devilish fellow as we passed by one another.*

The sea breeze whispered through the boughs of the carob tree, and the music proved just enough to restore him. He sat up and looked out to sea. *Would that I could forget the past. What bliss that'd be.* He crawled out from beneath the tree and knelt in the sand.

The elderly gentleman approached. 'Why you looking so maudlin? Back in my day, no one ever went out on the town looking like that. Grow a humour bone, I say.'

Jack refused to face him and eyed the waves instead. *Look there, the endless sea. It's something like the unconscious mind.* He thought of all the chemical reactions and impulses that drive a person to madness. *Won't I end up just like the old man? What a bloody terrible fate. For the rest of me life, I'll be confounded and obtuse. Fit to do nothing but wander the world and forage for me grub.*

The old man nudged him. 'At ease. I know what you're thinking.'

Jack shook his head. 'No, you don't. You're a tramp. You got no direction. I'm nothing like that. So, go away. I don't require a friend. The isolation, it's no trouble at all.'

'Bless you, dear boy, but you've got no hope, no, none at all, for you'd be possessed by all them impulses what bring a chap to ruin.' The old man suffered a few more mild seizures.

As the old man staggered away, Jack scurried back to the little carob tree—where he closed his eyes and listened to one last bough rattling on and on like an Egyptian minstrel's bamboo rain stick. *Music! Music!*

⁓

8 September 1917.

At midmorning, Jack discovered a second storm of downy feathers swirling all about his encampment. *I wonder if the feathers mean to tell me to avoid the barbershop back in the marketplace. Once I go in there, the Egyptian chap, he'll be sure to shave me head and leave me looking like an absurd bald fool, and the barber, he'll do it for no other reason than to take out all his aggressions regarding British rule, and then, once I exit the barbershop, all the little boys working their pushcarts up and down the narrow lanes, them lads, they'll roar at me something rotten, and the children's laughter, it'll be heartless and relentless.* Jack looked at the sky. *Where do me random thoughts come from?* He looked down from the sky because he knew the answer. *Me noodle don't work right.* He glanced in the direction of the village. 'I'll not let no one touch me hair, and that's a vow. Even were I to stay here ten more years, I'll grow me hair as long as an ascetic grows his.'

A few English soldiers marched by. 'You got no idea how much the locals despise the outrage of colonialism,' one of them said to the other.

'That's right,' the second one said. 'The natives long to be free.'

As the soldiers continued along, Jack glanced at them and then lowered his gaze. *I'm a coward. I'm a traitor.* The guilt was unbearable: he slumped his shoulders, shifted this way and that and broke out in a tepid sweat.

With the sun high and proud in the midday sky and the autumnal sea breeze whistling through the dunes, Jack's thoughts drifted back to the feathers. *How could a songbird grow so confounded as to pluck away all its plumage?* He breathed in the earthy scent of the beachgrass, and as he did, rubbed the heel of his palm against his chest. *Could it be the songbird has suffered some great trauma? Has the tragic thing lost the power of song? No, I got to think right and do away with all me random fantasies.*

An ocean breeze blew in from the east, and the plumes of water spray grew wild. What a terrific clamour, too. The gust awoke a nest of little sandpiper chicks lost in the dunes, and the winged creatures' cries commingled with a peal from somewhere out across the pier—what sounded like a sea captain's dissonant piccadilly bell.

Jack grabbed his deerstalker and strode off to the dusty roundabout, where he paused to consider the building standing at the summit of the gently sloping hill—an immense, Byzantine-revival opera house. *What a noble structure. Noble enough for Fitzroy Square.* He removed his hat, and as the desert sun beat down upon his scalp, performed a crisp nod.

From within the opera house, a few measures of song commenced: it was a soprano practiced in the technique of coloratura.

He refused to despair. *Soon enough, the opera company will depart. And when they do, maybe I'll take one of the dressing rooms and live there.* With a self-satisfied smile, he slipped the deerstalker back over his scalp and lumbered to the summit.

Before the lobby doors lay a big, dusty tuba. Beside the musical instrument, someone had stacked up a bundle of letters—the correspondence weighed down by a dozen seashells.

Down below and over to the side, a flock of goats appeared—and a dozen of them jeered and spat and bleated and screamed at him.

He watched them wander off through the landscape— the ruins of a Byzantine monastery made out of watermelon-pink limestone.

The desert breeze kicked up, and two little flower petals of sickly, pale-pear green drifted by.

The sickly colour reminded him of his stepmother's stationery, and as he stared at the correspondence, he wondered when and if he ought to write to her.

The desert breeze grew quiet, and down in the heart of the roundabout, a young, sloe-eyed Egyptian maiden holding an exotic, twelve-string *oud* beneath her arm came to sit beside the fountain. She studied the landscape awhile and shook her head as if she disapproved of the open ground and modest, unpaved, dirt-track road. Before long, she strummed a wistful melody and hit a false harmonic.

Jack studied her sun-scorched face and noted her drooping shoulders. *She looks right heartbroken.* He had heard about how cruel life in 'the Orient' could be, and now he tilted his head. *Maybe she's only just endured some awful indignity. The violence of genital mutilation. That's what it was.* Again, he cursed his habit of entertaining random, lugubrious thoughts.

The sad song continued, and a most uncanny warmth gripped him. Did the forlorn young lady expect him to come down to the roundabout to drop a few coins at her feet? He checked his pockets, but he found nothing more than a half-crown. *But I can't afford to give this away. I got to save me a tuppence here or there, or I'll go hungry.* He dropped the coin back down into his pocket.

The sad song concluded with an arpeggiated chord followed by a non-chord note. The Egyptian maiden placed the musical instrument at her feet. As sinuously as a belly dancer, she stood—and she stared at the mirror works on the other side of the roundabout.

Until that moment, he had not even noticed the humble manufactory. Now he studied the building's mundane, oblong shape and everyday clerestory roof.

The masonry, which looked to be porphyry, shone a dull shade of purple, not unlike that of a rotting Damascene plum.

Unimpressed, he gazed at the young lady herself. *Why not go up to her? Why not pay the maiden a few compliments and make repartee?* He had no talent for such things, however, and he knew it. *No, no. Don't go down there. Don't say one word to that Oriental maid. No, no.*

Down below, in the roundabout, the Egyptian maiden shook her head at the unprepossessing mirror works, and then she collected the twelve-string *oud*. She propped the musical instrument on her shoulder and marched off along the street that reached a half-mile back into the heart of the marketplace.

32

When she was gone, he cried out. As he fought back tears, he lamented the quietude of the roundabout and wondered why it did not attract more traffic. *Does no one use this route? Could it have something to do with the mirror works? The people who work there, maybe they're maniacal about keeping this part of town quiet. Who knows?*

The flock of goats bolted and vanished off in the direction of the wilderness to the north—the turquoise mines, the barren mountains, the ancient temples, the wishing rocks and windswept valleys.

A stunning, ghost-white flower petal drifted past his feet—what looked to be the remnant of a Bedouin wedding bouquet.

He gasped for breath. By now, he had come to realise how much he dreaded the power of beauty. *Yes, and because of that bloody undeniable fact, I'll always be alone. Unless I improve meself.* With leaden steps, he descended the hill.

No sooner had he stopped beside the fountain than the elderly gentleman, Mr Beddoes, approached from out of nowhere. 'Why you dawdle here?' the old man asked, pointing at the space between Jack's eyes.

'Go away,' Jack implored him. 'I'm perfectly content. The isolation and loneliness don't trouble me none.'

'At ease, boy. Let me ask you something. Do you think you've got the power to impress that Egyptian maid what stood here only a moment ago? No, lad, approach her and speak with her and all that, and you'll only manage to debase yourself, just like your own unconscious mind had willed it.'

Jack pushed himself up to his feet and planted his legs wide. 'I'm not a little boy. Don't require damn all from no one. So, go on. Go back to wherever you came from.'

Mr Beddoes dropped his hand to his side. 'I'd say your

unconscious mind compels you to debase yourself because your unconscious mind knows how your *conscious* mind operates, all of which explains why it puts out signals what say you don't belong but nowhere, aye, and it's just them signals what make everyone know to go ahead and feed off you, and you ought to believe it, too, because no matter what you think, you only ever get what you give, and that's just why a bloody rotten chap like you ought to learn to lay low, because back in my day, that's just what we'd tell someone like you.'

For the most part, Jack agreed with the elderly gentleman. Like a child, he fought back the tears. *No, I haven't any place in this world.* He looked at his frayed, untied shoelaces. *I've always been a dunce, a misfit, a dupe, an anomaly.*

The old man let out a few croup coughs. When he grew quiet, he tottered off in the direction of the shore.

Jack looked up at the opera house and grimaced. Even if the opera company were to leave soon, he did not deserve to live in such an opulent building. *Given my bloody failure to enlist, how could I deserve to sleep in a warm, regal room? For the duration of me sojourn here in the desert, I ought to refuse all extravagances.* He thought back to an elegy that his cousin, a veteran of the trenches, had penned. *What did he call it? 'For All Those Fallen at Flixécourt'.* Even now, the poem inspired in Jack more than a twinge of jealousy—especially the bold stanza in which Cousin Billy made a sophisticated allusion to the Battle of Marathon. *Meanwhile, I can't produce nothing good. Everything I write reads like sob stuff.*

The afternoon breeze blowing through the dusty roundabout, Jack turned his back to the opera house and sought to picture Cousin Billy's life back in England. *Barring some miracle, he should still be convalescing at that cottage hospital at Gallowstree Common.* By now, the dowdy nurses, each one of them a hopeless drudge, had probably fallen madly in love with him. *But why should he trifle with that lot?* Instead, Cousin Billy had probably befriended one of the other wounded soldiers. *No matter his own injuries, Billy probably had a habit of greeting the recent arrivals. Yes, he'll console whatever poor bastard who might've arrived from Liège or whatever godawful place.* Every now and then, too, Cousin Billy probably recited his poem for the other chap's pleasure. *I've got to learn to be good. Just like Billy Boy.*

The afternoon breeze blew harder, and something like the soft, mournful strains of a bugle resounded from the far side of the opera house.

The seeming bugle call made Jack think of a soldier's burial, so he endeavoured to hum the tune to 'The Last Post'. His muscles growing rigid, he could not recall just how the remembrance music went.

A scattering of thornbush leaves blew through the roundabout, the debris reeling around the fountain twice before settling at his feet.

I'm nothing. Just worthless. Jack kicked the debris away and struggled to quell his feelings of guilt. If only he had some good reason to oppose the war—the way the disenchanted, the conscientious objectors, oriented their minds. *But I'm nothing like that. No, no.* In truth, he had always admired the idea of service to king and country—and he had always pitied those soldiers who went lost in action.

A second scattering of thornbush leaves blew down through the roundabout, the debris darting off into a patch of ornamental onion boasting ashen flowers.

As ashen as me. As ugly as me loathsome visage. Jack trudged back to the beach. There, he lay in the sand and seagrass and patiently awaited the gloaming.

As twilight came and went, he thought of the soldiers. 'Lest we forget,' he thought out loud.

The sea breeze grew soft then. As solemn and as mournful as a bugler's evening hymn, the wind whistled through the bright green raisin trees swaying along the strand.

Listen to that. Bloody hell, it's the Last Post.

III.

Saint Petersburg, Russia. 19 September 1917.

Anastasia awoke to the odour of iron-oxide fumes. As she breathed in the iron dust, her mouth filled with the metallic taste of blood. 'What's happened?' she asked the fox. 'Do you know?'

'A wounded fox has crept into the house. Picture him, his ragged fur. That's the tell-tale sign of mange.'

'I don't believe a word,' Anastasia said. 'You're probably responsible for this latest hallucination, but why?'

'Just think of the poor fox. Imagine its wounds, the way it bleeds from its muzzle.'

She checked every corner of the house, but no matter how thoroughly she searched the various alcoves that gave the neo-Gothic floorplan so much of its labyrinthine character, she found no sign of a bloodied fox licking its wounds.

As she sank down onto the overstuffed divan, someone knocked on the front door. The visitor proved to be an old family friend—Mr Kabakov. When the elderly gentleman entered, he placed his top hat on the mirrored hallstand. 'I came to see how you're doing,' he said.

They sat at the dining-room table, and Anastasia smoothed the crimson chenille draped over it as she told him all about the re-emergence of her childhood Arctic-fox obsession.

Mr Kabakov patted the back of her hand. 'The disturbance you describe, it means you're not grieving your mother. No, at least not in some dignified way. That's why someday soon, you must determine some proper way to go free of the damnable creature.' With that, the gentleman wrote something down on a leaf of paper. 'Go to this address here,' he told her. 'On the twenty-seventh. Join the circle.'

She studied the leaf of paper in her hand. 'For what purpose?'

'*Group therapy*,' the gentleman answered. 'A gathering like this should remedy any relapse of girlhood hysteria. Especially one brought on by the death of a parent, your father.'

'Yes, maybe. In any event, you didn't have to check on me. Honestly, I'm quite the game girl these days.' She slipped the paper into her hobble skirt's inseam pocket.

When Mr Kabakov departed, she stretched out in the garden beside the little crushed rapunzel amid the bellflowers. Sleep eluded her, so she wandered down to Moskovsky Prospekt to think things over. *What a fool Mr Kabakov was. Therapy! How could some old physician help me appease a dream fox?* Down by the stationmaster's office, lost in reverie, she recalled the moment the night train from Arkhangelsk had pulled into Saint Petersburg back in 1907. As she disembarked, the conductor had helped the wine steward from the parlour car. What a terrible memory: the young man's left ankle bled profusely, as if some fierce beast had mauled him.

'Do you think the Arctic fox did that?' young Anastasia blurted out.

'Hush,' Mother told her. Then, holding the box of volcanic glass secure beneath her right arm, Mother guided her onward through the crowded railway station.

The door to the stationmaster's office opened now, and as a train engineer exited, Anastasia refocused on the present. *Yes, therapy. Maybe it could help me make sense of my memories. Who knows?*

She did her best to retrace the route she and Mother had taken that day so long before—and once she had made her way back home, she stopped at the table standing to the side of the banister. *All those years ago, the summer of 1907, Mother placed the box of volcanic glass right here on this very table. Yes. I remember.*

Mother had removed her coat and smiled affectionately. 'Why don't you go upstairs and check on Ludmila?'

At once, young Anastasia raced upstairs to check on her pet lemming—and as soon as she reached the nursery, she opened the wooden coop. 'Hello, Ludmila.'

Hopping to the floor, the lemming twisted itself all about, struggling to shed the plain-weave bonnet with which she adorned it. Having failed to dislodge the hat, Ludmila raced down the stairway.

Anastasia followed, but the lemming scrambled through the gap at the bottom of the back door. 'God, no.' Anastasia hurried outside into the garden bower, but Ludmila scampered past the place where Mother always sat when reading one of her Flaubert novels—and the creature got lost amid the brush.

A soft breeze sailed through the garden, whistling past the bronze representation of Peter the Great astride his warhorse. For the longest time, Anastasia stared at it—despite the fact that Mother's sculpture was a cheap replica of the piece Étienne Maurice Falconet had fashioned sometime after the

Battle of Waterloo. The triumphal figure loomed over young Anastasia, making her feel weak, worthless. With nowhere else to go, she trudged onward through the garden gate.

Outside in the street, she stopped at the curbstone—and the wayward lemming reappeared, twitching its nose.

'Come here!' Anastasia pleaded. 'You won't be sorry. I'll give you my best *matryoshka* doll.' She nodded. 'That's right, the Princess of Kiev. Yes, I'll put her in your coop so that she watches over you while you sleep.'

Despite the gracious offer, the lemming darted out into the avenue.

Anastasia followed—and Ludmila guided her down to the indomitable, wrought-iron gates of Count Orlov's palace. When the lemming darted onward through the rails, a flash of otherworldly light caught its eyes, and the wayward creature slouched across the courtyard to investigate the dreamlike glow: it proved to be the Arctic fox himself materializing not three feet from Count Orlov's majestic door.

Anastasia gripped the rails. 'Get along, Ludmila. Come back into my arms this minute. Don't let's tempt fate.'

The lemming ignored her and bared its teeth, as if to dissuade the fox from troubling himself with it.

'Come here,' Anastasia said softly. 'We'll go home, and we'll cuddle together, and we'll watch the midnight sun, and then maybe—'

Before she had even completed her plea, the merciless Arctic fox pounced on the lemming and consumed the screaming Ludmila in just one bite. Afterward, looking perfectly indifferent, the beast peered deep into Anastasia's eyes.

She rattled the rails. '*Diable!*' she cried out, tears streaming down her face.

The dream fox sauntered across the pristine courtyard and

stopped near the gate. 'It surprises you that I should consume a toothsome lemming?' the beast asked, a glint in its eye.

Gently, she placed her brow up against the cold of the crossbar. 'How could you? You're positively heartless. Heartless!'

'*Heartless*? The Russians, they're heartless. Let me tell you all about it. One day back when I was no older than a pup, a band of Russians came and planted a whole row of telegraph posts next to our den. And when Papa protested, do you know what the Russians did? They trapped him and skinned him alive and left his guts and giblets strewn all across the blessed tundra. I myself discovered Papa's remains. Can't you appreciate how deeply an ordeal like that should maim a wee innocent pup like me?' Without another word, the Arctic fox backed away from the wrought-iron gates and vanished.

Languidly, Anastasia's thoughts flowed back to the present—and she tapped on the table standing beside the banister. *No more awful memories. It's 1917 now. Yes, 1917.* With a flinch, she removed the leaf of paper from her skirt's inseam pocket.

The long, quiet day passed by. At dusk, she sat in the kitchen and revisited the idea that she ought to enter into therapy. Shaking, she checked the calendar on the wall. *The twenty-seventh, that's not so far away. Might therapy help me to placate the fox? Let's hope so.*

In the evening, she walked over to the window that afforded a view of Konstantinovsky Palace. *After Ludmila died, I stood in this very place. I'm sure of it. I watched a big fireworks display, skyrockets illuminating the city.*

Mother had come along then. 'There's a gala affair down at Konstantinovsky Palace,' she had explained. 'Shall we go? I heard a reliable rumour that your namesake should be there. The lovely Czarina. The Grand Duchess. *The* Anastasia.'

'No, Ludmila died today. I can't just attend some party. It wouldn't be right.'

'*Please,*' Mother protested. 'All day long, you've been brooding over that little thing. No more, I say.'

'But I'm in mourning. I can't go. Hire a governess to stay with me, and—'

'Tonight's function should be the last of the summer, and the palace guard means to shoot off their whole stockpile of fireworks.'

Young Anastasia did not respond. She retreated to the window that had always afforded a view of the plum-blossom garden. There, she wept for her pet lemming.

A young lady now, she marched off to that same window. *Ludmila, what has become of you?* Tapping the sash, she imagined the lemming's ghost materializing before the Governor's House in Siberia and consoling the Grand Duchess. *The one true Anastasia.*

~

23 September 1917.

Early that morning, the odour of iron-oxide fumes drifted all throughout her bedchamber, as usual. The taste of chemicals grew strong in Anastasia's mouth. She stuck her tongue out for a moment, and as she fingered the Huguenot cross, fixed her gaze upon the neo-Gothic vaulted ceiling. *Am I going mad? What could it be? The smell of blood?*

When she finally stopped fiddling with the necklace, she removed her housecoat and dressed herself in a simple gown. Outside, she followed the source of the odour to the gates of Konstantinovsky Palace. 'Are you awake in there?' she asked, looking down and rubbing her belly. 'How could you destroy my darling Ludmila the way you did, all those years ago?'

Deep inside her womb, the dream fox stirred to life. 'Forget the past. That's what you want to do. It's already happening.'

'How could you prey upon a little girl?'

'Please. How could I have ever mustered the power to resist? Think of all those cautionary tales.'

'What do you mean?'

'Always the wild, natural villain seeks to prey upon someone like the person that you once were. What a revelation, the corruption of innocence. There's no thrill that could ever compare to it, and there's nothing the villain may do to resist the compulsion.'

Three times over, she poked her belly. When her belly grew sore, she stumbled back to the Huguenot Quarter and stopped at her front door.

Strains of music resounding from the neighbour's residence bounced off the neo-Gothic frame.

What's that melody? My, how alluring. She wondered if the piece might be a composition by one of the great Huguenot composers. *Maybe* 'Suite Pour Le Piano' *by . . .*

The distant piano music discontinued, and as the whole of the Huguenot Quarter grew quiet, she ducked back inside and paused at the foot of the stairway. *What's wrong with me, anyway? Do I suffer from hysteria? Yes, I'm so excitable.* She inched her way toward the back door, drew a shallow breath, and pushed on into Mother's plum-blossom garden.

Deep inside her womb, the fox recited the first line of a Russian-language poem.

Anastasia pounded on the earth. 'Talk to me in English.'

The fox recited a French-language, Huguenot poem.

Anastasia exhaled loudly. 'Remember, my father was

British. So, talk to me in his tongue. I loved him dearly, I'll have you know. He was strong and beautiful and—'

'What are you doing out here in the garden?' the fox asked. 'Tell me.'

'What am I doing? Let me ask you something. Do you remember the time you chased my poor Ludmila all about out here?'

'Please. Forgive my past indulgences. That's what you wish to do. In times bygone, we all made our little mistakes. That's what you wish to say. Besides, the things you remember, they never happened at all. Think about it. Everything that happened, it was the stuff of dreams.'

Anastasia breathed in the scent of dead plum blossoms. Had any of her past trauma truly happened, and what if all her memories were tainted by a case of hysteria and little more? *If so, perhaps I dreamt up the Arctic fox.* Anastasia crawled deeper into the garden and stopped before a patch of weeds. 'If you didn't destroy Ludmila, then who did?'

'A stray bobtail cat devoured her. Maybe the animal had escaped from the zoo. Then the damnable creature leapt from the shadows of Count Orlov's palace, only to . . .'

Anastasia shook her head and crawled through the weeds. *Do I remember anything at all?* The autumn breeze sailed through the garden, the current gliding down her blouse and up her skirt.

From three blocks to the east, a street performer's barrel organ struck up a lively tune that sounded like a fragment from '*Trois Sonatines*'.

Not a moment later, the deafening roar of cathedral bells erupted—from the very heart of Saint Petersburg.

She did her best to cover her ears, as if that might make her feel safe. And she did feel a little bit better, too, until a wind-tossed, paper handbill came along and wrapped itself around her ankle. The piece of refuse made her think of all the frayed, fallen pamphlets forever tumbling about Ostrovsky Square, each little flier proclaiming some forthcoming Bolshevik rally.

How long before revolution destroys all of Russia? A violent shudder moved through her body. *I've got to escape all the mayhem and bloodshed, but where do I go?* She thought back to one of Mother's old acquaintances—Madame Jolivet, a famous Huguenot authoress who lived on a reindeer farm just outside of Smolensk. *European Russia? No, that won't help at all. I've got to go far, far away.* Anastasia's thoughts filled with memories of her late father—his many investments in Grahamstown, South Africa. *No, that'd be too far. Perhaps I ought to stay here and let the therapist confront all my hysteria until I've placated the fox.*

At last, the handbill blew free—and as the barrel organ grew quiet, the handbill tumbled off through the lifeless weeds and faded plum blossoms.

The cold autumn breeze kicked up, so she lay down in an expanse of dead cornflowers and held herself close.

The current filled the air with the exotic scent of oranges.

She breathed in, and the scent of the exotic fruit made her think of Spain. 'Ah, yes, *Le Méditerranéen*,' she thought out loud. Breathing in again, she went lost in reverie and imagined herself lying in a garden beside some exotic *pied-à-terre*.

The garden gate creaked softly, and the reverie concluded. With the autumn breeze stealing through her fringe—and how tender the sensation, something like the loving touch of a faith healer, she blew the Peter-the-Great statue an affectionate kiss and then ducked back inside.

Late that night, she tossed and wriggled in her bed. Alone

as she was, she feared that a night caller might come along to ravage her. *Why do I torture myself this way? To atone for my sins? Yes.*

The light of the moon crept through one of the windows and conjured shadows that resembled faces, funerary masks.

To distract herself from these imaginings, she climbed out of bed, scrambled off into Mother's room, and rummaged through some of the papers lying on the writing table—the last bit of business correspondence Mother had brought home from the House-of-Fabergé mirror works.

As Anastasia glanced at Mother's bookshelf, the fox spirit deep inside her womb twitched his long downy tail, making her womb throb in a way it never had before. 'Settle down,' she said, pinching her belly. 'Do you hear me in there?'

He did not answer, but through a gap in one of the windows in the little prayer room across the hallway, the nighttime breeze whistled a tune resembling Mussorgsky's 'Hebrew Song'.

Anastasia again eyed the books—the ones Mother had always seemed to covet even more than her French-language novels.

The music of the nighttime breeze grew increasingly lyrical, harmonic and impossibly dramatic.

Listen to that night piece. It's a mood in and of itself. So bewitching. When the current died down, Anastasia tapped one of the volumes—*Les mémoires de Saint Pétersbourg.*

Deep inside her throbbing womb, the fox leapt about. 'Go back to your room.'

Ignoring him, she flipped through the books. *Wasn't there one that included a freehand map that always interested Mama?* For an hour, Anastasia searched through the leaves of now this volume and that. Though she could not explain just why, she longed to locate the drawing. The map eluded her. *What do I do?* She crossed the hallway to the prayer room and tapped the Huguenot cross. *Shall I say a prayer?*

A force as of a ghost seemed to pull on a fold in her skirt. 'You must find that little map,' whispered a familiar voice that she couldn't quite place.

'What land did the map depict?' Anastasia asked. 'Just what country does the map represent? Even if you're nothing more than a hallucination, please answer.'

'Maybe it's a map of those places where your Huguenot ancestors once lived. How about a commune such as Gravelines?'

'Honestly?'

'No, it's nothing like that. Still, nothing less than your very fate depends upon your finding that map. Yes, that map should help you a thousand times more than any therapist ever could.'

Anastasia swung around, only to find herself standing alone. She studied the shadows falling about the prayer room. 'Come back. Tell me more about my fate. Tell me more about my future.'

The imaginary figure failed to reappear, so Anastasia paced about the darkened house—and as she did, the dream fox panted and hissed and shouted out several unintelligible protestations.

She stopped before the door to the guest room and poked her belly. 'Won't you ever go away? How do I rid myself of you? Get out.'

'You don't mean that. No, you love me.'

As the dream fox spoke, Anastasia intuited a fantastical presence at her back. *The ghost has come back.* Anastasia stared straight ahead into the empty guest room. 'Who are you?'

'It's Svetlana. I've come back to you. I'm standing right behind you, stroking my triple-pierced ear.' The ghost girl seemed to draw closer. 'Let's you and me find that map. Let's look among your mother's books, why don't we? Yes, please.'

Anastasia circled back to Mother's room and paused before the bookshelf. A thin novelette caught her eye: it was the tale of a killer who makes a deathbed confession and then draws a map to reveal the place where the authorities may exhume the murder victim.

Deep inside Anastasia's womb, the dream fox bit into her flesh. 'It's time for you to forget the past. Will yourself to do so. It's all too easy.'

Anastasia glanced at the window and espied a book lying beneath the antique enamel box standing before the lower sash.

Deep inside her womb, the dream fox yelped. Then he waved and wagged and twitched his long alluring tail. 'Let me fade back into your memories. The time has come.'

She winced. Still, no matter how discomfited she had become, she continued over to the windowsill. She pushed the enamel box to the side and read the book's peculiar title:

LE PHÉNOMÈNE DE LA RÊVERIE

She opened the book, and as the nighttime breeze whistled past the window, read the simple dedication:

'*à la mémoire de la Reine de Navarre . . .*'

Anastasia looked to the ceiling and then back again. Breathlessly, she leafed through the priceless antique. *Show me, please.*

Sure enough, on the seventy-first page, someone had sketched a map. The representation depicted a part of the Sinai Desert—and pride of place belonged to a seaside resort jutting out from an otherwise desolate stretch of coastline, the village of Al-Hubu.

For a third time, she sensed a presence standing at her back. 'What's so great about this place down there in Sinai?' Anastasia asked, her voice little more than a whisper.

'Don't you remember your mother talking about it every now and again?' the ghost girl asked in turn. 'Surely, you must remember something.'

No sooner had the ghost girl grown quiet than the dream fox spoke up: 'Go on. Think it through. *Concentrate*. With care. Affectionately.'

Anastasia stared sightlessly ahead, imagining the shimmery light of a bottle rocket flying through the clouds. 'I don't remember much. Mama told me that a famous natural philosopher lady once lived in a little seaside village down there in Sinai. What was her name? Émilie du Châtelet. Yes, that's the one.'

'Go on,' the ghost girl said.

Anastasia tapped the windowpane. 'Yes, didn't Émilie du Châtelet distinguish herself as a mathematician? Yes, she studied the physics of mirrors. And then, years later, she established a mirror works down there by the sea, a little bit like the mirror works that once employed my very own mother. Yes, an elegant mirror works.' Anastasia spun around.

Of course, no figure stood there—no menacing little ghost girl, no sinister, bald-headed spectre.

Anastasia reached out her hand. Like a little girl, she longed to believe it possible to register the spirit's invisible presence—its snug fur coat, the silvery diadem-spider brooch pinned to the lapel. 'What's it like down there in Sinai these days?' she asked once she realised that she could not feel a thing. 'The Egyptian people, don't they mean to revolt against the British Empire?'

No answer came, and as the nighttime breeze made its way through the lower sash and stirred the book's pages, she pictured herself sailing off to some port in Sinai. *Yes, how about Rosetta? Still, given the war, what if someone opens fire on my vessel? Oh, what does it matter?* She wanted so badly to go that she departed the house even now. *I'm off.* Just like an imprudent child, she broke into a sprint. *To Sinai!*

Not three blocks along, she came to her senses. *Thank goodness I didn't go too far.*

When she arrived back at home, she forced herself to continue upstairs. With a heavy sigh, she revisited Mother's quiet, lifeless, dimly lit room. The nighttime breeze made its way through the lower sash and stirred the pages of the book. She flipped through it again—back to the seventy-first page. Once more, she studied the freehand map. *Sinai.*

~

27 September 1917.

Once again, the odour of iron-oxide fumes awoke Anastasia. *There's that odd smell again. What could it be?* She climbed out of bed and drew a bath. *Today I meet with the therapist.*

In the tub, she relished the warmth of the water and sought to convince herself of the propriety in seeing someone. Sitting back, she thought up some questions. *As soon as I have the chance, I'll ask the therapist to explain the nature of evil. Once I come to comprehend, I'll never fear such things as diabolical dream foxes. I've got to remember to ask the therapist to explain all those primal urges that guide those who kill.* She arose from the tub and, taking care not to slip and fall, reached for her towel.

50

An hour later, when she finished her breakfast—still pondering on the taste of iron dust and chemicals in her mouth—she stood in the heart of the kitchen and called upon the fox.

'Yes, I'm here,' he answered. 'So, do you hear my voice? Why do you seem so sad today?'

She rubbed her temples. 'Why so sad? The whole of the human race, it's all so primitive. That's why.'

'Yes, even a healthful soul seethes with urges animalistic. No matter what mutation commenced humankind, each and every last one of you yet harbours the predator instinct inside your deepest unconscious. Ha!'

For a time, she ignored the fox. Humming the tune to a favourite Huguenot hymn, she washed and dried the breakfast dishes.

Deep inside her womb, the fox snickered. 'Don't deny it. You feel all kinds of vile, monstrous desires. The kind that only the emotion of shame might ever hope to countervail.'

As she dried Mother's favourite hand-painted teacup, the vessel dropped from her hand and shattered at her feet. Heartbroken, she crumpled onto the floor. *What have I done?*

When it came time to leave to honour the appointment with the therapist, Anastasia sat on the foot of the stair. *I can't go. I can't tell people my . . . secrets. No woman does that.*

Three times, the fox kicked. 'I know the problem. Biotic evolution has not just made you prone to wickedness. Biotic evolution has not just poisoned you with savage animal impulses all throughout the deepest reaches of your psyche. No, the primordial process of biotic evolution has not merely filled you with instincts primeval. More than that, you have inherited the malevolent propensity for *indifference*. Yes, *indifference*, my lady. *Indifference* to the matter at hand, the therapist, too, everything.'

The day passed by. At seven o'clock that evening, Anastasia wandered into the foyer and stopped. A memory came to her: three nights after the fireworks display out at Konstantinovsky Palace, her mother had completed her very first volcanic-glass table mirror.

When she had brought it home, she arranged a sheet of pink *cretonne* across the table standing alongside the banister. Taking up the newly completed volcanic-glass table mirror, she positioned it on the tabletop. '*Approuvez-vous?*' she asked.

Young Anastasia studied every detail. Despite some slight imperfections, how precious a treasure was Mother's very first volcanic-glass piece.

That evening, Mother rang a part-time governess and asked her to come over to the house—and not long afterward, Mother travelled off to Konstantinovsky Palace to locate a glove she had lost there. While she was gone, the mischievous fox crept inside. Up in the nursery, the invisible creature's downy tail brushed up against young Anastasia's thigh. Gasping for breath, she raced downstairs. There, she lifted the fine *cretonne* and crawled beneath the table.

Even if it seemed to be the best place to hide, it was not long before the intruder picked up her scent—and soon, the invisible fox lifted the luxuriant *cretonne* with his long pointy snout and crept forward. 'Hello,' the creature whispered. 'What a fun place for us to gather.' The tip of his tail slipped all the way through, and the tablecloth's hem dropped back down.

Young Anastasia recoiled. 'Go away.'

Sensually, the fox licked her shoulder, his tail tapping against a segment of the table's box stretcher.

What a foolish fox, she thought; the imprudent creature

should have been wise enough to intuit the possibility that he might knock the volcanic-glass mirror to the floor. Holding her breath, she crawled forward through the tablecloth. But once she had lifted herself up from the floor, she neglected to place the precious mirror in a safe place or to take the object with her.

But I just knew something would happen. So, why didn't I secure Mother's mirror? All those years ago, I should've proven myself to be someone dependable . . . someone much better than a dream fox.

Foolishly, she had wandered into the drawing room—where her governess had fallen asleep on *le tête-à-tête*. Young Anastasia settled herself beside her, and as she curled up, she was shaken by a terrific explosion—the volcanic-glass mirror shattering against the hallway floor!

The commotion awoke the governess. 'What was that?' She leapt up and marched out into the hallway. Upon spotting the shattered remains of the volcanic-glass masterwork, the woman shrieked.

And what happened then? Anastasia could not be sure. *I think the sitter reached beneath the table, only to discover the fox. Perhaps the creature's shame had somehow rendered him visible in that tense moment.*

If so, the sitter had probably grabbed the creature by the scruff of his neck—and then she would have lifted him into the air. 'No peace for the wicked,' she might have cried out. Then, the fox howling in agony, the sitter probably brought him out into the plum-blossom garden.

And in the end, maybe the sitter cut his throat. Maybe she did the deed with Mother's soil knife. And then the ghost of the dream fox went free. And then it drifted back into the house, only to slip into my womb. And he's still there . . . the spectre, the bearer of all my hysteria. And now it's 1917, and not only am I fatherless, I'm motherless, too. And oh so helpless.

Late in the night, Anastasia paced back and forth through the hallway. *I should've gone to speak with the therapist.* After a while, she imagined him standing at her back in the foyer. 'Do you think Man should ever triumph over barbarism?' she asked.

'Yes, of course,' he answered. 'Someday, Man will evolve into something much less bestial and much more angelic.' The therapist breathed in, as if he too detected the iron-oxide fumes. 'Why do you imagine the awful stench?'

'I suppose I'm ill.'

'Do you believe I hold the power to help you? Tell me. Do you believe in such things as psychological medicine?'

'I believe in Christian magic. And that's good, too, because I believe in the presence of evil. I do believe it exists.' She reached for her bottle of bath salt. 'Why does there have to be such an awful inhuman streak in humankind? Why all those animal impulses? Why does such primal savagery have to rise out from the unconscious mind? Why all the fiendish predation? Could it be that we inherited all that from the great apes?'

'Yes. Regrettably.' The therapist launched off into a lecture all about *der Libido*—the deepest reaches of the unconscious self, where humankind houses its primal instincts. 'Think of it as a most unfortunate side-effect of hominid evolution,' he concluded.

Anastasia walked through the place where the imaginary figure had stood, and she crept through the front door and stole through the street toward the therapist's office. *Oh, what's the point?* She stopped before a bent, broken lamppost.

A moment later, a vole approached—three little laurel

leaves in its mouth. The meadow mouse spat the debris out onto the pavement.

'Where did you come from?' She thought of the past, Ludmila—until whatever grand opportunity the idea of psychological medicine once represented was gone.

The odour of iron-oxide fumes re-awoke all around her. *Yes, the smell of blood.* As the laurel leaves blew about in the current, she clutched her cross and pendant and wondered if her own Huguenot collective unconsciousness had conjured the illusion. 'I'm a Christian martyr, someone unwanted,' she said, pointing at the rodent. 'I've got to save myself. Like a great woman would do . . . a prophetess.'

IV.

The Village of Al-Hubu, the Wilderness of Sinai.
4 October 1917.

The opera company travelled back to England that day—and already Jack found himself keen to move into the opera house. He could not do so, however. No sooner had he picked the lock on the door than he realised one of the less-accomplished sopranos had remained behind. Presently, she lived in one of the dressing rooms—and who could say just when the irksome woman might depart? Her ongoing presence vexed him, for every night the sea breeze had been blowing a bit colder all throughout his encampment down along the shore. His head hanging low, he backed away from the lobby door.

He watched as a half-dozen soldiers marched through the roundabout and raced off through the ruins of the Byzantine monastery. When they'd gone, he glanced at the lobby door and pursed his lips. *Maybe it's just as well.* Like so many times before, he questioned why he should even have a good place to sleep, what with all the soldiers huddled in the trenches. Returning to the marketplace, he donated ten pounds sterling—it was all the money he had—to the local charitable foundation. *I'm not a terrible person . . . no, I'm a good, dependable chap.*

At midday, he doubled back to his encampment along the sea—at which point a cold gust awoke. No matter his guilt, he longed for shelter. *Somewhere like that bloody restful dressing room. That would be perfect.* He wandered up the footpath a second time.

When he reached the dusty roundabout, he looked up the gently sloping hill and prayed that the singer might appear in the dressing-room window. *When she does, I'll glare at her. Yes, I'll unnerve her.* On and on, he waited. 'Show yourself,' he whispered beneath his breath.

The soprano remained inside. She performed a series of arduous singing exercises, a litany of arias that required intricate vocal trills.

Losing patience, he scowled and walked over to the oblong, porphyry structure standing on the other side of the dusty roundabout. No less than twelve dead, black roses lay upon the threshold of the mirror works. As he glanced around to see who might have left the roses, he espied the tall, homely soprano: she appeared upon the summit, the woman strumming a baroque harp she must have found somewhere in the opera house. He cringed. There could be little doubt she had noticed his recent comings and goings. If so, perhaps the woman welcomed his presence. *Bloody hell, she's got me gnashing me teeth.* He knelt beside the mirror-works door, arranged the dead roses in a heap, and then crushed them beneath his shoe. *Got the message, love?*

She ignored him. Had she even noticed him at all?

He could not help but wring his hands for a moment or

two. The conflict with the woman made him feel lonely, for the struggle served to emphasise just how much he longed to be in the company of a female befitting him. Hopelessly unaware of his arrogance, he prayed for just such a maiden to come to the village—and as the absurd prayer faded from his lips, he gazed upon the fountain and sought to envisage her. *When might she come knocking? Any day now.*

As the soprano returned inside, he trudged back to the beach, where the sea breeze grew increasingly cold. He wiped his runny nose on his sleeve. *I should've sought refuge in Tuscany, where it's good and warm. There, in some public house, a taverna with an exotic name, maybe Della Porta, I'd introduce myself to some fine Italian girl. That's right. A bird like no other.*

The sea breeze pushed him back a few steps, until he spun around. *I'll grab that soprano and throw her out on her arse.* He crept back up the footpath. *I'll fight her like an Egyptian driving off the colonists. Or maybe I'll tell her that I'm a rat, an informer, and I'm working for the revolutionaries.*

When he reached the fountain, Jack paused to count the coins shimmering up through the water. Then he checked all of his pockets, until he remembered he had nothing. *And you get nothing for nothing and precious little for sixpence.* His stomach growled, and he wondered how long it had been since he had downed a proper supper. *When the bloody hell should me old man think to wire more lolly?* Down about his waist, his belly rumbled again.

From inside the opera house, the soprano broke into song. Jack listened, frowning. The music sounded like a piece from *Die Welt auf dem Monde*. Whatever it was, the soprano's voice seemed hoarse. Had she scarred her vocal cords?

He fixed his gaze upon the dressing-room window and became lost in daydreams. *Just like me biological chemistry doomed me with the curse of all these youthful sorrows, the Fates should be me salvation. I know it. On the day I move into the warmth of the opera house, a suitable bird will arrive. A right fine damsel meant just for me.*

After what seemed like a long while, he turned back to the fountain and stared at one of the coins in the basin: a Victoria fourpence. The coin awoke a memory of home: he recalled that quiet afternoon when he had wandered into Bloomsbury Square to watch a lady street magician who had claimed to hold the power of telepathy. At one point, the woman fixed her gaze upon an unassuming gentleman dressed in a houndstooth coat—and the lady street magician described a dream that had apparently visited him the night before.

As Jack debated whether to drop his last Victoria fourpence into the woman's hat, a heckler accused the woman of witchcraft.

Her head held high, the lady street magician approached the heckler. 'Aren't you forgetting your scriptures?' the woman asked in a plainspoken tone.

'What scriptures?' the fellow asked in turn. 'You looking to put the hard word on me, are you?'

'Consider the time Pharaoh tested his magicians by demanding that they describe his dream *before* he himself revealed it. That's when young Joseph engaged his powers telepathic and described the vision perfectly, wherefore the king prized only the Hebrew's interpretations of the portent. Yes, only *his* and no one else's. And that's how Joseph ascended to the throne and ruled as prince of Egypt and helped the people of the Nile Valley survive the famine. Believe it, sir. Without the power of telepathy, who knows what might've happened? Perhaps the absolute extinction of all Egypt.'

Jack rested the small of his back against the fountain's

basin and thought back to the time he sought to teach himself the art of clairvoyance. One autumn afternoon, he read a few chapters of that famed study—*A Treatise on the Physics of Thought Transference.* Had he understood it, though? *No, no. Or maybe a wee bit.*

The desert wind played with some little flower petals, swirling them through the dusty roundabout. As he watched, a hazy autumn light shone down—and a soothing yet unnerving quietude persisted. Inside the opera house, the soprano broke the silence with another song—singing until her voice cracked.

Have one or two of her vocal cords collapsed? He shrugged half-heartedly. *Why not barge into the opera house and confront her? Yes, I'll shake me finger at her. 'With good grace, I'm here to tell you to nag off,' I'll say.* The desert wind blowing a little bit harder, he hummed the tune to a character piece he had composed about eight months before. Once he became famous throughout England, perhaps he could use it as a fetching interlude between two of his more ambitious works.

Little by little, he lost himself in daydreams of fame and fortune. *I know. I'll have some of me concert promoters and press agents tell everyone that I'd been possessed by the ghost of some deceased Bedouin minstrel. For that matter, why not change my name by deed poll? I'll take me a name to conjure with.* He fussed with his threadbare deerstalker for a moment or two, and as he did, debated whether he ought to purchase a better hat when he became a celebrity.

A strong October gust sailed through the roundabout, chasing off the diseased flower petals—and the current whistled about the majestic, Byzantine-revival columns that served to shade the lobby doors leading into the opera house.

He trembled all over, for the current made him feel thin

and malnourished—a thing doomed to waste away. The wind sailed down past the fountain and blew open the cracked windows that looked out from the mirror works.

He cringed. On the day of his audition at the Royal Academy, a gust of wind had sailed through the lobby window so hard it had managed to shatter a glass pane. As the desert wind blew harder and colder, he thought of his audition. Had he not debased himself that day? The moment he had concluded his performance, had he not stood there like a complete dimwit? *Yes, of course.* He nodded twice, and then he gestured to the instructors—for in that moment, he had still believed that he might be talented enough to study there. *Ah, but have I even got any faculty for music?*

Up in the opera house, the soprano belted out a few cracked notes. The woman's voice had grown alarmingly hoarse, sickly even.

Her vocal cords must be bleeding, but what do I care? He continued to brood over his failed audition. Picking up a shard of glass, he rolled up his sleeve. *Shall I carve some baleful symbol into me flesh?* Sometimes, it was all he could do to keep from cutting himself.

As the opera house grew quiet, he dropped the glass shard and circled the fountain a few times. He thought back to a tale he had read in *The Book of Great Victorian Horror Stories*—a tale all about an opera singer who let her rival be an earwitness to her devastation. *And she did so for no other reason than to convey the idea that neither should the other singer ever be talented enough to play any proper venue. What a shrew.*

He flopped down in the dust. The soprano in the story had succeeded in all her odious endeavours, for in truth, her competition was no better than her. The October sun beating down upon his brow, he revisited the story. The vindictive woman had played every last concert theatre in London. At one point in the tale, she had thought back to the previous autumn—when she had appeared at Endsleigh Gardens and some other pleasant square. At times, the soprano had even performed with a host of opera luminaries. During one recital, according to the tale, perhaps a dozen collared doves and firecrests had cooed and purred so as to provide counterpoint.

And here I am, an absolute nothing who never even managed a lowly recital. He gazed upon the mirror works. *I'm not a nutter. I'm a clever chap, strong and healthful. Just a wee bit lonely, that's all.* Shivering, he peered over his shoulder—as if someone must be there. *All me uncanny depression, it's bound to result in something extraordinary someday soon. Yes, indeed, but what?* A dozen times over, he plodded his way around the fountain—and the warm, lifeless day dragged on and on.

~

8 October 1917.

Jack awoke at dawn. *I'm bloody confounded. How should fate reconcile me accursed depression with me wonted loneliness?* For the better part of the morning, he wandered the waterfront. Then, as the sun rose ever higher, he lay between two dead corals. *Whatever fate decides, it's bound to be a bloody epiphany. Yes, I'm bound to come across the greatest mystery any bloke could ever confront.*

As the afternoon sky clouded over, he stumbled back to the dusty roundabout—where a tall English soldier with a parted-pencil moustache sat smoking a cigarette beside the fountain.

He studied Jack and seemed to realise how guilty he felt. 'You look terrible.'

'What do you know?' Jack said.

'I know plenty. I'm a medic.'

Jack nodded. 'I'm a terrible person,' he said. 'I want to talk to someone, but I don't deserve no one giving me the good cheer.' He fussed with his long unruly hair for a while and then looked the medic over. 'What're you doing?'

'Shining in the dust.' The soldier took another drag on his cigarette. 'I doubt you're such a terrible person. Maybe you're no different from any other chap.'

'No, in addition to all my sins, I'm someone maddened by depression, yet healthful enough to know and feel everyday loneliness.'

The medic remained quiet and tapped a bit of cigarette ash onto the ground.

Jack stepped back. 'I'm slothful. That's right. Self-absorbed as well.'

The medic put out the cigarette and stood. 'A case of mental depression is all quite natural. Here's the question. Why don't you strive to make something of yourself?'

'I do. I fancy myself a fine composer. A proper musician.'

'Oh? So, sing us a song of sixpence.'

Given the medic's friendly, even brotherly tone, Jack stood up straight. The prideful feeling did not last, though. He thought back to his schooldays—the way some condescending lout might speak kindly for a moment and put him at ease, only to tear him down for acting uncharacteristically mirthful.

A second time, the medic asked him to sing—but Jack refused. Then, as the medic checked the bandages and bismuth-magnesium tablets in his coat pocket, Jack looked to the opera house and revisited his daydreams—especially all those in which he imagined himself as a noble singer. For years, he had indulged in the most trivial daydreams. Shamelessly, he had fantasised about touring the world and performing at various cabarets and vaudeville houses. At times, he had even pictured himself making his glorious premiere at venues like *l'Opéra Bastille.*

At last, he looked at his feet: a bit of desert debris stirred about there, a few scattered hops along with a few little flower petals of coral pink.

The pretty debris made him think of the bouquet of roses that someone or other always presents to a great singer following a performance.

The medic cracked his knuckles and cleared his throat. 'Do you want to hear my boarding school *alma mater*?' With that, the medic broke into song.

Jack imagined a schoolyard bully standing at his back. *He's smirking. Just like all the louts back at Doughty Street Lyceum.* Jack thought of the sadistic children from his schooldays. Time after time, the insolent brats had baited him by repeating the words that he himself had said—and a few of the heartless children had even attempted to mimic his facial expressions.

The desert breeze kicked up, and the wild current pushed him back toward the fountain.

For a second time, he stared at the Victoria fourpence. *Why not pilfer the coin? No, a coward like me don't deserve it.* He clenched his fists, each one of his knuckles going white.

The medic must have noticed, because he concluded the song in what sounded like the middle of the bar.

'Tell me what's to become of me. What becomes of someone mad enough to feel great depression but also right enough in the head to want to resolve his loneliness?'

The medic eyed him awhile. 'Have you any talent? Have

you studied music? Do you know anything about composition and counterpoint? Here's a good question: Have you ever studied the traditional laws of harmony?'

Jack went lost in reverie and imagined himself living as a triumphal composer back home in London. *What a good life it would be. Day by day, all me many admirers, especially the comely young ladies, they'll obsess about me. Like a case of Lisztomania. And all the newspapermen and photographers, they'll follow me through the streets.*

The medic lit a second cigarette and studied Jack's hands, as if debating whether they seemed to be the hands of a proper musician.

Jack winced. 'Someday, I mean to be the finest figure in music, and once me entourage departs the concert hall, the newspapermen and photographers, they'll get all good and frenzied and chase us all the way back to me flat. And I'll be living in a splendid estate somewhere down about Saint James Park or Kensington Square Garden, and whatever the address, I'll have me a home no everyday working lad could ever hope to acquire, a flat as right spectacular as Holland House, as spectacular as . . .' Jack looked at his feet: the opera house cast strange, cat-shaped shadows across the roundabout. As the quietude continued, his thumbs quivered.

The medic flicked a bit of dust from his uniform. 'It's trying for anyone to work in a field that requires standards as high as that of music, don't you know? To command an audience, you must compete against many others, eh? Yes, and given the gramophone, too, you must compete against the great composers and interpreters of the *past*. Bugger, what hope have you modern-day buskers got?'

From the dressing-room window, a gramophone stirred to life and played a recording of a lyric tenor performing a cappella.

Jack eyed the opera house. *How to deny the power of recorded music?* Every note, every reprise, commanded the power to dredge up vivid memories and to bring forth emotion. *How to compete with such an extraordinary phenomenon?*

Up inside the dressing room, the tenor's song faded out the way some recordings do. In the quietude that followed, there was no sound but the dressing-room window's curtain lace snapping twice in the autumn breeze.

Jack stared at the cigarette butt lying on the ground. 'I got myself deep, youthful sorrows, yet I'm of sound mind.'

'No, you're not.' The medic marched off a few steps and then stopped to look over his shoulder. 'You remind me of Algernon Swinburne. True, he was a poet. But everyone who knew him well enough could swear he was a vampire.'

'I'm no bloodsucker. No, I'm not mad. Just a wee bit desperate. A wee bit lonely.' When the medic marched off, Jack traipsed back to the shore—where the roar of the surf brought him a measure of solace. For a time, he looked out at the Red Sea. What a dazzling, erotic sensation—the salty breeze, the warmth of the sun. He studied the Gulf of Suez, the endless waves, and then he looked straight ahead—to the vanishing point. *Don't lose hope. Someday, I'll be living life in essence. The love of my life, she's coming here. She'll probably be here no later than . . .*

The sands shifted beneath his feet, and from the corner of his eye, he noticed a female artist working at her easel not sixty feet away. 'What're you painting?' he asked, walking over.

She answered in French, and he did not understand a word—so he became lost in thought. *Perhaps she contents herself to make hackneyed, sentimental seascapes. Who knows?* The winsome Frenchwoman studied the waves awhile, as if she commanded the power to behold the world below them.

For the second time that day, he thought of *The Book of Great Victorian Horror Stories*—the tale of a woman artist who commanded the visionary power to paint the seabed, the myriad fishes darting about, all the pickled trout and unicorn fish, all the pearl fish and butterfly fish, too. He snapped his fingers. 'Let me look at your work.' He inched over toward her, but he stopped before he could catch a glimpse of the canvas. *How to trouble such a fine, sophisticated woman? I'm no one to do that.* He raised his hand and waved. 'Did you paint a school of jewfish, or what about a school of moonfish? Or a study of some solitary, diseased creature? What about a half-dead porcupine fish or a half-dead parrotfish lost amid the plume corals and sea feathers?'

For a second time, she spoke up in French. Her aloofness came as no surprise, for no artist would have travelled all this way to fritter away the time trifling.

By now, he had utterly confused the Frenchwoman with the woman in the story. Again, he snapped his fingers. 'Tell me how you do it,' he implored her. 'Tell me how to harness the power to look deep into the waters the way you do.'

The Frenchwoman ignored him, so he looked at his feet. *What the devil does she discern out there in the water?* He thought back to the story. *Yes, she perceives the wondrous ruins of a sunken city, a whole cosmopolis overgrown with a massive reef of mushroom coral.* He looked up and studied the waters. 'How desolate the lost world must be, the sea pumpkins and trumpet coral growing all so wild here and there. How bloody frightful.' He plopped himself down in the sand, the woman's shadow. 'I remember the tale, and I know what you see. It's a courtyard filled with purple seashells. Oh, yes. A goodly collection of seashells. Perhaps as many as six dozen right fine, resplendent tritons.'

The wind died down, and without so much as a simple *adieu*, the Frenchwoman gathered up her things and departed.

He wept awhile. *I'm a daft little boy. Unworthy of a woman's affection.* He stepped back from the surf, trembling. Even though no one else stood on the desolate shore, he broke out in a sweat and looked all around—as if a band of soldiers had concealed themselves somewhere so that they might judge him.

On and on, he sought to think of something pleasant. For a time, he hummed a melody he had always planned to plagiarise. When and if he did, he could take the lyrics from an obscure poem. *What about a translation of Novalis? That might do.* Again, he looked all around for any soldiers who might be about. A memory came to him—that evening when Cousin Billy came over and recited a passage from '*Hymnen an die Nacht*'. That windy autumn evening would have been the last time he had seen Billy—before he had sailed off to the trenches.

At dusk, Jack dragged himself back to his encampment. Agonised by the solitude, he gazed upon the golden sky and rubbed the heel of his palm against his chest. *I'm not so bad. I only long to meet someone. It's nothing more than loneliness. The kind of thing everyone must face.* His heart raced. Falling backwards, he contented himself to lie there in the sand. *Why should I be filled with so much trepidation? Why do I fiddle about the way I do? Why so alone? Day by day, I play me little games. Lost in me own world. How very sad.*

In the night, Jack bundled up in his coat. Still, the surf roared as never before—and the autumn winds blew so harshly that his teeth chattered. He struggled to convince himself that he had already grown good and warm. *I'm here in the sultry sands of the Orient, and things just have to get better and better. And all the irate Egyptian locals, they're bloody happy that I'm here.* The sea breeze grew stronger, and his teeth chattered even more.

Perfectly silent, a dozen or more British Army soldiers marched by.

He thought of the war, all the fallen soldiers. *Back home, everyone's attending memorial services to honour the dead.* He recalled the night he had almost attended an interdenominational service in Hackney Town Hall. Then he thought back to a few newspaper accounts describing the solemn memorial services in some cathedral city. *Was it Peterborough or Cambridge?*

A few medics strolled by—one of them the medic from earlier that day. Despite the darkness, there could be no mistaking his parted-pencil moustache. He raised his hand and pointed at Jack. 'Why you sleeping here, old boy?'

Jack could not take his mind off the fallen. 'Let me tell you something. I wish to make a proper confession. Do you know why I never attended no memorial service for any of them fine fallen soldiers? I suppose it's because I knew if I did, I'd only end up staring at all them comely young birds mourning the fine chaps. I'm a bloody knave.'

The two medics whispered to one another. The one with the parted-pencil moustache drew close and knelt beside him. 'Listen, I know about chaps like you. All the voices and memories of insults and such, that's what's got you feeling your presence here and there, always earwigging in your way.'

Jack averted his gaze. 'No, I'm just like anybody else. Just as healthful. Every bloke, he's only looking for love. An end to all his loneliness.'

'No, you got something akin to a beast's brain-wasting

disease, and that's what's got you tormenting yourself. It's the bloody emotional scars, all those memories of past debasements and epithets, trespasses. You can't get over the agony of it all, for you still hear the bloody blighters who took away your pride the way they did. Unless you get help, I imagine all the chemical reactions that comprise those terrible, tormenting memories should intrude on your thoughts forevermore.'

The harsh wind blew a torrent of sand back into Jack's eyes. When his tears finally washed away the grit, he looked up and blinked a few times. 'I know I'm not that bad. Just lonely. So, what happens to someone like that? Just what happens to a chap what's got big sorrows but still longs for someone?'

The medic fussed with his army patch. 'You must feel cold down here on the strand,' he said.

'Yes, but I deserve it. Just think of all them countless soldiers dying in the trenches, and were they to learn that someone like me schemed to sleep in some opera house, they'd be right cross, each and every last one, or do you think all them good Christian soldiers ought to excuse all me shameful cowardice? No, no, mate. Talk of absolution, that's the stuff of the olden days.'

The medic let go of his army patch and sneered. 'Don't you realise how confounded you are? You don't know whether you're coming or going.'

Jack scanned the length and breadth of his encampment, looking for a place to take refuge. The encampment offered no such refuge, however. Over beside a heap of seaweed, he had placed a few of his books. Off to the left, he had placed a handful of little seashells atop his stockings to keep them from blowing away.

The medic lit a cigarette. He said something unintelligible to the other and then looked deep into Jack's eyes. 'You've got to find some proper way to unlearn all the insults that rattle around inside your mind. You've got to determine some pioneering way to forget the past and erase all those tormenting memories. All your secrets as well.'

The scent of something wild, a fragrance as that of sea lilies, filled the air—and Jack closed his eyes and hummed the tune to a movement from one of his discordant, polytonal works. Soon enough, he pictured himself performing at a host of venues: the Theatre Royal, the Savoy, the Egyptian Hall in Piccadilly, maybe even one or two of the clubs down around Soho district. Perhaps most pleasing of all, he imagined a female accompanist—a comely, shapely, nubile woman all decked out in a beaded blouse and snug skirt. *What a beauty, too. A genuine goddess.* Now he pictured them sitting at a fortepiano, the two of them performing a piece for four hands—the love theme from the incidental music to some imaginary play.

The fragrance of the sea lilies abated, so Jack opened his eyes to find the medic standing there staring at him. *Bloody hell, why didn't I enlist?* Like a slow, listless cat, Jack crawled about his encampment—and like a slow, listless cat, he looked for a place of refuge. *I'm a ratter.*

The medic laughed quietly but scornfully, too. 'What's gotten into you? Why you acting like a wee little boy?'

'Tell me my fate. I'm to learn something, but what? What becomes of a person both mad with sorrows yet perfectly rational despite all his loneliness?' When no answer came, Jack fell asleep and had a dream—a vision in which he lay in the dressing room while a cool, wild breeze drifted through the curtain lace. Then the vision changed, and he imagined himself a cat staring out the dressing-room window—a lonely, grieving mouser yearning to reunite with a missing friend.

When he awoke from the dream, he found himself back on the beach—the whole of the waterfront illuminated by the soft, orange hues of the slowly unfolding sunrise.

As if he had been there all night, the medic approached from the back. 'Look, the bloody surf went and coughed something up onto the strand.'

Jack sat up some and studied the waters. He did espy something there, but that was not unusual. Time after time, the tide brought all kinds of refuse up onto the sand.

The medic tapped Jack's shoulder. 'Maybe it's your double, and he swam to his death, and then the Red Sea coughed him up, and now he's lying there dead, and if you were to rifle through his pockets, maybe you'll find a few shillings, or if he's still got a bit of life in him, maybe he'll tell you all you want to know regarding your fate.'

All atremble, Jack forced himself to stand. *I can't bear much more. No, no.* Half-naked, he raced back up the footpath and into the dusty roundabout. *I know I'm good. I'm sure I deserve real love.*

V.

Anastasia arrived at the seaside hamlet that had always fascinated her mother and checked into a lodging house—a hostelry resembling a Roman villa. She had come to the picturesque village because she believed that the mirror works must be the one true way to emancipate herself from the vile dream fox. During the journey across the desert, she had even devised a glorious scheme: she would master the art of mirror making, and then she would imprison the entity inside one of her creations.

Up in her room, she removed the volume from her travel bag and reread the curious title:

LE PHÉNOMÈNE DE LA RÊVERIE

A tap-tapping of paws caught her attention. Given her surroundings, she feared that a rabid desert fox, its gait uncertain, had stolen into the building. *Oh God, what'll the creature do once it enters my room? Perhaps it'll seek to convince me that its malady has made it tame. And if that doesn't work, maybe it'll scratch at itself with its sharp claws and draw blood from its pointy ears and long muzzle and . . .*

The sound of the uneven footfalls discontinued, as if she had imagined it—so she opened the book and studied the map. *I'm here in Sinai. I can't believe it. Sinai!* She retraced her steps downstairs to the lobby and exited the hostelry.

Inside her belly, the dream fox spoke up: 'Why did you bring us here?'

She paused in the heart of the marketplace and dropped her hand to her side. 'There's been a big change of plan. I'll not content myself to appease you. No, not at all. Instead, I aim to exorcise you. Do you hear? I aim to destroy you and take charge of my future.' She meant every word, too.

The fox breathed deeply, seductively—like a fine gentleman. 'Your affection for me must stop you. The love you feel for me, it's grown all throughout your being. Imagine life without me. Would you survive the aloneness? *No.* That's something you can't deny.'

She did not trouble herself to respond. Her hands at her sides, she bounded off down the long, dusty road. When she reached the mirror-making society's garden, she stood before the gate and breathed in the fragrance of the wildflowers—an odour as of spoiled rose-water lemonade.

Deep within her womb, the fox spirit laughed in a fatherly tone. 'Breathe deep the awful stench, my love. Already it's making you consider retreating.'

His subtle protestations vexed her, for who could say just what he might do if her current course of action continued to provoke him? In addition, her temples throbbed—and there could be no avoiding it either, for the harsh glare made her squint. She turned on her heels and looked back toward the village. Beneath her breath, she cursed herself: moments ago, as she walked through the marketplace, she should have purchased a paper parasol.

The fox spirit coiled around her heart. Then he twitched the tip of his downy tail so that the inside of her belly prickled.

She reeled back to the garden gate. '*Stop.*' With that, she opened the gate and continued as far as the shade of a fig tree.

There, an elegant woman sat in a rocking chair. For a moment, it seemed as if she had fallen asleep with her eyes open—just like Mother had often done. The woman stood up and bowed. Calmly, she introduced herself as Ernesztina Henreid and pointed toward the ceramic dish resting upon the Moroccan tea table standing to the side. 'Are you hungry?' she asked, offering Anastasia a date.

A fig leaf drifted down into Anastasia's fringe, but she barely even noticed.

Ernesztina laughed, as if impressed by the sensuality of it all. 'The fig leaf in your pretty hair . . . it makes you look a little bit like a witch.'

'Did you receive my letter? Will you grant me a post?'

'There's no reason to reject you. When summer ends and everyone goes home, we always require someone willing to stay the winter.'

With a sigh, Anastasia took the date into her hand and held it as if it must be something deadly—the flesh of the fruit tainted by the touch of some rabid animal's whiskers. *A terrible fox.*

Ernesztina slumped back into her rocking chair. Several times over, she rocked back and forth. Then the woman stopped and pointed at the fruit. 'Taste it, why don't you?'

As her temples throbbed, Anastasia placed the offering upon her tongue. When she bit into the fruit, she found that it tasted sour—as if streaked with something foul. *Yes, spoiled rose-water lemonade.* Worst of all, when she spat the morsel out into the palm of her hand, the date stone's distinctive contours served to recall the peculiar, egg-shaped pills that the physicians back in Saint Petersburg had once prescribed Mother. *Rest her soul.*

Ernesztina grabbed the partially consumed fruit and dropped it in the weeds. 'You wish to join our mirror-making society, but usually, Miss Ursula Georgiades sends us her personal recommendations. Like the girl from Moldova, the one that just left for home the other day.'

'I'm certain I'll do well,' Anastasia said, rushing her words. 'I learned at my mother's knee when she worked for the House-of-Fabergé mirror works.'

'Yes, you mentioned all that in your letter. And given your upbringing, I do believe it's possible you'd do good work. Perhaps your mother's artistic gift lives on inside you. More than that, I do pity you. When I was your age, my own mother breathed her last. I felt so alone, of course.' As the sea breeze continued to stir the flowers and trees, Ernesztina resumed rocking back and forth in her chair.

Her elbows held tight at her sides, Anastasia looked all about. *What a magnificent garden.* From what she had heard, Gertrude Jekyll herself had designed the whole expanse.

A solitary fig moth fluttered by, and Ernesztina rose from the rocking chair. 'Did you see that pest? I've got to save my garden.' She followed the little winged creature and vanished into the neighbouring thicket.

The fox squeezed Anastasia's heart in a pleasing way. 'Ernesztina has no desire to mother you. That's something you intuit on your own. Think, please. It's not so difficult to ascertain her intentions towards you. Let's be honest. She wishes to seduce you, and that's just what she'll do if you don't go home to Saint Petersburg this instant.'

At first, Anastasia refused to respond. She gazed upon the seashore awhile and then gestured toward the garden. 'Let's wait for Ernesztina to come back.'

The fox whistled a romantic tune. 'How do you feel about Ernesztina? Are you in love with her? Just think of what your mother would say! For that matter, it's a sin. Think of what all your Huguenot matriarchs might say. They'd consider you as disturbed as Joan of Arc.'

Fifteen minutes passed by, and when Ernesztina failed to show, Anastasia departed the garden. *I've got to bide my time.* Back in the hostelry lobby, she lay down on the sofa and had a nap—and as she slept, she dreamt of killing the dream fox.

When she awoke, the creature whimpered—as if he had peered into her mind and seen all her visions. 'You wish to destroy me. With not a little bit of zeal. For shame!'

~

That Same Day, Three O'clock.

Despite her confusion as to how she ought to feel about Ernesztina's intentions, Anastasia circled back to the garden gate. Once more, she breathed in the fragrance emitted by the wildflowers—an odour as of spoiled rose-water lemonade. The scent made her sneeze.

As if she had heard, Ernesztina reappeared. 'We've no reason to stand on ceremony,' she said with a bow. 'Come with me.' As gracefully as an aging ballerina, the sensuous woman guided Anastasia through the windswept thicket and onward into a quiet glade.

To one side stood a traditional English garden urn filled

with clam shells. On the other side of the clearing stood a tin-bronze mirror trussed up against a solitary white heath tree: the opulent piece stood as tall as a doorway but had a shape like an elongated teardrop.

Anastasia drew close. As she considered her faint reflection, she breathed in that same odour from before and doubted whether any flower could account for it. She stared into the mirror. Had the awful stench issued from some other dimension only to travel through the mirror's surface?

Ernesztina waltzed up behind her. 'Touch the tin bronze.'

With her right hand, Anastasia reached up and glided the tip of her finger along the gilded framework. Then, powerless to pass up the chance, she placed her palm flush against the uncanny cool of the tin bronze itself.

The merciless sun climbed ever higher over the distant, crimson-coloured mountains, and the reflection of the harsh desert light shone into her eyes.

Ernesztina brushed a bit of dust and debris from Anastasia's shoulder.

She snatched her hand away from the mirror. 'I didn't come to Sinai looking to have an affair.' She rubbed her aching temples. 'What do you do with your mirrors?'

Ernesztina did not trouble herself to answer. She merely recited several verses from some sensual poem—a fragment from the scandalous piece that Oscar Wilde had once written in praise of the sphinx statuette that he had always kept on his writing table.

Anastasia blushed. *She wants to seduce me. How flattering, but honestly!* The throbbing in her temples increased, so she closed her eyes. She had not anticipated how powerful the glare would be down here in a village hemmed up against the Red Sea shore. *Back home, even the midnight sun never*

78

commanded such might.

Ernesztina traced a fingertip down the length of Anastasia's spine.

She blushed again, and her body froze in place. *What do I do?* She harboured no prejudice against anyone, yet she had come to Sinai to exorcise the fox—and she had no ulterior motive for being here. *I'm a Christian. Yes, and I'm quite content to live the Christian life.*

Ernesztina stepped back a touch. 'Since 1717, only the finest mirror-makers have worked with us here. Prudence Xaviera Fleming, for one. Jude T Priestley as well. And back in the days of 1909, that's when Madame Bourriquet marketed her mirrors. With great success. By the last days of the Veiled Protectorate, she even employed her own *attaché de presse.*'

Anastasia opened her eyes and gazed into the darkness of the tin bronze—the soft shadow light. At once, she had goosebumps. Given the immeasurable beauty of the piece, she pictured herself stumbling forward and passing through this very mirror and into some other realm. As foolish as it must have looked, she even sought to push her hand through the surface. When all efforts failed, she dropped her hand. 'What's wrong with this piece?'

'The tin bronze can't retain its magic indefinitely,' Ernesztina answered. 'After a while, it grows lifeless.' She touched the nape of Anastasia's neck. Once more, the woman traced a fingertip down the length of her spine.

Anastasia pulled at her ear. By now she felt quite certain that Ernesztina longed to entice her into an affair. *I'll just play dumb. Why not?* Anastasia fingered the Huguenot cross dangling from the chain around her neck. She knew she had come to the place where she belonged. *Yes, that's right.* Still, how many mirrors would she have to make before she became skilled enough to draw forth the dream fox and to send the vile spirit into that dimension lying within the tin bronze? Gazing at the sky, she closed her eyes and whispered a prayer.

The light pounded against her scalp, and as the piercing quietude of the desert descended upon the garden, the searing ache in her temples spread throughout her body.

Ernesztina studied her own reflection in the mirror—where her unsmiling, heart-shaped face presently appeared over the likeness of Anastasia's shoulder. 'Why did you wish to come work with us here?'

Anastasia folded her arms. 'It's a secret. Just know that I have to do this. Sometimes an act of labour is the only way to achieve a sense of redemption. Even if what ails were nothing more than a flight of fancy.'

'So, you believe the mirrors ought to heal you of some spiritual disorder?'

Anastasia held her breath and nodded.

For a third time, Ernesztina traced a fingertip down the length of Anastasia's spine. 'Meet me at my mirror works. At sunset.'

'Yes, madam.' Certain that Ernesztina had given her the position only so that the woman might have the chance to seduce her at some future date, Anastasia clenched her jaw and glanced westward—and she found herself blinded by a merciless glare, the sun acting like a vindictive, jealous god.

As she made her way back toward the village, the fox spirit slipped back down into her womb. 'Sail home. That's what you wish to do.'

'Enough with all your mischief,' Anastasia said through her teeth.

'No, we must leave. If you sell yourself to Ernesztina, someday soon you'll be sorry. God Almighty should challenge you and punish your wickedness. That's what you believe. He'll send down His angel of wrath.'

'It's just like you to say such things.' Anastasia sauntered off into the crowded marketplace, where she paused to look up to the arched tin roof that sheltered the narrow lane. How cool was the shade: It made her smile, until she intuited someone's eyes upon her. Breathless, she shot a glance at the telegraph office.

There, standing beside the door, a young man gazed upon her—and the youth did so as if spellbound. Whoever he was, his pallid skin made it rather unlikely he was a local.

She studied his attire: he wore a good linen shirt, strong woollen trousers and a traditional, tweed-cloth deerstalker. *He's English.* She marched past an empty pushcart and approached the young man, drawing very close. 'Have you had your pennyworth? If so, how's about a halfpenny change?' With that, she stomped upon his left foot.

The scoundrel did not even look at her. Neither did he say a word. He only raced off through the marketplace.

Lovingly, the fox spirit laughed. 'Tell yourself you'll have it that easy when the angel of wrath comes to punish all your wickedness.'

'Oh, hush.' She scurried over to the curiosity shop across the way and studied some of the paper parasols on display.

Like a gentleman nibbling on her ear, the fox spirit picked at and toyed with the heart of her womb. 'You think I fib, but it's a sin to serve someone as irreligious as Ernesztina. That's something you cannot deny. She'll teach you to fashion *occult* mirrors.'

Anastasia should have ignored all. More than anything, she should have purchased a parasol. Instead, she re-examined her scheme to banish the fox. Did the idea even make any sense? Perhaps her stratagem was nothing more than the stuff of whimsy. She thought of the process by which a proper mirror-maker smelts the tin with charcoal, and she endeavoured to grasp the intricate methodology by which an accomplished artisan arranges all the compounds and elements. *Do any of them contain the kinds of occult properties that someone like me would require to thwart an aberration of the psyche?*

Scratching at her temples, Anastasia found her way back to the hostelry. For a time, she paced about the lobby. When she climbed the stairway to the rooftop, she bumped into one of the hostelry's elderly tenants.

In a thick Greek accent, the old woman introduced herself as Philemon. Then she knelt beneath a large patio umbrella. 'The hostelry keeper tells me you wish to find a post down at the mirror works.'

When Anastasia failed to say much, the old woman removed an ornate *huqqa* pipe from her shoulder bag. 'Please talk,' Philemon said then. 'I see great sadness in your eyes.'

'Sadness?'

'Could it be the women down there at the mirror works don't require an apprentice just at the moment?'

'*No.* Everything went well, but that's the trouble. Suddenly, I've got the notion that someday soon the Lord ought to punish me for what I'm doing.'

Philemon smoked her pipe for a while, and then she dropped the pipe hose. 'Of course, the Good Lord must make you pay. What a villainess, Ernesztina. She's godless, *blind*. No scruples. *Kýrie eléison.*'

Anastasia wrinkled her nose. *Does the old woman speak the truth?* She fussed with her Huguenot cross. *What if the sensuous Ernesztina hopes to corrupt me? What have I gotten*

82

myself into? Her temples throbbing yet, she looked out across the flat, parapeted rooftops of the village.

Deep within her womb, the dream fox leaned back—as if repulsed. And now he hissed and yelped and howled like a baby.

She scratched her chin and sought to convince herself that in coming here, she had decided wisely. *Once I'm liberated, I know I'll feel so good. I'll take my place in society. I'll make something of myself.*

Philemon removed a leather flagon from the basket at her side. 'Maybe you drink something?'

The water should have tasted sweet; however, when Anastasia downed a mouthful, she found that it tasted sickeningly tart.

The old woman puffed upon her *huqqa* pipe and pointed the end of the hose toward the horizon. 'We must flee village. Up at Saint Catherine's, there lives a monk named Papachristou. Maybe we strike a bargain, so he help us travel up north.'

'What makes you think I want to do that? I'm not afraid of anyone.'

'Please, we sail for lovely Naxos, and you no regret nothing. Mount Zeus make a good home for you. All the desert islands of Hellas make very good home. The Venetians, they come years ago, and they build all such lovely villas and towers and piazzas.' The old woman puffed upon the pipe one last time and cracked a grin. 'No you worry.'

Deep inside Anastasia's womb, the fox spirit twitched his tail. 'Listen to the old woman. Go away. Tonight. When the moon glows shimmery bright.'

The sun beating down upon her scalp, Anastasia placed her hand upon her belly and caressed the skin around her navel—until the dream fox sighed.

A moment later, as the desert breeze whistled across the rooftop, Philemon dropped the flagon. 'Maybe we go inside and pack our bags, yes?'

Anastasia winced and shook her head. Then she knelt beside a marble krater stuffed with Egyptian willow. *I'm not going anywhere.*

~

That Same Day, Almost Seven O'clock.

As the sun continued its descent, Anastasia departed the hostelry and traipsed back into the marketplace.

Softly, the fox spirit twitched his tail. 'You leave me no choice but to challenge you in the most insolent way. If you'll not cease to conspire against me, and if you'll not sail home, then I must drive you to madness.'

'Oh, leave me be.' As she waded through the crowded marketplace, she noticed that same pallid youth from before.

Once more, the peculiar young man stood beside the telegraph-office door. As soon as their eyes met, he hurried over toward the curiosity shop across the street. For the longest time, the puzzling stranger acted as if enthralled by the little Persian inkhorn standing in the heart of the display table.

What a dunce. At a steady pace, she passed by a shop selling paper parasols and sidled over to the moneychanger's shop to rest her back against the white stucco wall.

The youthful stranger did not approach, as if the earlier encounter precluded all. He glanced at her, though, and then averted his gaze—as if ashamed.

She noticed that his bladder gave way—and no sooner

had the fool fouled himself than he darted off in the direction of the produce market. She shook her head. *What's a girl to make of all that?*

Deep inside her womb, the fox spirit twitched his tail slowly against the lining of her womb—as if to please her. 'As feckless as that English lad, that's how powerful I'd be. You know that to be true. It's something your powers of intuition tell you. Don't deny it.'

'*No.*' Three times over, she poked at her belly.

'Please, you must sail home. And soon. Leave this place. If you don't, I swear you'll never recover from my magic.'

She meandered along through the marketplace, only to step into a heap of camel droppings as malodorous as rain-drenched hemp.

The fox hissed and panted and yelped. 'What makes you think someone like you could ever perform some kind of exorcism? And what makes you think the mirrors around here should be magical enough to imprison me? Don't you appreciate my powers?'

She continued through the marketplace until she emerged from the shade of the tin roof and into the soft, soothing light of the sun. Further down the road, she washed the sullied sole of her button boot within a grandiose fountain standing in the heart of the dusty roundabout. Then she looked at the sky and closed her eyes. In that moment, what a delight it was to listen to the splash of the fountain's jets.

By the time she opened her eyes, the soft, pink, silvery-orange light of dusk already stretched out across the sky.

How lovely. She checked her timepiece, and then she paused to consider the beauty of the mirror works.

'What's that place there?' the fox asked. 'Tell me.'

'That's where I'll destroy you, one fine day.' She approached the structure to look inside, but the awning window revealed little more than a long, wooden worktable in the foreground and a shearing wheel in the back.

Not five minutes later, Ernesztina appeared along the dusty path winding its way up from the seaside garden. When she reached the mirror-works door, she let Anastasia inside.

The modest workshop boasted all kinds of machinery, and on the walls hung an array of tools and supplies—punches and chisels, specialty hammers, pump sprays, leather aprons and matching gloves. The bookshelf along the eastern wall contained jumbles of papers and sundry jars of tin chloride.

When Ernesztina guided Anastasia outside, the woman pointed toward a little donkey-drawn tumbrel cart just then approaching from the north. 'That'd be the tinsmith. He's bringing us a whole new consignment of tin bronze.'

When the tinsmith reached the mirror works, he let go of the reins and greeted Ernesztina. When he climbed down, he gestured politely to Anastasia.

Her temples throbbed anew, and as the fox spirit deep within her womb gently twitched his tail, the muscles all throughout her pelvic floor churned. 'Stop,' she whispered, looking down at her belly.

The tinsmith waddled off to the back of the tumbrel cart, where he severed the cord that bound the metallic sheets together. As soon as he set the sheet down, the tin bronze hummed like a quartz bowl.

Once he had hauled that first sheet into the mirror works, Anastasia followed Ernesztina inside and helped her to gather up some of the metallurgical books strewn about. When the tinsmith hurried off to collect another sheet, Anastasia approached the one he had left leaning against the cracked, blistering wall. 'How long does it take to transform such a grainy surface into a mirror?' she asked over her shoulder.

'Sometimes it takes nine whole months,' Ernesztina answered. 'Just like a woman who seeks to carry her baby to term.'

Deep inside Anastasia's womb, the fox spirit nudged the lining of her womb. 'Go home this instant. To willingly serve a woman as sensuous as Ernesztina, that's a sin. If you don't go home, I'm sure God Almighty must exact the most unspeakable retribution. He'll never forgive you. Let's not forget you're a Huguenot. You live in defiance of Vatican City State.'

Her head spinning, Anastasia wandered outside—just in time to espy that same pallid, peculiar English youth: he passed by, a little crust of bread in one hand and a milk jug in the other. She looked at the stain on his trousers and realised, with a sneer of disgust, that he had not even troubled himself to clean up.

Without a word, he crossed the roundabout and climbed the hill. Removing his deerstalker, he continued into the opera house standing atop the summit. A moment later, a soft, muted, creamy, seemingly electric orange light shone from one of the upstairs windows.

What's he doing in there? She poked her belly. 'What have you to say about this?'

The fox darted about her womb. 'I know nothing about that foolish lad. Still, he's one more good reason for you to go home. That's something you agree with, deep down.'

She snuck forward to study the light, and when the youth peeked from behind the window's left-side jamb, she grabbed a pecan-shaped stone lying nearby and hurled it at him.

The stone dropped some fifty feet short, without a sound—but then, off to her right, a strong, valiant, manly voice called out: '*Brava.*'

The voice belonged to a tall, athletic British Army captain strolling along in the direction of the marketplace. What a striking figure, too. The officer had deeply set, amber-coloured eyes, a perfectly chiselled jaw and muscular thighs. In addition, his regimentals could not have appeared more immaculate: his perfectly tailored khaki tunic boasted brass buttons and a noble sleeve badge, and his trouser crease looked impossibly sharp.

Oh dear. Until that moment, she had no idea that the War Office had billeted any soldiers nearby. More than that, as he continued forward, she wondered if she had ever witnessed anyone looking so beautiful. *Send me.* All the time rolling the very tip of her tongue over her gap tooth, she gazed deep into his eyes—until her bosom heaved. *Go easy.* At last, she smoothed out her blouse and then dropped her hands to her pleated skirt.

The officer stopped three feet away and tipped his hat. 'Give the enemy the everlasting knock,' he said.

The tinsmith's donkey whuffled and squealed. Had the officer impressed the animal?

Her mouth slack, Anastasia could not respond. Without question, the charming soldier wished to trifle with her. She sucked in a quick breath. Then she considered his scent and recognised it as a pleasing blend of aloe wood and musk. *How befitting a captain.*

The soldier gestured toward the pebble at her feet. 'Cast that stone there and knock the whole opera house down. Just like an Egyptian revolutionary might do.'

She straightened her posture. 'So, there's a citadel down by the seaside? That's a big surprise. I should've thought that the British Army might be garrisoned up the coast a mile or so, defending Sharm al-Sheikh.'

'Name, rank, and number. Captain Holywell, number 5373739. I shan't tell you anything more.' With that, he pointed at her Huguenot cross and pendant dove. 'A French-Protestant lass, are you?'

'That's right. For what it's worth, though, I'm from Russia. My mother's side of the family followed Gustav Fabergé to Saint Petersburg. The Huguenots, we're all quite loyal to one another.' A movement caught her eye, and she noticed the tinsmith exiting the mirror works with his familiar, waddling gait—Ernesztina following along at his heels.

He handed Ernesztina an invoice. 'Forgive high price,' he told her. '*Aiwa*. Tin futures to blame.'

Ernesztina grimaced and folded up the slip of paper. With neck bent, she took refuge inside.

The tinsmith grabbed the donkey's worn leather noseband and guided beast and tumbrel cart off in the direction of the caravansary.

Deep within Anastasia's womb, the fox spirit sighed. 'Repent. Leave this place this very instant. It's what you want to do.'

She ignored the dream fox and paused to consider the mild breeze. *Could it be that the weather patterns of Sinai include the phenomenon of Goose Summer?* She certainly hoped so, for she had always delighted in those warm autumn days when old cobwebs crumble apart such that the gossamer threads float off on the breeze.

Before she could mention anything about it to Captain Holywell, the officer saluted her and marched off in the direction of the marketplace.

As she watched him go, she could have swooned: the soldier held himself so straight and so tall, and what broad shoulders, too.

The dream fox snarled. 'Imagine what must happen to you if you don't go home. One day, you'll awaken to find that I've gouged out your eyeballs. You heard me right. That's something you've always feared.'

She barely registered the message. The whole time that the dream fox fulminated, she could not take her eyes off the soldier. *Oh God, I'm so confounded.* Before long, she staggered over toward the fountain. Without even thinking, she ran her hands up and down her chest and bosom and neck. *What's happened? What am I feeling just now?* She had no answer. Like any other innocent maiden preparing for her very first assignation, she could no longer distinguish between the cold ache of horror and the burning thrill of lust.

VI.

The Village of Al-Hubu, the Wilderness of Sinai.
2 November 1917.

Early that morning, Jack awoke and found himself in the opera-house dressing room. For a time, he studied the shadows falling on the walls. No matter the relative warmth of the building, he shivered uncontrollably. Only yesterday, he had learned the new arrival's name. *Anastasia. How lovely.* Given his recurring dreams of someone coming to greet him lovingly and to lie at his side, he longed to believe that certain someone must be her. *Yes, Anastasia.*

Already, his loneliness had beguiled him into believing that she desired him as much as he desired her. Like a telepath calling upon someone far away, he spoke up: 'Anastasia, come visit me.'

No response came, of course.

He broke into tears. *There's no one here. Naught but shadows in an empty room.*

When he finally picked himself up, he wandered into the marketplace—as he had done yesterday. And just like yesterday, he pined for the young lady who had recently arrived in the seaside village.

By chance, she passed him by—though she did not make eye contact. Even if she had, what would it have mattered? He knew it was unlikely that she would wish to watch him wallowing in self-pity. Moreover, as timid as he had always been, he would not have been able to muster the nerve to introduce himself. As he rubbed his hands on his dirty trousers, he slouched over to the telegraph office. Standing there with his legs parallel to one another, he rubbed the back of his neck and stared at the ornate papyrus print hanging on the otherwise barren wall. The print depicted the Eye of Horus: a falcon's eye complete with a black teardrop-shaped marking that made it seem as if the deity must be weeping.

Jack stumbled a little bit closer to the telegraph-office window, for the pupil seemed to peal very softly—like a sea captain's brass bell. He listened for ten minutes. Then, as he made his way back from the marketplace, he stopped beside the fountain that stood in the heart of the roundabout. His hands shaking violently, he discerned the uncanny presence of an old footman standing at his back. 'What's your name? Never mind, I'll give you one.' Jack thought awhile and then clasped his trembling hands together. 'I'll call you Mr Albéric T Sylvius. That's the name of me former chemistry instructor. And just like him, you prefer to dress yourself in a derby and threadbare sack suit. Right?'

The apparition tapped Jack's shoulder, and for the very first time, a disembodied voice spoke up: 'Why you always twiddling your thumbs, aye, why don't you do something with your life?'

Jack dried his tears and paused to consider the spectral figure's voice itself. *Why does he sound like me? He talks like me because he's a creation of me own noodle.* Jack leaned his head to the left. 'Why must you hector me? Can't you appreciate the angst I'm feeling? I ought to be living in essence, and God willing, maybe I'll be doing just that soon enough. It's just that I've got to overcome me bashfulness if I'm to make Anastasia's acquaintance.'

'No, you'll never manage that. It all comes down to your slothfulness, aye, and the sin of sloth, it's disgusting, so why don't you concentrate on your work and find a concert promoter to help you along with your sterling career, aye, or get yourself a press agent?'

'Someday soon, I'll do all that. For now, though, I got to think about Anastasia. I've got to find some way to introduce myself and . . .'

'You should be so lucky. Nobody wants nothing to do with a halfwit like you. Not even a hallucination like me.'

Inexplicably, the earflaps on either side of Jack's deerstalker burned—so he dropped the hat at his feet. As an awkward silence continued, he sniffed at his armpit. *Bloody hell, I pong like a fox. A dead fox.*

One of the locals, Ernesztina, passed by with gliding, ladylike steps.

Jack scratched at his oily scalp and watched awhile. The woman's pleasing gait resembled the sensual way his stepmother had always slunk about the house back home.

When he collected his deerstalker, he studied the mirror works—the place of business where the beautiful new arrival lately worked. A second time, he dropped his hat. The tweed cloth burned like a ball of fire. *I'm loused. Bloody hell, I'm losing the plot.*

The old man tapped upon Jack's shoulder. 'You ought to make advances and seek the damsel's hand and ply her with a fine gift, and no, it can't be no bit of debris what the surf coughed up. It's got to be something bespoke, so how about a tortoiseshell plectrum?'

'I can't do that.' For a second time, Jack scratched at his scalp. 'Bloody hell, I can't speak to no beautiful bird.'

'Why not?'

'Because I *can't*. Whenever she passes by, I get to feeling like I'm two of eels. And then, me heart in me mouth and all, I can't think of anything to say. Like I'm all in a muddle.'

'That can't be true, mate, so, go speak with her even now, because back in my day, that's what I'd do, and in all honesty, you got nothing to fear because I'm quite sure she should fancy you, for you've got yourself such long, lovely, wavy brown hair and such big blue eyes, aye, what a fine, beautiful lad.'

Jack stared at a thin, little thorn tree standing over to the side of the mirror works. 'Back home in Bloomsbury, I'd never go up to some bird what didn't even know me. If I were to do that, she and her friends, they'd probably fall about laughing.'

'*Enough*. She's only pretending to be disdainful, I say. You've got no cause to fear the gracious new arrival, for she's no ordinary girl, aye, and for all you know, she'll sympathise with a chap like you.'

Jack's spine burned, as if he had been sitting in a wooden chair all day with his back up against the sunbaked splat.

The warm desert wind gusted, meanwhile, and over alongside the mirror works, the thorn tree rattled like a Spanish maraca filled with pumpkin seeds.

All the dust and sand made Jack sneeze, and he wiped his nose upon his sleeve—and suddenly even his linen shirt became impossibly hot to the touch, and now the tip of his nose burned.

'Go speak with the bird,' Mr Sylvius said. 'Take her in hand and tell her she's got the deft touch. "My, but you work like the dickens," you'll say.'

'No, I *can't.*' Trembling, Jack glanced at the mirror works and imagined the young lady working inside.

From within the mirror works, a shrill noise rang out. Had she activated some kind of electric die grinder?

He kicked at a few of the faded wildflowers that had sprouted up alongside the fountain's basin.

At his back, Mr Sylvius let out a fatherly sigh. 'I must insist you call upon the object of your affection sometime soon, because it won't do for you to simply gaze into her eyes, because that kind of thing, it bloody well unnerves the gentle sex.'

'Right.' Biting at his lips, Jack collected the deerstalker and tucked the hat beneath his arm. 'I'll come speak with her the first chance I get. Cross my heart.'

From the direction of the mirror works, the shrill din grew louder—as if Anastasia must be cutting something apart, shaping some crucial piece.

Holding his breath, he marched up the hill to the opera house—where the lobby door's burnished-bronze knob burned in his palm like a lump of hot, soft bitumen.

No sooner had he drawn his hand back than the die grinder grew quiet.

For a moment or two, he paced—and he resisted the urge to turn back in the direction of the mirror works. *What if she's standing at the window looking my way? What would I say?*

At last, he continued inside. Upstairs in the cool of the dressing room, he paused before the cracked stage mirror to check his reflection. 'Look here, you. It's time for you to get yourself a stratagem. You've got to chalk things out if you wish to win the heart of a bird.' With that, he tiptoed over to the window and tucked a tattered old shawl over the top rail—as if the darkness might give him strength and make him feel more secure. *How about some music? Yes, that should do me good. Why rush meself? No reason at all.* He edged over to the gramophone that the soprano had left behind and secured the horn to the elbow. Once he had wound up the whole apparatus, he arranged the stylus upon one of the soprano's opera recordings—and following a few pops and crackles, a pleasing duet from *La traviata* commenced. *Cheers.* He lay upon the divan, closed his eyes, and imagined himself the tenor singing Alfredo's part. *Yes, I'm a fine young provincial French chap.*

Twenty minutes later, when the music concluded, he opened his eyes and listened to the stylus skip over the last groove in the recording. *I got to do something, eh? I've got to overcome me fears and kick things off with Anastasia.* As the stylus bumped up against the label, he shifted onto his side and studied the dressing-room walls: each one shone eggshell white, not unlike the traditional *couturière* chair that had always sat in his stepmother's boutique back home.

His head snapping back, he recalled that autumn afternoon when a lovely Italian girl stopped by the shop and asked him to attach a lace veil to her silk parasol. At first, he could not speak. Over and above her beauty, the Italian girl had always mystified him. Time after time, he had noticed her traipsing along Charlotte Street—the peculiar figure mumbling in her Tuscan dialect and cursing some unclean spirit that had evidently taken possession of her.

The stylus bumping up against the label yet, he covered his ears against the click click click click of the needle. *Maybe*

*if I wait here long enough, Anastasia should come to me. Yes, I'm
sure she'll visit.*

Despite the shawl hanging over the window, a warm,
fresh desert breeze crept into the dressing room. Gently, the
current stirred a few pages of the frayed book that the soprano
had left behind—*The Age of Fable* by Thomas Bulfinch.

For the second time that day, Jack broke into tears. *The
age of fable has passed me by, and now there's nothing left but
the tedium of modern times. The absence of miracles, telepathic
bonds between loving boys and girls.*

Wheezing from all the dust, Jack stood up from the divan
and dragged himself over to the gramophone. He lifted the
stylus from the recording, and then he knelt and polished a
few minor scuffs showing upon his walking shoes—anything
to convince himself that he was much too busy to visit
Anastasia at the moment.

Midafternoon, he crept downstairs to the opera stage
and stopped before the glass harp—a set of glass dishes fitted
about a long, narrow rod holding everything in place over a
long water trough. Not two weeks earlier, he had discovered
the contrivance in the opera-house attic—and he had resolved
to teach himself how to play the archaic instrument. For the
very first time, he stepped upon the treadle to make the dishes
reel through the water. Gently then, he glided his fingertips
over the edge of this dish and that and performed a ghosted
note or two.

What an otherworldly sound—something like the music
that an accomplished busker might perform on a set of lead-
crystal wineglasses and goblets.

*Or the music played by the piper at the Gates of Dawn. That's
right.* As the desert breeze sailed through the music hall's tall,
majestic windows, Jack played a simple étude.

The antique plum-crystal chandeliers tinkled as the desert breeze moved through them, and a section of the pleated brilliantine drape danced in the soft remnant of the current.

As the last delicate peal died out, Jack gazed out of the window, where a profusion of light poured into the orchestra stalls. The soothing, hazy, white-smoke glow, unlike the light of the desert sun, seemed all so *nostalgic*, suggesting as it did the soft October light of home. He revisited his life there—all his melancholy daydreams, his vain longing to be some celebrated composer.

From the direction of the mirror works, the din of the shearing wheel rang out as it had before: industrious, beautiful Anastasia cutting a sheet of tin bronze.

Anastasia, oh my. He shuddered and laughed bitterly. Like a fool, he picked at a few of the nicks on his chin where he had shaved the day before. *If only I had some way to make her love me.* A second, violent shudder moving through his torso, the whole of his body burned—until, from down below and out across the dusty roundabout, the din of the wheel died down.

Directing his gaze downward, he noticed not twenty feet away, in the stalls, something shining as brightly as a knight-errant's breastplate.

When he inched his way forward to investigate the matter, he determined the mysterious object to be nothing more than the tin of apple curd that his stepmother had sent him some two weeks before. By now, though, the mice had consumed the contents. *How's all this for a moment of bathos? Ah, but I probably deserve it.* He collected the empty tin and studied his reflection. *Might I be good enough for the bird over there in the mirror works?* Suddenly, no question could ever be so paramount. Nevertheless, he could not quite manage an answer. *Would a beautiful girl like her approve of my rather distinctive Greek nose?*

The scent of Guinea pepper filled the air as the spice merchant's buckboard rolled through the roundabout.

Jack looked out the window and watched Ernesztina climb down from the buckboard and stroll off barefoot through the dusty roundabout.

As the buckboard continued along, she passed by the marble fountain and stopped at the mirror-works door—as if to say something to the young lady inside.

A moment or two later, her arms crossed, Ernesztina departed the mirror works and slunk off around the corner.

They must've been talking about me. That's right. He slouched back to the empty apple-curd tin. Again, he studied his faint, distorted reflection. *I'm a dosser. I've got to learn to care for others, the poor and all. If so, I'll be deserving of someone. Maybe even a bird like Anastasia.*

A pink Jerusalem mealybug fluttered down into the metallic box—as if the apple curd's lingering aroma had deceived the creature into thinking that a few grains of sustenance might still be there.

Why not show the poor thing a measure of mercy? He coaxed the fly onto the tip of his finger and placed the empty tin upside down on the windowsill. Then he flicked the creature onto the floor. *No, what if the blighter comes buzzing about upstairs?* He paced for a while, and then, as selfish as he was, crushed the harmless insect beneath the sole of his right shoe.

An hour later, back in the dressing room, he stared at his carriage clock, transfixed by the incessant ticking. *Shall I go talk to Anastasia?* Like a humbled subject, he knelt before the clock for a moment. Coming out of his trance, he took the device into his hand and studied a few of the case screws. *Shall I take it apart and check the crown wheel?* At last, he succumbed to the urge to dawdle—anything to delay the inevitable for a few more days. *I'll talk to Anastasia some other sunny afternoon. Right, once I've willed me angst to go away.*

~

8 November 1917.

Late that afternoon, Jack peeked out the lobby door and looked down to the roundabout. *Are you anywhere about, love?* Both of his hands going limp, he fixed his gaze upon the mirror-works door. *I'm thinking of you. Do you read me thoughts? Please answer.*

As the beauty of that found moment washed over his person, his eyes widened: a dozen balls of tumbleweed rolled along this way and that, and to the south of the dusty roundabout, the desert breeze rattled a few of the opera company's wooden cycloramas presently standing amid a thicket of date palms. *It's the perfect moment to speak to Anastasia. Perfect.*

Awakening from the dreamlike interlude, he noticed the way the setting sun reflected on the mirror-works windows. *Why not call upon her before she locks up? Right, that's just what I'll do.* Having decided to tidy up first, he retreated into the darkened lobby and hurried off into the ladies' powder room. Beside the washbasin, where he had arranged his ditty bag, he felt at some of the stubble on his cheeks. When he looked inside the ditty bag, however, he realised that he had no more shaving soap.

From the direction of the waterfront, there awoke the unmistakable thumping of soldiers' ammunition boots.

Glancing out of the window, he saw a tall, steadfast

captain marching a whole company through the roundabout. Jack cringed and looked at the floor. The soldiers' presence only served to remind him of his own cowardice. More than anything, he thought of Cousin Billy and the terrific array of shrapnel scars he had sustained whilst serving with the Cheshire Regiment outside Flixécourt.

'I got no regrets,' Cousin Billy had told him at the homecoming party. 'A proper bloke has no choice but to slip the king's coat over his shoulders.'

The sound of the soldiers' ammunition boots trailed away, and a dissonant clamour awoke from the direction of the mirror works—the die grinder.

Jack crept back to the lobby, where he heard something stirring outside. When he opened the door, he found the source of the scrabbling to be a ball of tumbleweed having rolled all the way up to the threshold.

Chin lowered to his chest, Jack trudged down the hill. When he reached the fountain, he noticed a foul odour—something like stale custard. As he retreated from the basin, he debated whether he ought to flee. *Why not postpone things till tomorrow?* He forced himself to face the fountain. *I've got to introduce myself to Anastasia, as diffident as I am.*

Two figures approached from the east. As they came closer, the party proved to be the engineer who worked for the Sinai Public-Works Department, together with his little daughter.

Jack bowed to them. '*Ahalan.*'

The engineer greeted him in broken English and placed his wooden toolbox beside the fountain. Without explanation, the engineer stopped the pump—and the triumphal jets vanished.

As the waters grew quiet, Jack wondered what he should say to the Egyptian worker. *Why not apologise for British rule and offer a few words of encouragement?* When he spoke up at last, the engineer ignored both the apology and the lame attempt at upliftment. With a frown, Jack tugged at his crumpled club-collar shirt and fussed with his woollen trousers—wondering if the locals might be more accepting of him if he were to dress in a fine, ankle-length robe. *How about a woollen* dishdasha *in Egyptian blue?*

The engineer opened the wicket, and a torrent rushed out of the basin. As the water flowed off in all directions, he helped his daughter up into the fountain—and the little girl lunged this way and that, gathering the many coins into an earthenware jar.

What if Anastasia comes along at this very moment? Weaving in place, Jack glanced at the mirror-works door. *How to engage a fine bird, what with these villagers standing here?*

The engineer belched rather noisily, and the desert air filled with the odour of pistachio *couscous.* Seemingly unashamed, the engineer took the earthenware jar from his daughter and belched a second time.

As Jack watched the engineer and his daughter stride away, Anastasia emerged from the mirror works. She closed and locked the door, and then, looking down, shuffled forward along a narrow section of the roundabout where the earth remained dry.

His knees shook, and his heart thumped. Still, as the comely young lady drew ever closer, he willed himself to advance. *Say something. Go on.* As she passed him by, he tried to catch her big blue eyes. *My God. She walks in beauty.*

And then it was over. The exquisite beauty vanished. Had she hurried off into the marketplace?

He stumbled back a few steps. *What a calamity. How to bear such a bitter defeat?* His knees still weak, he lurched over to the fountain and looked into the basin.

Miraculously, the little Egyptian girl had missed a coin: a Victoria fourpence shimmered brightly just there beside the riser pipe. Before he could pocket the coin, though, the fountain's drainpipe spewed forth one last burst of water—all over his trouser cuffs.

When he looked up, he saw Ernesztina reappear down the street.

Her eyes flashing, she strode forward and stopped. 'I passed by Anastasia just now, and she told me that you made her feel quite ill at ease by staring at her. Why must you vex her the way you do?' Ernesztina's face tightened. 'Look there,' the woman said, pointing toward the ornate Egyptian pantheon neatly hewn into the fountain's black marble basin. 'Gods such as these would never tolerate your insolence.'

The tips of Jack's fingers burned, as if he had touched a hot coal. 'I weren't looking to be insolent.'

Ernesztina knelt to the earth, and with her finger, tapped upon the veil concealing some godly visage. 'This is Isis, goddess of magic. And do you know why she hides her face? If she failed to do so, a mortal could look into her eyes and learn his destiny. And what a grave crime that'd be.'

The uncanny burning sensation spread from Jack's fingertips and into his wrist and up along his forearm.

Ernesztina seized his arm at the elbow and squeezed. 'You remind me of some scoundrel hoping to deceive Isis and lift her veil and learn his destiny.'

As he pulled his arm away, strains of music commenced—an intimate, soothing, lyric-contralto voice humming a dreamlike tune.

The melody resembled a piano piece that he had once taught himself. Gulping, he stuttered, 'Do you hear the music?'

'What are you talking about? What music?' Ernesztina tapped upon the veil a second time before standing.

'You don't hear the music? What mood. What dynamics. It's so lovely. *Andante espressivo.*'

Ernesztina merely shook her head. 'Are you ribbing me? It sounds like you're sick in the head. Like you've contracted a brain fungus.'

He did not answer. Instead, he raced off toward the marketplace. From there, he followed the dreamlike melody all the way to the telegraph office—where the humming grew much louder and faster. His head swivelled right and left as she sought the source of the music. Then he looked through the window and espied the papyrus print depicting the Eye of Horus. *Of course. Of course.*

Even if it were nothing more than an auditory hallucination, the wondrous music seemed to emanate from the black of the falcon god's pupil.

His mouth falling open, Jack debated the matter at hand. *Perhaps me nerves have conjured an illusion. No, it's no illusion. It's magic. It's a miracle.*

When the music ceased, a trick of the light compelled the darkness of the pupil to sparkle—as if the Eye of Horus must be alive, as if the entity commanded great powers and had resolved to send the young man a telepathic message here and now.

Jack trembled as he advanced closer to the telegraph-office window. *Horus means to tell me something, do he? Blimey, it's the same way the fountain carvings speak to Ernesztina.*

As the black of the Egyptian god's pupil flashed the colour of a pristine bronze Victoria fourpence, Jack drew a deep breath. *Tell me what to do about Anastasia. How do I speak to her? Do you know? Please explain. I'm poised for action.*

That's right. I'm longing to live in the essence.

The whole of the eye seemed to wink. 'You will speak with her *telepathically*, just like a clever street magician. Now call upon your beloved.'

'But what do I say?'

'Vow to compose a piece of music for her. A love song.'

'A love song.' Jack's shoulders jerked and sagged as all the tension left his body. Suddenly, he possessed the answer to all his woes. *Yes, but what should I call me song?* He would have to give the work a fine name. *I'll call the piece 'Ode to the Memory of Anastasia'.* He decided against it—for the title did not seem fashionable enough. *How about something austere? I could name the piece 'Egyptian Lyrics'.* He scratched his head. *No, I'll call the piece 'Reminiscence'.* Soon enough, he revisited the idea of calling the work 'Ode to the Memory of Anastasia'. *Would that be right? Maybe I could give her name an exotic spelling? How about Anastasiia? Would that work?* Hands clenched into fists, his thoughts turned back to Tuscany. If he had chosen to sojourn there, he would have so many appealing options: 'Tuscan Lyrics' or 'Tuscan Music' or perhaps even a formal-sounding title such as 'Lines Written in a Tuscan Marketplace'. *Or maybe 'Lines Written in a Tuscan Café'.* Jack's eyes grew wide, and his body went still. *What am I doing here? A real composer writes the bloody song first.*

A dozen soldiers marched by, their presence shaking him out of his reverie. Like so many times before, he again envisioned all the valiant British soldiers huddled in bolt-holes somewhere along the trench line—and as he pictured them there, he slumped. *Enough with the trenches. And to hell with me inadequacies as well.* In an effort to get his mind on something else, he pulled his deerstalker low and sought out the most extravagant hotel in the village. When he reached the establishment, he stopped before a fallen Egyptian white-lotus petal. *How romantic. Yes, indeed.* As he loitered there, he pictured Anastasia sitting in her room. 'Do you read me thoughts?' he asked in a wavering whisper. 'Please answer.'

The hotel chef, a gentleman reeking of toasted seeds, wandered outside—as if he alone had received the telepathic message. He glared at Jack and sauntered off—and the alluring scent of toasted seeds died out.

Shall I go on inside? No, don't. Jack looked at the balcony above. 'I know how lonely you must be feeling here in the Orient, but don't pother. Everything's all dancing, for I know how to serve you. On wings of song, I'll prove me love for you. And then we'll be together. Just like real love.'

Anastasia should have transmitted a response, but he neither sensed nor heard anything unusual.

He gaped at a weathered pushcart bearing an empty birdcage. 'A birdcage?' A second time, he stared at the balcony. 'Don't be affrighted. I don't mean to lock you up, girl. Remember, there's no one so fond of you as me. Honest, love. Fancied you at first blush, I did.' No response came, so he shook his head and wended his way back to the telegraph office. For a second time, he stared at the wondrous papyrus print.

The Eye of Horus throbbed with heartrending emotion, a longing to fulfill the most shameful erotic fantasy.

Jack gasped. *I'm only projecting. Yes, I'm the Eye of Horus.* Jack's chest caved as a sigh wracked his body. With bent spine, he made his way down to the seashore. *I got to be hopeful, that's right. Hopeful.* He forced himself to stand up straight and imagined a lady artist working off to the right—that same fine Frenchwoman standing before her easel, her colourful canvas depicting the Temple of Poseidon complete with fairy shrimp and devil rays flitting about.

'I don't require your kind no more,' he told the imaginary Frenchwoman. 'Pack up your easel and off you go. I've got me own lovely bird, and we've got the power to read each other's thoughts. Which proves how deep our bond is, eh?'

A few English soldiers marched by, and as Jack fidgeted, they dumped a crate of empty cream-sherry bottles over to the side.

'What're you doing here in Sinai?' a lance corporal asked him. 'Oi, it's a mystery to me, but I'd say you look old enough for mobilisation.'

Jack sought to say something, but the shame left him speechless. His cheeks burned, and he wondered if his lingering guilt might explain all the burning sensations he had felt of late.

A second soldier approached. 'Maybe this stripling considers himself a pacifist,' the soldier said in a working-class London accent. 'Maybe the fellow despises war.'

'Or maybe he's just a bloody coward who prefers to enjoy the springtime of his life,' the lance corporal said. 'So, which one would it be, then?' he asked, pointing at Jack.

No matter how hard he tried, Jack could not bring himself to answer. Struggling to breathe, he gave the two soldiers a blank look. *What have I done? I should've joined up.*

When the soldiers were gone, he removed each one of the bottles from the crate and brought them up to his former encampment and stood them in a row. *There you are. Smashing.* He tapped the glass bottles in the hope that he might stumble upon some heartfelt prelude—the beginnings of a love song. *That's right. A love song.*

VII.

The Village of Al-Hubu, the Wilderness of Sinai.
23 November 1917.

In the darkness before dawn, Anastasia awoke with clammy hands. *Somebody's here.* Before climbing out of bed, she listened for the presence of an intruder. She heard no one, so she leapt up. As she dried her hands on the hem of her nightdress, she struggled to recall her dreams from seconds ago. *Yes, I know. I dreamt of that peculiar youth climbing in through my window.* There could be no avoiding such visions. By now, she could no longer bear Jack's preternatural talent for silently gazing at her whenever she strolled through the marketplace. *Does he wish to devour me with his eyes? What does he want?*

Just before the break of dawn, she climbed out onto the hostelry rooftop to contemplate the crescent moon and to collect her thoughts. At once, however, images of Captain Holywell clouded her mind. Soon, the lust intensified— for the more her disgust with the enigmatic youth grew, the more passionately she yearned for the bold officer. *That fine soldier, he's everything an Englishman ought to be.* In a swoon, she swayed back and forth. *Captain Holywell. Yes, Captain Holywell.*

The moon's glow shone upon a passing cloud, and the wintry wind shifted such that the current's shrill whistle resembled a traditional Huguenot lullaby—the very one Mother once sang to her.

She climbed back into her room and settled herself in bed. *There's nothing to fear.*

Deep inside her womb, the fox cried out like a baby.

She kicked her feet in the hope of chastening the fox. *Today, I'll find some way to crowd him out of me. That's what I'll do. By the end of the day, I'll be free of him.*

Three hours later, when Captain Holywell stopped by the hostelry, she invited him to stay for breakfast. Tapping her feet to a mirthful tune playing in her head, she went into the upstairs kitchen and prepared a dish of mashed field beans and barley bread. They brought the repast out to the little mosaic table on her balcony.

Deep inside her womb, the fox spirit held his downy tail perfectly still. 'Why should you be sweet on this soldier boy here? He could never adore you the way I do.'

Anastasia leaned over the wrought-iron balustrade, where a thin ray of light poured through the posts. Only yesterday morning, she had noticed a layer of hoarfrost enshrouding the railing cap—a shimmery crystalline coating that wasn't there today. Now she looked out across the rooftops. *If I noticed a frost yesterday, then it could only mean Goose Summer must finally be here.* A series of strong unladylike tremors awoke all throughout the muscles of her pelvic floor, and she arched her back. Impulsively, she glided the tip of her tongue over her gap tooth. 'Let's sleep together down by the seaside tonight,' she said.

At her back, the officer remained quiet. Did he mean to embarrass her? Whatever his intention, he made no sound at all.

'You'll bring an army bedroll,' she continued, 'and we'll find a place in the bluffs where the sand feels good and soft. What do you say?'

When she glanced back in his direction, Captain Holywell held his chin high and smirked. 'Don't be so coy, love.'

His irony made her wince. When she turned back to the balustrade, she looked down through a large gap in the arched tin roof that sheltered the marketplace.

How quiet the narrow lane was now that the last of the summer-holiday crowd had gone home.

A glistening strand of gossamer drifted past the tip of her nose. Simultaneously, a wondrous dreamlike note of music whistled all so softly.

What's that? As much as anything, the sound made her think of the way a guitar player makes harmonics—the musician plucking one of the strings while barely touching the fret, the harmonic note ringing out like a soft, velvety chime. Time and again, that sound had always filled her with wonder.

Another strand of gossamer drifted by—and a note with a lower pitch resounded, as if the guitar player had moved his fretting hand further down toward the headstock.

She looked out across the rooftops. *Could it be that here in Sinai the strands of broken cobwebs make fantastical sounds as they sail through the currents?* Her hands growing moist and cool, she rubbed them together to warm them.

The clamour of a pushcart with rusty wheels awoke from the marketplace, and she looked down. As if he sensed her gaze, the little boy working the pushcart stopped and looked through the gap in the arched tin roof. He glowered at her—as if, she thought, he knew all about her scheme to bed Captain Holywell and could not believe how unchaste she must be to even consider the notion of surrendering her virginity.

She held fast to the balustrade and sought to convince herself that she had lost her innocence a long time before. *In Peterhof. Oh, but does that even count? No.*

Again, she glanced back at Captain Holywell. This time, though, she pursed her lips. *What an eyeful.* She averted her gaze and admired the faded gold braid upon the stern, dependable officer's forage cap—anything to get her mind off his natural beauty.

Whatever he said, she did not hear—for something soft hit her right shoulder blade. *Did the little boy throw a date at me? Oh please. I must be imagining things.*

Not a moment passed by before another dreamlike, non-existent date struck her in the very same place on her right shoulder blade.

She decided to bide her time, but it would not do. Filled with righteous indignation, she slammed her palms against her thighs. *My nerves have gotten the better of me. Am I descending into madness?* She marched back inside and grabbed the paper parasol she had purchased one week before. *I'll show that street urchin.* Ignoring Captain Holywell's confused call, she ran out her bedchamber door and raced down the stairway.

Outside in the marketplace, she charged the little boy and poked him with the ferrule—right in the gut. 'You think I'm damaged goods, do you?'

The little boy grimaced, as if baffled. Then he stepped back some and kicked her in the shin.

At that point, a shopkeeper who must have recognised

her as Ernesztina's helpmate came along and pulled him away.

With her free hand, Anastasia took a dried date from the little boy's pushcart and brushed the fruit against her gown's finely pleated flounce. A moment later, her palm glistening, she popped the treat into her mouth. The dried date tasted like cocoa and honey.

Captain Holywell happened along then. 'Why did you run off?' he asked.

Fearful of rejection, she dried her palms on her sleeves. 'Do you wish to join me down by the seaside tonight? Yes or no.'

'Maybe,' Captain Holywell answered. '*Damn*. If my commanding officer learns about any of this, he'll drum me out of the army. He's a bloody killjoy, that one.'

A striped hawkmoth fluttered by, only to float off past a display of evening bags embroidered with Mecca stones.

She thought of the unnerving English youth always staring at her. *I've got to be strong, austere, unchanging. Like a Mecca stone. I must ignore the vile creatures passing my way.*

As several more hawkmoths fluttered past her ear, he looked up and down the length of the street. At once, she intuited someone's fevered stare all over her person. *It's got to be that maniacal youth, but where's he hiding?* She threw her hands over her head and looked around. Clutching at her gown, she thought back to her schooldays. Back then, whenever a knave had thought to trouble her, she could always ask someone big and strong to escort her about so as to make the other think that she had already found someone.

Captain Holywell tapped her wrist. 'I ought to get back to the citadel,' he said.

She pretended she did not care and twirled the ends of her golden hair that slid across her shoulder.

Captain Holywell tilted his head before strutting off with a conceited gait. Anastasia flinched: she suddenly realised that not far down the street, the peculiar English youth sat atop a bag of compost, the demented fool silently gazing upon her. *With cow eyes. That scoundrel, he's relentless.* Stroking her throat, she collected an evening bag with her free hand and tapped a Mecca stone that shone the same turquoise blue as the English youth's eyes. *Shall I look again?* She glanced back in the young man's direction—but he was gone.

~

Later that Same Day, Three O'clock.

Anastasia ventured out into the marketplace. *I've got to get back to the mirror works. I can't just laze about the hostelry all day. I've got to make progress.*

Deep inside her womb, the fox spirit purred like a cat. 'Think of what you're doing. You think you stand to accomplish something? No. Imagine how terrible you'll feel when you give your body to someone else. Your warm, precious womb belongs to me. Yes, your womb grants me *life*.' The dream fox breathed deeply. 'If you should betray me this night, I swear I'll avenge your wickedness. Yes, I'll gouge out your eyes.'

She poked herself in the belly. 'Silence.' As she transmitted the abrupt message to the fox, Jack emerged from the colonnade. She intuited his longing. Even worse, his gaze seemed to tear at her person like the atrocity of violation—as if his eyes assailed her, poked at her glory.

The fox inside her purred even more softly. 'Imagine how you'll feel if that wretched scoundrel reaches out his hand and

113

gropes you. That's the way you'll feel if you go through with the tryst. You'll feel as if Captain Holywell has ravished you.'

She barely registered a word, for the English youth would not take his eyes off her. Like a fool, she stepped back and then lurched forward. Trembling all over, she debated whether to tell the louse to go wash his long greasy hair. *No, don't do that.*

The fox spirit rose in her throat. 'What if that chap there means to strangle you to death? Afterward, he'll escape punishment. I know. He'll tell everyone your passing was a case of erotic misadventure and nothing more.'

Her neck constricting, she raced off down the narrow walkway. Out of breath, she ducked down a pedestrian mall paved in faded tessarae. *This way.* She ran along awhile until she reached the curiosity shop.

As fate would have it, the display table no longer boasted the usual wares. Instead, the shopkeeper had arranged a mother-of-pearl box in the heart of the display table. Moreover, an exquisite Moroccan lantern shone onto the antique such that the box seemed *sacred*—too sacred to touch, much too sacred to open.

She looked down to consider the fired-glass street tiles at her feet, then raised her eyes to study the mother-of-pearl box again. '*Si beau,*' she whispered, thinking out loud.

Several soldiers passed her by, the young men reeking of ripe desert pumpkin. One of them even tipped his hat to her.

In no mood to trifle, she refused to make eye contact for more than a second. Averting her gaze, she breathed in the fine, leathery scent of the Syrian moneybags dangling from a nail in the curiosity shop's doorframe.

Deep inside her womb, the fox spirit whistled like a little bird. 'The soldiers, they delight in your shapely figure.'

She pulled in a deep breath. 'Are you jealous?'

The dream fox made no sound, not even a snarl. 'What if I were to feel a touch covetous?' he said after a long pause. 'I ought to feel that way. That's something you've always known. We belong to one another, forever and ever and ever.'

The shopkeeper stepped outside and bowed to her. '*Sabah al-Khayr*. Do you approve of lovely box here? You wish for to haggle with me little bit? What was you willing to pay? Please to name your price.'

'Never mind me.' Without another word, she raced off. A muscle spasm awakening in her back, she did not get far. With a groan, she stopped before the butcher's shop—where the carcass of a pheasant dangled from the smoking trolley like a sacrifice awaiting the altar. She stretched her back until the ache died down. When she reached the mirror works, she paused inside the door to study the opera house. *He must be watching me.*

Starting work, she dragged an elongated, teardrop-shaped sheet of tin bronze from the shearing wheel and arranged the piece upon the worktable. *On to the next step.* She opened the little jar containing the compound that prevented buckling, and as the air filled with the odour of something like ether oil, she coughed. To disperse the fumes, she took a palm frond from the handcart and waved the leafy bough this way and that.

Ernesztina appeared at the door. 'I just stopped by to ask you to join me in the garden this evening. I've got a fresh squid from the fishing village down the coast. I shall cook the beastie for you in its very own ink. How's that?'

Anastasia dropped the palm frond. 'No, thank you. Not tonight.' She took up the mop brush, dipped the bristles into the jar and proceeded to apply the first coat.

'Have you other plans?' Ernesztina asked, her voice full

of wonder.

'Yes, I'll be very busy tonight.' Anastasia brought the mop brush over to the washbasin to run some water through the bristles.

Ernesztina pointed toward the tin-bronze sheet. 'I'm happy that you've made so much progress, despite that Jack Wylye always making such a nuisance of himself.' Ernesztina clasped her hands together and tapped her foot awhile. 'The way you move, it reminds me of that stage actress, Gabrielle Ray. Have you heard of her? Ever attended any of her picture shows?'

'Are you maybe infatuated with this Gabrielle Ray?' Anastasia asked.

Ernesztina did not answer. She smoothed out her gown instead. 'Years ago, I had a lady friend who looked a little bit like Gladys Constance Cooper. Have you ever attended any of her picture shows?'

Her head bowed, Anastasia inched over toward the door. 'Sometimes I think you hired me to work here only because you fancy me. Maybe you hoped to entice me into some kind of affair.' The breeze sailing through her gown, Anastasia looked at the ceiling. 'I've come to Sinai for one reason only.'

'Tell me why.'

Broomstick in hand, Anastasia peered out the door to the dressing-room window that looked down upon the roundabout. *I'd love to do something to that lout. Yes, I ought to bash him over the head. With all my strength.*

Ernesztina tiptoed up to Anastasia and touched her arm. 'Haven't you ever attended the picture shows just to admire some stupendous actress? You've never felt anything for one of them? No infatuation?'

A dull ache pulsated in Anastasia's gut, and the whole of

her body quivered. 'If I spurn your advances, what happens then? Do you aim to remove me from my post?' She dragged her fingers down her cheeks. She debated whether she even required the position. *If I were to conceive life tonight, surely that would be enough to convince my deepest unconscious that the fox could no longer possibly occupy my womb.*

Ernesztina traced her finger down the length of Anastasia's arm—from her elbow to her wrist.

Anastasia placed her hand between her legs. If she were to surrender her virginity this very night, might she conceive life? She looked out at the marble fountain. *No, if my monthly has come, this ought to be the safest time. Wouldn't that be right? Yes, I think so.*

A moment passed by, and then she spotted the English youth: his upper lip tucked, he lumbered through the roundabout and dragged himself up into the opera house.

Not five minutes later, a discordant instrument of some kind cried out a series of descending sigh figures—the awful music drowning out the sound of the autumn breeze.

Closing her ears to the racket, she pictured herself down by the seaside—gladly lying beneath Captain Holywell's body, the crescent moon miraculously shining as brightly as the glorious midnight sun back in Saint Petersburg. Breathless, she looked up to watch a delicate, glistening silken thread drift past the tip of her nose. What a lovely sound the gossamer made, too, as if the guitar player had positioned his finger upon the highest string—just there atop the thirteenth fret. The silken strand whistling yet, she held out her hand and sought to catch it. When she failed, she followed it back to the worktable.

The thread came to alight upon the tin-bronze sheet. Slowly, the silken strand melted into the surface of the metallic sheet—the gossamer thread vanishing into some other dimension. Had she only hallucinated the effect? Even if she had, her lips parted. *Someday, I'll send the accursed fox into the tin bronze.*

Down in the depths of her womb, the fox hummed along with the theme emanating from the opera house.

'Stop that.'

The fox complied. 'Tell me something. Why do you seem so hopeful?'

She did not answer, for she espied yet another silken thread dancing upon the breeze—and now she listened to the harmonic sound the thread made, the wistful peal. *It's a sign. A sign of freedom. Yes, I'll be going free this very night.*

Gently, Ernesztina traced a fingertip along the angle of Anastasia's jaw—and the sensuality of it all made Anastasia jump. She made her way back outside, where a date stone promptly wedged itself into a crack running along the sole of her button boot. Wincing, she limped over to the fountain, where she removed the hard, irksome pit and then paused to study the pantheon of Egyptian gods hewn into the fountain's base. *What artistry.* She dropped the date stone to the side, knelt on the earth, and touched the veil enshrouding Isis— until a warm healing sensation, a feeling as of some elixir drifting through the veins in her fingers and hands, made her realise just how conflicted she was. 'Please, don't let me conceive. Summon my monthly. Let it start.'

When she stood, Anastasia crossed her arms tightly across her chest and then hobbled off to the caravansary. There, she sat upon a little olivewood bench standing beside the stables. In time, she lowered her brow. *Do I feel Jack's gaze upon me?*

If the young man had followed her to the courtyard, he did not show himself. Several journeymen in Kurdish dress stopped by the inn, but no one else.

She tipped her head back. *Wouldn't Jack be aghast if he knew what I've got planned for tonight?* She sucked her cheeks in and lay across the full length of the wooden bench. *Rest.* She closed her eyes. *Enough with my obsession. I've got to come to my senses. Sleep.*

~

Later that Same Day, the Twilight Hour.

When she awoke, she looked all around: the dying light of dusk glimmered like black honey, and the stone courtyard basked in a tangerine-orange glow.

Over to the right, atop an old shrine, an object gleamed as brightly as a heap of pink pearls.

What's that? When she drew near, she recognised the object as the mother-of-pearl box that had so enthralled her earlier in the day. As her hands grew clammy with fear, she had to wonder if the English youth had placed the box there to intimidate her. *Yes. Oh, who knows?*

The mother-of-pearl box glistened all the more, as if a sorcerer had cast a spell in the hope he might cajole her into lifting the lid.

Do I dare? She bit her lip, struggling to resist the temptation. Her hands and fingers trembling, she patted her belly. 'Do you know what's inside the box?'

'Think about it. Maybe there's a terrible plague swirling around in there. That's what you believe, and that's why you long to run.'

As the box gleamed in the dying light, a pharaoh eagle-owl soared past the caravansary's east tower and winged its way off in the direction of Mount Sinai.

The seeming portent of good fortune filled Anastasia with hope. *Go on.* At last, she lifted the lid and peeked inside. The box contained some broken seashells, nothing more. She scratched her cheek, struggled to make sense of the discovery, and closed the lid.

The early evening sky now a dazzling starscape, she strolled down to the seaside—where a malnourished, yellow-orange Abyssinian cat writhed about beside a dried dying shrub. *Poor thing.* The cat made her think of all the motherless Siberian kittens wandering the streets back home in Saint Petersburg. She listened to the rumble of the surf until the clock-tower bells counted out the hour.

As the last peal died out, Captain Holywell appeared at the citadel gate. He held a big shoulder bag in his left hand and had an army bedroll tucked up beneath his right arm. In the silence that followed the clock tower's tolling, he stopped to say something to the sentry standing beside the juniper bush—and the sentry snickered like a little boy, as if Captain Holywell must have said something indecent.

She raised her right hand high and snapped her fingers three times. 'Here I am!' she cried out. Dropping her arm to her side, she stepped back. *I can't believe I'm doing this.*

Upon greeting one another properly, they made their way down to the waterline and then ambled off westward.

Softly, the fox spirit wept. 'Think of how dirty you'll feel if you prove to be unfaithful to me. That's something you'll come to regret.'

As a strong, cool rush of sea froth tumbled across her feet, she paused to pound upon her belly.

When she finally continued forward, she bumped into Captain Holywell, who stopped.

He pointed at a lifeless spotted zebra shark lying some three feet ahead, the beast's eyes a shade of slate blue in the bright moonlight. Facing the waters, he thrust out his chest and recited a mock elegy:

Come hither, all ye empty things.
Ye bubbles rais'd by breath of kings.
Who float upon the tide of state;
Come hither, and behold your fate.

She had no interest in any kind of diversion. She pinched her nose, hurried past the carcass and climbed the ruins of a stone staircase reaching into the bluffs.

When Captain Holywell followed along, she guided him into the lemon grass—and they settled upon a sandy hollow. A collection of empty cream-sherry bottles standing in a row over to the side suggested an encampment, and she hoped the former lodger would not come back.

Deep inside her womb, the fox spirit grew very quiet. 'With all my heart, I beg you to consider my feelings for you. If you don't, who knows what challenges may beset you? Think about that.'

She sat and fingered the Huguenot cross dangling from the chain around her neck. *How good it feels to spite that inexorable fox.*

Deep inside her womb, he seemed to blow her a kiss. 'What if you conceive? By any measure, it's a terrible sin to carry a misbegotten child. Yes, all of polite society should spurn you. Are you even ready for such an ordeal?'

'Oh, please,' she whispered, looking at her lap. 'Do you think I'd even care if others were to frown upon me? No, I'm strong enough for anything.'

Captain Holywell knelt on the earth and opened the shoulder bag. 'I brought us some tommy,' he said. 'How about a cup of lentil soup?'

'I'm not hungry.' Arranging herself seductively on the bedroll, she studied the officer's heroic profile. 'Take off your boots and come here. Come close. Give me a Hollywood kiss. Just like Douglas Fairbanks.' She looked into the officer's eyes. *I'll do my best to show him a proper, womanly, come-hither look.*

Captain Holywell removed his boots and flashed a broad smile.

She barely heard him whistling 'Save Your Kisses till the Boys Come Home', for deep inside her womb, the fox spirit had burst into tears again.

The parlour song faded from Captain Holywell's lips when he joined her on the bedroll. 'How about a cuddle and a kiss?'

As the malevolent fox spirit wept and snorted and hissed, she lay upon her back and fixed her gaze upon a star. Before she knew it, she found herself beneath Captain Holywell— the warm weight of his body pinning her down. Once he had hitched up her gown, she lost herself in the business at hand. *Oh, my days.* She laughed like a baby. When she climaxed, she let out a shriek—and when she did, she wondered if she sounded as wild as a trumpeter finch.

Captain Holywell climbed off and lay down by her side. Before long, the handsome officer fell asleep. Thankfully, he did not snore. Even better, over to the side, a soft, almost-imperceptible music tooted and sputtered and rasped into being.

At first, she believed it to be a song thrush. *But no.* The music sounded more like a pan flute. She sat up and looked this way and that.

The music proved to be nothing more than the sea breeze blowing all about the mouths of the empty cream-sherry bottles. Meanwhile, along the edge of the hollow, the same Abyssinian cat from before danced in time—as if the music held the creature spellbound. How enchanting, too, the way the cat's eyes glistened: they shone like a pair of freshly minted coins.

She crawled over and knocked the bottles down; consequently, the cat sauntered off across the moonlit dunes. A burning sensation awoke between her legs. At once, she recalled her childhood in Russia—that fateful night out at Peterhof Riding School and Livery Stable. She had just snuck back into the post-and-beam horse barn to visit her beloved piebald pony. 'Let's ride off somewhere,' she had whispered into the beast's ear. 'I'll arrange your bridle, and we'll visit that palace the emperor of China built for the czar. Yes, and we'll sleep in the garden.' Later that evening, as the pony took her through the woodland, a trickle of blood emerged from between her legs: the tender flesh of her maidenhead had broken apart against the saddle.

'You're ruined,' the Russian moon seemed to whisper. 'Just look at all the blood where it's seeped through your riding breeches. For shame!'

For a long while, she begged the moon's forgiveness. When no response came, she placed one hand down onto the pony's well-trimmed throat latch and the other hand upon the creature's crest. 'Say something,' she pleaded. 'Forgive me, won't you? Surely, I deserve some kind of absolution.'

Her pleas proved to be in vain; with a stern tone of voice as that of an irate czar, the moon launched into a Russian-language lecture. In addition, the sphere adopted a retrograde orbit—as if to shame her into thinking she had done something so awful the heavenly body had no option but to shun the laws of nature.

She dismounted the pony and backed into the shadows of the forbidden forest. Her cheeks burning so, she concealed herself beneath a heap of fallen chestnut leaves—and there she remained until the search party discovered her the next day.

The desert breeze washing over her face, she studied Captain Holywell and shook her head. 'Don't look so smug,' she whispered.

A sound of a ship's bell rang out, the faint, wavering, coppery peal reverberating across the bluffs.

She jumped up and looked out to sea. As if heavily laden, a cumbersome cargo vessel steamed along. She caressed her belly. *Did I conceive?* If so, perhaps the miracle of life had already driven off the fox spirit. She pressed her fingertip into her navel. 'Hello? Are you still in there? Please go away.' She clenched her fist. Whether she had conceived life, how long would it be before Ernesztina tired of her and sacked her? Like a foolish, shameless little girl, she placed her hand over her Huguenot cross and pendant dove and whispered a prayer. Looking at her feet, she whispered, 'Please, Father. Hear me. Maybe Ernesztina means to send me packing as early as tomorrow. That's why You must let me conceive this very night, so that my body may expel the fox spirit once and for all.'

Once more, the ship's bell rang out—and this time it sounded like the blast of a fox-hunting horn.

She stared at one of the cream-sherry bottles lying at her feet. *How do I endure the endless obligations of motherhood? Always burdened with family cares, I'll have to give the baby away. Oh God.*

For a third time, the ship's bell rang out—and this time it

sounded like the long, mournful wail of a huntsman signalling the time for going home.

She closed her eyes, picturing her baby in some other woman's arms. Her hands moist and cool and pale, she scowled like a little girl mad with jealousy—until the baby took on the appearance of a rabid animal foaming at the mouth. At last, she staggered down to the seaside and poured several handfuls of frigid saltwater over her head— as if an impromptu forgiveness ritual like that might change anything.

VIII.

The Village of Al-Hubu, the Wilderness of Sinai.
2 December 1917.

Early that morning, Jack awoke to the sound of someone calling out his name in a most unfriendly, mocking tone. Stepping outside the dressing room, he breathed in an odour as of smelling salts strewn with baby powder—the kind of odour that might envelop a sportsman, a footballer. And did he detect cigarette smoke? *Or what about a musty stench? Both musty and sour.* Convinced that an intruder had come along, he retreated into the dressing room. *Could it be someone's come to have a row with me? Maybe it's that army officer.* Jack smacked his lips and realised that, because he had only just awoken, his breath reeked of boiled cabbage. *I'm bloody disgusting.* He closed his eyes. *Let me cease to exist. Then I'll observe the world from some other dimension. Just like a bloody ghost.* His thoughts turned to the past. Day by day, whenever he had noticed Anastasia in the marketplace, he had gazed into her big blue eyes and had telepathically pleaded for her affections. *What else could I do?* Even if he had wanted to speak up, he would not have had the power to do so; presently, his voice had grown so hoarse that he could only manage a soft rasp. The condition had probably followed from a sensitivity to the various desert microbes awoken by the winter rain. *I suppose so.*

He opened his eyes and convinced himself that he had not detected any alien scent in the opera house. *It's just me nerves. Nothing more.* Twice, he retched.

Downstairs, he stopped before the glass harmonica. *Why not work on me song?* He shook his head and crept back upstairs. *No, no.* He preferred to laze about the dressing room. Spreading himself out on the floor, he listened to a few of the recordings that the headstrong soprano had left behind. Then, as he picked his nose, he closed his eyes and pictured himself standing face to face with Anastasia. *In that glorious moment, I'll show her the sheet music. And then she'll transmit a telepathic thank you.* His muscles growing tense, he opened his eyes and glanced over toward the doorway. *Do I detect any odour? Could it be someone's come to have a row?*

At midday, he dragged himself to the telegraph office. Standing in the street, he studied the papyrus print depicting the Eye of Horus. 'What do you think about me love for Anastasia? Do you doubt me fantasy should ever come true? Do you scoff at all me timidity and irresolution?'

From time to time, a familiar sound rang out from the pupil—the peal of a brass bell, the kind that tends to grace a ship captain's table.

Even if it were nothing more than the stuff of aural hallucination, the mirthful sound of the bell served to sustain him. *No matter how ghostlike I feel at present, me woes should resolve themselves some fine day. Just like magic.*

Finally, he dragged himself into the telegraph office and

took the papyrus print down from the wall.

The falcon's eye flashed like a gold sovereign. Or did it? Jack could not decide. *I'm a spectre, a being wholly estranged from reality. How should I ever know what's what?* His heels tingling, he imagined the whole of his person must be levitating six inches off the floor. *Am I a ghost? Yes, I think so.*

When it seemed as if his feet had landed upon the floor, he dropped the print. Then he reached his hand toward the table holding all the telegraphy instruments to check whether his palm might pass through the wireless key.

The young clerk—his name was Hamza—emerged from the back room. 'No you visit today,' he said. '*Aiwa.* Captain Holywell, the one from the Camel Corps, he guard marketplace today. And the captain, he know the way you look at Anastasia. Maybe the captain smite you good.'

Jack placed his hand over the orbit of his eye and for a moment or two sought to picture his face once the officer had socked him.

'Go back to the opera house,' Hamza said. '*Yela!*'

'No, the sacred Eye of Horus, it won't never let anything happen,' Jack whispered as loudly as his hoarse throat would permit. 'The sacred Eye of Horus, he'll entrance me nemesis with the power of song.'

Hamza frowned. 'What song? I think you suffer terrible illusions. Like desert mirage on hot summer afternoon. You must be very ill, my friend. Throat cancer, too.'

'A fat lot you care.' For a second time, Jack sought to move his hand through the wireless key—and when he failed, he raised his hand to touch his swollen neck.

Hamza sat down at the table, copied out a text, and then reached out to adjust one of the wires in the clock board. 'Now I send message to my uncle up in Cairo.'

'What's that you say, lightning slinger? Listen. I ain't paying for no cablegram.'

'Uncle Djibril, he's clever enough to remedy any affliction. You travel there, and he give you tonic, maybe ointment made from tallow, baby oil, and calf suet. Or maybe a little bottle of featherfew. Whatever he give you, maybe you spread it all over your neck. Yes?'

'Don't be daft,' Jack said, his voice but a raspy whisper. He collected the papyrus print and held it high. 'Look at this teary-eyed falcon god. Give *him* your tuppeny medicaments.' His throat burning, Jack threw the print in Hamza's face and ducked outside.

A winter storm blew in, the rain a steady cannonade against the arched tin roof shielding the narrow lane. Down near the dry-goods mercantile, a section of the rooftop collapsed with a metallic, crashing tumult—and a pillar of rain exploded through the gap, the frantic downpour bouncing off the cobblestones.

How to proceed? He suspected that the force of the rain would wholly dissolve him—for how could something so wispy survive such an onslaught? His feet shuffling, he thumbed his ear and debated whether he ought to take shelter until the storm abated. *Very well, why not?* As he hastened back toward the telegraph office, he collided with the baker's wife. *Bloody hell.* She greeted him in good English, so he returned the civility the best that he could—despite his failing voice.

The woman strolled off down the street, and when she reached the place where the section of the rooftop had collapsed, she hobbled through the rain—plainly oblivious.

The woman's elegance and boldness made him cringe. *Me, I'm worthless. A piece of refuse what the surf coughed up.*

Across the street, a burly unshaven soldier emerged from

the nickelodeon lobby, his regimentals in complete disarray.

He must have fallen asleep in the stalls last night, Jack thought. He averted his gaze, for the very presence of a soldier filled him with shame. *Do I feel dizzy? Have I got me a headache coming on?* As guilty as he felt, he broke out into palpitations.

Like a drunkard, the soldier staggered forward. 'Aren't you that daft buck always ogling that bird Anastasia?' The soldier belched. 'You must be bloody mental.'

Picturing himself with a bruised mouth, Jack blinked rapidly. *What dishonour to have me a wound spreading across me upper lip. Like a blood-red moustache.* He held up his hands, but he said nothing. When he finally dropped his arms, he fussed with his long woollen topcoat. By now, he wondered if he detected a fluttering in his chest—as if his shame had touched off an irregular heartbeat. The notion that his heart might be pumping blood at a slow rate made him sweat even more.

The soldier smirked. 'You're a lovesick fool. The village idiot. And you think you'll have your wicked way with Anastasia, do you? Not bloody likely. Why should a graceful bird like her let a knavish bastard as piddling as you stuff your wee mutton dagger up into her fine receipt of custom? You're a bloody nothing. Not even fit for the gas-pipe cavalry.'

Given the fact the soldier spoke just like Jack did, he wondered if the soldier might be nothing more than a hallucination. *How to tell? Who's to say?*

When the soldier finally let him go on his way, Jack raced off through the pillar of driving rain.

Back at the opera house, the cats seemed to plead with him to let them inside. As selfish as ever, he ignored their appeals and closed the door behind him. When he reached the warm, dry dressing room, he lay upon the divan, stretched his legs and lamented his own hardships.

Nightfall came, and the rain grew harder—and all throughout the roundabout, the cats cried out. Did they fear the storm clouds had consumed the precious desert moon?

At midnight, the lobby doors opened with a heavy thud and then slammed shut again. Slow footsteps crept through the house and ascended the stairway to the darkened dressing room. 'Are you awake?' a woman's voice asked.

He pushed himself up from the divan, but he could not readily discern the visitor's identity. 'Ernesztina?'

With her catlike stride, the woman slunk over to the window and removed the shawl from the top rail. Quietly, she dusted the gramophone's sound box with a few of the ruffles adorning the shawl's hem. 'I can't let you keep gazing upon Anastasia the way you do,' the woman finally spoke up. 'You've got Anastasia sorely affrighted.'

'That can't be true,' he whispered, his voice barely strong enough to carry over all the caterwauling outside. 'Please don't interfere.' He picked himself up and grabbed the shawl. 'Me and Anastasia have ourselves a secret telepathic bond. Brought on by the gods of Egypt. That's why it wouldn't be cricket for you to help me. If you did something like that, the gods of Egypt must deem me love song all in vain.' Without another word, he arranged the shawl so that it dangled from the window's top rail just like before.

The woman sighed. 'You must not debase yourself any longer,' she told him. 'Reclaim your *pride*.'

Down in the roundabout, the cats fell silent—and the woman departed.

In the morning, Jack stumbled down the hill. As he breathed in the pungent, earthy aroma drifting through the roundabout, he suffered a grave coughing fit. There could be no avoiding it, for the rain had rejuvenated the desert such that many of the wildflowers had released an array of spores into the air. Even worse, as he continued off toward the marketplace, he realised that the rooftop drainpipes had flooded every street; in some places, the dirty water had risen as much as four inches. Hungry, he trudged onward anyway.

A dove fluttered past his shoulder, a seemingly fresh crimson laceration running across the songbird's crop. A moment or two later, a Barbary falcon boasting blue feathers barred with amaranth pink followed along in hot pursuit.

Stricken by the violence and melodrama of the chase, he did not even notice Anastasia standing up ahead near the nickelodeon's little booking office.

When their eyes met, Anastasia turned her back on him. Immediately, she crossed her arms about her bosom and held her elbows wide from her body. *How could anyone fail to recognise her exasperation?*

He stopped and fixed his gaze upon a fold in the centre back pleat of her coat. 'Why so brassed off today?' he said in an imperceptible whisper. 'Could it be your many burdensome labours? Yeah, it's a slave market the way Ernesztina has you working in that mad mirror manufactory. What I wouldn't do to set you free. Ah, but don't lose hope. Any day now, I'll complete me love song.' Leaning forward, he awaited the telepathic response.

She did not reply. Instead, she adjusted her stance by planting her legs a little bit wider.

Overcome by a second coughing fit, he spat up a torrent of phlegm—and he hoped and prayed she had not noticed. Recovering, he glanced in the curiosity shop window.

What perfect desolation: a frayed thread of saffron lay in the heart of the display table, nothing more.

Bugger all. A sharp winter breeze played upon his coat collar—and he slipped and tottered. *I'm weightless. I'm ghostlike. As inconsequential as the scent of coriander presently lingering in the air.* He approached Anastasia through the floodwaters, his shoes and stockings drenched. As he passed by, he permitted the back of his hand to brush up against her thigh. Did she even register his spectral presence? Even if she had not, *he* had certainly felt the warmth of her body. *How beautiful. How perfect.* He raced off into the oncoming crowd and did not stop until he reached the bakery.

The morning rush had left the establishment in shambles, and dozens of muddy shoe prints had sullied the floor.

He pointed at the empty shelves. 'There ain't nothing left,' he complained, his voice little more than a cracked whisper.

'Come you back tomorrow,' the baker said, his hands flapping.

'What about today? Haven't you got a few fresh cakes? What about a few savories, or what about a few pieces of shredded phyllo dough?'

'Tonight, I bake date-fig bread. Come you back tomorrow.'

'Right.' Over at the long walnut-wood table, Jack gathered up what few acceptable crumbs and fragments remained.

'You must be hungry,' the baker continued. 'You sound ill, too. I think malady like that come from sleeping in opera house this time of year. No gas furnace in there. No nothing.'

Jack grew warm and itched all over. 'Please help me. Be a friend. Arab tradition obliges you to show me a measure of hospitality, no? So, please help me.'

The baker stood up and dropped his apron to the side. 'Don't go. I come back in a moment.' With that, the baker darted off into the back room.

Jack looked at the cashbox. *Shall I pilfer all that?* He

blushed like a fool and dashed to the doorway. *Out of the way of temptation.*

The Barbary falcon fluttered down from the eaves, and Jack realised why it had failed to dispatch its quarry: the falcon had only one eye, the left socket empty but for an accumulation of yellow pus. *I'm no better. I'm damaged, worthless.*

As the hapless falcon fluttered off, the baker doubled back. 'You take these spices,' he said, handing Jack a silver-gilt ginger jar resembling a chrismarium. 'You discover many good things inside. Elder flowers and parsley. They cure your coughing.'

'It's some kind of elixir?' As he took the jar in his hand, Jack half-expected the mysterious vessel to fall through his ghostlike fingers.

The baker drew closer. 'You stay away from Anastasia. Yes, because she love that big tall soldier. And the prudent one, he know to stay away from another man's dish.'

Jack squeezed the spice jar hard. When it failed to shatter, he wondered if he ought to cast everything against the baker's big stone oven. *Why should some bloody fool presume to counsel me? How could anyone be so bloody condescending?* His posture stiff, Jack strode off.

Down near the nickelodeon, the Barbary falcon reappeared: the half-blind creature fluttered down to the flooded street and focused its one good eye upon the spice jar, as if yearning to breathe in the aroma of its contents.

Very well then, let's have ourselves a sniff. Jack removed the lid, only to find that the elixir reeked of hyssop. Instantly, he gagged. *Bollocks.*

The wounded dove fluttered from out of the shadows, and the songbird glided about the nickelodeon's booking office once or twice before alighting upon the finial that crowned the cupola. Curiously enough, the wounded dove held within its bill one of the falcon's distinctive feathers—a plume of deep Prussian blue barred with brightest amaranth pink.

As if greatly chagrined, the falcon hopped about the flooded street—until the dove let go, at which point the falcon's feather fell into the waters lapping up against the nickelodeon's doors.

Jack dropped the spice jar and flinched. For the very first time that day, he intuited the presence of Mr Sylvius standing at his back.

'Was you hoping to elude me?'

'Bugger off, I say.'

'What do you mean to do today? Working through obstacles, are you, then? Making progress on your song, are you? No, no. I say you mean to fritter away the whole day, aye, just like you always do.'

As Mr Sylvius giggled, Jack kicked the spice jar into the gutter.

~

8 December 1917.

In the evening, Jack visited the seashore to study the waters and will himself to make some progress on his song—and soon. His belly rumbling, he removed a crust of bread from his coat pocket. As he did so, he imagined Mr Sylvius standing at his back—the spectre reaching out to take the sustenance from him.

'*Please,*' the old man spoke up. 'Don't you wish to do good, dear boy? Don't you wish to provide alms and all that? Every good boy deserves favour, but—'

Jack stuffed the crust of bread back into his pocket. 'I got nothing for you. Go away, you scoundrel.'

Mr Sylvius wandered off.

His shoulders pulled as low as possible, Jack made his way back to the opera house. When he reached the dressing room, he found Ernesztina waiting for him. 'What're you doing here? Haven't you got busy work to do?'

'Never mind me. What do you do all day? Do you listen to your gramophone and imagine what it'd be like to engage Anastasia?'

'No, I'm working. On me song. Take heed. Anastasia should love me once she reads a few measures.'

'You're a daydreamer.' Ernesztina removed the shawl from the window, and the moonglow streamed in through the sash.

Jack scrubbed a hand over his face and considered the hazy cherry-pink shaft of light reaching across the floor. 'Please put the shawl back where it was.'

'Tell me something. Why did your parents send you here?'

'For all you know, I'm a runaway. And maybe it took great valour for me to come all this way.'

Ernesztina folded the shawl into a neat square and held it up against her bosom. 'Have you noticed all the Abyssinian cats huddled about the fountain?'

'What about them?'

'Don't you pity the little creatures?'

'No, I got me own damn plight to address.'

'Why don't you at least bring the kittens inside?'

'I can't do that. I've got to complete me song for Anastasia. That's why it won't do to have them bloody cats buzzing about. It'd only be a matter of time before one of them knocked over the glass harp.'

Ernesztina scraped her hand through her greying hair. 'Illusory love, it's neither infatuation nor the mere overestimation of the sex object. No, a thing like illusory love, it'd be nothing more or less than the descent into madness, derealization, the dissociative state, the phenomenon of detachment. I'm talking about temporary insanity.'

'*No*,' he whispered as loudly as his hoarse throat could manage. 'I talk to Anastasia all the time. It's just that when we talk, we employ the art of telepathy.' He took the shawl from the woman, unfolded it, and placed it back where it had been so that it dangled from the top rail—and as Ernesztina departed, darkness pervaded the cold little room yet again.

At midnight, he completed the first two sections of his song. *I did it, didn't I?* Once he had bundled himself up in his duffle coat, he stuffed the sheet music into the garment's ticket pocket and exited the opera house. Despite the late hour, he resolved to call upon Anastasia and show her what he had done. *And then she'll transmit a telepathic thank you. And she'll come to the door, and without words, we'll embrace. And then I'll hold her close.* Without any further hesitation, he faltered along through the roundabout and back into the marketplace.

When he reached the darkened hostelry, he fretted whether he looked presentable enough. *If only I had me a proper topcoat. And a proper hat as well.* Removing his deerstalker, he gazed upon the fanlight. 'I'm here,' he whispered beneath his breath. 'Wake up, love.'

When nothing happened, he looked down at his deerstalker and impulsively twisted the earflaps out of shape.

A light shone from the villa next door, meanwhile, and an old woman reeking of *oodh* charcoal looked down from her window.

He stared at the hostelry door. 'Shall I get down on bended knee?' he asked in hushed tones. 'Shall I pledge me undying devotion? I got a better idea. Come here, please. I'm keen to show you something. Me song! Come read the notes. Savor a song artfully crafted.'

Down the street, a British Army flatbed lorry rumbled to life—and the headlamps blinded him in two beams of indomitable light.

The lorry crawled forward. When it stopped, a soldier boasting a ruddy drinker's nose leaned out the passenger side. 'Why'd you break curfew?'

Jack wrapped his right hand about his throat and tapped his gullet with the webbing between his thumb and first finger to signal his powerlessness to speak.

The two soldiers climbed down from the cab, and as the driver gawked at him, the other shook his head.

'The bastard can't speak a twopenny bit,' the driver finally announced. 'I'd say this bloody bastard here, he's got himself a bad case of lockjaw.'

'I'd say he's a bloody tramp,' the other soldier said. 'Just look at his long tousled hair, all unruly and oily-like. And what about that ragged-arse coat he's got on, and what should we make of his soaking-wet threadbare shoes?'

As the driver laughed malevolently, Jack slipped back into his now absurdly misshapen hat and fixed his gaze upon the driver's ammunition boots. *Why didn't I serve?* Blushing like a crestfallen child, he drew a few deep breaths. *I'm nothing.*

With the tip of his service rifle, the driver tapped Jack's lapel. 'You go on back to where you came from, right? And you don't come around this here hostelry no more neither.'

As Jack made his retreat, the soldiers climbed back into the lorry—which idled for a time before lurching forward.

As the lorry followed along at his heels, the heat of the headlamps beat down against the nape of his neck.

Relentlessly, the lorry kept pace with him—all the way to the bakery. When he stopped there, the lorry's brakes hissed. One of the soldiers climbed down from the cab and cast a stone at him.

What do I do about this fine predicament? Jack held himself as still as possible. *Don't panic, eh? I'm a ghost. No, I'm not even here just now.* For a moment or two, he even sought to levitate. When nothing happened, he sucked in a quick breath. Then he turned to the bakery and considered the aluminium grille concealing the storefront's decorative façade.

The soldier cast a few more stones, one landing near Jack's heel and another one shooting past his ear. 'Get off the bloody streets,' the soldier said. 'Why are you breaking curfew?'

If only he had not lost the power to *speak*. Still, even if he could speak up, the soldiers would surely laugh in his face. He wiped his runny nose upon his sleeve now, and he fought back tears. Perhaps he deserved all this abuse. After all, he should have served. *The army life would've benefited me as well. After a while, I'm sure I'd get to feeling bold and strong.*

Up above, the baker opened the window over the storefront cornice and shook his fist at the soldier. 'Go away!' he shouted. 'This *my* country. To hell with your godless empire.'

The soldier climbed back into the cab, and when he slammed the door shut, the driver gunned the engine.

The clamour made Jack think of a deadly Vickers FB12—the shrill drone he had always imagined resounding from the engine. His gaze bounced from place to place. *I should've enlisted. But no, I despise war.* The more conflicted he felt, the harder he pressed his palm against his chest. *Me heart, it's not working right. Me heartbeat, it's too bloody slow.*

From the direction of the seaside, the report of a rifle resounded—so Jack fell to his knees and cowered behind a heap of rubbish. He did not pick himself up until the lorry finally slipped into reverse.

As the lorry rolled away, the baker tapped upon the windowsill. 'Do you finish the healing elixir?'

Jack shook his head no and then paused to observe his distorted reflection in the floodwaters.

The baker scowled. 'So! You don't even take it.'

Jack suddenly recalled that time down at Billingsgate when an elderly fishmonger had noticed him wandering all about the docks, looking forlorn. Put to shame, perhaps, the fishmonger had wrapped up a large bundle of cockles and mussels and had insisted that Jack take it. He had not hungered for the offering, however. Indeed, the odour of cockles and mussels had always sickened him. Later, as he had prepared to depart the fish market, he stopped beside a barrel and dumped the cockles and mussels inside. He sauntered off, and only then did he realise that the elderly fishmonger had been watching his every movement. The old man stared at him, mouth agape, as if he had never before witnessed an act of such obscene ingratitude.

For a second time, the baker tapped upon the windowsill. 'You wait, please. I come down there to tell you something.' The baker darted away then, and a moment or two later, lifted the noisy grille from the inside. 'Come you here,' the baker said in a fatherly tone. He snapped his fingers.

Jack averted his gaze. 'I haven't got your chrismarium.' Powerless to keep still, he sought to conceal his face behind his long unruly hair. 'I'm certain a thief must've stolen into the opera house and taken it. Yes, just a few nights ago.'

Jack cleared his throat. *Did me deceit sound at all convincing? Probably not.*

The baker clapped his hands. 'I only wish to talk. I am good friend. Only wish to ask you something.' Barefoot, the baker trudged into the flooded street. 'Do you know why those soldiers behave so bad? They behave that way because you always *alone.*' The baker scratched his beard, and then he stabbed the air with his finger. 'I think maybe people fear your solitude because your solitude maybe show you lack power to make the good relations with others.' Slowly, the baker retired into his place of business and closed the aluminium grille.

For a second time, Jack studied his distorted reflection in the floodwaters—and then, like so many times before, he imagined a presence at his back. *Mr Sylvius. Yes, it's him.*

Had the old man snuck up from the beach? Perhaps he had been performing music by tapping upon all those cream-sherry bottles. Mr Sylvius sniffed at Jack's ear. 'Hello,' the old man whispered. 'I only wish to tell you that the baker has it right, aye, I got it on excellent authority that solitude must be nothing more nor less than the stuff of *madness.*'

Jack dropped his chin to his chest, and he squeezed his eyes shut. 'Please go away and leave me be.'

'Feeling oppressed, are you? *Why?* You got no reason to feel that way with me standing here. I'm your imaginary friend, and I'm the only friend you've got.'

'You're not even there.'

'No, I'm real. A lonely old man. Never had a wife. Never had any friends. Then me mum perished. Destroyed by a cancerous tumour on her heart. And now she's gone, and there's no one to talk to but you.'

Little by little, the wintry rain fell anew. Minute by minute, the downpour grew steadily stronger. On and on, it pounded upon the tin roof that shielded the street.

The old man tapped upon Jack's back. 'Get down on your knees and rub my heel, why don't you? At the moment, I'm sorely afflicted by a rupture of my Achilles tendon. Help me, please.'

Jack looked up. 'You just want me to feel guilty. You just want to add to the shame everyone's already dumped all over me.'

The apparition howled with laughter. 'You deserve to feel deepest shame, and you know it. Chaps your age, they're fighting for life and limb in battles what leave the wounded and dying scattered hither and thither.'

Jack thought of the army life as he never had before. He closed his eyes and sought to picture the trenches crowded with other blokes—everyone dirty and cold and hungry. When he opened his eyes, he placed his hand over his aching heart. 'I would've enlisted, but me parents, they made me sail off to Sinai. You got to believe me. No, I weren't no bloody coward. I'm quite sure I would've served honourably enough had I been given the chance.'

As the apparition howled with another round of laughter, Jack bowed his head and trudged back to the roundabout. There, no matter the hard driving rain, he knelt before the fountain and looked upon Isis. He touched the veil that obscured her face. 'I've always got you, and that's a blessing because I'll always require your friendship.'

IX.

A nastasia awoke to perfect silence. *The baby gestating inside me . . . has it crowded out the dream fox?* There could be no doubt the dream fox was gone, for any and all tension had left her body. The revelation should have made her celebrate in some way. At the very least, she should have parted her lips and opened her mouth in wonder. She did no such thing, though. Even if the little baby had, in fact, crowded out the mischievous fox, she still had Jack's relentless presence to unnerve her. *Why does he have to gaze into my eyes the way he does?* She sighed now, for she just knew that anyone else would have discerned her total disinterest. Moreover, she had made a point of holding Captain Holywell's hand whenever they loitered here or there in the crowded market. Still, the many recurring displays of affection had failed to dishearten the maniacal youth. *No. He'll not be dissuaded. In all likelihood, he's bound to kill me someday soon.*

The cold, rainy, late-December breeze rattled the window

sash. As the current died down, she sat on the edge of her bed and whispered a solemn Huguenot Christmas prayer. How to avoid it? Only yesterday, on Christmas Eve, the War Office had decided to ship Captain Holywell off to a command post in the jungles of India.

At nine o'clock, she poured herself a cup of breakfast tea and wandered outside onto the balcony. *Has he already sailed off?* She pictured a battleship pulling away from the pier down by the citadel, and now she cursed all her luck. Still, she could not quarrel with the British Army's decision to send him somewhere crucial to the empire. What a magnificent person he was. *On the one hand, he's distinguished himself as a gentleman as moral as any other. Ah, but on the other hand, as an officer, he's manly enough to win any battle.* Her mouth opened and closed several times over. *I miss him already. Captain Holywell.*

An hour passed by before she looked down at the balcony railing and realised that she had not even touched her tea. 'Captain Holywell, please come back,' she whispered, scanning the seaside.

Late that morning, she visited the seashore and pictured his ship vanishing into the horizon.

The surf coughed up the carcass of a baby lemon shark, which landed at her feet and immediately reminded her that the assignation from before had left her pregnant.

A trio of English soldiers escorted her back to the hostelry. Keen to keep them there, she sat them in the Syriana chairs facing the reception desk and poured each guest a glass of Turkish coffee.

One of them, a gangly weapons engineer named Patie Mulroy, tapped her right knee and grinned. 'What shall we do about Jack, then?'

'Who knows? It doesn't bear thinking about.' Anastasia collected the broom and swept a section of the lobby floor.

'We got to give the bastard a measure of retribution,' Private Tushingham spoke up just then. 'The maniacal lad, he's gone off his onion, hasn't he? Aye, the little cutthroat reminds me of Jack the Ripper. Remember that woman of pleasure down on Mitre Square? He chopped that charity dame up and downed her gallbladder like it was a red blush pear, he did. And that's no gobshite. Read it in the Sunday papers when I was only a lad.'

The third soldier, Iain Meicklejohn, gestured toward Anastasia. 'Did you ever read about them Whitechapel atrocities? Every night, murder was afoot. One of the halfpenny papers quoted the chief constable, who recollected a story about the time some patrol sergeant went down to the city morgue to look long and hard into some dead strumpet's face on the wee chance her eyeballs might still somehow reflect Saucy Jack's face. Sadly, them peepers didn't reflect anything, and that's just the kind of thing what put Jack's quarry into the lap of the gods.'

Patie Mulroy sat back and tugged his sleeves down some. 'I'll tell ye something. Me own auntie served on the Whitechapel Vigilance Committee. She told me all about it. With every new murder, her blood went cold.'

A series of violent contractions and bladder spasms awoke all throughout Anastasia's belly. Blushing, she grabbed her belly.

An opaque black glass jar caught her attention. It was nothing out of the ordinary, just a little vessel of pomegranate hummus that the hostelry keeper had left standing on the edge of the reception desk. Nevertheless, as she gazed into the dusky glass, she could swear that she heard a dissonant noise emanating from inside. *It's just my nerves acting up.*

The din grew louder, as if the source of the noise had escaped the jar and presently buzzed about her left ear—like a cloud of gnats. And now the imaginary gnats seemed to enter her person, each one of the tiny intruders buzzing all about her optic nerve.

The broomstick fell from her hand. She sat in the hostelry keeper's chair. Her body growing numb, she struggled to keep from falling to the floor. More than anything, she wondered if she were about to *transform*—as if the whole of her life had transpired for no other reason than to bring her to this moment. Her eyes tingled. She gave the soldiers a curt nod. *Something great must happen. Maybe I'll acquire the power to see for miles. What a miracle that'd be.*

Patie Mulroy sipped his coffee and then looked up. 'I know. The next time Jack comes at you all mumchance, you ought to do something right foul. Maybe you ought to belch or pick at your nose or scratch at your knickers. That rummy, he'll pipe off once you stop flittering about looking all prim and proper. Remember, lass, it's your own beauty what gives rise to a lad's fiendish, devilish illusions. God strike me blind if I bear false witness. You mustn't do nothing to enhance the suffering bastard's illusions.'

'I've got it,' Tushingham said. 'Just you hide your golden hair beneath a beastly fright wig.'

'*No,*' she said, giving the soldier a sidelong glance.

'Tushingham, he's got it right,' Iain Meicklejohn insisted. 'Who'd think to pluck a feral bird running about looking like Shylock's daughter?'

Patie set his coffee glass down and held his knees and legs tightly together. 'Right then, it's like this, love. You can't let the deranged lad weigh upon your nerves too much. Even if

146

he comes around in the night and pinches your frillies, you mustn't panic. Remember as well, if the bloody bastard sends you inappropriate gifts and tawdry things and such, you've got to preserve everything and get it to your solicitor.'

Several more contractions rattled Anastasia's body. *God, it's as if I consumed a whole mouthful of glass shards.* Without delay, she marched off into the powder room and slammed the door shut. *Mercy.* She lifted her skirt, only to notice a trickle of blood streaming down her right leg. *Blood?* She sat upon the cool chipped bidet.

Not a moment later, she suffered a miscarriage. '*Mon Dieu. Le bébé est mort.*'

She grabbed a cotton rag. Carefully, then, she wrapped up the warm bloody miniscule discharge. Overwhelmed to the point of delirium, she let out a self-deprecating laugh and then dropped the tiny lifeless jumble into the flush toilet.

Someone knocked upon the powder-room door. 'Are you feeling well?' one of the soldiers asked.

'Yes, of course,' she lied. Given all her anguish, she could not manage to say another word. How she longed to speak with someone, though—a parson, perhaps, a good Huguenot minister. Her body all atremble, she stared at the ceiling.

Once more, the soldier knocked. 'I apologise if we discomfited you any. We was only having a laugh. I do beg your forgiveness. What do you say? Give us grace, love.'

Very slowly, she slipped back into her skirt. When she opened the door, she told the soldiers nothing. *There's probably no point.* She approached the reception desk, eyes tingling as they had before. *What's that?* The strange sensation would not relent, so she paced awhile. Up until that point, she had been planning to spend the day reading a novel she had recently found lying about the hostelry. Just yesterday, she had discovered a copy of *Middlemarch* beneath the lobby sofa. Now she wondered if reading a demanding work like that might prove to be too much of a strain. *I've got to rest my eyes.*

The telephone rang. It proved to be Ernesztina calling to ask that Anastasia return to work.

Five minutes later, the three soldiers escorted her to the roundabout. Then, as the trio followed the faint pathway down to the citadel, she reeled around the fountain. *My eyes, they're burning.* She lunged over toward the mirror-works door. *What's happening to me?* When she continued inside, she took hold of the shearing wheel. *I've got to commit to my goal and find some way to imprison the dream fox within the mirror. That's my charge.* The smouldering in her eyes grew worse, as if she had been staring at the midnight sun through a telescope. Finally, she faltered back to the door. When she stumbled outside, she placed the palm of her hand over her belly. Truly undone, she breathed heavily and revisited the moment of her miscarriage. *God, forgive me.*

From the direction of the opera house, a high-pitched tune struck up—the drone of the discordant, uncanny music reverberating across the roundabout like the howls of a thousand or more hungry Arctic foxes.

Anastasia held her hands over her ears and knelt on the earth. *Enough.* No matter how much she prayed and pleaded and protested, the awful music would not relent.

How to come to terms with the miscarriage? She prayed for some miraculous force to reveal why the travesty had happened.

The cacophony faded until no sound remained other than the seeming drone of a spectral gnat buzzing about the fountain. Before she could welcome the silence, a distant howl rent the sky. Or might the sound have been nothing more than the stuff of hysteria?

She thought she detected the odour of Russian permafrost. *Oh yes, the tundra. Could it be the Arctic fox coming for me? Does he intend to leap back inside me?*

A torrid ghostlike being sniffed at her right heel. At least, she imagined as much. Had the fox perhaps learned all about the tragic miscarriage? If so, the ghostly being would surely long to reclaim his place inside her womb.

Her skin having grown mottled by exposure to the heat of the spectre, she crawled back inside and concealed herself beneath the worktable. 'Go away!' she cried out. 'I'll never let you back inside my body.'

Someone entered the mirror works, the sound of the footfalls unmistakable. When the other party passed by the worktable, there could be no doubt it was a woman: whoever it was, she wore traditional Egyptian sandals with golden-winged buckles.

It's probably Ernesztina. Beneath the worktable, Anastasia held her breath. She could only guess that Ernesztina had come by to trifle. *But I'm a proper Huguenot girl, and I can't be doing things like that.* She hoped and prayed the woman would exit. *Go away.* She thought of home, the time one of the Russian girls from school invited her to Pushkinsky District and what proved to be a cat party—a girls-only affair.

When Anastasia decided to leave much too early, a girl from Petrogradskaya followed her all the way back to the railway station.

'Why don't you wish to stay?' the girl asked no sooner had Anastasia passed through the gate. 'Don't you fancy girls like us?'

'It's nothing like that,' Anastasia said. 'You must

understand that I'm not like any other person in the world. I'm a Huguenot. And not only that, but a Huguenot mystic. God Almighty demands that I live the Christian life and that I do the kinds of extraordinary things that others may learn from. My life, my experiences, must unfold like a book. A magical, dreamlike story filled with deep symbols.'

Once Anastasia had boarded the train for home, she looked out the window to find the girl from Petrogradskaya sitting atop an abandoned steamer trunk and sobbing uncontrollably.

The memory made Anastasia sit up straight, and she bumped the top of her head against the raw, unfinished, unsanded bottom of the worktable.

Whether Ernesztina had heard the gentle thud, the woman breathed in loudly and then departed very quickly—like a cold indifferent cat darting away from someone unworthy of its attention.

Anastasia rubbed the little bump on the top of her head. *Am I bleeding?* She crawled forward and pushed herself up onto her feet. Swaying dangerously to the right, she collided with an old elaborate bench vice.

⁓

That Same Day, Five O'clock.

Back in her room at the hostelry, Anastasia fell into a troubled sleep that did not last long before a dream of the miscarriage jerked her awake. Lying in bed, she soothed her temple with the cool of her fingertips.

The light of dusk streaming through the window looked all so promising, as if the twilight was the light of dawn. The headboard of her bed shone where it had been inlaid with polished camel bone.

Am I even worthy to sleep in a bed like this? She trampled downstairs into the warmth of the lobby, where she took a handful of kindling from the firewood basket. Once she had cast the twigs into the hearth, she lay upon the sofa. *Don't think about the miscarriage.* She closed her eyes. *How could I let something like that happen?*

Outside, a British Army lorry rumbled to life. Like a train rolling down the tracks, the lorry's engine rattled and hummed.

She pushed herself onto her side and went lost in another round of agonizing, guilt-ridden dreams. She awoke in tears and sat up. *If only I could forgive myself.* As the fire in the hearth died out, she rubbed her arms and shivered.

The army lorry drove off, and the lobby's sudden reversion to absolute quietude made the space seem drab, unpleasant.

More than anything, the silence made her think of the Arctic fox. *How long before the entity steals inside my body?* She stretched her arms. *What will the Arctic fox say to me in that moment? Perhaps he'll wish me a 'Merry Christmas'. Then he'll laugh in his nervous, derisive way. And then he'll twitch his tail. 'Even if you were to bathe in holy water, the blessed solution should never be strong enough to cleanse your defiled flesh.' That's what he'll say.* She patted her body—up and down. *He's coming back to me.* As her hands jerked this way and that, she slouched back into the sofa and braced herself. *At any moment, he'll be here.*

Sure enough, the sound of footfalls echoed from outside, but the footsteps passed by the lobby door.

What if it's Jack skulking out there in his way? How passing strange is his habit of staring at me. The more she thought about it, the more her belly throbbed. She lay on her back and gazed at the cracks in the ceiling. *Whenever that maniacal fool stares at me the way he does, how rapt he appears. And his blue eyes never fail to smoulder with a fugitive's passion.* She placed her hand between her legs. *Oh God, it feels just like I've been violated.*

Outside, someone passed by the hostelry's one shuttered window. Whoever it was, the person crawled along at a languid pace.

Maybe that'd be Jack. Perhaps this very evening, he'll go on and make his way into the hostelry. Maybe then he'll hold me at knifepoint. She twisted her Huguenot cross awhile. *What might Jack look like in that moment he comes inside here? Perhaps he'll look enraged, a fiend with a corded neck.* She dropped her hand and twisted the pendant dove that dangled from the cross.

A winged creature—could it have been a dwarf honeybee?—stole through the lobby and glided past Anastasia's nose.

I'm wonderstruck. She stood and sought to catch the little thing in her hand—and when she failed, she paused to look upon the opaque glass jar of pomegranate hummus yet standing upon the edge of the reception desk.

From somewhere outside, yet more footfalls resounded. Before long, someone or some*thing* bumped up against the hostelry door—hard enough that the glass jar fell to the floor and shattered to pieces.

She studied the glistening black shards strewn about the tiles: each piece shone as brightly as a fragment of volcanic glass. No matter the scent of pomegranate hummus spreading through the air, she thought back to her childhood—the tundra's permafrost, the way it reeked during that ethereal night journey to Arkhangelsk. *And what about that vile, conniving Arctic fox?* There had to be a sensible explanation for what had happened to her that fateful night. *Could it have been some kind of psychological breakdown, some kind of nighttime terror tantrum? Yes, that'd explain everything. None of that harrowing encounter ever really truly happened at all. No, no, no.*

A harsh winter breeze whistled through the darkened lobby, and something rattled. The object in question proved to be a flail that the hostelry keeper had mounted upon the wall, the relic's three beaded tails swinging back and forth in the current. Outside, a sound as of footsteps approached the door.

I'm not alone. She fixed her gaze upon the cross rail. 'Who's there?' When no one answered, she tiptoed over to the door. Holding her breath, she set her ear against the scarred wood and listened. Despite the howl of the winter breeze and the ongoing rattle of the flail's three beaded tails, she could swear that she heard some kind of creature sobbing where it stood on the other side of the door. *Could it be the spirit of the Arctic fox?* For the longest time, she sought to envision the creature—his eyes agleam with lust, desire, desperation. *I won't let him slip back into my body. No. Never.*

The footfalls trailed away, and once the whimpering had ceased, she could not resist the urge to open the door. When she found no one there, she hurried back to the mirror works.

That evening, she thought she detected the odour of permafrost in the air. *The scent of the tundra.* Again, her eyes tingled and burned. *What could that be?* She recalled Russia's wild woodlands and pictured a cloud of hungry gnats buzzing about some dying Arctic fox.

From the direction of the opera house, the English youth's music recommenced—the sound a discordant, glassy drone.

She intuited the approach of a ghostlike being. *Yes. He's*

drawing close. And he's sniffing at my right heel. She gasped for breath and stood. 'You've come back to me, haven't you?' She pounded her fist on the tabletop. 'I'll never let you come back inside me. Go off and find someone else to taunt and ruin and whatever else. Do you hear me?'

There was no response, but the unrelenting music continued to split the night.

She looked this way and that. 'Listen here, you. Each and every day, I'm getting better at making mirrors, and it's only a matter of time before I surmise the proper way to banish you and send you off into the tin bronze. So, why don't you hurry off? Go on, I say, while you still have a chance.'

Yet again, there was no response—only Jack's dreamlike music. Had the disturbed youth broken into a discordant variation on a Christmas hymn?

A voice as of a fox spoke up. '*Bonsoir,*' the creature whispered.

She covered her mouth with her hand. 'Leave me be. I don't want anything to do with you. You've got my nerves frayed. I can't even bear the thought of you. Keep away. Come any closer and I'll trap you inside one of my mirrors. And you'll never escape.' At last, she staggered back to the shearing wheel. Nostrils flaring, she sought to pull the spindle apart—until she grew so exhausted that she slumped to the floor. *Shall I hide?* The music ceased, and the mirror works grew quiet enough that she could hear her own heart beating—as slowly as that of an old woman resigned to impending death.

Later that Same Christmas Night.

Back at the hostelry, she crawled into her room and lay in the corner. *Why not sleep? Maybe my dreams will show me how to imprison the fox inside some tin-bronze mirror. God, I hope so.*

Something stirred in the shadows. 'I know what you'll dream about,' a voice as of the dream fox whispered. 'All through the night, you'll dream of the most primitive things. The art of hunting, the art of trapping this or that wild beast. You'll envision yourself some kind of gamekeeper commanding authority over barn owls and English game fowl alike.'

She lit a candle and looked all about. 'Are you here?' When no response came, she slipped into her housecoat and inched her way downstairs into the warmth of the lobby. *If only the hostelry keeper were here to keep me company.* She longed to ask him to help her to purchase a proper foxhound. Perhaps the presence of a hunting dog would quell her fears and convince her that her old adversary had no hope of assailing her.

As it so happened, the hostelry keeper had travelled north to participate in an anti-colonial demonstration—and he would not be trekking back for a while. There was nothing unusual about that, however. During the winter months, when the hostelry keeper did not have very many tenants, he often left—and for several days on end, too. He did not seem to feel the least bit guilty, either. It had been weeks since he had told her to start doing things for herself.

She lay upon the sofa, and she listened as a mysterious cloud of gnats buzzed all about the lobby window. *They're not there. It's just my imagination.* A jagged shard glistened in the firelight and caught her eye. No matter how often the cleaning lady had swept the lobby, the old woman must have missed that one last remnant of the pomegranate-hummus jar. Anastasia curled up into a ball. *Sleep.*

As she fingered her Huguenot cross, a ghostly kind of footfalls approached the sofa. 'I aim to leap back inside your body,' a familiar voice spoke up. 'I suppose you'll be in a state then, but what do I care?'

She decided that she had hallucinated it all, so she closed her eyes and fell asleep. What a fitful slumber, though; she dreamt of the miscarriage, the Arctic fox, all her miseries.

She awoke with her hand caressing the pendant dove, where it lay nestled within her neck dimple. *I'm so alone.* She stood and lit another fire. Then she looked at the keys strewn across the reception desk. *There's no other tenant this time of year. Not a one. If only someone else had stayed the winter . . . a Russian girl, someone in whom I could've confided all my sorrows. All my fears.*

Like a palpable mist, the savoury scents of rice, lentils and garlic drifted into the lobby. Had one of the neighbouring households begun some monumental celebration?

Her body perked up. *What might the occasion be? Could it be a wedding?* She wondered whether she ought to step outside to look. If she did, perhaps she might identify the source of the banquet. As she stole across the lobby, she very nearly stepped upon that one last remnant of the pomegranate-hummus jar. With a heavy sigh, she opened the door. The savoury scents died out, and it made her body posture sink. *Find the fox.* She marched outside and looked all about. The cold wind tearing through her housecoat, she tiptoed down the desolate street.

Over to the left, the winter breeze whistled through a

broken cockfighting chair lying on its side. A moment later, from no more than three blocks to the south, an array of lively footsteps approached.

She braced herself, for the footfalls did not sound human. 'What could it be?' she asked out loud.

From the shadows of the alleyway over to the right, a whole troop of sand foxes appeared. Given how blindingly white their coats and how purple their eyes, the animals appeared fantastical—a troop of ghost foxes that had only just wandered in from the desert.

'We've come to haunt the village,' one of the vindictive creatures said. 'We're looking for the Egyptian huntsman who shot and killed us.'

Anastasia shook her head. *No. I'm dreaming. I'm sleepwalking.*

Dream or not, the sand foxes circled her very slowly—as if debating whether to rip her to pieces. As the sand foxes continued to circle her, what strange energy they exuded— the sordid impulse to devour some other's flesh.

Her arm ached, as badly as an archer's bow arm following some long, trying hunting expedition. *What do I do?* Her bare feet growing cold and numb, she held her hand over her belly. Much too tense to permit herself to bolt, she exhaled very quietly. *A death by mauling, that's got to be the worst way to go. Heavens.* Holding her breath, she peered in the direction of the seashore and sought to convince herself how much worse it would feel if a great fish were to consume the whole of her person in just one bite.

Whether they were even there at all, each one of the ghostly sand foxes grew still and sniffed her feet.

Hopelessly surrounded, she held up her hands.

How to appease such creatures' unrelenting hunger?

Each one detected in her the promise of sustenance. How to forestall the depredation? They did not pity her. What did they care about all her childhood trauma? For that matter, what did they care about the cumulative effects of a demented youth's habit of staring at her?

Thankfully, the sand foxes did not pounce. On the contrary, one of them licked her big toe—tenderly, too. Afterward, the whole of the troop darted off.

The harrowing encounter left her profoundly disoriented. Her hand splayed out against her chest, and she was lost in a torrent of childhood remembrances—memories of the night journey from Saint Petersburg, the excursion to Arkhangelsk and back again. As her eyes prickled, she looked at the clouds. Most of the formations moved much too quickly to study, but it was not so long before she espied a stationary one—which resembled a heap of bulgur wheat and shone the colour of bone broth. *Yes, that one there.* She focused on that very cloud. 'Father, tell me what's happened to my eyes. My intuition makes me think you mean to grant me great power. Could it be the power to see across vast distances?'

The deity refused to answer. Something as of a warm, little pillar of sand came bounding up her leg, however. Then, as her thighs throbbed violently, she thought back to that night with Captain Holywell. *What a mistake it was to surrender my virginity the way I did. Yes, what a waste. I got nothing out of it.*

The Arctic fox slipped back into her womb, and he laughed and sneered and twitched his downy tail. 'So, did you miss me? Tell me true. Of course, you yearned for my triumphal and joyous repatriation. That's something you cannot deny.'

She bit her lip and staggered back several steps. *Damnation.* She pushed down on her belly and attempted to drive the fox spirit from her womb. When it would not go, she adopted a hunched posture and drew a deep breath. 'Please go away.'

The fox laughed and sneered and twitched his downy tail that much more. 'I'll never leave you. Believe it.'

She plodded along in circles. *I'm only dreaming, nothing more.* Her body shaking all over, she looked to her feet and kicked a little blue pebble into the gutter.

Down the street, meanwhile, the ghostly sand foxes cried out. Had they only just arrived at the huntsman's house?

No matter how preposterous the whole notion, she hurried forward. The tip of her nose growing warm and itchy with anxiety, she ran along for several blocks but could not locate the sand foxes anywhere. *That's because they were dream foxes.*

Up above, the clouds dissipated. She saw a shooting star; it appeared as an abbey-white stripe in the sky above, complete with a crooked tail.

The wonder of it all filled her with awe such that she staggered back on her heels.

As the meteor streaked across the sky, the sand foxes' anguished howling fell silent—and the dream fox inside her screamed and barked and squealed.

Once the shooting star had vanished, Anastasia poked at her belly. 'Please tell me what's happened.' But she already knew the answer: she had experienced a dazzling dream *of* and homage *to* something impossibly profound. *The thrill of the hunt and the glory of the kill.*

X.

The Village of Al-Hubu, the Wilderness of Sinai.
The Day After New Year's Day, 1918.

Back inside the opera house, Jack sat in the orchestra pit and thought of Anastasia. *She's grown all so forlorn. I do wonder why.* He blamed himself: if he could just complete his song, he could perform the work. *And then she'll love me. With all her heart.* As the morning light poured into the orchestra pit, he crawled over to the darkened corner. *I got to think. Once Anastasia accepts me hand in marriage, I'll have to talk to her. And take her to bed as well. Which means I'll have to muster the ability to perform.* Subsequently, he would have to provide for her—and that would require him to compose the kind of music the public might actually embrace. Did he even have enough talent to do that, though? In truth, he could neither live *with* nor *without* Anastasia—and he fully understood the paradox.

Midmorning, he dragged himself down to the citadel to beg for some English fare—a tin of smoked herring or whatever else the mess sergeant might give him. As it so happened, no one guarded the gate that day—not even a sentry dog. Thankful, he ducked into the bailey and then paused beside the dry-stone clock tower. He studied the soldiers lazing about. *Do they know I've come to Sinai for no other reason than to avoid serving? If so, they must despise me . . . and why not?* Beads of sweat rolled down his neck. He glanced over at the pointed arch in the wall. There, a lance corporal sat feeding his bore brush through the barrel of his pocket revolver. *The bloke looks like he's sixteen. Did he lie about his age when he enlisted?* Jack continued over to the cookhouse. 'I'm here to beg some grub,' he whispered as loudly as his hoarse throat would permit.

'Later,' the mess sergeant told him. 'Just now the god *wallah* means to deliver another one of his right inspiring sermons, don't he?'

The beadle came along then, the young officer dragging a weathered, mid-Victorian cedarwood table into the heart of the courtyard.

The chaplain, an elderly man dressed in a black Geneva gown, climbed onto the tabletop. 'Now hear this,' he cried out. 'I know just what ye must be asking yourselves at present. What's this excitable Nazarene mean to tell us today? Could it be something about the languid approach of Candlemas? No, no, mates. I'll not vex ye with tales of the Holy Virgin's purification rite. But the dead of winter envelops us all, so I tell ye this. Ye ought to consider what a purification rite *betokens*. Yes, indeed, a noble rite such as Candlemas betokens the purification of a Christian's soul. Do ye hear, lads? Listen up, each and every one of you. No, no. Don't trouble yourself with the Holy Virgin's burdens. Ye must mend your *own* sinfulness. Ye must mend your *own* sloth.'

Jack wrinkled his nose at the sickly sweet odour pervading

the air. The fumes reeked of antifungal medicament and seemed to be coming from the stone well standing to the side of the gatehouse. *Patience. Listen to the sermon.* He noticed the chaplain studying his long tousled hair and tried to avoid his eye.

'*Sloth!*' the chaplain shouted, shattering the silence of the courtyard. 'That'd be the very deadliest of all sins, for the righteous man never puts off till tomorrow what he might just as well do today. No, soldier boys, only the sinfully slothful kind fritters away their time. Oh yes, that's right. Only the sinfully slothful daydreamer prefers to indulge the *self* and let everything go to the dogs rather than live the right, upstanding *Christian* life.'

Jack's belly rumbled, the noise loud—like the wail of a dying animal.

Everyone must've heard, he thought. He bowed his head, half-certain the soldiers must be staring at him. Knees wobbling, he looked all about for somewhere to hide. Shaking, he tottered over toward a crate of breech-loading rifles.

More than a few soldiers gawked at him, as if he must be the most peculiar anomaly in all of nature. Perhaps they knew nothing about the curse of depression.

He stumbled toward a field gun standing in the shadow of the battlements. *Go on. Leg it.* He could not move, for his foot had fallen asleep.

The chaplain thumped his clothbound Bible a few times and raised his voice. 'I'll tell you what happens to a sinful, slothful daydreamer. Little by little, his whole life slips away. The older he gets, the more he daydreams of the various things he should've done and would've done had he been industrious enough to have *lived*. And by the time he's ready to haul ashore, he realises that there's no time left to torment himself with regrets. In fine, he realises his whole life was nothing but a grand paradox. And so, the wastrel meets his end.'

Jack trembled. *The chaplain, he's talking about me. Bloody hell, I know it.* He studied some of the dark unsightly stains splashed across the curtain wall. *That might as well be me own repulsive reflection there.* He looked at his tattered trousers and battered shoes. *The chaplain must find me right disgusting, and why wouldn't he think that?*

The sea breeze kicked up, and something tumbled past his heel—a faded halftone print depicting a dying Egyptian revolutionary.

The image made Jack's cheeks burn, for the agony in the revolutionary's face reminded him of how little he had ever suffered. The sickly sweet odour from before wrapped itself all around his person until he gasped. He pulled back as slowly as he could, as if that might serve to make the retreat a touch less conspicuous. When he finally made it to the stone well standing to the side of the gatehouse, he breathed in. *What's that? It's the stench of death, that's what.*

Twice, the chaplain stomped his foot. 'No, no, don't let yourselves fall out of heart,' he exhorted the soldiers. 'Don't ye scuttle your dreams like the sinful and slothful do. For ye will be a long time dead, lads. That's why each one of you standing here today, you've got to go on and purify yourself of all your indolence and youthful sorrows. Bear up, I say. Otherwise, ye might as well shun life and go the way of Judas. That's right, brave soldier boys. If ye will not cease with all your petty daydreams, then ye might as well bowl off.'

Jack swallowed hard. *Bowl off?* Until that moment, he had never once considered a measure as extraordinary as suicide. Still, what better way to remedy his anguish? If he could neither live *with* Anastasia nor live *without* her, then why not meet his death willingly? Would suicide not be the perfect solution to the dilemma at hand? *Yes, the perfect solution.*

A shadow darted across the courtyard, and he glanced up to see a milk-white heron fluttering over toward the east turret. There, the majestic creature settled atop the armoured cupola and called out as if to tell him to come along. But the heron sailed off, vanishing into the slate grey of the northern sky—where he could not follow.

On the other side of the bailey, an army lorry came to life—and as the engine rumbled on and on, he made haste and continued through the citadel gates.

When he reached the dusty roundabout, he knelt before the fountain to study the noble pantheon etched into the basin. He tapped upon the veil concealing Isis. 'What do you think?' he asked, his voice a rasp. 'Shall I end it all?'

Jack sensed a presence drawing near, and Mr Sylvius rematerialised at his back.

'You're bloody bent,' the vision said.

'*No,*' Jack whispered. 'These days I'm knocking about in fine feather.'

'Just listen to yourself talking with bated breath the way you do. I've never known anyone so pitiable as you. Crossed in love and as hopeless as Lady Montague's rotten kid.'

Jack's knees ached, but he could not bring himself to stand. *Curses.* He debated whether he should face his foe, but decided against it. Instead, he fixed his gaze upon Isis for the second time. 'So,' he croaked, 'have you any counsel to share with me?'

Mr Sylvius cackled like a witch. 'Just think of how dishonourable you'd be, lad, aye, and did any other bastard anywhere ever think to solicit his tormentor's opinion? Back in my day, no one did that, and are you so daft you actually presume a concept such as constructive criticism even exists?'

'*Please.* Why must you denigrate and deride? Help me, why don't you? Tell me whether it'd be wrong for me to die by my own hand.'

'Enough,' the old man said, his tone of voice mirthful. 'Make your own decisions, aye, think for yourself, mad Romeo, aye.'

Jack touched a few of the figures carved into the marble fountain's basin. He pointed at Isis. *There you are. Yes.* He touched the veil that obscured her visage.

'If you do decide to blot yourself out of existence, you won't require no Veronese apothecary,' the apparition said after a while. 'I'll tell you the very best way to bowl off and exit this world.'

'Go on,' Jack whispered as loudly as his aching throat would permit. 'Tell me how to do it. I'm listening.'

'Make tracks down to the seaside, aye, and then you'll pass by the citadel, aye, and then you'll roll into the waters, and then you'll keep going, and you'll swim, aye, until you haven't the strength to go no further, and soon enough, you'll drown.'

Jack's jaw went slack. *I can't die like that. A suicide has got to be good and blissful and harmless and clean.* He held out his hands, palms up. 'Drowning? Swallowing salt water? That's much too agonizing. I'd much prefer to fall asleep and never wake up.'

From within the mirror works, the cacophony of the shearing wheel started up—and it did so, Jack thought, for no other reason than to augment the grim tenor of the discourse and to make the nasty old man's words seem even more disagreeable.

Jack picked himself up and considered the opera house—
the bold, Byzantine-revival columns standing before the
lobby doors. *I should go on inside. Maybe I could take shelter
back in the dressing room.*

The old man must have produced a spectral dagger, for
now Jack could swear that his nemesis poked him in the
back. *Bloody hell. What do I do?* Jack's heart beat rapidly as
he sought to picture the old man's blank expression. 'Put the
knife away,' he whined.

Mr Sylvius gasped. 'I got no knife, lad. Have no fear, aye,
it's true, I honestly pity you, and that's no fib, aye, it's true,
and I shed a tear along with you.'

The shearing wheel in the mirror works fell silent, and
the old man's flat, emotionless voice descended into a series
of incoherent murmurs.

For a second time, Mr Sylvius poked him in the back. 'I
know why you hesitate, aye, you don't wish to drown at sea,
only to have the surf cough your body up onto the shore, and
more than that, by the time someone collects your remains
there, your flesh and bones should be in an advanced state
of decomposition, and that'd only make things even *more*
undignified, aye, you wish to *disappear*, to die *free*, aye,
somewhere far away, somewhere no one should ever find you,
aye, you wish to let it be as if you wasn't ever here.'

'What's all this?'

'Aye, there's no doubt about it,' Mr Sylvius continued.
'You wish to affect the awe and mystery of *vanishing*.'

In the hope that a seeming air of detachment might serve
to augment his image in that moment, Jack remained silent.
*The art of silence, it's as powerful a weapon as insolence. That's
right.* He recalled his schooldays. Whenever contrite, he would
beg some instructor's pardon—but the vindictive, tyrannical

instructor had always remained silent in those moments, as if he had intended for the silence itself to augment the shame.

Jack glanced up as Anastasia exited the mirror works. Looking perfectly inscrutable, she locked the door.

How long before Anastasia notices me standing outside here? Once she espies me loathsome presence, she'll do something. If nothing else, she'll hurry off and find some bastard soldier to come along. And then me and him should have ourselves a big row. Jack cringed. He had no idea how to fight or to wrestle. For that matter, a proper soldier would have no reason to overestimate a frail youth's capabilities. On the contrary, any serviceman would know how to size up the enemy and how to obliterate him with one swift, devastating body blow.

Her head bowed, Anastasia ambled off in the direction of the marketplace.

As the old man snickered and snorted, Jack ran back to the opera house and ducked inside. On the apron of the stage, he stopped before the glass harp to study the musical instrument.

Mr Sylvius approached at his back again, belching. 'Think of all those times the wee sadistic imps back in the schoolyard laughed at you. Back then, you didn't have no good way to preserve yer honour, but now you do, lad, aye, lest someone else play this rarefied glass harp and compose a medley of song superior to your own piece, you ought to get to feeling real hard and shatter the whole bloody device, aye, remember, lad, the thoroughgoing preservation of honour always requires *sacrifice*.'

'Cheers for that, Mr Sylvius.' As pointless as it would have been to destroy the glass harp, Jack welcomed the idea. Still, he lacked the nerve to destroy such a precious object. His hands fell to his sides. Ignoring the old man, he crawled upstairs to the dressing room.

The shawl had fallen from the window's top rail, and the desert wind whistled through the sheet music strewn about the floor.

He packed up his belongings. *I'll simply vanish from this place and find somewhere to die. That's just what I'll do.* He paused to look at the dressing room one last time. 'I'm going away,' he whispered. 'I'm ready to bowl off.'

~

That Same Day, Two O'clock.

Jack took up his bags and lumbered down toward the citadel—the lorry park where the Royal Mail van had always pulled out when heading back to Cairo.

From the direction of the citadel, the mournful bright rattling crack of a snare drum resounded.

That sounds like funeral duty. A death march. He had never noticed any corps of drums before, and he sought to picture the drummer. When he could not do so, Jack sought to count the time. *It's much too slow. No more than forty beats per minute.* As the precise metallic drumbeat rattled on, he wondered if he heard a dog coming up from behind—the animal dragging both of its hind legs. When he looked, he espied nothing there. He placed his hand over his chest and moved it over toward his left breast. *Me heartbeat, it's much too slow. I'm afflicted with some bloody grave malady.*

For a second time, he hallucinated the sound of a dying dog at his back. Soon enough, he even heard the poor animal lose its balance and fall over onto its side. 'What's happened to you, then?' he asked. 'Afflicted by a severe increase in blood pressure? Would that be it?' He looked as he had before, but again, there was no animal there.

The sun beat down upon Jack's scalp, and he stumbled forward and back. The dizzy spell made him wonder if perhaps a blood vessel in his brain had burst.

On and on, the solitary drummer's hard dry snare drum slowly, steadily rattled and hissed.

The current grew strong, and a dead raisin bush tumbled across the lorry park.

Jack kicked one of his bags and then wrapped his hands all about his head. *I know what's got me coming apart. That drum corps; it's making me feel bloody guilty for not serving.*

A medic and a wounded soldier came along, and as they crossed through the lorry park, the wounded soldier fell to his knees.

I'm a coward. The worst kind. He looked at the sky. 'I'll be gone soon, so don't be too cross with me. And when I'm gone, there will be no need for no drum and bugle corps mourning me memory. I don't deserve it, anyway.'

A few more soldiers traipsed by, the young men talking about some recent, harrowing battle out along the Hejaz Railway.

Jack's fear and dread made him shiver—until his teeth chattered. *No more talk of war and death. No more, please.*

The drumming resounded yet and would not relent—and as the beat slowed down even more, Jack pressed his palm against his left breast. *How long till me heart pumps so slow I end up dying right here, right now? Bloody hell, where's that van?*

In a cloud of hot swirling yellowy dust, a vehicle with a powerful engine approached from just around the bend.

Look there. It's the bloody courier. At long last. Jack waved. When the Royal Mail van stopped, he hitched a ride. *I'm on the journey.*

Out beyond the sand dunes, the driver turned off the thoroughfare and pulled out onto the long, winding, sun-scorched desert highway.

Jack looked out the window and watched the desolation passing by. 'What happens if we get lost?'

The driver snorted. 'I got me a good map,' he answered. 'There's no chance I'll forget the way. Trust me, eh?'

'All the same, if we run out of petrol, don't worry about me. I'll tramp off on me own merry way. It's no trouble.' Jack laughed like a giddy fool. As the van passed a caper bush, he looked back.

Already, the quiet seaside village had vanished amid a series of barricades—sand dunes and rocks.

'Goodbye,' he muttered beneath his breath. 'Let the mystery of me vanishing haunt you forever and ever, Anastasia. End of story.'

Midafternoon, as the mail van crossed a narrow bridge spanning a perilous wadi, the passenger-side front tyre burst—and the vehicle swerved.

'A bloody blowout.' Cursing and muttering, the driver applied the brake and climbed down from the cab.

Jack opened the rear hatch and hopped down. 'Can I help you?'

The driver, busy removing the flat tyre, waved him off. Jack tucked his shirt into his trousers and wondered at the distant mountains.

What a sight: amid the endless jumble of metamorphic rocks and boulders, a dozen or so veins of basalt quartz shone as resplendently as fool's gold. Moreover, it seemed as if the basalt quartz sparkled with the energy of life—as if at any moment the various crystalline minerals might transform into a legion of Egyptian gods.

He bowed to them. 'Ye ought to know I've reached the point of no return. No, I can't live with nor without Anastasia, and that's why I've got to deliver meself from this bloody heartless world.'

A soft, deep, booming illusory voice answered: 'It's a sin to destroy the life we gods granted you. A crime as well.'

He dug his hands into his pockets and gazed at his shoes. 'Why should bowling off be some kind of crime?' he asked in a whisper, glancing at a few of the rock formations. 'A chap ought to have every right to end his life.' His arms growing heavy, he pictured Isis assuming the shape of a milk-white heron and fluttering down to his heels. *Yes, she's standing right there. The goddess of healing.* With a sigh, he sought to picture the heron's long featherless legs. And now the creature seemed to peck at his calf. He winced. Then he sought to picture the heron's pinkish bill. 'Stop that,' he whispered, running his hand through his long brown hair. 'Why must you go and make trouble for me? If I seek to bowl off, do you aim to stop me? What then? Do you aim to throw me in some penal colony?'

The milk-white heron did not answer, so he wheeled around—and in that moment, he half-expected to find the creature standing there.

No heron awaited him, but a dark plume drifted past.

He studied it. *Could it have fallen from some wayward creature? What about a wading bird's black feather crest?* For a moment or two, he chased after the object—through a scattering of cracked sandstone boulders and dark grey pebbles.

The elusive plume vanished amid the rocks hidden by the oddly shaped shadows falling across the sandstone plains and hills.

A soft desert breeze whistled through the columns of

volcanic stone standing to his right, and the heartrending sound resembled the music of the glass harp.

As the music died out, the driver lifted the spare tyre onto the wheel studs—and Jack watched him work, until a blast of wind blew through the mail van such that a dozen or so leaves of the sheet music sailed off upon the current. *Strike me pink. There goes me work, me song.* No reason I should want to save it, Jack thought, though every impulse told him to retrieve it all. His heart racing, he chased his papers all the way to the edge of the ravine.

Some ten minutes later, once he had collected the last of the leaves, he held the papers up against his stomach and peered down into the ravine. *Am I ready to bowl off? Yes, I think so.*

A fluttering of wings passed by overhead: a pale-brown desert lark had only just taken flight. Twice, the winged creature circled the gorge. As he watched it, the desert lark came to alight upon a nearby boulder shaped a little bit like a reclining female nude.

He peered deep into the shadowy ravine. *If only me accursed noodle worked right. If only I could forget all the insults what've come my way.* He thought about the way children come to forget traumatic events. *Then what?* Many years later, the person comes to recall the repressed memory. *And the wound, the scar, festers on and on.*

The desert lark hopped a few times. Then the winged creature chirped and buzzed, and the noises made it seem as if the bird must be passing judgement on him.

The sheet music slipped from his hands, and he grabbed for it. As he held it tight, he let out a forceful breath. The sound of the lark made him feel self-conscious, much too withdrawn, emasculated, bloodless even. At last, he looked at the sky. 'What makes the coming-of-age process so bloody miserable?' he asked in as soft a whisper as he could manage.

A kind of response announced itself; from perhaps as far as two hundred miles away, a faint bell seemed to reverberate.

Even if he had imagined it all, he stared in the direction of the seaside village. *Could it be the Eye of Horus, the blackness of its pupil? Yes, that's right. The blackness of its pupil, it's calling out to me. Of course.*

The desert lark made a sound as if laughing at him— perhaps even deriding his immaturity, his penchant for whimsy.

Jack glared at the animal. *What's this? You laughing at me?* The more he listened, the more foolish the lark sounded. If nothing else, the bird sounded like some lonely, introverted fool who cannot stop giggling in one of those rare moments when he finds himself the welcome party to some friendly, albeit temporary, gathering. Still, if that were the sound that the lark intended to make in this moment, then the lark's message to him could not have been less unequivocal: *he* must be that same kind of lonely, introverted fool.

Back along the sunbaked road, the driver finally succeeded in mounting the tyre onto the wheel's frame. Sweating profusely, he lumbered with a waddling gait over into the shade of a dead acacia tree and flung himself down on the grass to rest awhile.

For a second time, the faint bell seemed to resonate—and this time the sound made Jack's temples throb. He studied his sheet music, and he read through a few of the measures. As he did, he thought of Anastasia. *Day by day, what might she do now that I'm gone?* The current made the boughs of the dead acacia tree clatter, and the hot wind flapped at the sheet music such that he had no choice but to hold them up against his chest and wait. When the wind dropped, he looked up. *Someday, she'll notice I'm not there to give her no longing gaze.*

A flock of desert larks burst out of the faint, ghost-white clouds and soared overhead. Gliding above the quiet desolation of the desert road, they winged their way to the seashore.

As they vanished into the horizon, he stood up straight. 'Anastasia, do you read me thoughts just now? Did you realise I've reached the point of no return? That means *you've* reached the defining moment, too.'

The wind picked up again, shook the dead acacia tree, and bent the crown back from the road—until the biggest bough crashed to the earth.

The driver sat up and stared at Jack—and he stared at the debris. 'Anastasia, what do you think of me? Tell me true. Maybe you suppose I'd be mad, eh? Like me noodle went funny.' He sighed. *Well, if Anastasia does think of me that way, I can't say I blame her. Ah, the curious case of Jack Wylye.*

A hare came hopping along, and the creature stopped to look at him awhile. Plainly indifferent, the hare scraped its clawed fingers in the sand.

Jack kicked a pebble toward the animal and looked closely to see if the disturbance might have brought about at least a shift in its breathing.

The hare did not seem to notice what he had done. The creature continued to scrape at the earth with its clawed toes. *Why must I assail a harmless creature? I know. I'm a coward looking to compensate, that's why.* As the hare loped away, he closed his eyes and sought to picture himself back in the village. *Just how long before Anastasia might come along? When she did, she'd probably seek to intimidate me.* Perhaps she would ask one of the taller soldiers, a lithe and lofty former footballer, to accompany her as she passed by the very place where he stood. *Or why not recruit one of the stockier ones? Yes, why not recruit some bearded, musclebound former footballer? Why didn't one of them soldiers bash me when he had the chance?*

A few minutes passed, and as the sun continued to beat down on his scalp, Jack imagined a pair of English girls standing at his back. *Each one must be looking at me with absolute fear and revulsion in her eyes. Their mouths agape and their faces wrinkled.*

He imagined one gesturing to the other and speaking up in a loud, illusory, contralto voice: 'Do you see him? He's mad. Yes, and he's a wicked brute. This here's the one who longs to ravish poor Anastasia. Yes, it's true. Do you know what I'd do to such a reprobate? If I only could, I'd imprison him for decades and decades. And I'd sprinkle saltpetre into his tea, so that he wouldn't even command the power to fantasise about pretty girls. He'd suffer a fate worse than death. Chemical castration, that's what I'd call it. Then, at the end of his life, if for some reason I permitted him to go free for a few months, he'd still have to make amends and serve others. Just like a penitent.'

On the verge of tears, Jack stumbled forward—but now he imagined yet another pair of vindictive English girls marching toward him. *That's right. They must be schoolgirls, old friends of Anastasia.*

One of them, the brunette, glanced at him and made eye contact and smirked. 'I know your secret,' she told him. 'You long to murder a comely, innocent maiden. You're a beast.'

He lifted his chin. 'No, I was lonely. That's all it was.' Spotting the driver waving, Jack raised his hand. *Damn them girls. They're not even real.* Jack scuttled back and followed the driver over to the van.

When the driver settled himself behind the wheel, Jack climbed inside the mail van. As the driver turned the engine, Jack looked out the window and bit at the inside of his cheek. Then he let his posture go limp. *Whither? How much farther shall I ride along, and how do I bloody well die once I've arrived at me destination?*

The driver released the clutch, and the mail van slipped into gear—and picked up speed.

Jack closed his eyes and became lost in a daydream. He imagined that some forty years had gone by, and now he found himself in Kenya. The driver happened to be Anastasia's husband, a game warden from a noble English family. And the mail van was a Sheffield-Simplex armoured car—the kind only military officers drive. *And what the devil might Anastasia say when me and her well-proportioned husband arrive at their estate? Will she even remember my face?*

The mail van bounced over the rocky surface, jerking Jack upwards. He opened his eyes and looked all around. *I'm back in Sinai. Thank God.*

XI.

The Village of Al-Hubu, the Wilderness of Sinai.
The Day Before Saint Valentine's Day, 1918.

As she lay in bed that morning, Anastasia finally
acknowledged Jack's absence. He no longer appeared in
the marketplace to make eyes at her, and she no longer heard
his discordant music as she toiled away in the mirror works.

She climbed out of bed and stood at the window. *He
could play, I suppose, after a fashion.* The quietude made her
feel alone, regretful. *Did he die of a broken heart?* At first,
the notion made her laugh—but as the darkness turned to
light, the idea made her feel sick. She cupped her hand over
her mouth. *If only I'd befriended him, then maybe I could've
shattered his illusions. And he'd still be among the living.* She
peered down through the window, dropped her hand from
her mouth, and gasped: an animal looking like either an
Icelandic sheepdog or a diseased, tame-acting desert fox
circled all around before darting off into the marketplace.

A rush of air blew through the hostelry, making her
think of home—the unforgiving Russian winter. Shivering,

she dawdled along down to the lobby and lingered by the hearth. As she gazed into the dying fire, the sickly scent of the firewood made her think of the waterfront—the citadel, the dead creatures constantly washing ashore. As she struggled to find her breath, her stream of consciousness drifted into thoughts of Captain Holywell. *Where might he be this morning?*

The dawn breeze whistled like a glass harp, and her thoughts drifted back to the peculiar youth—his sudden, puzzling absence, his utter inadequacy. She blamed herself. If only she had commanded as much character as Captain Holywell always had. Now she paused to consider how extraordinary she might have been if only she commanded a more sensuous nature. Her lips trembling, she gasped and tittered. *If I'd been a caring, loving trollop, maybe I could've healed the troubled youth with the pleasures of the flesh. Yes. Oh God, that's so absurd.* As the breath rattled out of her, she imagined Jack standing at her back. *Yes, I suppose he's cut his hair and changed into clean clothes. With eyes unblinking, he's probably staring at my bottom.*

She just knew what he would say. 'You was wrong about me. It weren't never me goal to kill you. So, please forgive me trespass. I never intended to misspend me youth. Just happened, it did. An accident of history.'

She turned around to look at him, and when she found herself standing there all alone, a curious prickling sensation commenced all throughout her eyes. At first, she did nothing about it. Lost in thought, she drew her shoulders down and stretched her neck. *Am I right to think all my experiences here have served to transform my very nature?* Her hands fell to her sides. As the strange sensation continued to flitter about her eyes, she sensed that something magical must be unfolding. *At any moment, I'll acquire great powers. Oh yes, godly powers.*

The fire dwindled, and the last three dying embers emitted a scent as sweet as cedar.

She collected a long immaculate piece of driftwood that the hostelry keeper had brought up from the shore several weeks earlier, and she dropped the refuse across the andirons. Three times over, then, she poked the log with the blackened fireiron.

As the flames grew, the fox spirit deep inside her womb kicked. 'Do not think that I've forgiven you for my recent exile. Furthermore, I know you've come to this village for no other reason than to bring me to ruin. For shame, I say.'

'Hush.'

'That's the last thing I intend to do. And remember, no matter what you scheme to put me through, I shall have the last laugh.'

Surreptitiously, the first light of dawn slipped through the lobby window and shone onto the stone floor.

She poked the length of driftwood three more times. 'No matter what you say, you'll never defeat me. This I promise. No matter how many times you interrupt my life, someday I'll know everything a girl must know to banish a terrible thing like you from her body. And I'll be free of you forevermore.'

The dream fox snorted, and then the whole of his being seemed to fly from her womb and into the orbit of her left eyeball. 'You'll never thwart me any. Never in a million years. Yes, and remember this. If you won't behave, then soon, very soon, I'll gouge out your globes. With all my strength. That's just what I'll do.'

'Not if I gouge out yours first.' Anastasia dropped the fireiron to the floor and pushed down upon her belly, trying to drive the insufferable fox spirit from her womb and back down her leg. When all efforts proved futile, she staggered

179

away from the hearth. Wringing her hands, she looked out the window.

What a perfect dawn: three bright orange ribbons glowed all so triumphantly amid the otherwise blackened sky.

The hopeful sign only served to emphasise her predicament. Once more, she pushed down upon her belly. Again, she sought to drive the fox spirit out of her womb.

He leapt and yelped and kicked even more. 'Have you no shame? Have you no knowledge of animal cruelty?'

She continued to push down for a while, but when an ache awoke deep in her belly, she had no choice but to relent. By now, the whole futile endeavour had only served to remind her of the miscarriage—the ease with which her body had expelled the ill-formed embryo. *My baby.*

The dawn sky grew a little bit brighter, and before she knew it, the morning light shone as triumphantly as the midnight sun back home in Saint Petersburg—and from one of the nearby minarets towering over the village, the solemn call to prayer rang out and echoed through the streets.

When the village fell quiet, a dreamlike thud resounded; the noise resembled a cast-iron anchor thumping to the seabed and settling in the sands.

She crossed her arms and looked down. Had she merely imagined the uncanny sound? A big part of her refused to believe it. Without question, she had heard something as of an ethereal ship's illusory anchor catching the hypothetical seabed only to rest in its immaterial sands. *It's a miracle.*

As the morning light grew strong throughout the lobby, the beauty of the incandescence made her think back to her old *Société-Biblique* edition of *Le Nouveau Testament et le Livre des Psaumes*—its gilded edges. *What about that book?* Once, when she was just a little girl, she had flipped through the pages to one of the epistles and had read a passage about hope as a steadfast, indomitable anchor that preserves the soul from all manner of iniquity.

Several more times, a series of soft, illusory thuds resounded—as if a whole ghostly, invulnerable, fantastical flotilla had berthed somewhere down along the waterfront.

Lulled by the steady beat, she slipped into the hostelry keeper's coat, wandered outside and poked along down to the seashore. As far as she could see, the waters seemed desolate—no sailing vessels anywhere. 'Please, God. Give me a sign. *Quelque chose.*'

The surf coughed up a drenched tawny woollen cloche— and the bell-shaped hat trailed past her ankle.

What if the captain's daughter lost it? Yes, it fell from her head. Anastasia scanned the horizon in search of at least one dreamlike galleon. *Where could she be?*

~

Later that Same Day.

At one o'clock, Anastasia unlocked the mirror-works door and slouched inside. As she looked around, a burning sensation itched at her eyes. Taking a step back, she gasped. A procession of gleaming geometric shapes danced before her. She shook her head and rubbed her knuckles against her eyelids. Nothing helped, and she stared in wonder at the complex shapes, trying to puzzle them out.

As she watched them, a host of cones and trapezoids and pentagrams mutated into a series of vivid kaleidoscopic effects—all of which conjured an orange and pink and fluorescent-blue aura.

181

She poked her belly. 'Oh, why must you try me like this? You got me full of jubilant confusion. What's the meaning of this?'

'You think I'm to blame? No, it's not me. I'd say the fox gods have chosen you for some great charge. That's why they've ordained your magnificent . . . transformation.'

'*Transformation?*'

'Yes, I say. Soon, very soon, you will command the power to see for miles and miles and miles.'

'What use will that be?' Anastasia staggered forward, wondering if her eyes might be reacting to one of the potent compounds she had lately applied to her work in progress— an ambitious mirror that she hoped might prove wondrous enough to imprison the dream fox. As disoriented as she was, she stumbled into a country chair and knocked over a wooden barrel that sometimes stood in for a proper grinding stand.

As she struggled to put the barrel right, the sensation of a wild Arctic breeze crept into the mirror works.

Deep inside her womb, the fox spirit kicked. 'I detect a sweet little Huguenot ghost girl drawing near. Yes, she's come to take away your old eyes and replace them with magical ones, the eyes of a goddess, enchanting blue eyes strong enough to see all the way across the dunes and valleys and wastelands of Sinai.'

Anastasia fell to the floor. Lost in dreamlike delirium, she imagined herself crawling across the seabed and coming upon the mystical anchor she had heard earlier in the day. 'I know what this means,' she whispered. 'I'm saved. The King of Glory, He'll never forsake a Huguenot prophetess like me.'

As the dream faded, a pleasing noise as of a baby's toy rattled.

Anastasia blinked and peered across the room. 'Who's

there?' she said, fixing her gaze upon the washbasin.

The ghost girl materialised in the shadows—a fragile little thing all decked out in a long black linen skirt and traditional Ukrainian folk blouse embroidered with bright spring flowers and little green diadem spiders.

'What a lovely blouse,' Anastasia said. 'Where did you get it? A blouse like that must've cost a fortune.'

The ghost girl remained quiet. As for the seductive rattling, the source proved to be a silvery dice cup; the girl held it in her hand, shaking the vessel as if it were the begetter of her magic.

Anastasia picked herself up and pushed herself away from the worktable. There could be little doubt that she hallucinated the ghost's presence, but why? Given the many compounds with which she had treated all the metallic sheets, could it be that her eyes had grown diseased enough that she could not help but envision the most disturbing, nightmarish phenomena? As gently as possible, she rubbed her eyelids with her knuckles. 'Who are you? What is your purpose? Please tell me.'

'Ah, but you know my purpose,' the ghost girl said, with a downturned mouth. 'I was never anything more than . . .'

'*Please*,' Anastasia implored the apparition. 'Tell me your true purpose.'

'Ah, but you know my true purpose,' the ghost girl said, laying a hand against her breastbone. 'Your psyche always intended for me to personify your own animal impulses and teach you what volatile instincts dwell in the deepest, darkest reaches of a person's unconscious mind.'

'I suppose that makes sense.' Anastasia retreated several steps until her bottom bumped up against the edge of the worktable. As she rubbed her belly, she drew a deep breath.

'Does the ghost girl speak the truth? What do you know about all this?'

All throughout her womb, the fox spirit leapt about. 'I think the glorious fox gods have summoned the Huguenot ghost girl. Yes, she's come to bestow upon you the most magnificent powers.'

Despite the many kaleidoscopic effects yet clouding her view, Anastasia lunged toward the dreamlike vision.

Without a sound, the mysterious spectre dissolved into an array of blinding white sparks, like those emitted by crucible steel when tested against a powerful grinding wheel.

Again, Anastasia fell to the floor. As the sparks vanished, she crawled outside to the fountain in the heart of the roundabout. 'Help,' she cried. 'Please. Anyone. Something has gone wrong with—'

A trio of Egyptian schoolgirls rushed to her aid.

'What's happened?' the dark-skinned girl, Ghalliya, said. Before Anastasia could answer, Ghalliya reached out her hand to help her up. 'Your eyes look red. *Aiwa.* Like maybe you weep all the morning long. Something bad you learn?'

Anastasia glanced at the opera house. *Something's gone. Yes, but what? The shawl that once dangled from the dressing-room window's top rail.*

Ghalliya followed her eyes. 'Are you thinking about the English madman who lives up there?'

Anastasia paused to think for a moment. *What's become of that English chap?* She blinked several times, struggling to put an end to the kaleidoscopic effects and restore her vision.

The green-eyed girl, Khulood, tugged upon the side seam of Anastasia's skirt. 'Do you think maybe the madman die of fever?'

'I suppose it's possible,' Anastasia answered, looking at

the third schoolgirl—the quiet, *hijab*-clad one who called herself Miss Hajek. 'What do *you* think?'

'I no think he die from no fever,' Miss Hajek said. 'I think maybe he suffer the terrible curse of *al-Asra*, and he die only because he fall in love with someone. *Aiwa*. Maybe he fall in love with *you*.'

With a series of short jerky movements, Anastasia pushed herself up onto her feet. 'You little ones stay here,' she said, dragging herself up the hill to the opera house's columned portico.

Disobeying her, the three schoolgirls followed along. Together, they pushed through the doors.

Once inside the lobby, Anastasia paused to breathe in and test the air for the stench of rotting flesh. She did not detect anything, so she strode into the house itself—where several beams of hazy light poured through the windows. Though she longed to call out, she decided against it. Instead, she cocked her ear and listened for any sign of life.

The opera house remained perfectly quiet but for the sound of mice quarrelling over an array of breadcrumbs that lay scattered at her feet.

The hazy light shifted, and a solitary ray fell across the stage and illuminated the glass harp.

There. She passed by the orchestra pit and climbed onto the stage. Gently, she tapped one of the glass dishes with the tip of a fingernail. As the chime died out, she inched over toward the stairwell to the left. 'That's the way.' She marched past the proscenium arch and tiptoed up to the dressing-room door. *I'll bet he's lying in the foetal position. Yes, the poor fool ought to be right there on the floor.* Holding her breath, she peeked inside.

Thankfully, no corpse lay on the floor. The space proved

to be empty but for a divan, a gramophone and a vanity table.

She breathed a sigh of relief. Biting her lip, she strode over to the window and tapped the catch. 'What's become of him?' she said, pinching her belly.

'He's probably gone off across the desert,' the fox spirit answered. 'Perhaps he's looking for a pleasant place to breathe his last. Maybe he intends to perish in a meadow of bright blue mushrooms. Bright, bright blue. Shimmery blue.'

'Tell me more. Tell me what's happened to him. And don't you fib.'

'Who knows? Maybe the poor youth will survive his ordeal out there in the wild, and when he footslogs his way back from some faraway land, decades from now, you'll notice the lad down there in the roundabout, where *he* must be the one to shun *you* . . . the old, faded beauty.'

At once, Anastasia registered a sensation of estrangement that she could not readily comprehend. *What an odd feeling to be* un*wanted.* As repulsive and as unnerving as Jack had always been, his sudden presumed indifference toward her made her feel a little bit lonely—perhaps even unworthy.

The dream fox must have intuited her discomfiture. Deep inside her belly, the creature snickered and twitched his tail even more.

She summoned her strength and battered her stomach, hoping to will her body to expel the spirit—and again, the futility of it all only served to recall the miscarriage. As she revisited that awful day, the kaleidoscopic effects seemed to swirl about that much faster—as if she had been staring at fireworks so intense that the display had served to rupture her eyeballs. Several times over, she blinked. Stumbling sightlessly, she bumped into the gramophone and very nearly knocked it to the floor. *I've got to come to my senses.*

When her condition failed to improve, she kicked the dressing room's baseboard with the toe of her right button boot.

Over to the left, the ghost girl reappeared, eyes glowing—the dice cup silent in her hands.

Through the fog of her blurred vision, Anastasia recognised the hallucinatory being—its triple-pierced ear. *She's not just any Huguenot ghost girl, but Svetlana.* Her jaw tight, Anastasia offered the apparition a flat gaze. 'What do you want?'

'I've come to confess,' the dream figure spoke up. 'I've come to tell you what happened all those years ago. It was just a chance encounter, nothing more. Yes, I existed . . . but never as a supernatural being. I was a bad little girl, that's all. A hoaxer, a rogue. Someone who delighted in the opportunity to poke and prod someone.' The dream figure leaned in until the tip of her nose touched the tip of Anastasia's chin. 'So, do you feel a little bit disappointed?'

Anastasia recoiled. Heart beating wildly, she stepped back from the spectre. *I must stay calm.* She did no such thing. Realising she could see little more than a hot glaring yellow mist streaked with flourishes of blinding electric-lime green, she fell back onto the divan.

~

Later that Evening.

When her sight returned to normal, Anastasia sat up. 'Anyone here?' She stumbled out of the dressing room and looked for the three schoolgirls—but the trio had already departed. 'What about you, Svetlana? Are you here?'

The dream figure was gone, too. At least she did not

say anything.

Anastasia exited the opera house. Lips pressed tightly together, she circled back to the mirror works. No sooner had she reached the worktable than the kaleidoscopic effects reappeared in full force. 'What's gone wrong with my vision?'

The dream fox refused to answer. Deep inside her womb, he only laughed like a sadistic, insecure little boy.

She made her way back outside into the roundabout. From there, she faltered over to the fountain and knelt before the pantheon of Egyptian gods hewn into the marble base.

The three schoolgirls reappeared, and Miss Hajek attempted to pull her away. 'No, you come too close to false gods,' she said, speaking through her teeth. 'False gods be wicked angels, nothing more. *Djinn*! They fall from grace long ago. In the beginning of time.'

Despite all, Anastasia reached for Isis. And as soon as she touched the marble veil, she heard the same peculiar noise that she had heard earlier: a dreamlike thump resounding without even the faintest hint of an echo, a disturbance as that of a cast-iron anchor and its pointed crown catching the seabed and settling in the sand.

The skin below her thumbnail tickled, and as she rolled the tip of her tongue over her gap tooth, she fingered her Huguenot cross—and the precious pendant dove.

At last, the dream fox ceased with his laughter. 'Do you believe the sound of the anchor to be a sign of hope? Yes, of course, you believe the Saviour has brought about the miracle.'

No matter the creature's ironic tone, she had no doubt. Something like a castaway living on some distant shore, the Holy Trinity had communicated with her—and for no other reason than to let her know that she stood on the cusp of transforming into someone extraordinary. She closed her eyes and beheld a procession of swirling dreamlike colours—pale, milky, futuristic shades of white. *Yes, someday soon, I shall acquire great mystical powers.*

The schoolgirls sought to pull her away from the fountain, and one of them even let out a shriek.

Anastasia broke free, reached for the representation of Isis and clawed at the idolatrous veil.

As Anastasia's fingernails cracked and bled, all three schoolgirls chided her and sought to pull her away again. When they failed, Miss Hajek looked at the sky and recited a brief prayer.

Anastasia stood and faced the distant sea. Due to the kaleidoscopic effects swirling all about, she strained to catch a glimpse of the horizon. 'There's a ship out there,' she said, full of emotion. 'Oh yes, I've heard her anchor. God the Father, He's let me hear it because He'll not have me lose hope.'

'*Halas!*' Ghalliya took Anastasia by the hand, and the little girl pulled her away from the fountain.

Anastasia's eyes burned badly. *If a Huguenot parson stood before me in this moment, what might he think? Who knows? Maybe he'd blame me for my whole ordeal.*

As her eyes watered, the three schoolgirls guided her off down the road winding its way back into the village.

She stopped and shot a glance back in the direction of the mirror works. 'Have you no idea how sinful I was to believe that objects of vanity such as mirrors might command magical properties? Ernesztina and her kind, they have no answers. Women like that, they believe in the cultic, the taboo, the stuff of heresy. *Blasphème contre le saint esprit.*'

The three schoolgirls guided her along anew, but as soon as they reached the heart of the crowded marketplace, the unmistakable rattle of a little dice cup resounded.

189

'Where's it coming from?' Anastasia asked. 'The telegraph office? Do you hear that rattle? Could it be a friendly game of backgammon?'

Whatever it was, the noise grew increasingly dissonant—until the dice resounded like castanets made from cracked yew.

Oh, what if it's Svetlana? Oh God, she's come back. Oh God. Her lips parting, Anastasia prayed some divine force might suddenly fall from the sky and force the ghost girl to dissolve into sparks.

Deep inside her womb, the dream fox sneered. 'Svetlana, she's well-versed in the art of predation. Any moment now, she'll smite you in your temple. Yes, just like some poor proud brute aiming to assail the first obtuse fool who passes by.'

The whole of her body growing numb, Anastasia swayed back and forth—until she stumbled forward. At the last second, she caught Ghalliya's arm. *Be strong.*

Ghalliya squeezed Anastasia's wrist. 'You look a little bit sallow. Maybe I help you back to hostelry. You go up there to bedchamber, and maybe you rest. After little while, you feel very good.'

Anastasia broke free from Ghalliya's grasp and lurched forward. Thankfully, by the time she reached the telegraph office, the resplendent kaleidoscopic effects had mutated back into a series of almost-imperceptible geometric shapes. *Am I getting stronger?* She turned toward the curiosity shop. *What might be there in the very heart of the display table? Maybe the shopkeeper has arranged an antique backgammon board and matching dice cup.*

The uncanny rattle sped up and reached the most enthralling crescendo, only to cease—and in that instant, Anastasia's world went black. 'Why has everything become dark? It cannot be that night has fallen. Has there been a solar

190

eclipse? What's gone wrong?'

The dream fox should have answered, but he did not. Deep inside her womb, he only wagged his long downy tail.

She reached out for the schoolgirls. 'What's happened? Why has it grown so dark? Do any of you know? Ghalliya, are you there? Say something. Khulood, are you there? Please say something. Miss Hajek, are you there? Speak up.'

None of the little girls did—as if the trio had grown affrighted by the presence of some sinister entity.

Deep inside her womb, the dream fox grew still. 'I'll tell you what's happened. You've gone blind.' The dream fox whimpered and snickered simultaneously. 'Yes, blind.'

'*Blind*? That's impossible.'

'I always told you that I'd gouge out your eyes someday. Yes. It's retribution for all your sins. And even if you repent, no, I'll never grant you amnesty. No, never.'

She groped in the gentle darkness that surrounded her. 'Give me back my eyesight. With all of my heart, I beg you. *Please*.' She must have unnerved the three little girls, for she heard the trio darting away—their footsteps reverberating for a moment before trailing off entirely.

As Anastasia leaned against the wall and wept, an elderly Egyptian woman, or so it seemed, came along and greeted her. Gently, the old woman took her by the hand. 'Don't panic, my friend, but I think maybe you suffer from a grave eye disease.'

Anastasia shook her head and rubbed her chin. For a moment, she even reeled about in circles.

'Please stay calm,' the Egyptian woman told her. 'I'll take you to the doctor's office.'

'No, take me back to the hostelry and find my copy of *Middlemarch*. My love of books will restore my vision, and then I'll get some reading done.' Anastasia made a step in what she believed to be the direction of the hostelry, and then she stopped. In that moment, she suddenly thought of a mystery drama—the confounding, suspenseful prelude. She recalled the way the actors perform the first sequence in sound only—the silent assailant and the talkative victim but a pair of silhouettes standing in profile behind a translucent curtain that permits the whole of the audience to *hear* the act of villainy without actually discerning the murderer's identity. Anastasia felt for the elderly Egyptian woman's hand. 'Are you still there? Don't leave me all alone.'

The elderly woman patted Anastasia's wrist. 'I'm still here.'

Several shopkeepers and villagers gathered around them, everyone speaking in hushed tones. Anastasia's condition concerned them, obviously.

Her body swayed. *Have I gone into a mild state of shock?* Her thoughts flowed back to the dramaturgy of mystery plays—the detectives standing about the crime scene, each one of them struggling to decide which clues matter and which must be the stuff of misdirection. *Yes, and someone always solves the mystery. So, there's no reason for me to despair.*

The Egyptian woman took her by the hand. 'Come with me.' With that, the woman guided her onward through the streets.

The sense of shock suffused Anastasia's person—until she could not know where her thoughts terminated and the real world began.

When they reached the local dispensary, the Egyptian woman sat Anastasia on the lumpy leather sofa in the waiting room.

She reached for the Egyptian woman's hand. 'Do you maybe know how this mystery play ends?' Anastasia asked.

192

'Have the detectives perhaps noticed anything peculiar missing from the slain girl's room? Do they think the culprit might have taken the purloined item home to keep as some kind of grotesque trophy?'

The Egyptian woman tried to calm Anastasia and stroked her cheek.

The woman's efforts did no good. Anastasia stood and reeled. 'When do you think the detectives should interview the various suspects and adjudge the merits of their alibis? And just when do you suppose the murderer ought to write a letter to taunt the detectives?' Once more, she reeled all about.

A set of footsteps approached, and a woman introduced herself as the nurse.

Anastasia took hold of the nurse's wrists. 'Do *you* maybe know anything about mystery plays?'

The Egyptian nurse sighed. 'Please, friend. No you panic. I help you.' For a time, the nurse spoke to the elderly woman in Arabic.

Anastasia pulled her hand away. 'When the final act comes around, shouldn't the hero resolve just about every question? Yes, why should a proper theatregoer tolerate anything less? The mystery play, it ought to end in that moment the chief constable issues the murder warrant.'

Finally, the nurse succeeded in compelling Anastasia to sit. Then the nurse placed what seemed to be a proper liquid-in-glass temperature gauge beneath Anastasia's tongue.

When the nurse walked off, the cool, salty, late-winter breeze sailed through the window and stirred some kind of plant standing on a table at Anastasia's side.

The sensual sound made Anastasia think more lucidly— and soon enough, she reached out her hand and sought to locate the plant. 'What might this be?' she said. 'A medicinal plant?'

'No, it's just a Congo fern,' the elderly Egyptian woman told her. 'The strong wind has its blades scraping against the wall.'

Anastasia dropped her hand to the pot, at which point she detected the presence of a young curled little frond. 'Something terrible has happened,' she whispered, as if she held the power to speak to any living thing. 'I've gone blind.' Now she tore the leaf and popped it into her mouth. What an awful taste, too—like that of an Egyptian radish. She spat it out into her hand. *No, don't do that. Maybe it'll cure my blindness. Yes, let's hope so.* Like a foolish belligerent little girl, she popped it back into her mouth and swallowed. *Heal me. Help.*

XII.

Cairo. 2 March 1918.

That evening, Jack brought his sheet music out onto the hotel balcony and assumed his usual place at the little coffee table.

Ever since his arrival in the Egyptian capital, he had found one excuse after the next to postpone his suicide. At present, he had convinced himself that he could not depart this world before he had completed his opus. *So, go on, then. Work.* Without a glass harp, though, the task proved trying. He struggled to picture the musical instrument. Then he glided his fingertips over the imaginary glass dishes that would reel around the imaginary rod that would dangle over the imaginary water trough, and he endeavoured to resolve a few of the more intricate passages. *It's bloody impossible. I'm undone.* At last, he sat back and contented himself to look out upon the river. As the wind whistled through the towering trees that overlooked the Nile, he imagined the mournful sound as the music of a nightingale—the accursed song that promises the songbird's eventual death. Given how sentimental the whole idea was, he sobbed.

A familiar, sickly sweet odour drifted by—and a stench as that of some potent antifungal medicament suddenly pervaded the nighttime fog.

I've dreamt up the smell of death. I know it. The odour made him think of Mr Sylvius, and he imagined the nasty footman standing at his back—right there on the hotel balcony. Jack grimaced. 'So, have you come to taunt me? Go away.'

Mr Sylvius laughed malevolently—wildly, too, as if the nasty old man could not speak for laughing.

'What do you want? Did you come to gift me a litany of abhorrently rude, psychosexual insults?'

'What if I did?' the old man said. 'Why should I show you a sign of respect? You'd be the hapless kind, aye, someone unrequited in love, which would be why you don't *deserve* a bloody sign of respect, nor do you deserve any kind of approbation.'

Jack fidgeted awhile. Then he draped his duffle coat over his shoulders and approached the balcony railing. 'How'd you ever find me here?' he asked, folding his arms across his bare chest.

The old man did not answer. 'Why you standing there?' he asked. 'When will you complete your song?'

'When the devil goes blind.'

'What a pity, for when the hotelier forwards the bill to London, your parents should be terribly cross with you, eh? An establishment like this ought to cost a packet.'

Jack shrugged. 'It's got to be. What can I say? I'm a bitter-ender.' Little by little, the sickly sweet odour in the air grew stronger—until it made him sneeze. His eyes darting like those of an anxious, affrighted little boy, Jack gathered up the sheet music and staggered back into the darkened hotel room. With nowhere to go, he slumped against the wall and looked down to study a few of the folds in the little patchwork fur rug.

When the old man followed along inside, Jack drew his legs up and rested his brow against his right knee. *I got no reason to pother. In a few more days, I'll complete me grand opus. And then I'll bowl off and rest right easy. And in the morning, the chambermaid, she'll discover me body, and then she'll fall to her knees and lament me and wonder why anyone so beautiful should wish to throw his life away.*

Mr Sylvius sat upon the edge of the bed. 'You shan't destroy yourself.'

'What do you know?'

'I know plenty, aye, I'd say the will to live ought to stop you. The will to create more music will proscribe any attempt at deliverance.'

Jack sought to look up and to do something to retaliate, but his body froze in mid-movement. He drew his legs up even more. 'I'm going away,' he whispered, as loudly as his fragile voice would permit.

An olive-leaf moth fluttered into the hotel room. Mysteriously, the winged creature came to perch upon Jack's knee.

Why not crush the little bugger? He cupped his hands together, and he soon captured his prey. Then, as the insect's wings flapped wildly against his fingers and palms, he paused to ask himself just what it would feel like to reduce a creature of that size to a warm, sticky puddle of mush. *Don't do it.*

Mr Sylvius gave Jack a harsh squint. 'Go on and destroy the living thing,' the old man whispered. 'Show me just how selfish a chap like you should be.'

A cold bead of sweat running down the length of his

frown line, Jack opened his hands to let the moth go free.

Mr Sylvius waved to the creature—which soon came to perch atop his shoulder. With a sigh, the old man turned to the bedrail. 'Why so irresolute, lad? Why didn't you crush the bloody moth? Could it be you're beginning to prize life as much as you prize your music? *No.* You just didn't want to get your hands dirty.'

Jack collected some of the sheet music and studied the key signature along with a few of the half notes. Mostly, he fretted over the lyrics. Not only were they insipid, he had plagiarised the better part of them. Over the course of the past few days, he had lifted dozens of lines from W H Iveley's *Guide to Arte Lyrica*.

The old man snapped his fingers. 'Even if you was to translate everything into a tongue such as Ecclesiastical Latin, the many instances of plagiarism should still be obvious.' The old man crossed his legs, and then he wrapped his hand around his ankle. 'Go on home, aye, maybe some physician could help you, or at the very least, he'll determine just how much your troubles follow from your biochemistry and just how much of your troubles follow from your well-to-do upbringing, so go on home, then.'

'Why don't *you* go home?'

'You want me to leave?' The old man coaxed the olive-leaf moth onto the side of his index finger. 'What would you do if me and this here wee little bug pissed off just now?'

'I don't rightly know. Maybe I'd visit the Arab market. It's well-nigh time for me to get myself a soporific.'

'So, that's how you prefer to meet your death?' At that point, Mr Sylvius sang a bit of doggerel:

Ashes to ashes and dust to dust,

If the Lord shan't take you, so the devil must.

Jack studied a painting on the wall—a Cairo streetscape boasting a horse-drawn, double-decker omnibus rolling down Fatimid Boulevard. He imagined that the vehicle happened to be transporting his corpse to some forgotten cemetery out in the Sahara. Impulsively, he licked his lips. 'Why not swallow some pleasant soporific? Why not drink some powerful deathly elixir? That'd be a right peaceful way to go.'

'But the blooming soporific might not be strong enough, aye, even a bundle of hemlock might fail, or what if you choose to inhale some deadly blossom? Maybe the aroma should bring you hallucinations but not necessarily *death*, aye, and from that moment on, maybe you'll suffer incurable brain damage, aye, you'll grow docile, unaware, *unassuming*, as if you haven't got any memories, and what a laughable, incongruous creature you'll be, aye, pitiable only to fellow celibates and losers.'

'No, no. I know what I'll do. I'll visit a bottle shop somewhere in the market, and I'll down the sedatives with a good strong spirit.'

'Yes, how about fig brandy?' the old man asked. 'Might I recommend an imported variety? How's about something from Tunis, or what about Casablanca?'

'Sure, that'd be aces.' Jack stretched his legs out flat against the floor, crossing his right ankle over his left. Another bead of sweat ran down his left frown line, followed by a tear of self-pity. He dropped the sheet music onto the floor. His big toe growing very cold, he wondered what kinds of bottle shops did business in a city like Cairo. An illusory lump throbbing in the sole of his foot, he thought back to his childhood—

all those times when he and a few friends might give some lowlife the funds to enter some shop to purchase them a pint of this or that spirit. Always, the lowlife would slip out the back door. *Bloody hell, it never failed. No.*

As gracefully as a butterfly, the olive-leaf moth fluttered down to the rug and then darted this way and that before settling upon the sheet music—the treble clef, to be precise.

Kill the little bastard. Go on. A tightness in his eyes, Jack slammed his fist down—but as luck would have it, the curious creature darted off just in time.

From somewhere outside, the report of a rifle rang out. Had the British Army shot to death some revolutionary?

Jack leapt to his feet and folded his arms across his bare chest. *Out there in the streets of Cairo, they're fighting for their freedom. And here I am, drowning in self-pity.*

The olive-leaf moth fluttered all about yet, and the sickly sweet odour grew stronger—as if the frantic creature's wings served to diffuse the stench in all directions.

By the sound of it, Mr Sylvius had detected the odour. Gagging, he marched over to the cheval mirror.

Jack collected one of his shoes then and hurled it at the apparition, the heel striking the old man in the back of his head.

'Very well, lad. In the twitch of a bed staff, I shall be moving on.' Mr Sylvius slipped through the floor mirror, its immaculate surface—and with that, the old man vanished into worlds unknown.

Late that night, Jack left the hotel and wandered off into the marketplace. *I got to get me the things I'll require. A soporific and strong spirits.*

Very few shopkeepers conducted business at that hour, but two blocks up ahead, along a narrow lane adorned with nutmeg trees, a dimly lit apothecary's shop beckoned. Jack raced forward and sought to keep pace with a team of grey flea-bitten steeds running in the same direction. When he reached the apothecary's shop, he let the riderless horses go on their way. Pulling his shoulders low, he peeked inside the place of business.

The establishment proved to be dark and cluttered, the walls dominated by a series of mahogany cubbyholes containing an array of elixirs.

'Come you in,' the apothecary called out. Though obviously very old, the apothecary had a pleasant aspect. He wore a very long beard without a moustache. Most appealing of all, he had a prayer callus on his forehead—and the bump made him look exceedingly wise and giving. 'You wish to cash prescriptions?' he asked.

'I haven't got a prescription, but I've got me a bloody bad case of . . . insomnia,' Jack lied, blinking once or twice. When the apothecary did not immediately respond, Jack fixed his gaze upon a merchant's scale. 'So, could you help me? Please, sir.' Jack looked into the apothecary's eyes and sighed like a girl. 'You've got to believe me. Now that I can't sleep no more, I'm wending me way through life with a face like yesterday.'

The apothecary tugged at his beard and shuffled over toward a gilt-wood showcase before shambling off into the back room. After quite some time, when he finally reappeared, he presented Jack with a blown-glass phial filled with a pale yellow concoction.

'What's all this, then? Do you think it'd be strong enough to remedy a real bad case of sleeplessness?'

'Yes, this remedy we make from the mandrake root,' the apothecary told him. 'No you drink too much, though. Yes, please. Just you drop a touch of the elixir into a glass of milk at the bedtime.'

'*Aiwa.*' Jack paid for the soporific and then hurried outside—where he paused to feel the nighttime breeze blow through his long brown hair. A cat with a blue-cream coat passed by, a bloodied finch trapped in its jaws. The wounded songbird struggling all the while, the blue-cream cat darted off through the dimly lit marketplace. Jack sauntered off in the same direction because he knew of no other way to return to the hotel.

Two blocks over, the beguiling cat peered down an alleyway running alongside a boys' *madrasa*. There in the narrow passage, an elderly drunkard in traditional Coptic–Christian dress lay asleep beside a bottle of what looked to be Egyptian whiskey.

Take it. Go on. Jack looked in both directions and then inched ever closer—until the drunkard awoke, took hold of the whiskey bottle, and glared at him.

Jack almost swallowed his tongue. 'Do forgive me, eh?' He gave the old man a slow nod and then, wheezing all the while, fled in a sprint.

~

Cairo. 8 March.

At midday, a riot consumed Cairo—and Jack watched the loud, violent melee from his hotel balcony. *I'm too craven to serve. Too craven to bowl off.*

Not twenty minutes into the disturbance, two soldiers opened fire on a large number of revolutionaries running up and down Sultan Jaqmaq Boulevard.

The violence had Jack in convulsions—both because

of his sympathy for the people and his endless guilt at not enlisting. He crawled over to the chair where he had placed his belongings and grabbed his duffle coat. Pulling until his face shone red, he tore the sleeves apart.

Little by little, a series of hateful, reproachful voices— they must have been the voices of imaginary soldiers— reverberated all throughout his stream of consciousness.

'Maybe you ought to bowl off,' one of them said. 'You don't look right. Maybe you've got some kind of fluid building up in your airways. Yes, indeed, that'd explain what's happened to you.'

'Maybe so,' a second voice agreed. 'Just look at Jack's drooping face. The poor bastard doesn't look good at all. I wonder if the bloke even has the strength to raise his arms over his head. Probably not.'

'Right,' yet another voice spoke up. 'It's a good thing this frail coward didn't serve. Who would want to share a funk hole with him?'

'No one would ever have to share no shelter with this one here,' a booming fourth voice spoke up. 'If a chap like Jack were to arrive at Rollestone Camp out there on the Salisbury Plain, they'd take one look at him and then send him home. Why should anyone think he'd be capable of learning fieldcraft and that? And even if that didn't happen, and maybe this prat completed his phase-one training, the officers would have no choice but to grant Jack a mental discharge, because what good might someone like him be to the Training Reserve? None at all.'

No sooner had the fourth voice spoken than Jack wrapped his arms and hands around his head. On and on, he rocked back and forth—the hotel-room floor creaking noisily beneath his body.

By two o'clock, the riot dissipated—but Jack found himself so overcome that he finally resolved to forsake the demanding opus and to end his life already. *Let's do this already. No more dawdling.*

From the direction of Coptic Cairo, a church bell played. Calmly, methodically, it counted out the afternoon hour: four o'clock. As the last peal fell silent, Jack stumbled downstairs and dumped the sheet music into a rubbish bin standing outside the hotel. When he went back inside, he swallowed a mouthful of the soporific and gagged. The peculiar concoction tasted sickly sweet. *Just like some bleeding antifungal medicament. What else?* In need of a chaser, he poured himself a tall glass of Turkish coffee. 'To the very best in Christendom,' he whispered, his voice cracked with tears.

Once he had downed everything, he wandered out onto the balcony. *What do I do?* He studied the movements of the river. As he watched the water swirl and eddy, he asked himself whether he believed in some fanciful hereafter. Looking up, he studied the clouds as if seeking an answer from them. *How could anyone believe in such a thing as an afterlife?*

After a while, a violent fit of paroxysmal coughing came upon him. *God, I'm choking to death.* He slumped at the little coffee table, his head propped on his hand. *I got to chill me beans.*

From the corner of his eye, he saw a milk-white heron flutter across the Nile. As it flew eastwards, the winged creature let out a grating scream. He watched as the heron took refuge within the boughs of a date palm towering over the opposite riverbank. *Look at him. He's found a good place to laze about.* Determined to die in his big, beautiful bed, he crawled back inside and collapsed on the four-poster, his arms and legs so ponderous, he thought they must be fettered with wrought-iron chains.

He lay there awhile until it seemed as if the soporific must be cracking his bones apart. Despite the agony, he reached out his left hand, letting it dangle over the edge of the bed. The chambermaid will discover me this way, he thought, and marvel at the dramatic pose—as if in the moment of me death, I sought to take hold of some exquisite, imaginary jewel. 'Goodbye then, Anastasia.' With that one last utterance, he closed his eyes. *Have no fear. Sleep.* Swiftly, he lost consciousness.

Some six hours later, the shadows of night having already pervaded the room, he awoke to a phantasmagoria of uninvited, ghostly voyeurs gathered about the footboard. Most of them looked vaguely familiar. *Might they be schoolmates? Yes, from Doughty Street Lyceum.*

A lad with bad acne shook his head. 'You didn't die,' he blurted out. 'All that caffeine inside the coffee ground went and blended with the mandrake root. Hence, all the hallucinogenic effects. You might as well have overdosed on blooming morphine.'

'True that, you've made yourself drug addled,' a second figure added. 'Though the lad looked very young, he wore a khaki-drill uniform. 'You've gone as mad as a March hare,' he continued, shaking his head all the while. 'No wonder the army never wanted you any.'

Jack let his eyes adjust to the darkness and then peered at the two apparitions, trying to identify them. *Do I know them? When did we meet?* He hauled himself up. 'Who the devil are ye?' he said, pointing at the strange figures.

From the far corner of the hotel room, a ghostlike version of an old acquaintance approached the bed. 'You can't do anything right,' the spectre said. 'You should've concluded your affairs and drawn your last baleful breath, but no. You must be some kind of simpleton.'

Jack shook and shivered. 'What's happened? Might this be a reunion? Have all the schoolmates come back together to talk about all the sods like me? Why must ye do that kind of thing, eh? Wasn't it enough that ye ruled the roost back in our schooldays?'

The old acquaintance raised a hand. 'That's enough of that. If you'd had a better place in the pecking order, you would've persecuted just as many as we ever did.'

A little boy, an old friend from Doughty Street Lyceum, approached the bed now. 'What's happened t–t–to you, Jack?' the little boy stuttered. 'T–T–To all appearances, you look like a vagabond, the pitiful k–k–kind always sleeping rough down in the railway station.'

Jack reached out his hand. 'What's your name, old friend? Malcolm? Gilbert? No, how about Clive? No, Colin. Colin Cockerham. Could that be it? Help me. Remember, once upon a time, we was the best of friends.'

The little boy twisted and pulled at his clothing. 'T–T– Teach me how to play two-fingered tremolo.'

'I got no time for that,' Jack said. He closed his eyes for a moment or two, and when he looked again, the little boy had vanished.

Like something out of a dream, the visitors from Doughty Street Lyceum transformed into a cluster of shimmery, floating diadem spiders.

Jack closed his eyes tight and curled up—but as he lay there, the diadem spiders insulted him with veiled references to every little mistake he had ever made back in his schooldays. And the more detailed the insults regarding his hygiene habits and clumsy, callow manners, the more disingenuous the diadem spiders' tone—as if the merciless creatures just knew that their feigned innocence would only serve to intensify his debasement.

When the cluster finally grew quiet, he opened his eyes and looked up. 'Why do ye pretend to be all so proper and polite? Ye wouldn't be no better than me. Can't you show me a measure of mercy?'

One of the freakish spiders ascended to the top of the nearest bed knob. 'Just look at what you've gone and done!' the illusory creature bellowed. 'You've gone and jimmy-riddled all over the hotel's posh linens!'

Jack climbed out of bed and knelt over the cool stale puddle in the mattress. Teetering, he removed his stenchful trousers and sullied shirt. Naked, he staggered into the washroom and illuminated the pendant light. When he checked his reflection in the mirror, he shrieked. By now, his pupils had contracted so much that each one appeared as little more than a speckle of black powder. *I've got the wild eyes of a madman.* Despite his state of undress, he raced out into the hallway. *I've got to find help.* In a frenzy, he tripped over an ice pail. As soon as he collected himself, he looked up ahead; at the very end of the corridor, Anastasia trifled with a pair of tall, handsome English soldiers. Though they had to be hallucinations, he hurried forward. 'I never thought I'd see *you* again! Please stay right there, and we'll have a friendly chat. You'll see I'm not so bad. That's right, you'll see I'm worthy to talk to you and all.'

She did not answer. Quickly, she followed the soldiers into the broom closet and closed the door behind them.

'Anastasia, don't go.' When he opened the broom-closet door, he found himself face to face with Rudyard Kipling.

The famed author laughed at him. 'Have you no shame?'

he asked. 'You smell like you've just spent a penny all over yourself. You look to be in a flat panic as well.'

'Where did Anastasia go?'

'Tell me something. Why are you buzzing all about as naked as nature made you? What did you do with your ammunition pouches? What did you do with your braces? For that matter, where did you put your entrenching tools? And what about your water bottle?' Rudyard Kipling looked up and moaned. 'Do you realise you haven't even got your rifle? What did you do? Did you give it to the Germans? Did they take your bayonet as well?'

'Please, sir, could you help me find Anastasia?'

'*No.* Forget your wife. You're already dead. Methinks that'd explain what's become of your vestments. Your widow must've gone and arranged your robes and sandals and things all about your headstone. That's because Bedouin tradition obliges her to do so. That way, all the poor may come along after the service and claim whatever they'd be lacking.'

Dizzy, Jack propped himself up on the broom-closet wall and looked at his feet to keep himself from falling.

As he teetered back and forth, Rudyard Kipling took hold of his manhood. 'Don't you pity all them grim, grieving Bedouin widows? Imagine how ghastly it'd be to go through life all the time confronted by lowly beggars and the like doddering about the encampment all dressed up in your old man's clobber.'

As soon as Rudyard Kipling let go, an emaciated, ghostlike pharaoh hound materialised at Jack's feet. 'You'd better get your work out of the rubbish bin,' the spectral beast whispered, looking up into his eyes. 'If the goddess Isis won't furnish you with a preparation deadly enough to kill you, then you might as well rescue your sheet music.'

'Right, me sheet music.' Jack stumbled down the stairway, wandered through the crowded lobby, and tottered out the door. He stopped then; given the narcotic effects clouding his mind, the city did not even look real. *Am I back home? Might this be Fountain Lane?*

Down the street, a sonorous thrum rang out—and now the whole of the casbah slowly transformed into an expanse resembling Portobello Market, which subsequently metamorphosed into an expanse resembling Manchester Square.

The miracle of it all had him so dumbfounded that his body went still. *Me eyes must be deceiving me.* When he looked in the direction of the Nile, no less than Putney Bridge suddenly materialised. *Cor blimey.*

A whole crowd marched over from the other side of the river. What an alarming mob, too: the throng included the London street gangs that had accosted him over the years—even a pair of hooligans who had assailed him late one winter afternoon in Victoria Park.

'Go away!' he shouted. 'Go back where you came from, eh?' He ran about in circles awhile before collecting his wits. *Go on. Find the sheet music.* When he finally reached the rubbish bin, he found the receptacle empty but for a handful of rotten cucumbers.

Over to the left, another phantasm appeared. The figure proved to be the Italian girl from his past, her face obscured behind the fine veil dangling from her parasol. 'Why did you think to terrorise Anastasia the way you did? Just what did she ever do to deserve such mischief? Do you know something? She happens to be a good friend of mine. As a matter of fact, she's just like a sister to me. And I wouldn't lie about something like that.'

'Please help me find me sheet music. If I'm not to perish, then I must locate me work and complete everything. If nothing else, it'll help me become a noted musician.'

The bewitching Italian girl's mouth fell open. 'The dustman already came by to collect the refuse.'

Struck dumb, Jack fell to his knees and wept. 'I've thrown it all away. All me work—it's gone forever. All me work.'

The Italian girl laughed in the most impolite manner, and then she took a few quiet steps in this direction and that. 'No, there will be no swansong performance for you. Everything's gone. Still, what kind of song was it, anyway? The work you've been composing, it was not a song but a suicide note.' With that, the Italian girl gazed inwardly. 'Yes, a suicide note.'

The nighttime breeze kicked up, and the medicinal odour of muskroot came swirling through the alley. Did an Egyptian physician live nearby?

Whatever the reason for its presence, the muskroot had a tranquilising effect on Jack. Having forgotten all about his shameful nakedness, he crawled over to the phantasm's feet and bowed. 'Please help me find me precious sheet music.'

Like wisps of blue flame, the Italian girl's eyes shone through the lace. 'Why must you mill about without a stitch? My word, you didn't even think to slip into a singlet?'

He looked himself over. 'For pity's sake,' he muttered, puffing and panting. Then he looked up into the Italian girl's eyes. 'What did you do with me nightshirt, you Guinea wench?'

Her gold belt buckle glowing like a star, the Italian girl laughed the way heartless little girls laugh. 'You're a miserable clown,' she told him then, rushing her words. '*Che miserabile pagliaccio.*'

He stood and attempted to backhand her across the jaw,

but he missed. Confounded, he fell to his knees. Then he crawled back to the rubbish bin and reached inside. Grabbing a rotten cucumber, he pivoted to face her.

She fixed her gaze upon his unimpressive manhood and laughed in the most sinister way. When she grew quiet, her belt buckle glowed brightly a second time. 'You're a total nothing,' she told him. '*Si certamente.* I have no reason to threaten you. I'd have nothing to gain from threatening a worthless imp.'

'Why'd you pinch me clothes? Where the hell did you put everything?'

'Maybe I put your clothes in the old Theatre of Pompey. Yes, right there in the debating chamber. So, why don't you go get them? If you begin the journey now, you should be there by the Ides of March.' With that, the Italian girl pointed at a long procession of hushed, wounded protestors—local Egyptians who had perhaps only just participated in a demonstration that very night.

A moment or two later, as the procession continued past the alley, the Italian girl turned back to Jack. 'All those people there, it's the Senate of Rome. Follow them, yes? Maybe they'll show you the way.'

At last, he hurled the cucumber—which sailed right through the spectral figure's immaterial being.

As if chastened, the vindictive figure relaxed her posture. Then, without a word, she dissolved into the ether.

The sudden solitude made him think of Anastasia. 'Do you hear this wee telepathic message? Where are you on a night like this? Where are you? Will I ever see you again?'

As he spoke, the breeze compelled a few leaves of crumpled newspaper to come tumbling forward from out of the thick nighttime fog.

211

He grabbed the filthy papers and held them up against his body, for he could not be too particular. In that moment, he had to reclaim his humanity. At the very least, he had to reclaim his modesty.

XIII.

The Wilderness of Sinai. 23 March 1918.

Just before the break of dawn, Anastasia awoke to a soft late-winter rain resounding from outside her hostelry-room window. She opened her eyes. *I'm still blind.* Several times over, she blinked. Then she pulled in a deep breath and held it. No matter how indomitable the darkness seemed at present, she lately hoped her diagnosis might prove to be nothing more than a temporary case of hysterical blindness. Only yesterday, Ernesztina had read a newspaper article that had alluded to the many shellshocked doughboys who had served in the trenches of war-torn France, only to develop the very same malady. Anastasia exhaled now and listened.

Unrelentingly, the rain fell—several drops bounding through the window and then bouncing off the night table, only to glide past the tip of her nose.

Once more, Anastasia blinked—but nothing happened, no miracle. *I've gone blind for good.* She patted her blanket. For the first time, she ran her fingers over the embroidery— the geometric patterns woven into the wool. Some had a shape like that of diadem spiders, and that curious fact made her think of the ghost girl. *Long ago, travelling on that train, was it all a dream? A nighttime terror?*

If, on the other hand, Svetlana had truly appeared before her that fateful night, then there had to be a logical explanation. *Could it be the precocious girl had fancied herself something far more sophisticated than an everyday hoaxer? Perhaps she had always boasted a brilliant, evil intellect. What if she had engaged in acts of devilry for no other reason than to satisfy some esoteric, misanthropic, sadistic impulse?*

Given how vague her memories of the incident were, Anastasia had no answers. *I'll never know what happened that dreamful night.* From the depths of her unconscious mind, a thought arose; quite possibly, Svetlana had always longed to forge a career as a performance artist. *If so, perhaps she had hoped that the staging of elaborate escapades and practical jokes might help her to learn something about the psychology of her hypothetical audience. Might that explain everything?*

The late-winter rain grew a little bit stronger now. By the sound of it, some of the raindrops drummed against the window's upper sash. How pleasing the rhythm was, too—alluring enough to make Anastasia get lost in reverie—until she imagined Svetlana standing at the foot of the bed. *Yes, she's here.* The ghost girl had come for no other reason than to torment her—just the way she had done all those years ago. *Or what if she aims to murder me? Perhaps she'll bide her time, only to drop some deadly poison into a cup of tea . . . the same way a vile woman might poison her husband in the hope she might collect on a lucrative insurance policy.* Anastasia sat up and struggled to detect the odour of a lethal concoction perhaps lingering in the air. Though she failed to sense anything out of the ordinary, she could swear that the ghost girl did, in fact, stand there at the foot of the bed. 'Svetlana, are you here? If so, please speak up and greet me properly.'

No voice spoke up, but what did that prove? For all Anastasia knew, the ghost girl stood there, glaring at her—the merciless spectre staring at her with murder in its eyes. *Yes, of course, she's giving me the evil eye.* At the very least, the ghost girl had a dirty look on her face—just the way a politician's eyes glaze over when some unfortunate circumstance compels him to listen as his rival speaks. *Or what if Svetlana's eyes register no emotion at all?* The thought seemed quite possible: the ghost girl looked upon her with utter indifference. *No, I know what Svetlana would be doing.* Anastasia pictured the ghost girl mocking her plight by frantically bowing an imaginary violin.

As a peal of distant thunder resonated in its godlike way, Anastasia scowled and wetted her lips. 'Please go away. Let me go back to sleep.'

'*No,*' the ghost girl whispered, almost imperceptibly. 'I've come to help you. I've come to admonish you and prepare you for the future.'

Anastasia reached out her hand—as if she ought to feel the cool warmth of the ghost girl's presence.

'Things look dire at the moment,' Svetlana's whisper continued, her voice rising. 'Things have gone from bad to worse. Struck with blindness as you are, it means you have failed in your struggle to thwart the fox. So, he grows stronger. Strong enough to destroy you from the inside.'

For the longest time, the ghost girl remained silent—and during that dissatisfying interlude, Anastasia contented herself to listen to the rain.

In time, the ghost girl invited herself to sit on the edge of the bed. 'Honestly,' she whispered, 'the whole idea that you might wield the power to throw the fox into the mirror someday, was that not all terribly foolish?'

The rain fell harder until several drops bounced through the window and splashed against the tip of Anastasia's nose.

She felt for the ghost girl. When Anastasia detected no presence, she climbed out of bed and waved. 'Where did you go?'

No response came. The room remained quiet. Indeed, the whole of the hostelry remained perfectly silent but for the lilt and flow of the falling rain.

She staggered forward three steps until she stubbed her big toe hard against her steamer trunk. 'What hope have I got? How do I free myself from the fox? What do I do?' The torrential rain resounding louder, Anastasia found her way back to her bed.

~

Later that Same Day.

Someone knocked upon Anastasia's door and then continued into the bedchamber. 'Are you awake?' a woman's voice asked. 'It's me here. Ernesztina.'

At once, Anastasia sat up in bed and dropped her feet to the floor. No sooner had she stood, though, than she bumped into the night table, only to topple a jar of Aleppo pepper that had been standing next to her comb ever since she had absent-mindedly brought the spice in from the kitchen. Overcome by the harsh burning alkaloids suddenly drifting about, she sneezed three times.

By the sound of it, Ernesztina took it upon herself to tidy up the room. 'You look very thin,' she said. 'Are you trying to starve yourself? Maybe I ought to cook something savoury for you. What about a bowl of spicy Ethiopian chicken stew?'

Anastasia rubbed her belly. *Why not starve myself? If I do, maybe the fox will leave my body at long last. Who knows?*

Another peal of thunder bellowed. Soon, the downpour fell so hard that a chorus of caterwauling resounded from the rooftop.

Guided by the sound and feel of the wind and rain, she made her way over to the window and took hold of the sill. Her hands shaking, she listened closely; up on the storm-tossed rooftop, the caterwauling grew worse—the tempo reverberating more quickly, the pattern expanding into this rhythm and that. *Sounds like a whole pounce of dying Abyssinian cats.* She should have done something to help, but now she hesitated: an impulse deep inside her mind willed her to imagine the ghost girl standing to the side of the window's casing.

'*Privet,*' Svetlana's soft, throaty illusory voice seemed to say.

'Go away,' Anastasia whispered beneath her breath, quietly enough that Ernesztina could not hear. 'You're nothing but vile fantasy, a dreamlike being. So, go away.'

'Do you remember that night the fox crept onto the train?' the ghost girl said. 'When you opened the cabin door, you left the natural world behind, yes, because I had come to call you to *adventure*. So, what did you do? For no good reason, you thought better of your decision to open the cabin door. And you refused to comply. And that's just what any would-be heroine does. No, it never fails.'

Anastasia fingered her collar. 'Be gone,' she whispered.

A sudden wild gust of wind stirred the sash weights so that they thumped against the casing.

Ernesztina drew close to Anastasia and tapped her wrist. 'I think you should sail away from this place. Travel off to London.'

'Why London?' Anastasia asked.

'*Why?* Some of my contacts and associates in the mirror-making society have told me that certain London colleges of medicine employ pioneering physicians who might be able to restore your sight.'

Anastasia became lost in thought, and she imagined some forward-thinking English physician checking her eyes with some kind of prism. And now she imagined herself gradually reacquiring the power to discern the spectrum, the whole colour continuum. *Oh, what joy that'd be. Pure joy. I'd be healed.*

The sash weights fell silent, but up on the roof, the cats cried out even more.

She tapped the windowpane and sought to picture the village. *On a rainy day like this, the streets should be desolate. Down in the marketplace, all the shops should be closed for business.* And what if some solitary window happened to be shining a soft light down onto the colonnade? *It'd be the huntsman's house, and behind the curtain lace, his daughter, maybe she'd be painting an array of wooden, Egyptian-goose decoys . . . the kind clever enough to deceive a ruthless fox.*

Up on the roof, the caterwauling died down. Had the better part of the pounce darted off somewhere? Soon, by the sound of it, only one solitary cat remained. Endlessly, the poor thing shrieked—not unlike a little baby girl, the cat's voice all so human-sounding.

As a motherly impulse took hold, Anastasia wondered if she might bring the creature in from the rain. '*Oui, fais le*,' she thought out loud. Feeling her way with outstretched arms, she staggered past her wardrobe trunk and groped for her housecoat. *There.* One last time, she sneezed—and then, still holding her hands out, she made her way across the bedchamber.

'Where are you going?' Ernesztina asked, her tone a little bit apprehensive. 'You shouldn't be out and about. Not in your condition.'

'I'll be right back,' Anastasia told her.

'Just what do you think you're doing?'

'Finding my way,' Anastasia answered. With that, she made her way down the cool, drafty corridor. At the end of the hallway, she climbed the stairway to the rooftop and pushed open the coarse heavy rooftop door. 'Here, kitty,' she repeated several times over.

The cat grew quiet. Moreover, the rain fell harder all the time—and the whole of the hostelry seemed to rock this way and that.

Anastasia looked up. She imagined herself standing upon the deck of a doomed plague ship, the vessel adrift upon some merciless sea.

Again, the building seemed to move back and forth. One moment, the hostelry pushed to port—and then the whole of the structure seemed to pull off to starboard.

Ernesztina followed along and grabbed Anastasia's arm. 'Come back inside,' the woman implored her. 'We've so much to discuss, young lady. We've got to decide just what to do about your eyes.'

Jerking her body forward, Anastasia broke free. 'Quiet, please.' She strained to hear any sign of the stubborn animal.

The cat remained perfectly silent—as eerily silent as Jack had always been whenever he might stare at her with that pinched expression of his.

Deep inside her womb, the dream fox twitched his tail. 'Are you enjoying your rounds up here on the roof?'

'Silence,' she whispered, lowering her blind eyes. The rain streaking down her brow and shoulders and back, she placed her hands over her belly and drummed in time with the ongoing downpour. 'I remember when you spoke affectionately with me. You'd tell me what to do. Yes, and you'd tell me why I said what I said or whatever. You always wanted to entice me, but now you no longer try. You've changed, and so your voice has changed. Does that make sense?'

'Are you cross with me? Listen, please. I haven't changed at all, and I'm sorry I had to gouge out your eyes. Ah, but you would not listen to a single word I said. That's why I had no choice but to do what I did. Just like Apollo, forced to discipline that cold, unfeeling nymph, whatever her name was. If you reject a magical being's love, then you must pay.'

'Do you know what I'll do? Here and now, I'll pray to God Almighty and ask that He come down out of the clouds and slaughter you.'

'Oh? And just why should God Almighty concern Himself with something as wholly inconsequential as me?' For a time, the fox breathed in and out. 'I think I know. Perhaps you've convinced yourself that the King of Glory must serve your desires and answer your prayers, only because He's got some grand purpose for you. Yes, that's the answer. You believe that someday He'll ready you for some noble charge that He'd have you fulfill. Yes, that's the foolish kind of thing you believe in.'

She pinched her belly. 'Hush up, you.'

Several times over, the fox bit at the lining of her womb.

She flinched and pulled back. Once more, she willed her body to expel the entity—and once more, the futility of it all served to recall the miscarriage. *Will I ever forgive myself?*

Her lips trembled. She stumbled and fell, bumping her head against a marble krater standing over to the side. *Have I drawn blood?* Given the endless rain, she could not tell for certain. *Am I going delirious?* Her thoughts ran wild. She imagined the hostelry as a seaborne vessel. *I've boarded a steamship bound for Saint Petersburg. Maybe I won't even survive the perilous voyage, for who could say whether a German submersible might suddenly appear off the starboard bow?* Her shoulders tightened. *Even now, there must be countless treacherous U-boats haunting the steamship lines. Those U-boats, they're everywhere.*

Ernesztina checked Anastasia's wounds and sat her beside the hostelry rooftop's knee-high parapet wall. Anastasia rested her aching brow up against the cool rain-soaked stone. *Oh, that feels good.* She smiled and recited a simple Huguenot prayer.

Ernesztina sank down next to her and sighed. 'I'm sorry we ever agreed to terms. You weren't the type who ought to work as a mirror-maker. You're such a *spiritual* girl, the beautiful kind. The type who tends to be too wise for the sensual world and much too clever for marriage.'

The wind blew harder, and with a snort and a wheeze and an air-rending cackle, the rain-soaked cat recommenced its mournful shrieks.

Anastasia thought back to her childhood—all those books about the Russian shipping lines and how they always encouraged the sailors to bring cats aboard. 'Why do the Russians bring cats onto their ships?' she asked, feeling in vain for Ernesztina's hand. When no answer came, Anastasia continued to scrabble about, seeking her friend's fingers.

With an audible sigh, Ernesztina leaned forward and took Anastasia's hand. 'Maybe the sailors hope to preserve the galley from vermin.'

Anastasia shifted on the wet marble tiles and frowned.

'No, there has to be some mystical reason.' Once more, she imagined herself aboard a seaborne ship. *Yes, and she's a dazzle ship. A powerful dreadnought. Oh, but there's a German vessel drawing near. At any moment, the German officer will call out to me. What a clever adversary he'll prove himself to be, too, an expert in the art of war. He'll know everything pertaining to the science of psychological warfare. If I hold forth with propaganda and misinformation, he'll disbelieve every word.*

Ernesztina tapped Anastasia's arm. 'Let's go back inside and get warm and dry, why don't we? Are you not hungry? If you're not in the mood for chicken stew, I could make you a bowl of Egyptian spinach soup.'

'Have you any idea what it feels like to go blind?' Anastasia asked. 'Even now, as we speak, how do I know I'm not simply dreaming? What if we've already weighed anchor, and we've already set sail for some glorious port?' Anastasia glided a fingertip across the contours of the parapet. 'Who's to say the Imperial German Navy won't come along to sink the ship?'

Ernesztina laughed in a loving way. 'The loss of your sight has brought you to heel and vexed you in ways I never anticipated. You're prone to hallucinations. What a pity. Don't lose hope, though. When we get you to London with its modern hospitals and the like, the physicians will examine your eyes, and who knows what they'll find?'

Deep inside Anastasia's belly, the Arctic fox darted about. 'You must not let Ernesztina take you anywhere. No, I'll not stand for it. You belong to me, and that's why I prefer that you remain blind. Without your eyesight, I'll have a much simpler time controlling you. That's the essential point.'

Ernesztina clutched Anastasia's forearm. 'What're you thinking?' she asked, her tone of voice vaguely servile. 'I've got it. You regret coming here.'

Anastasia's thoughts drifted back to the fantastical notion that she must be sailing on the high seas. 'Let the Germans fire their torpedoes,' she thought out loud.

Ernesztina responded with a weary laugh. 'Come to your senses. We're not sailing aboard some ship.'

'Once the enemy opens fire, they'll have the blood of our dear, innocent lives on their hands,' Anastasia continued. 'And nothing should save the wicked kaiser from having to make costly reparations. No, not even the art of diplomacy.'

Again, Ernesztina laughed—and this time it floated in the air like a prayer chant. 'No more trifling,' she said afterward. 'Blindness doesn't oblige you to indulge yourself in fantasy.'

Anastasia struggled to her feet and, clenching her fists, fumbled her way onto the slippery parapet wall. 'Have no fear. I'll find some way to appeal to the German captain's humanity. I'll quote a fine German poem. What about a selection from Goethe's "Faust"? What about the verse in which the harridan breathes upon Faust's eyes and renders him blind?'

Ernesztina grabbed hold of Anastasia's right ankle. 'Enough with all these childish games. Let's go back inside. We'll go down to the lobby, and I'll sit you by the fire, and then I'll go back to the kitchen and make you supper.'

'Yes, of course.' Anastasia glanced downward and endeavoured to picture the desolate courtyard below.

And in that very moment, the Egyptian schoolteacher who lived in the adjacent house cried out: 'You there! Move you back please! No you fall!'

She refused to comply. Instead, she willed herself to teeter forward.

Down below, the Egyptian schoolteacher clapped his hands. 'You there, why you act with such impropriety? Please to go back. Maybe you slip on a puddle, or maybe you slip on some of the cat droppings. Take you care, please.' Once more, he clapped his hands—and then he whistled loudly, as if with his fingers.

As Anastasia lurched forward, Ernesztina grabbed her around the waist and pulled her back from the parapet.

Down below, the schoolteacher recited an Arabic-language blessing.

⌐

Late that Same Night.

Anastasia's thoughts drifted back to the mirror works. *Now that I've gone blind, I'll never complete the work in progress.* Given that sombre fact, she realised she had no hope of driving the dream fox into the reflective tin-bronze surface. *What a terrific waste of time my sojourn here in Sinai was. Though I've studied with the celebrated Ernesztina Henreid herself, it's all been in vain.*

When she heard the rain dash against the window, Anastasia put her hand on the cold brittle pane of glass and remembered the way she had once studied her sombre reflection in the tin bronze. Now she imagined a magical old-fashioned looking glass hovering at her side—so she tapped the imaginary frame and stared sightlessly into the surface. *Will I ever be cured of this blindness?*

Summoning her shadow vision while feeling the current against her body, she ventured out onto the rooftop yet again.

Deep inside Anatasia's womb, the dream fox kicked. 'You'll never go free of me. No, I'll haunt you till your dying day.'

Anastasia clenched her fist and thought about the futility

of all her endeavours. Then, as the nighttime rain battered the rooftop, she grasped the Huguenot cross and very nearly tore it from her neck before a memory of her mother stopped her. From deep inside Anastasia's darkest unconscious recesses, she recalled how childlike, how girlish, how innocent Mother had seemed in the weeks leading up to her death. By contrast, Mother had seemed so strong and so womanly when they had made that trek to the White Sea. *Long after crossing that place where the Arctic fox always compelled the train to stop, we arrived in Arkhangelsk. And then we found our way to the waterfront. There, we collected the volcanic glass. In that moment, I should've grown strong and wise . . . until no Arctic fox could ever stand in my way. Oh, and the return trip should've occasioned some glorious act of redemption. Victory, rebirth. Yes, healing.*

Several times over, the dream fox kicked. 'Stop thinking about the past. What happened had to happen.'

Inundated by the wild scents of the desert, Anastasia let go of the Huguenot cross and felt her way back inside. Downstairs, she slipped out of her wet things and dried herself in the lobby washroom. A raindrop dripped down her temple, and she wiped it away. Taking hold of her right ear, she squeezed. *One of these days, I ought to get a triple piercing.* She placed the tip of her first finger and thumb on either side of the lobe and pulled as hard as she could.

The desert fox hissed. 'How beautifully Svetlana's three earrings always shone in the soft glow of the midnight sun. And they gleamed that way, too, in that moment I crept onto the train and strode through the caboose door and called on *you.*'

Anastasia felt her way out from the washroom and warmed herself by the fire. Then she stumbled and groped and made her way upstairs to her room. Once she had slipped into a clean bedgown, she found her way back to the windowsill.

Up on the roof, a solitary cat shrieked in its childlike way. The shrill rasp resembled a lemming's squeak.

For a time, she thought back to her childhood pet. *How long has it been since I even thought about my Ludmila?*

From somewhere outside in the marketplace, a soft explosion as of shattering glass resounded—most likely a gang of youthful scoundrels vandalising someone's front-door lantern.

Whatever it was, she revisited that moment Mother's volcanic-glass mirror broke apart against the floor. *Wasn't I to blame?* Anastasia sighed; she never should have guided the Arctic fox down below that hallway table, and in that moment she had resolved to depart, she should have thought to take the table mirror into her trembling hand and to safeguard the piece. *Why didn't I think to do that? I must've been a foolish little thing. Or maybe a big part of me was wicked, and I wanted the fox to topple it.* Now she gripped the edge of the windowsill and stood unmoving. *Yes, it's true. Some evil impulse must surely exist deep inside my psyche.* Would that not explain why she had chosen to sojourn here? In addition to her longing to send the dream fox off into one of the mysterious tin-bronze mirrors, she had hoped to banish, too, that ignoble imperfection that had always afflicted her own character. *Yes, I've always been a terrible person.* Crumpling against the window frame, she gripped her hands together.

Down below, the hostelry keeper called out her name—but lost in her gentle blindness, she decided against responding.

He came to her. Quietly, he stood in the doorway. He must have been looking into her blind eyes. 'I hear what happened, so I come back,' he finally spoke up. 'I am sorry.' With that, he changed the subject to the British Empire. 'We no wish no bad on you. We good people. We the Egyptians only wish to be free. *Aiwa*. Nothing more.' The hostelry keeper laughed nervously.

At once, she recalled her schooldays in Saint Petersburg—all those unguarded moments when she herself might laugh only because some other little girl would be doing so. *How should laughter be contagious that way?* Now she laughed—the confident way that a scholarly woman might do. Scratching at her scalp, she asked herself why anyone laughs and giggles. *Could it be the stuff of fear? Or what about some other irrepressible instinct?*

In the end, she grew quiet. Ashamed of herself for having laughed for no reason, she revisited memories of the peculiar youth always staring at her in the marketplace. *Jack.* The mere thought of him amused her. *What's he doing just now? Maybe he's sitting all alone at his supper table. Then what? When he shifts in his chair, the chair's leg will make a sound as of a person passing gas. And because of the mortifying din, he'll have to cough and to make even more little noises. As if to do so ought to make it clear that he had not committed any repulsive indiscretion the moment before. And then he'll pass gas for real. And he'll probably just sit there, the sick fool breathing in the foul odour.* She shook her head.

The rainfall continued—and the hostelry keeper breathed noisily, as if the downpour affrighted him. Downstairs, the lobby door opened anew—and perhaps thankful for a pretence to depart, the hostelry keeper did just that.

The wind grew stronger, and up on the rooftop, the solitary cat's shrieks grew increasingly plaintive.

In tears, she pictured the poor thing—a rain-drenched runt, a creature wholly unfavoured by natural selection, an animal unworthy of *life*.

Downstairs, the hostelry keeper spoke with the visitor. Before long, she heard footsteps on the stairs.

'Who's there?' she asked, creasing her brow.

'Ernesztina.' Following a long pause, the woman entered the room and drew close. 'If you choose to sail away for London, you must take care once you arrive. God only knows what could happen to you in a city like that. On a night like this, you'll be at some reception, and then some gentleman takes you into another room and slips a drug into your cognac, and then just like that, he's climbed on top of you.'

Anastasia recalled some of the crime stories that she had read in the papers over the years. Often, the obtuse, unsuspecting female had wandered off alone—and in modest dress, no less. Later, once she had gone missing, the papers had often blamed the victim herself—as if she should have known how many deviants plague society, as if she should have known, too, how often such villains hide in plain sight.

'I'm puzzled,' Anastasia said.

'Why?' Ernesztina asked.

'The stakes, they've grown so high. What do I do? Even if I journey on from this place and even if I survive a big city like London, I wonder where I belong.' Anastasia felt for her steamer trunk and sat down atop it. She remembered some of the tales Mother had told her regarding their family history—a matriarch who sailed for England, where the refugee lived out her life as a weaver.

According to family legend, the woman had grown delusional and had come to imagine herself one of the Fates. *Or was it one of the Norns?* Whatever it was, the demented Huguenot woman believed the tapestries she made on her loom determined the destiny of the universe itself.

Anastasia kicked her heel against the steamer trunk.

'What might be my destiny, my future, my purpose?'

Ernesztina approached quietly and ran her knuckles gently down Anastasia's cheek. 'Go to London. I'm sure you'll learn the answers to all your questions there. London, that's the place that always offered the warmest refuge to woebegone Huguenots.'

From all around, the rainfall rattled against the rooftops. As for the cat, it continued with all its caterwauling. The cacophony sounded alien and primal—the call of a diseased fox, its hind legs paralysed, the cold, hungry, feeble creature pulling itself along with its claws.

Somebody, anybody, save the poor thing. Please, please, please. Anastasia bit her lower lip and shivered. *There's no one but me. One last time, I've got to venture outside. Save the cat, go on.* She arose from the steamer trunk and froze.

Though it might have been little more than her imagination running wild, a sound as of a tapestry rattled and hummed over on the other side of the hotel room.

She listened for a moment, swaying this way and that. *It could be one of the Fates spinning the thread.* She listened for footsteps and felt certain that she heard them. *It could be yet another one of the Fates, the one who measures the length.* Standing still and holding her breath so hard her kidneys throbbed, she cocked her ear and awaited a shrill metallic sound as of shears slicing through something. When she thought she heard it, she gasped, knelt beside the steamer trunk, and exhaled. *That must've been the last of the Fates, the one who cuts the thread.*

XIV.

Cairo. 18 April 1918.

Early that morning, Jack awoke in the fever hospital where the constabulary had housed him a few days before. 'Anastasia!' he called out, his head snapping back. How he longed to come back to her. *If I can't exit this world, then I've got to reunite with my beloved. Posthaste.*

He had little hope of leaving Cairo. Convinced he must be disturbed and unstable, the authorities had forbidden him from checking out.

At eight o'clock, he wandered out into the hospital grounds. Though a fierce, howling sandstorm had left the city under a terrific pall, he still preferred to fritter away most of his time outside. The endless gusts blowing through his hair, he studied the walls and looked for a section here or there that he could scale.

The barrier stood at a right angle and offered no holds.

When he finally turned from the wall, he raised his hands to shield his eyes and marched deep into the storm-ravaged hospital garden. As the yellow wind tore through the boughs of an ailing strangler fig, he collapsed. For the very first time, he noticed the limestone boulder around which the tree had spread its roots; some ancient artisan had hewn the visage of an Egyptian ram god into the rock. *If only the visage could speak. Would he tell me my fate?*

The sandstorm continued to rage, and the Egyptian ram god looked upon Jack with an expression devoid of emotion. 'Let this be a lesson to you, my friend,' the god spoke up then, its voice a miraculous telepathic message. 'Without torment and intellectual dissatisfaction, there should be no way to create great, inspired art. Do you hear me? If you were to forget the spiritual violence that the sadistic children visited upon you back in your schooldays, you would have but nothing to inspirit your music.'

The interlude left a ringing in Jack's ears, and he staggered this way and that as he wondered whether he had imagined the voice.

The figure of a tall portly gentleman wearing dust goggles emerged from the swirling sands, and he waved—his fingers moving up and down inappropriately.

'Who the hell are you, then?'

'Dundreary's the name,' the gentleman said. 'I work as liaison to the consul general, the chaps who detained you here.'

'Bugger off,' Jack told him.

'Listen up, friend. The party's over. We've learned your identity, haven't we? In point of fact, you'd be none other than Jack Wylye. From Bloomsbury, London. Am I right?'

As the winds let out a deafening howl, Jack turned to the sundial standing on the other side of the garden. *They've learned me name.* Suddenly, the workings and machinations of the world seemed all wrong—as if the progress of time itself were passing by much too quickly. For a moment or two, he studied the yellow wind blowing through the hospital grounds: the thick, dark sandstorm whipped and bolted a touch too swiftly. *How could that be?* His shoulders slumped, and he studied Dundreary's weak chin.

The gentleman smirked. 'Actually, we've known your identity since mid-April. But we failed to act on it, didn't we? Blame it on a clerical error. A mislabelled file. Now, then, please come along with me, and let's get out of this dust storm.' With that, Dundreary grabbed Jack's arm, dragged him up into the gazebo, and sat him in one of the straw-plaited chairs. 'I suppose you'd have me explain just how we puzzled out your name, yes?' Dundreary removed his dust goggles and sat in the other chair. 'It's quite simple,' he continued, kicking his feet up onto the table. 'A fine woman came by, the renowned mirror-maker, Ernesztina Henreid. She's told us the whole sad story, and now everything's a good wicket. So, tonight, you sail for Liverpool. Your doting parents have agreed to collect you there. I do believe they mean to send you to a nursing home.'

Jack stood and smote the nearest gazebo post. 'Do you honestly think I'll let you take me off to Liverpuddle? Hell, no. I'll do a bunk.'

One of the hospital attendants, a young Cairene holding a comb and a pair of shears, emerged from the cloud of dust.

As the attendant continued into the gazebo, Dundreary snapped his fingers at Jack and then pointed to the chair. 'Why don't you sit back down and let this good fellow here do away with that tousled bob of yours? We can't let you sail home to England looking like someone from the House of David.'

'Listen here, you bloated aristocrat. No matter what you

say, I'm not going home.' Jack shook his fist like a foolish little boy having a tantrum.

The attendant drew closer, and no matter how pitiful he must have appeared, Jack weaved this way and that—just like he had seen the bare-fisted pugilists do.

Dundreary laughed maliciously. 'There's no reason for fisticuffs,' he said, dropping his feet to the floor. 'Blue blazes, what do I care if you wish to go home to England looking like a homely Hebrew princess?'

The attendant walked off, and as he did, a fierce squall rattled the gazebo's spindle walls so badly that a whole segment of the wooden screening tore off and vanished in an instant.

Just as he had before, Jack sensed time itself ticking away too quickly. *This can't be happening.* He rubbed the heel of his palm against his chest. *If I depart Egypt, I'll lose Anastasia forever.*

After a while, the attendant made his way back through the sandstorm. He placed a dish of chickpeas and a basket of flatbread on the table.

'Go on, then,' Dundreary told Jack. 'Have yourself one last savoury breakfast, why don't you? Once you're seaborne, you'll be none too pleased. It'll be nothing but yesterday's admiralty ham for the likes of *you.*'

The hot, yellowy sands swirling all about the gazebo yet, Jack listened to the all-powerful winds—which made the ringing in his ears grow louder and more dissonant. More than that, the moan and groan of the winds served to recall the mournful sound of the glass harp, all of which made him think of Anastasia.

A storm of feathers came flying, swirling and darting through the gazebo—each filthy yellowy plume twisting and bending at an absurdly rapid rate.

Yet again now, he discerned the movement of time itself proceeding along much too quickly.

The yellow wind droned on and on, meanwhile. And soon, the howl sounded something like a booming monotone voice struggling to pronounce some magical word—a deity's taboo ineffable name.

All the time shielding his eyes, Jack descended the gazebo steps and made his way back to the strangler fig.

Already, the high winds had nearly torn the roots away from the boulder. And now the sandstorm's booming monotone voice seemed to utter a word:

'*Banebdjedet! Banebdjedet!*'

Immediately, Jack dropped to his knees. He looked into the ram god's eyes, wondering if the invocation might be the captive deity's immemorial title.

The sandstorm's voice grew deeper, louder—like that of a cyclone:

'*Banebdjedet! Banebdjedet!*'

At last, Jack cackled. When his loud peal of laughter grew hollow, he pointed at the visage. 'Go free, you bloody bastard.'

With a sharp crack that pierced the yowl made by the winds themselves, the strangler fig snapped and fell over.

Look there. Bleeding hell. Jack grabbed hold of the ram god's horns, each one visible for the first time in what must have been two thousand years. 'You're finally free, you bloody lucky bastard. Free!'

Midmorning or thereabouts, once Dundreary had completed all the paperwork, he pushed Jack into the back of the consul general motorcar. Then a muscle-bound soldier climbed in, sat beside him, and tapped twice upon the stock of his rifle.

When the motorcar turned into the windswept street,

Jack looked out the window. No matter the torrent of dust and soot blowing all about the city, he could still discern a few villas with their exotic, double-arched windows.

The burly soldier tapped upon the rifle's action bar, and he whistled the tune to a parlour song.

Jack recognised it as 'Take Me Back to Dear Old Blighty', and he wondered if the soldier hoped to provoke him.

As the driver stopped to let a procession of modestly dressed Egyptian women go by, the soldier discontinued his song and nudged Jack's left shoulder. 'You know something? I've been here in Cairo four whole months, and I still haven't had me a chance to shoot no one. Not even some wily Oriental gentleman.'

The motorcar slipped into gear and continued along for a few blocks before stopping a second time—this time alongside a vast Fatimid palace.

Open the door and run. Jack reached for the door handle, but no sooner had he done so than a fleecy ram emerged from the storm. *A ram here in the city?*

Bleating loudly, the beast rubbed its snout against the window. Then the creature shifted some so that its right horn scraped the glass.

The motorcar slipped back into gear, and once the driver had made it through a busy roundabout, the driver put on speed.

Beneath his breath, Jack cursed all his excitability. *I know I only ever imagined the bloody ram.* He thought he knew why, too; the lingering hallucinogenic effects must have followed from the way the caffeine in the Turkish coffee had commingled with the mandrake root in the soporific. Again and again, he wiggled his toes. Breaking out in a warm sweat, he stared down at his hands. *I should've bloody well bolted when I had the chance.*

The soldier elbowed him. Then the soldier whistled a few more measures of the parlour song. Afterward, he tapped his rifle's stock as he had before.

Meanwhile, the consul general motorcar turned the corner and stopped before the railway station.

Bloody hell. We're already here.

The next few hours passed by quickly—as if the train journey from Cairo took no more than two minutes. As he sat by the window, he pictured himself as an old man who had only just come to call on the elderly Anastasia. *Will she even remember me? What if she thinks to ring the authorities? At the very least, she'll ignore me. Or else her husband will show me to the door and tell me to go and never come back.*

Late that afternoon, when the train reached Alexandria, a second guard detail collected him at the crowded concourse and then guided him onward through the Old Town.

Not far from a signpost pointing the way to the famed Caesareum, Jack stopped and clasped his hands together. 'Why keep a beady eye on me, then?' he asked no one in particular, his tone effeminate and servile. 'Let me go, eh?'

The lieutenant knelt to loosen the wool puttee wrapped around his lower left leg, and then he looked up. 'If I let you take your leave, then it's my arse on the peg.'

'The blighter don't deserve to go free anywise,' the colour sergeant added. 'What's the lad been doing for the past year? He's been wandering about the whole blooming empire, that's what. No salt to a herring.'

'Yeah, that's what I heard as well,' the lance corporal spoke up then. 'The lad's been fiddling about on permanent holiday while everyone else fights for dear life up there in the trenches.'

Jack searched the soldiers' narrowed eyes and then looked at his trouser cuffs. *I'm a turncoat. Something a thousand times worse than the wicked Hun.* The ringing in his ears droned on and on, as if for no other reason than to add to his sense of shame and torment.

As the party continued in the direction of the sea, the demoralizing odour of rotting flounder came wafting through the storm. Seconds later, they reached the waterfront.

As pieces of used dunnage tumbled about in the yellow wind, Jack paused to consider the invincible-looking steamship berthed at the pier. She had a lofty foremast, four colossal, basalt-black smokestacks, and a most curious name emblazoned across her bow: RMS *Arianrhod.*

A crewman emerged from the wheelhouse and descended the gangway. He introduced himself as the boatswain. Following a terse, unfriendly interview, he escorted Jack up onto the ship's deck. 'Don't try my damn patience,' the boatswain told him then. 'I'm the deck boss on this tub, and I'll not stand for any attempt at slipping the collar.'

Jack pouted like a child, and he did not say anything. Still, he did manage to acquiesce with a slight nod.

The boatswain turned away and gestured to a big fat oaf presently tormenting a few Mediterranean gulls with his bean shooter. 'Hey, you there.'

'Aye,' the shipmate answered, slipping the weapon into his hip pocket.

'Mind this lad here,' the boatswain told him. 'Take care the ponce don't broom it back down into the harbor. For that matter, don't let him nick nothing from the helmsman's quarters neither.' As the boatswain ambled off, a few more beautiful Mediterranean gulls with fine, white flight feathers fluttered by.

Without hesitation, the surly fellow reached for his bean shooter and fired at one of the innocent creatures.

Jack curled up in a wobbly deckchair and closed his eyes. *Patience. I'll be free soon enough.*

~

That Same Day, Just at Dusk.

Jack opened his eyes, only to meet the big oaf's glare. *Mercy me. Caught in a trap.* Jack averted his gaze. With a lump in his throat, he looked at the quay.

Down below, a storm of sullied, white feathers blew this way and that in the endless yellow wind. As the feathers tumbled off, a convoy of fast-moving, drop-side lorries pulled up alongside the steamship.

With a furrowed brow, he studied the vehicles. *If I could make it down the gangway and conceal meself inside one of them lorry beds, I could escape. So, how do I get meself down to the jetty?*

Two dozen or so deckhands approached the convoy and proceeded to unload the freight, which proved to be an army of granite statues—each one a winged lion.

The raped antiquities should have sickened him. Instead, he sensed only that same uncanny sensation of time itself marching forward much too quickly: the strange phenomenon manifested itself in the wispy way his body felt—as if at any moment all gravity would cease and permit him to float into the clouds.

The big oaf sat down in the deckchair to the right. 'I know what you're thinking,' he announced, picking his nose. 'You mean to send me off on a fool's errand, and when I'm

238

gone, you'll roll down to the pier. Ain't that right, lass?'

'Sure, sure. Right. Whatever you say, governor.'

'Yeah, I've got it. You think you'll beg a cup of black tea, and you'll promise to wait here whilst I scrounge up the brew. Well, you ain't getting no tea.'

'Yes, sir.' Jack pinched his bottom lip and rubbed his ears, as if that might help to make the ringing stop.

The big fat oaf removed his finger from his nose, and then he pointed at the nearest smokestack. 'Don't tell me you've to slake your thirst none. You never got parched till you've gone down below and worked the firebox there, and don't I know it? I'm the coal-tender on this here tub. I'm the stoker.'

Jack turned back to the quay. Swiftly, the tower crane's winch boom descended toward a singularly immense piece enshrouded in wrinkled white muslin. No matter how badly the yellow wind made his ears ring, he focused on the carefully wrapped piece. *What's that there? Just what could it be?* He thought back to his schooldays, a social sciences lecture in which the instructor had alluded to the Egyptian god of fate. *How good it'd be if this piece here were the god of fate, the deity what determines the span of life. Bloody perfect.*

Soon enough, one of the deckhands wound a rope around the figure—and then he proceeded to coil the very end of the cord around the jib's steely hook, at which point the tower crane hoisted the plunder into the air.

He remembered some of the lecture; the instructor had described the way the venerable god of fate stands beside the great scales and weighs the lifeless pharaoh's heart against the most sacred object in all the heavens—the Feather of Truth.

As soon as the figure came to dangle over the cargo hold, Jack hurried over. If he timed things well enough, perhaps he could lift the muslin and have a look. The simple sensation of shame should have kept Jack from reaching for the muslin; nevertheless, he grabbed hold of a fold in the cloth.

'Get your hands off the goods,' the stoker cried out. 'All that booty belongs to the right honourable Earl of Derby as of now. You do harm to anything, and I'll slice off all four of them raw-boned limbs of yours.'

Jack let go, and the enshrouded figure descended through the hatch and onward into the bowels of the steamship.

The yellow wind bellowed, the gust nearly pushing him into the darkness below. As two different awnings sailed off from the direction of the marketplace, he dragged himself back to the wobbly deckchair. Careful not to make eye contact, he pointed at the stoker. 'How could it be right that we plunder such treasures? Do they not belong to the Egyptian people?'

Without the least bit of shame, the stoker broke wind. 'Why don't you close your eyes and feign another nap? If I think you've nodded off, maybe then I'll leave my post. That's right, and then you'll piss off back into the wilds of the Orient.'

Yet again, Jack readily discerned time passing along much too quickly; as the awnings sailed through the waterfront, his body felt immaterial, abandoned by gravity. When he failed to float off, his thoughts wandered back to the matter at hand. Soon, he would be in Liverpool, of all places. *And what's to become of Anastasia?* Back in the village, perhaps she had already found someone else to court her. *Maybe they've already had it off.*

Sometime later, as twilight turned to darkness, the howl of the ongoing sandstorm blended with the roar of the empty lorries driving back into the city. Then, when the last of the convoy had vanished, a noise as of a creature blinded by rage resounded from deep within the cargo hold.

What a row. That might as well be the god of fate. His ears ringing yet, Jack plodded along back to the hatch and looked down. There, amid the winged lions, stood the one immense enshrouded piece, a ship's lantern illuminating the wrinkled muslin so that it shone like gold leaf.

At eight o'clock, the harsh, dissonant bells of a Greek Orthodox church pealed and resounded across the waterfront.

The hymn ringing in his ears, Jack looked about for the stoker. *Has the bloody bastard gone below?* With an uneven stride, Jack crept over to the gangway. Rocking slightly, he studied a few of the broach spires dotting the skyline. *There's got to be so many places to hide over there in the Greek Quarter.* He hopped up and down—like a giddy little girl. *Go! Move!* At last, he raced over to the gangway.

Down below, a fleecy ram suddenly blocked his path. The dreamlike creature bleated noisily—its fierce call a piercing otherworldly lamentation.

He stood still. Did he merely imagine the ram's presence? He struggled to convince himself that the creature must be nothing more than a hallucination. *That's right.* He looked to the storm-tossed pier and fixed his gaze upon a heap of green-glass fishing buoys. *There's no bloody ram down there.*

When he finally turned back, the apparition had vanished. *Cheers. Off we go.* He took two steps down the gangway, but then he stopped; two fine womanly figures had just emerged from a cloud of dust and soot rolling eastward across the waterfront.

As they drew closer, one proved to be Ernesztina and the other Anastasia. Each one looked so true to life, too. How could *they* be hallucinations?

His knees trembling, he inched his way backward a few steps and concealed himself behind the mast house. *Anastasia means to board this vessel?* Over and over, he sought to swallow, but could not do so. *Anastasia!*

A moment or two later, Ernesztina guided her onto the ship's deck—at which point they strolled off in the direction of the galley, each one looking perfectly oblivious.

He came out from behind the mast house, looked this way and that, and then staggered back to the gangway. The ram was gone, but what did it matter? Suddenly, he realised that there was no reason to flee. *For crying out loud, Anastasia's come aboard. She's here.*

At ten minutes past ten o'clock, the ship's horn emitted two long blasts to signal her leaving her berth. And then RMS *Arianrhod* calmly put herself to sea.

Over on Pharaoh's Island, a midshipman appeared in the lighthouse door. 'Send her victorious!' he shouted.

RMS *Arianrhod* steamed farther and farther from the ancient, exotic pier—until the lights of Alexandria faded into a haze of midnight blue.

Jack climbed the stair to the promenade deck, where he lay down outside the smoking room and bundled himself up in a heap of hessian cloth.

A short, stocky crewman came along and kicked him in the thigh. 'Have you noticed any ironclads about? They'll be darning the waters, so just you preserve the watch.'

'Bugger off.'

'What's that? Let me tell you something. I've had more sea miles than you've had pusser's peas, and that's why you'd be right clever to listen to what I got to say.'

Jack sighed and shook his head. The unpleasant exchange reminded him that the war dragged on, and that there was no guarantee he would even make it back to England. *But I want to live. I don't want to die just yet.*

The captain's mate came along and ordered the crewman to help him with something, and the little fellow hurried off.

Two minutes later, the boatswain stopped by and nudged Jack's foot. 'Why don't you go down to the galley, or might you be supping with Duke Humphrey tonight?'

'Don't pother. When we pass by the kaiser's sugar boat, I'll ask the boy steward to throw me some bloody *kreppel.*' Jack scrambled to his feet, gathered up the hessian cloth and marched off toward one of the lifeboats. Alone then, he lay back down and listened to the sea breeze.

As softly as a reed flute, the current whistled through the ship's railing—the fine music a solemn incantation.

With her familiar, catlike stride, Ernesztina emerged from the wireless room. As she drew near, her sable hair shone a soft, silvery gold in the glow of an oil lamp dangling from above.

He stood and approached the balustrade. 'How could you betray me? Thanks to your meddling, I'm going home. And when we berth up there along the Mersey Wharf, have you no idea how repulsive it should be? Me stepmother should be ogling me like Potiphar's wife ogled *her* prey. And me old man, he'll be standing there in a stew.'

Ernesztina touched his hair. 'Why must you grow your locks so long? If you must grow such a wild shock of hair, maybe you ought to grow a beard, too. You'd look more manly.'

Jack rubbed the back of his neck. 'What's with Anastasia, then? Why did she come aboard? She's bound for Liverpool as well?'

'No. At Brittany, we'll transfer to a ship bound for the Port of London.'

'The Port of London? Take me with you. After a little while, as we're crossing the channel, you could introduce me to the girl. And then someday quite soon, maybe not much longer than a fortnight's time, I'll be ready to serenade her with me song. Wouldn't that be the perfect end?'

'*No*, you're not ready to go home just yet. First, you must learn to triumph over all your melancholy and all the strange illusions that your melancholy brings about. Until you do, you shan't be strong enough to take your place in London society.'

He turned to the waters, gripped the ship's railing and prayed that a German submersible might open fire. *The blessed torpedo will rip through the hull, and down by the firebox, that vile stoker will be the first to drown. Then the cold waters, they'll rush into the cargo hold, where the captive gods will cry out in a ghostly chorus . . . none of them quite so plaintively as the dismal god of fate.*

Ernesztina snapped her fingers in Jack's face. 'You resent my counsel, do you? Yes, and at any moment, I suppose you'll begin to fuss and bellyache like a little girl. That's because your bitterness has come to emasculate you. Like a eunuch. But that's just why you must take the time to improve yourself. Remember, only when you've truly conquered your youthful sorrows will a winsome girl divine a trace of something honourable in you.'

Jack looked into Ernesztina's eyes. 'Something honourable?'

'Yes. An air of aplomb. That's what serves to attract a desirable female. An air of aplomb means you ought to be a challenge. And a worthwhile one at that.'

He scowled. Then he shook the balustrade, hell-bent on ripping the whole of the ironwork from the weathered base rail.

Ernesztina placed her hand on his shoulder. 'Please, I didn't mean to defame or provoke you. *Enough.*'

Jack grew calm and bowed his head. Only when he felt his body going limp did he look up again. From out of the northern sky, a bright green sandpiper fluttered down to the side of his shoe. All the time waddling about with its teetering gait, the shorebird studied him. Then, as if spooked, the sandpiper took wing. Jack looked down the length of the ship's railing, and his heart fluttered. Anastasia stood no more than twenty feet away, her long fine golden hair dancing in the sea breeze as wildly as his own.

Like a dozen times before, he experienced that same peculiar sensation—the progress of time passing by much too quickly. *Yes, the laws of gravity have ceased.* He looked at the stars and trembled. *At any moment, I'll float off into outer space.*

Ernesztina tugged upon his sleeve. 'I think I hear something, some kind of appeal, some kind of heartfelt entreaty.'

Sure enough, from out across the waters, a magisterial song had commenced. Could it have been a pilot whale calling out in its timeless language?

No matter the beauty of it all, Anastasia seemed indifferent. If anything, she appeared to be half-lost in a hypnotic state. Had something vexed her eyes?

The whale song rattled him until he wondered if he had been the one lost in a hypnotic state—but now the mesmerist's keyword had only just awoken him. And now he doubled over, for the whale song had cleansed him; in an instant, he realised that all those times whenever he might walk past Anastasia back in Sinai, she had only ever shunned him. *As if me very presence had her feeling greatly repulsed. No, she never wanted me.*

The sea breeze kicked up, and as it whistled through the deckchairs, the whale song grew more and more erratic.

He looked at his feet, wondering if he and Anastasia had ever even enjoyed any kind of telepathic bond at all. The revelation should have shamed him, and it did. All those times he had stared at her, the maniacal misbehaviour must have unnerved her. To be certain, the oddity of it all must have incensed her. *What a miracle she never asked some burly bastard soldier to bash me good.* He kneaded the ship's railing, for how alarming it was to think that he had lost touch with reality the way he had. *It must've been a temporary case of insanity.*

As he let go of the ship's railing, the whale's erratic song concluded. Suddenly, no sound remained but the current— which whispered like a thousand little children.

His head tilting back, he tapped his foot and pictured himself as an old man slow in speech. *An old man what can't even comprehend time. An old man what loses his train of thought as he speaks and then invents words the moment he continues.*

All around, the waters grew quiet—as quiet as a lifeless pond.

A moment or two later, he recognised the sensation of time slowing down and returning to its proper pace. *What's happened, then?* For a moment or two, he scratched at his scalp. Had the revelation eased his stream of conscious just enough that his much-tormented faculties had restored themselves? *Maybe.* The ringing in his ears ceased.

Ernesztina looked deep into his eyes. 'Do know what's happened to Anastasia? Did you know she's gone blind?'

'*Blind?*' His mouth fell open, and he looked here and there with a wandering gaze.

Not a hundred feet away, out along the port bow, the pilot whale finally breached and then vanished back below the waves. A second time, then, the creature propelled the whole of its body out of the water.

How to turn away from such a magnificent creature? With a growing fervour in his heart, he gazed upon the animal. *What majesty. What dignity.*

XV.

London. 23 May 1918.

Anastasia awoke early that morning, and her jaw dropped. Though she had been living in England's capital for over a month, she could not remember where she was. *Am I in London already? Yes, I do believe so.* She rubbed her blind eyes. *Yes, and it was only yesterday the eye doctor promised to remedy my blindness.*

The morning breeze sailed into the room, the current alive with perilous, aggressive, manly scents and secretions—pheromones, chemicals with calming powers, odd chemical components with traces of what might have been some kind of stupefying effect.

She sat up and dug her fingernails into the linens and mattress.

Deep inside, the fox laughed. 'I think that murderous scoundrel has come for you. Yes, it's that English youth. Jack. He's giving off his odour because he's only just climbed in through the window.'

She shivered and breathed deeply. As she did, she detected

the stench of armpit sweat commingling with his cologne. What a cheap cologne, too, she thought: she could not discern any infusion of leather notes nor incomprehensible notes, only a mundane blend of mint flowers with notes of everyday lemon.

The noise of the capital rang out: distant voices calling, the roar of traffic, the blaring shriek of a bobby's whistle.

Despite the ongoing din, she listened for the sound of someone's breathing. The window open as it was, she failed to hear anything. Holding herself as still as possible, she listened for the sound of someone's heartbeat. *I hear nothing.* She shook her head and exhaled. Perhaps her unconscious mind had deceived her. In truth, it only hoped to tell her that she ought to fear the idea of predation and, as a consequence, ought to prepare. *I've got to will my other senses to grow strong enough to compensate for my blindness. More than that, I've got to will my spirit to develop much better intuition.*

The morning light shone into the room, and the warmth of the sun against her face made her think of the past. Her failure to say anything to Jack had made her feel guilty all throughout the voyage home. One morning, as she lay in her stateroom, she thought she heard a goddess, one of the Fates or perhaps one of the Norns, working her loom over to the side. The sensation of guilt intensified then—and much to her dismay, the tormenting shame had come to augment the ailment afflicting her eyes. By the time she had reached London, she had feared that one of the merciless deities had already severed her thread and had already thrown the fragment back into the Well of Fate.

Oh, the Well of Fate. She placed her hand over the warmth shining down upon her face, and she wondered if perhaps she might never be cured. *What if not one solitary oculist proves knowledgeable enough to help me? What then?*

Someone knocked upon the doorjamb, and she heard a set of soft, hesitant footsteps as someone entered the bedchamber.

'Are you awake? I think you ought to get out of the house today. You've got to learn to live in light of your blindness. Honest, it won't take much time at all before you know your way around London town.'

Anastasia recognised the voice as belonging to Fiona. *Yes, I'm lodging with Fiona.* On the third of May, a shrewd parson down at the London Huguenot Society on Chapel Street had located a Huguenot girl in need of a flatmate—and a church official had brought Anastasia to this address and had graciously helped her to move in.

Fiona shook Anastasia's foot. 'Did you hear what I said?' As Anastasia rolled onto her side, Fiona read out loud from the morning paper. What a lurid story, too: a dodgy woodcutter had discovered a woman's lifeless body in Southend only the night before. Fiona sat herself down on the edge of the bed. 'It's the girl's own fault,' Fiona said. 'A bird ought to know you don't go wandering about the countryside all alone.'

'Enough,' Anastasia said. 'For the last month, you've been reading stories like this and blaming the victim.'

'But I'm right,' Fiona said. 'A girl ought to know what might happen if she wanders out along some woodland walk. Maybe someday Southend should have rows of terraced houses, but there's nothing out that way just yet. So, why the devil go mucking about there?' Fiona flapped the newspaper and then resumed with the article.

Anastasia sat up some. 'You're a radical,' she said. 'As a matter of fact, you adore the dregs of society. That's why every time you read the newspapers for my benefit, you interject your liberal commentaries. Always, you oppose Scotland

Yard. Anytime they arrest someone, you presume it is a case of entrapment. And most irksome of all, you insist on providing excuses and pretences for the offender. Time and again, you've done that. No matter what the evidence clerk says, either. If the suspect seems to have endured a hard life, you're certain to take the position the courts ought to deem the thug just as pitiable and important as the actual victim.'

Fiona did not answer, nor did she seek to console Anastasia. Over the course of the past week or so, Fiona had proven to be less than ideal. Though descended from a long line of pious, principled Huguenots, she had not kept the faith. From all that Anastasia had discerned, Fiona had embraced secularism whilst studying at Saint Paul's Girls' School. Evidently, a prideful, opinionated prefect had encouraged Fiona to study the writings of various left-leaning social reformers and sexologists associated with the London School of Economics—a progressive institution where the apostate presently read for a business degree.

Fiona pulled Anastasia up into a proper sitting position, then pulled her feet down to the bedchamber floor. With that, Fiona placed the wooden support cane into Anastasia's hand.

The eye doctor himself had presented Anastasia with the support cane only yesterday, and he had explained how simple a proposition it would be for her to get around: 'You must learn the precise number of footsteps between this destination and that, and once you commit that number to memory, you'll always command the power to undergo said journey.'

Already, Fiona had counted the number of footsteps from her door to the tearoom down the street—and Fiona had insisted that Anastasia commit the figure to memory.

Fiona sat back down on the edge of the bed and poked

251

Anastasia's arm. 'I won't let you stay indoors all day.'

'But something has muddled my mind.' Wilfully, Anastasia pretended that she could not distinguish between her present-day life and the voyage from Alexandria itself. Feigning a bout of hysteria, she even cried out—as if she believed the SMS *Helgoland* had just fired upon the doomed vessel.

'I'm quite sure you know you're in England, love. And this here's the best place in the world to be. The Land of the Rose. The sceptred isle. So, seize the day. A week hence, I'm sure you'll be leaping along.' With that remark, Fiona nudged Anastasia's foot and exited the room.

Anastasia pulled her arms and legs into her core. She thought about Jack lazing about wherever in the world he might be at present—the peculiar, demented youth indulging all kinds of bad habits. *I've got to do better than that.* At last, she dropped her bare feet back onto the cool floorboards.

In time, the faint aroma of raisins crept into the bedchamber. Without a doubt, Fiona had gone downstairs to the kitchen to brew a kettle of Darjeeling white tea.

Anastasia inhaled. Before long, it seemed as if the white tea's exotic aroma had conjured an array of magical, spectral raisins that hovered all about the room—each one reeling all about in a perfect circle over the bed. Smiling, she reached out to catch one—but the sweet, dreamlike creation eluded her touch.

Fiona returned from down the hallway. Again, she knocked upon the door jamb—just once. Anastasia heard her footsteps continue inside, and she felt Fiona reaching for her to place a cup of tea into her hands.

Though her feet had grown cold, the warmth pulsating through the thin, fragile china soothed Anastasia so. She let her body sway gently. Then she jumped slightly when Fiona kissed the apple of her right cheek.

'I got me an early lecture down on Houghton Street this morn,' Fiona said. 'You'll manage?'

'Yes, of course.'

'Splendid. You could visit the tearoom. I think I left one of my schoolbooks down there last week. *The Wealth of Nations*. Could you ask the hostess what's become of it?'

Anastasia hesitated to answer, for a promise to collect the book would oblige her to go through with the daunting journey. She sipped her tea, and she wondered if she might invent a melodramatic story to explain why she could not go. Perhaps she could swear that she had heard the invasive, high-pitched hiss of a rat lurking in the alley. *Yes, I'll feign some kind of hysterical fear of mice, and I'll convince Fiona that I'm affrighted by the notion that if I depart the flat, one of those repugnant creatures should race across my foot and nibble my ankle.*

On the other side of the room, Fiona tapped her foot against the floor. 'Are you dreaming up some excuse why you can't check the tearoom?'

Before Anastasia could respond, a flower girl struck up a song in a bold lilting voice somewhere outside.

The music should have filled Anastasia with hope, but no. She fumbled for the night table and set the rattling teacup down.

'Feeling green about the gills, are you?'

'No,' Anastasia insisted. 'It's just that it's not so easy to get about without the power of sight. Moreover, a gentleman smells no different from a knave. So, how to distinguish between them?'

'Enough of that. Listen. You know the count. Take a

left at the door, and it's only thirty-seven steps to the corn chandler's shop. Then it's twenty-three steps to the pawnshop, and then a mere seventeen steps and you're standing before the tearoom door.'

Anastasia trembled. *Who's this brash ideologue to pressure me?* Her hands scrabbling on the night table, she finally managed to collect her teaspoon—and she tapped the end against her knee. 'I don't belong here. I've got to live with the spiritual kind. Maybe that's the trouble.'

Fiona did not say much. She wished Anastasia godspeed. Then she marched off and was gone.

Anastasia dropped the teaspoon onto the night table. *I'm all alone . . . except for the fox inside me.* She wrapped her hand around the warmth of the teacup. 'Say something.'

'Don't make me cross,' the fox told her. 'Already, I've decided if you won't obey my words, I'll force you into a most consequential crossroads. A terrible turning point. A crucial catastrophe.'

~

Later that Same Day.

Anastasia had still not dressed herself. She still lay in bed, and every once in a while, still strained to hear the rattle of a loom.

Outside, the sounds of the city rang out: several motorcars came and went, and then the flower girl's wondrous lilting voice reverberated anew.

Deep inside Anastasia's womb, the dream fox kicked. 'Don't listen to that music. Go back to sleep.'

'Yes, of course,' she said softly. 'You want me to stay here all hopeless and miserable and woeful?'

'Yes, because you're *mine*. Don't go strolling here and there. Stay in bed. If you go out, some knave should touch you. And that'd be a crime, because you belong to me. Only I should enjoy the warmth of your body.'

She sat up and groped for the teacup. Though the warmth once pulsating through the china had long since faded, she held the teacup awhile. *If only the vessel contained something as potent as pennyroyal tea. I'd down every last drop and then will the toxins to destroy the entity in my womb.* Breathless now, she revisited the miscarriage back in the village. *Should I ever forgive myself?* She climbed out of bed and faltered over to the window. There, she sought to detect any kind of pleasing aroma wafting up from the flower girl's basket—but there was nothing.

The dream fox yelped and panted and darted all about inside her. 'Get back into bed this instant.'

'Does the flower girl affright you? Why? Has she some great, godly purpose?'

If the fox knew the answer, he did not say.

Out of spite, she fumbled her way over to the wardrobe and felt about for her taffeta-trimmed cardigan and her best cotton-twill walking skirt. Once dressed, she scrabbled to locate her support cane before making her way downstairs.

The dream fox panted. 'If you don't obey, I'll have my vengeance. Do you know what I'll do? I'll pray for transformation, that's what. Yes, yes, yes. I'll pray that I change into a giant, hideous, gruesome, grisly diadem spider. Think about that. Instead of a graceful fox inside your womb, you'll have something truly vile lurking inside you. Ha! A terrible beastie.'

She dismissed all that as an idle threat and continued

outside, where she paused beside the letterbox. The May breeze a little bit cold against her face, she listened to the sounds of the city.

What a commotion the hustle and bustle of Oxford Circus was: the motorcars, the clatter of steely horseshoes, too. Suddenly, from some several streets away, the flower girl called out again—and what a bold, lilting, grandiose voice she had.

A series of manly odours sailed by—the allure of cheap cologne, the power of a labourer's underarm sweat, the pheromones within.

She breathed in five times over. *Are my remaining senses growing stronger? How to intuit the dissimilarity between someone good and someone evil? What if it's impossible?*

The fox spirit moaned. 'That flower girl out there, she's no flower girl at all. I think she's a fallen angel. *Wicked.* She'll cast a spell on you and make you starve yourself.'

'Well, then, we ought to track her. Maybe by starving myself, my body should become much too inhospitable for you. Yes, and you'll be destroyed. Afterward, do you know what I'll do? I'll find the flower girl, and she'll sell me some lovely flowers. Maybe she's got some good fresh yarrow, or what about sweet pea? Whatever blossoms the flower girl might be selling, I'll bring home a whole bouquet to celebrate your demise.'

'You shouldn't say things like that. Besides, once the flower girl destroys me, do you know what she'll do? She'll destroy you because she knows you're a sinful one. All winter long, what've you been doing? You've been trifling with sensuous women like Ernesztina Henreid, and a Huguenot girl should know better than to do things like that. Dearie me.'

As the fox panted deep in her belly, Anastasia blinked

several times and sought to picture the city standing before her. *Do I remember how many steps to the tearoom? I've got to think for a moment. Yes, I remember.* Without even thinking, she unbuttoned the very top button of her cardigan. As she did, she debated whether she ought to continue.

Deep inside her womb, the dream fox twitched his downy tail. 'Turn back, I say. We've got to maintain the midnight watch lest one of the U-boats sink us. Yes, we've got to get back to your stateroom. It's the only safe place on a passenger steamer like ours.'

With a sigh, Anastasia dropped the support cane. 'Do you honestly think you'll confound me by acting like that?'

The dream fox howled. 'We're back aboard the ship, I tell you. Don't you hear the rumble from the engine room? What about the steam whistle? Please, we've got to get back inside and find a warrant officer, a proper brass-bounder. Maybe he'll give us a newfangled depth charge, and we'll use it to panic the Germans.'

With yet another sigh, she picked up her support cane. Three times, she tapped the tip against her heel. *Go on.* She ventured one step out into the walkway—when just by chance, the pavement rumbled beneath her feet. *Oh God.* At once, it seemed as if she stood upon a narrow, unsure footbridge spanning a bottomless chasm. Teetering a little bit, she even sought to steady herself against the imaginary railing. *But I can't even find it.* Coming undone, she grabbed a fistful of hair and pulled.

Deep inside her womb, the fox spirit kicked. 'Do you feel the rumble? I'd say it's the angels awakening Behemoth. Yes, that's what happened.'

'Oh, it's probably just the Twopenny Tube.' No sooner had she spoken than the rumble died out. As the morning train passed along, she fixed her hair. *Just thirty-seven footsteps to the corn chandler's shop. Go on.* She stumbled forward and, tapping the end of the support cane here and there, counted very carefully. *Two, three, four.*

The fox leapt all about inside her and snarled. 'Let's go home. What if some fiendish, knavish blighter passes by? What's to keep him from squeezing your dairy arrangements in his hot little hands? Or what if he gropes your bottom? We must retreat.'

As the fox spirit continued with his taunts, she placed her one free arm across her bosom to shield herself. When the spectre laughed, she clenched her fists and drummed upon her belly several times over in the hope that the awful creature might come spilling out of her body then and there. And once more, she thought of her miscarriage—until she thought that she heard a lemming's hiss. *Or did I only imagine it?* She chewed on one of her fingernails, and then she leaned back—for she hoped to rest her weary spine and shoulders against the strong cool of that wrought-iron gate standing before Count Orlov's palace. *Saint Petersburg. If only I were there now.*

Whatever the dissonant noise had been, the hiss-like sound abated—so she willed herself to advance and went back to counting off her paces. Further down the street, as she counted out her thirty-seventh step, she detected the odour of cat dander and bird droppings. *So, I've reached the corn chandler's shop.*

The clatter of footfalls approached, a stranger's heels resounding loudly—as if the soles of his shoes must be fashioned from desert ironwood.

Immediately, she placed her free hand into the moist warmth of her right armpit—and she pressed her free arm as tightly as possible across her bosom.

The fox panted. 'Here he comes. And remember, if he can't get at your Isaac Newtons, so the lecherous bastard's sure to smack your arse. Yes, that's just what he'll do.'

She held her breath, braced herself, and let the stranger pass by. *Oh my my.* She exhaled, removed her hand from her armpit and shambled forward. *One, two, three.* Step by faltering step, she drew ever closer to the pawnshop. *Seventeen, eighteen, nineteen.*

The fox spirit kicked three more times. 'There's no hope for you. When the fancy-goods dealer notices you creaking along, he'll come after you. Yes, that's just what he'll do.'

She refused to listen and continued to tap the support cane here and there. Of course, she resumed the count, too—until she reached her twenty-third step. *Now I ought to be standing beneath the three gold orbs that dangle above any pawnshop door. Am I, then?* She raised the cane and waved it back and forth until she hit something up above and heard a clank as of something metallic. *Yes, I'm here.*

A door opened, and a shopkeeper's bell resounded. 'You go lost?' the old pawnbroker asked in a thick Hungarian accent.

'No, sir.' Once the pawnbroker went back inside, she poked her belly. 'There. The old man didn't do anything to me.'

'So what? London's a big town, and we've got plenty of scoundrels chasing about. Just like lemmings. Ha!'

She tapped the support cane's heel against the toe box of her shoe, and she struggled to envision the path before her. *How long before I bump into a lighting bollard, or what about a post box?* She fidgeted, and her hands refused to settle.

The pavement rumbled anew; another morning train passed along somewhere below the streets around

Oxford Circus.

She clenched her jaw. Just like before, she imagined herself standing upon some narrow, unsure footbridge spanning a vast, bottomless chasm. Still, no matter how much she longed to reach out with her free hand and to take hold of the imaginary railing, she resisted the pointless urge. Then, once the train had passed by, she poked her belly one last time. 'All those years ago, what did you do to my Ludmila? Yes, I remember. You ate her. What a heartless rogue you are.'

The dream fox kept quiet. Had the spectre made himself small? Even if he had, his shame did not last long. Soon enough, he grew as ponderous as before—and he kicked.

From thirty or so yards to the right, meanwhile, the flower girl called out in her bold lilting voice: 'Blossoms for sale!'

Anastasia blushed. How to reconcile such unusual musicality with the otherwise mundane cacophonous sounds of the city?

The dream fox sighed. 'If you don't go back to Fiona's place this instant, I swear I'll metamorphose into a diadem spider and gobble you up from the inside.'

Anastasia marched onward, for she had only seventeen steps to the tearoom. *One, two, three, four, five, six, seven, eight, nine* . . .

When she reached the tearoom door and stepped inside, she heard the sound of footsteps approaching.

'May I show you to a table?' the hostess asked, her breath heavy with the scent of *crème* Chantilly.

'No, I don't require a table. I've come in search of a book. My friend, Fiona, she's reading economics, and—'

'*The Wealth of Nations*,' the hostess blurted out. 'I'd wager a quid to a bloater that's the book you're looking for. Found it just the other day, I did.' Not a moment later, the hostess placed the musty-smelling book into Anastasia's hand.

~

Later that Evening.

Anastasia had still not found her way back to Fiona's flat. Upon leaving the tearoom, Anastasia had become lost. At present, she sat between a lone street lamp and what seemed to her to be an outdoor sculpture. *How did I get here? Where do I go? What do I do?* She bounced a foot and fingered her necklace.

The flower girl recommenced her flamboyant song, but as soon as Anastasia pushed herself up onto her feet, the flower girl grew quiet—as if she did not want Anastasia to home in on her voice.

Gradually, Anastasia sensed the woman's powerful gaze upon her body—as if one of the flower girl's eyes had discharged a ray of light that bathed the whole of Anastasia's person in a warm misty glow. For a moment, she longed to believe that the mysterious flower girl might very well be an angel. *And she's watching over me.*

Deep inside Anastasia's womb, the dream fox kicked several times. 'You've got that book, so why don't we leave? Go on. We ought to hurry home before a gang of hooligans comes along and takes it from you.'

She groped for the sculpture's foot. 'Yes, that's right. I've collected the book. Now we've got to find the lovely flower girl.' As the fox spirit darted all about, Anastasia tucked the book underneath her free arm.

The scent of tulips swirled all about her.

She breathed in. *Could it be the flower girl drawing near? Oh, maybe she's standing over to the left. Yes, I think so.*

The scent of the tulips grew stronger until the spring flowers emitted a fragrance as of apple trees—the finest, sweetest apples.

Anastasia raced forward, neither counting out her footsteps nor tapping the end of the support cane against the pavement. 'I'm here!' she cried out.

At last, she bumped into what she believed to be the tearoom door—at which point she realised that she had not detected the scent of tulips but the aroma of fresh tealeaves. *Apple tea, more than likely.* She backed away from the door and whispered a Huguenot prayer.

The fox spirit gnawed at her womb. 'Let's go back to Fiona's house. And please hurry, won't you? If you refuse, I swear I'll transform into a diadem spider this very day. That's right, a great big disgusting diadem spider, right here in your womb.'

Anastasia pressed the book tightly against her ribs. 'No, we'll find that flower girl. And then she'll exorcise you and strangle you to death.' In her confusion, she dropped both the book and the support cane. 'Now look what you made me do.' Her muscles sagging, she knelt to the walkway and patted here and there with the palms of her hands.

Hearing a procession draw near—five or more sets of heavy footsteps—she wondered if it could be a band of soldiers, the whole troop lurching along single file.

She moved her head to gauge their position and flashed a friendly smile. Her thoughts ran wild. She revisited a newspaper story Fiona had read for her some time ago—a report on a band of soldiers. They had survived the trenches, but the war had left them blind. And now, ever since the fire had burned their eyes away, the blindfolded soldiers would falter about the city, all in a line. *As blind as a labour of weary little moles.*

Once the seeming procession of blinded soldiers had passed by, a peculiar noise resounded—a jeer as of several large rats hissing.

Her upper lip curling back, she imagined she had fallen off some narrow footbridge—only to reach the darkness at the bottom of some dreadful chasm. *The Well of Fate.* Looking up, she sought to picture the bridge from which she had fallen.

Someone, a gentleman smelling of roast lamb with *Moutarde de Dijon*, drew close. 'You dropped your things,' the gentleman said, setting a volume into the palm of her left hand. 'Right, and here's your pikestaff,' he continued, arranging the support cane into her right.

She held the book against her ribs, and she gripped the wooden cane's crown so that the nose dug into her palm. 'Please, sir. Help me back to the pawnshop and see that I'm standing beneath the three gold orbs.'

'By all means.' With that, the polite stranger accompanied her all the way back to the pawnshop—and when they reached the establishment, he helped her to stand just where she wanted. 'Cheers,' he said, his voice friendly, perhaps even brotherly.

Despite the scent of the roast lamb, she discerned the faint aroma of his cologne and wondered if it resembled some kind of timeless Japanese pepper.

The gentleman made a bit of repartee, meanwhile—but overcome by the peppery scent in his cologne, she did not hear a word. Then she thought for a moment. *I've only got to go twenty-three steps back to the corn chandler's shop. From there, it's only thirty-seven more steps back to the flat.* She thanked the kind stranger and continued along. *Homeward bound.*

Back at Fiona's place, not a foot from the door, Anastasia

heard the crunch of broken glass beneath the sole of her shoe. The debris forced her to reflect on how perilous her life would be from now on. *But I've got to be strong. I must learn from my adventure today. I'll learn to be valiant . . . just like a prophetess, a saint, the Maid of Orleans.* Anastasia groped for the keyhole and then continued inside. When she called out, no one answered. There could be little doubt that Fiona had not come home from the London School of Economics just yet. *What a letdown.* The book fell from her hand.

Then the evening breeze came drifting through the house, the current alive with the scents of chemicals, armpit sweat and mint flowers.

With faltering steps, she climbed the staircase. Inchmeal, she advanced down the corridor leading back to her room. 'Jack, are you here? Don't you touch me. Go away.'

What if he were there, and just what might he say in that moment? She imagined the odd, unkempt youth standing alongside her window. 'I'm not here,' he would tell her. 'I'm just like the ghost girl, or the flower girl for that matter. Or the dream fox inside you. We're all of us no more than terrible illusions dreamt up by the deepest recesses of your unconscious.'

'But why?' she asked. 'For what purpose does my unconscious torment me the way it does?'

When no one answered, she forced herself to advance toward the window and to feel here and there. *No, there's no one here.* The curtain lace blowing into her face, she placed her hands upon her belly and pushed down. 'You in there. Are you quite serious about changing into some kind of spider? Why? Why must you or I torment myself the way you and I do? Won't you tell me the answer? Please explain.'

With a quiet rumble, the spring breeze grew strong—and

the curtain lace blew into her face several more times before the rumble sounded much less like the current and much more like a loom.

The tapestry of life!

XVI.

The North of England. 2 June 1918.

Jack awoke late that morning and looked all about his room. *I'm still here. Bloody hell.* As soon as his ship had reached the Port of Liverpool, his father had committed him to this oppressive establishment—Plumbland Nursing Home.

Looking out the window now, he considered the fact that the nursing home happened to be situated in the heart of the countryside. *How to escape a place like this? Where do I turn?* His shame only intensified—until he crumpled onto the floor, at which point the guilt compelled him to revisit his misadventure back in Sinai. *The whole time I lived there, I only ever debased meself before Anastasia. What was I thinking?* His shoulders curling forward, he imagined some ideal young man in Anastasia's employ standing over him. *Me accuser. He stands very tall. Over six feet. And he's got the body of a sportsman. He weighs just under fourteen stone. And not even a trace of fat along his waist.* Jack's belly grew severely unsettled, as if he had been sitting in the back of a motorcar and riding for hours on end.

As he picked himself up from the floor, a dozen or so aural hallucinations followed—his accuser charging him with any number of crimes against Anastasia and threatening to bring him to trial. And what a perfect voice: Anastasia's champion spoke in a deep, resonant timbre. *The kind of tone colour what a bird finds ideal.* Jack sought to speak up and to make his own voice sound more like a strong breathy baritone, but it would not do. Moreover, he stumbled over his sentences. *I'm nothing.* He hid his hands in his pockets and paced.

Midmorning, a serene ghostly presence seemed to sail into his room—with a sound resembling the sinister whisper conjured by gases escaping a lifeless body. Might the whole effect have been nothing more than the wind?

He sought to ignore it all, and he tapped his toes. When he permitted himself to stand still, he could not feel even the faintest breeze blowing in through the window. *It can't be no current. So, what could it be?*

For the longest time, the ghostly sensation played through his long brown hair—until he closed his eyes. No sooner had he done so than he imagined the presence as a very gentle hand touching him. *Yes, a woman's hand. A woman who loves me.*

When the presence drifted off, he opened his eyes. *Where did it go?* He returned to the window and fixed his gaze upon the big grey windmill standing atop the distant hill. Soon, he recalled an episode from his childhood—a splendid fortnight's holiday at his Aunt Vera's dairy farm. How to forget the comely girl who had lived in the big grey windmill standing a half mile up the rutted country lane? *Europa Menzies, that was her name.* To the best of his memory, she would have been the very first girl he had ever fancied. *Europa.* He shook all over and wondered if the colour had drained from his face. *Europa.*

Despite the ongoing absence of any afternoon breeze, a few of the wind harps dangling from the hallway ceiling stirred to life.

He glanced at his door. Ever since his arrival, it had amused him the way the hospital staff had adorned the nursing home's corridors with all those little wooden lyres.

Suddenly, the melody seemed to reach the middle eight— and the abrupt change in the tune suggested a fragment from his lost composition.

How could it be? He wondered if the gods had entreated the wind harp to accomplish the feat. Now he raced over to the tallboy, and he gathered up whatever papers he had. The length of a frayed booklet envelope standing in for a rule, he lay upon the floorboards and drew up a leaf of make-do sheet music complete with a grand staff and all the necessary staves. Then, as the wind harp continued to perform the melody, he listened closely and wrote down each precious note. *Amen.*

A sound as of a bellwether pealed. Had a flock of Suffolk sheep come wandering the countryside? The bellwether went silent, and the wind harp died down.

God, no. Bring me music back. He stood up from the floorboards, cocked his ear and strained to hear. The wind harps remained quiet, so he sat on the bed and rubbed his legs.

A pair of footsteps approached his door, and a burly hospital attendant peeked into the room. 'It's time for your session with the disorders analyst,' the young man said.

'Thanks awfully, but not now. I've got busy work to do. I've got to do the lyrics and render everything into Latin. Bloody fooking hell, I've got to retrieve me great opus.'

'Please come along. Dr Allcock only wishes to find some way to heal you. Don't you want to get better?'

'Just tell the bloody bastard to put a mustard plaster on me chest. And from that moment on, I'm quite sure I'll be right fine.' Jack made his way back to the window and endeavoured to focus his attention on the Indian-bean tree— its trunk and crown standing all aglow in the hazy light.

'Feeling blue-devilish, are we?' the young man said in a womanly intonation.

'Bugger off.' Jack averted his gaze from the Indian-bean tree, and he studied the syringe in the stocky young man's hand. The attendant had filled the pump with what looked to be the customary canary-yellow sedative.

The attendant advanced into the room. 'Come, come. We can't permit you to laze about, pouting like a child. Your parents brought you to Plumbland so that we should help you. And how do you think they'd feel if you won't let us do that? Not a little bit chagrined, I'd say.'

Jack turned back to the window and gazed upon a few of the moorhens fluttering about the marsh.

The attendant stopped at the foot of the bed. 'Don't make me stick you. Let's go.' With steady steps, the attendant drew closer. 'Do you wish to escape into the Borderlands?'

Immediately, Jack looked at the faint, coin-silver moon— just barely visible against the bright blue of the midday sky. 'Escape? No, I prefer rotting away here. What's more, I bloody well adore Dr Allcock. Why wouldn't I delight in the chance to sit around all day, every day, listening to some old mountebank while he rattles off all his right clever theories? No, if I was back in London, I'm sure I'd be as miserable as a rat in a tar barrel.'

'So, why don't you hotfoot your way home? You could go tonight. Who'd stop you? But listen here, lad. It's down to this. Even if you manage to escape jolly old Plumbland, you'll never escape *yourself.* That's why you'd be wise to stay right here, where Dr Allcock might talk to you and help you contend with your depressive psychosis.'

Jack turned from the window. 'Depressive psychosis? Can't we give me diagnosis a more poetic name? What about the slough of despond?'

Despite the deep undying stillness in the air, a few wind harps hanging in the hallway resounded.

No matter the jumble of random atonal melodies, there could be no mistaking the occasional quote from the lost glass-harp piece. At the very least, certain notes did have the power to remind Jack of selections from his lost composition. He cupped his hand around his ear.

The attendant held his head high. 'You hear the music, then? Dr Allcock says those wind harps hold the power to remedy almost any affliction. Don't it sound like a wee band of angels strumming upon their lyres up there in the creamy clouds?'

Jack stumbled back to his make-do sheet music and threw himself on the floor. Lost in his work, he didn't even notice when the attendant knelt to shoot him up with the overpowering elixir.

The state of delirium that followed seemed to last for two hours or more. Breathing much too rapidly, he imagined himself a British soldier having been taken captive by the Germans and brought to some labyrinthine castle in the Rhineland. 'Torture me all you wish,' he said out loud at one point. 'I'll not betray England. I'll not tell you anything you want to know.'

When the effect of the sedative wore off, Jack opened his eyes and found himself huddled in a corner of Dr Allcock's study. According to the clock on the wall, only twenty minutes had gone by.

The physician sat in his chair, arranged his watch and chain about his waistcoat and then crossed his legs by putting his right ankle across his left knee. 'Don't you wish to speak with me today?'

'No, not especially. I don't belong here. I'm fit as a flea. I've got no reason to bowl off no more, so go ahead and send me home. I want to be free.'

Dr Allcock said nothing. Instead, he stood to stretch his back. Then he limped over to the east wall to study the watercolour hanging there. With quiet steps, then, Dr Allcock limped back to his chair.

Jack studied the work of art: the painting depicted an ancient youth lying beneath a beam of moonlight.

'Do you recognise the theme?' Dr Allcock asked. 'The malevolent moon goddess has put Endymion to sleep, and the shepherd should never wake up. Sad, don't you think? As the lad dreams on and on, the outside world passes him by. And that includes all the pretty girls. Day by day, they trifle with this lad and that. Ah, but the young shepherd may never participate.'

Just like earlier in the day, Jack registered a gentle sensation—the erotic touch of some ghostly visitor. Feeling warm, he stood and faced the French doors.

Their glass panes did not provide much of a view. Outside, a few faded, long-dead camellias swayed back and forth.

The dead flowers reminded him of the dead lying forgotten on the battlefields all throughout the continent. *And I'm here, good and snug. A nothing, a coward.*

Dr Allcock removed a corncob pipe from his coat pocket, packed the bowl and lit it with a match. The smoke appeared as a pulsating shapeless presence—and as the physician puffed, the room filled with the sweet vanilla scent of his pipe tobacco. 'Tell me about your adventure down there in Sinai. You must've endured a heartrending rejection during your sojourn. That'd explain why you test me the way you do. You wish to know if I'll reject you as well.'

His left leg jumping, Jack opened the French doors and strode into the desolate camellia garden. *Don't look back. Run for the hills.*

From the window just above the study, a wind harp broke into yet another tune from the heretofore lost work.

He shook all over. How to leave this place before reclaiming his opus? He picked one of the dead flowers, promptly dropped it to the earth, and then raced back inside. 'Let me go back to my room. Please, sir.'

For the next two days and nights, Jack worked and worked. Then late one night, twenty minutes to midnight, the erotic touch of what seemed like a ghostly visitor awoke him—and he sat up in bed and looked all about. 'Who's there?' he asked, studying the shadows.

Like a breeze, the presence glided through his nightshirt. Then, as the current caressed his body, the moonlight shone down upon the sheet music to his opus—which he had completed just a few hours before.

He climbed out of bed. As the moonlight grew brighter, he gathered up the sheet music and stumbled over to the door. *Right, let's do this.* He tiptoed down the hallway and continued down the stairwell and into the darkened day room. Holding his breath, he groped for a box of matches and lit a candle. Then, when he sat on the bench before the cabinet upright, he stretched his wrists, hands and fingers. *Am I ready?*

At last, he placed his fingers upon the keyboard. '*Lento.*'

The ghostly presence caressing his calf, he performed the song in its entirety. 'There we are.'

As the final note faded into silence, only then did the illusory presence seem to drift off through the window.

The candle's flame dying out, Jack checked his timepiece and suddenly realised what he would entitle his work:

Anastasia's Midnight Song

He looked up and stroked his chin. How to translate the title into Latin? Would the genitive case do? *Anastasiæ carmen mediæ noctis.* Or why not something like *Mediæ noctis carmen Anastasiæ*? Or what about the ablative case? Now he debated which version would sound more artistic: *Carmen Anastasiæ mediæ nocte* or *Anastasiæ carmen mediæ nocte.* He shook his head, for he could not decide.

One of the other patients, Owen Mercier from Newton Heath, Manchester, emerged from the darkened kitchen. 'Jack Wylye, would that be you there? Shite. Who the hell taught you how to play? Roderick Usher?'

Jack winced, for he took the reference as an insult.

Owen must have intuited as much. The young man ducked back into the kitchen and then returned with two dishes of hasty pudding. He placed one on the table next to the settee, and he sauntered off with the other.

As the day room filled with the sweet scent of maple sugar, Jack lost himself in a vivid memory of the childhood holiday out at Aunt Vera's farmstead. Licking his lips, he recalled that quiet evening when he shared a dish of hasty pudding with Europa. As they downed their dessert, her mother told them all about how the Royal Highland Telephone Service intended to drum up publicity for their new line to Liverpool by ringing out a medley along the route. Evidently, a fine chap in Glasgow had intended to perform the opus upon a newfangled electrical musical instrument, a telharmonium, and the telephone service had planned to broadcast the futuristic composition through each and every telephone-pole horn between the two cities.

No sooner had her mother explained all that than Europa had patted Jack's hand. 'On the night the music plays, you and me should have ourselves a dance. Won't that be fun? We'll dance a proper jig or maybe some kind of reel. Depending on our mood, eh?'

From here and there throughout the nursing home, the soft strains of the wind harps awoke with a jumble of random notes.

He glanced at his sheet music. *Memories of those moments with Anastasia, they're all that's left for me now.* He arose from the piano bench, lay himself down upon the settee and then curled up into a ball. *Sleep.* Sometime before dawn, a nightmare seized upon him.

Without a word, Mr Sylvius guides a blind Anastasia through the gates of the Hermitage and onward into the museum lobby. From there, Mr Sylvius helps her down an empty portrait hall and into a powder room containing a large glass box in which Jack himself stands beside a diadem spider the size of a dog. Mr Sylvius reaches into his coat pocket. 'Shall I remedy your blindness so that you may enjoy the exhibition?' he asks. With that, he produces a pair of celluloid opera glasses and holds them up to Anastasia's big blue lifeless eyes.

The opera glasses heal her blindness, and now she smiles and looks all about. Then, as soon as she notices the two captives standing within the glass box, she steps back. 'What're they doing here?' she asks.

Mr Sylvius points toward Jack's groin. 'Behold.'

Jack drops his trousers, picks up the giant diadem spider

and performs the act of sodomy upon the ghastly creature. Over and over, he strokes and thrusts back and forth in a shameless, animalistic manner.

'Do you grasp the point?' Mr Sylvius asks Anastasia.

'No, I don't,' she answers. 'At least I don't think so.'

'This here atrocity exhibition seeks to illustrate what happens to a person who has no direction in life,' Mr Sylvius explains.

'That's right!' the diadem spider cries out. 'Everyone else, a whole generation, they're proving themselves down there in the trenches. And what's Jack Wylye doing? He's content to have me put my pudding up for his treacle.' The ghastly creature laughs then. And he laughs in the most malevolent way—just like sadistic children out in the schoolyard.

Little by little, the outburst came to merge with the true-to-life dawn chorus of all those songbirds outside in the hospital grounds—a blush of excitable robins just then fluttering past the day room's canted bay window.

Jack opened his eyes and brushed his right hand across his lap, as if to push aside the diadem spider. Leaping from the settee, he knocked over the table.

The dish of hasty pudding fell to the floor and broke in half. Meanwhile, the dawn chorus grew louder and increasingly dissonant.

He yawned, stumbled over to the left blind and cursed the winged creatures. Then he doubled back to the upright to study the sheet music. As the radiance of dawn grew brighter, he considered the title:

Anastasia's Midnight Song

For a second time, he asked himself just how to translate the title into Latin. *The genitive case? The ablative case?* Despite all his indecision, he offered the songbirds outside a weightless gaze—for he did register the peculiar sensation of finality.

~

The North of England. 8 June 1918.

Early that afternoon, Jack honoured his daily appointment with Dr Allcock. There was no reason to resist, but the conversation dragged. Mostly, they spoke of Jack's guilt regarding his failure to serve.

In time, Jack retreated to the glass French doors and looked outside. A profusion of orange lilies had lately replaced the dead winter camellias.

Dr Allcock crossed his legs. 'You're looking out of countenance today. Maybe you think too much about the war. You worry too much about what others might think of your not having participated. I could help you with all that, though. I'm sure I could make the shame go away.'

'No, you can't.'

'I could hypnotise you. Forthwith. And then I could redirect your thoughts and produce upon your faculties a measure of good cheer and perhaps even condition you. Truly, you've no idea how far-reaching the power of suggestion is.'

'Stuff and nonsense.' Jack studied the watercolour: the shepherd Endymion looked all so blissful, perhaps even grateful the moon held him spellbound. Jack held his hands loosely behind his back, and he glowered at the physician. 'Prove your powers.'

Dr Allcock fussed with his watch and chain for a moment or two and then sat up. 'Close your eyes and hold out your arms to either side.'

'Right.' Standing perfectly straight, Jack did as he was told and stretched out his arms as far as he could.

'Now imagine you're holding a solitary feather just there

276

in your left hand.'

Jack did just that.

'Now imagine you're holding an iron dumbbell in the right.'

Jack played along, and he did just as Dr Allcock had ordered him to do—and soon enough, the arm holding up the imaginary dumbbell did indeed ache. Then, when Dr Allcock finally told him to open his eyes, Jack could not deny the fact that his right arm did indeed droop badly—as if his right hand did indeed hold a ponderous dumbbell. 'The fine art of mesmerism, it *works.*'

'And so it should.' With a knowing grin, the physician stood and approached the watercolour. 'Never mind the moon goddess and how she mesmerised Endymion,' Allcock said, his tone unmistakably prideful. 'In modern times, the art of mesmerism promises to set a captive lad free.'

Without a word, Jack opened the French doors. *What if I were to escape this place one of these nights? Where would I go? Maybe there's an army post somewhere nearby. I could show up at the gates and ask to join.* Jack ducked outside, kicked some of the orange lilies and then made his way back around the outside of the building and retired to his room.

For the rest of the afternoon, he planned his escape. At supper, he nicked a few extra crusts of bread. Then, just after midnight, he arranged his sheet music and personal effects in his leather satchel and crept out into the hallway. *No more dawdling. I'm bloody well going free.*

Outside, he raced off toward the hill. Swiftly, he followed the moonlit footpath through a field of Queen Anne's lace— until he reached the summit, where he donned his deerstalker.

A low, steady, unnerving, full-tone clamour resounded from the other side of the big grey windmill. *What the devil?*

When he stumbled forward, he recognised the source of the commotion to be an array of honeybee houses. *Bugger.* He held the deerstalker's front bill over his eyes and hurried forward a few steps before stumbling over a weathered old beekeeper's veil lying in the weeds. A dozen or so steadfast scouts gave chase. They pursued Jack through the thick rolling fog and all the way down into the valley—where a lone farmhouse stood amid a spinney of Scots pines. When the scouts finally relented, he lay beside an oily telephone pole and revisited the memory of Europa. Specifically, he recalled that hot, summer night when they had ambled off to join everyone around a telephone pole down in the village square. What a miracle—at that moment the wires crackled with life—and the telharmonium's mirthful futuristic music emanated from the tin horn mounted above the transformer. *And then me and Europa, we danced and danced. Until we lay down to rest in that layby. What a night. What a bloody magnificent night.*

The memory concluded, and he discerned a familiar sensation in his hair—the curiously erotic touch of a ghostly visitor. *What's that, then? Could it be nothing more than the nighttime breeze?* Whatever it was, he crawled into a patch of gillyflowers and slept peaceably—until the break of dawn, when the nightmare from before presented itself anew.

For a second time, Mr Sylvius guides Anastasia into the Hermitage. And for a second time, he presents her with the magic opera glasses.

Just like before, Jack appears in the large glass box, everyone ogling him as he performs the act of sodomy upon the horrid diadem spider.

After a while, the ghastly creature speaks up—but this time, how displeasing is the diadem spider's voice. The creature sounds like a recording of Jack's own inelegant voice. And now the spider laughs and laughs.

And just as the earlier outburst had merged with the true-to-life dawn chorus of robins just then fluttering about the hospital grounds, the present outburst merged with the true-to-life dawn chorus of all the robins just now fluttering about the countryside. This time, though, Jack merely half-awoke to the cacophony—and in his half-awoken state, he hallucinated the presence of a diabolical dream spider that had managed to remain upon his person. 'Go away!' he cried out, gasping uncontrollably.

'I'll brass along when I'm good and ready,' the dream spider told him. 'In the meantime, how's about a show? Take hold of that bean tosser of yours. Let's see you flog the bishop.'

Breathless, Jack managed to remove his right shoe. He knocked the dream spider away from his person and thrashed at the hallucination, which dissolved into a glaring royal-purple mist. As he sank back exhausted and feeling defeated, the light of dawn shone a shade of pale harvest gold across the horizon.

Bloody hell, I've squandered the night. He grabbed his satchel and raced off through the lush wild meadow—until he stumbled upon a thatched barn. His belly rumbling, he wondered if he might jump the fence. *Why not nick some provisions from the root cellar?* No sooner had he taken hold of the top rail than something stung him not far from the base of his spine. *It's one of them honeybee scouts.* He let go of the fence. *Mind the grease and run.* No matter how badly the sting burned, he raced along—the angry honeybees following close behind.

The morning light grew brighter and brighter—until he longed to slake his thirst. *So, look for a fresh bubbly brook.* Only resting every now and then, he trudged forward for the better part of an hour and a half but found no watercourse from which he could drink. *I'm cursed.*

At last, he stopped before a medieval well made of well-dressed and properly moulded fieldstones. At the same time, a sound as of ghostly, dreamlike footfalls approached at his back—and then it sounded as if the person let out a huff. Jack dropped his satchel to the earth and crossed his arms. 'There's no one standing there. It's just me imagination, so go on.'

'No,' someone seemed to say, and in Jack's own voice. 'I'm your double.'

'Me double?'

'Yes. And I've only come to admonish you not to drink from this bloody well. Even if you could reach the water, it'd be right toxic. Bound to make you quite ill. Then you'll lose all sense of time and think maybe it's yesterday. Or maybe you'll think it's already mid-June. No, no. I'm quite sure you won't know anything.'

Jack did not answer, for he presumed that he had only hallucinated the voice. *It's got to be the voice of me bloody accuser. Some fine chap looking to defend Anastasia.* With a very soft whimper, Jack looked down at his weak, trembling hands. Twice, he kicked at the earth. Then he gripped his hands together, and he drew very close to the well and breathed in.

Much to his chagrin, the waters reeked of various clay minerals and gave off a strong sulphurous odour.

He collected his things and continued along—until he reached the ruins of what looked to be an eighteenth-century bog house. And now he found himself awestruck; up ahead, just beyond a thicket of pussy willows, stood a massive structure that just happened to look like the precise duplicate of Plumbland Nursing Home—from the exceptional decorative stonework and distinctive medallions to the hipped roof and fine louvered cupola. *My sainted aunt. What's happened here?*

The presence of the fantastical structure standing there in the morning light seemed to indicate that he had departed the world that he had once known, only to reach some fantastical dimension.

Atop a distant hill carpeted with Queen Anne's lace, the blades of a big grey windmill creaked to life.

Strike me blind. As he watched the sails revolve, he realised that he had not reached some other world at all. In truth, he had misspent the night walking about in a terrific circle. *I boxed the compass, didn't I?* His breath laboured, he shook his head and continued down to the nursing home's back door.

Languidly, a smirking, sneering attendant stepped outside. 'So, where have *you* been?' he asked.

'No place special. I slept outside last night. Like a soldier.'

'Your story beggars belief,' the attendant insisted. 'No, I don't believe it. Not for one dicky minute. I'd say you meant to take French leave. Just like a cowardly soldier who thinks to abandon his post and run home to his mum.'

'Bugger,' Jack shouted. 'If I'd intended to flee, why the devil would I be back with the milk?'

'Maybe you never intended to come around this fine morn. Are you quite sure you haven't been walking around in circles?'

Jack turned away then, only to espy a honeybee scout. Though deprived of its stinger and surely dying, the wobbly creature darted past his right shoulder and soared upward through his window. *Hello.* He stumbled inside and retreated to his room. *Where did the bloody pest go?*

The creature lay upon his pillow and writhed about as if

it had only just discovered a patch of clover, which obliged it to perform the glorious dance by which any loyal scout maps out the precise coordinates where the virgin wildflowers await the swarm.

Given the bee's extraordinary powers, he could not help but blush. 'I do envy all your wisdom. I'm a directionless fool, I am. Can't do nothing right.' He collected the creature by pinching its forewing between the tip of his finger and thumb. *Am I a fool?* His chest tightening, he gazed into the honeybee's vast compound eye—the way a madman might do in the hope that he might register some miraculous sensation, a feeling as of atonement. At last, he shook off the whole idea. *No, I know what's happened. What if some incomprehensible, unconscious impulse intended that I should go round and round last night? Perhaps deep down inside I always knew that I must come back and grow healthful.* At last, he did as any proper youth might do: he cast the dead honeybee into the rubbish bin.

When he continued out into the hallway, the same attendant from before stopped him and looked into his eyes. 'Where you going?'

'I'm off to get some breakfast,' Jack said.

'Not until you hear me out. You've got to stop thinking about soldiering. You're a musician, right? So, tell yourself you don't belong in no war. And just keep saying it, like you aim to hypnotise yourself.'

Jack nodded his head. 'I know all that. I've got to grow healthful now. I've got to get me noodle working right. So that I'm strong enough for love. Strong enough for a woman.' Quietly, he followed the attendant downstairs—and they had breakfast together.

XVII.

London. 19 June 1918.

In the darkness before dawn, a dream awoke Anastasia—it was a nightmare in which the dream fox inside her willed itself to metamorphose into a large hideous diadem spider.

She did not fall asleep again for an hour, and once she had, a foul odour awoke her for good. *What could it be?* She sat up and pinched her nose shut. Sensing warmth against her face, she realised the room was bathed in the morning light. The odour lingered, too, so she climbed out of bed and crawled off to her left, following the smell. Soon enough, she discovered what she believed to be the carcass of a rat lying to the side of the footboard. *A dead rat. It's an omen of something awful.* When she finally mustered the nerve, she groped here and there for the tail and collected the lifeless creature. Then she stood, felt her way over to the window and dropped the dead rat into the alley below.

After she had washed her hands, she stumbled back to the window. *What to think of something like that?* She revisited the dream. *Could it be a sign the conniving dream fox inside my*

*womb has already transformed into a monstrous diadem spider?
If so, what happens next?*

Outside, the streets grew quiet—and the lull made her twist the Huguenot cross. For a time, she paced. Wringing her hands, she debated what kind of pathology might be responsible for envisioning something so disturbing as the metamorphosis fantasy. Every now and then, she sat in bed and rubbed her belly—and in those moments, she brooded. *Someday soon, I'll deliver the diadem spider. Just like a woman gives birth to a little baby. And then the hideous thing will probably tear me to pieces and consume my remains, and why wouldn't it?*

Once more, she paced. At times, she sought to calm herself—all in vain, though. Even if nothing existed down inside her womb, she could not be sure of just what her fears might make her do. *One of these days, the hysteria could get the better of me. Maybe as I make my way to the produce market, I'll feel the compulsion to do something drastic. Yes, I'll throw myself into the roar of the oncoming traffic.*

One last time, she stopped at the window. *I've got to do something about this. It's now or never. I've got to find some way to triumph over all my fears, my hysteria, whatever the diadem spider represents.*

The morning hours passed by until the strains of a wistful serenade filled the room: the singer sounded like the flower girl from before. At present, she sang as boldly as a noble opera singer.

Anastasia stood in the heart of the room and listened. *Does the flower girl wish to help me?*

With each one of its legs, the diadem spider tapped upon the lining of Anastasia's womb. 'Do you think the flower girl wants to teach you how to think lucidly? Do you think she wants to teach you how to let go of your fears? Do you think she yearns to fill you with transcendent hope?'

Anastasia said nothing, for the flower girl's voice did fill her with hope. She clasped her hands together. *Yes, I feel my mind growing strong.* She stumbled back toward the window, and as the unmistakable scent of fresh pimpernel drifted into the room, breathed in. Intoxicated, she slipped into her things. *I've got to find that flower girl and ask her what to do about the diadem spider.* She groped for the crown of her support cane and then found her way down the hallway, where she reached out her hand and felt for the newel post. *There.* Gliding her free hand along the length of the softwood banister, she shambled down the staircase. *Hurry. Don't lose her in the streets.*

Just as she reached the front door, the diadem spider inside her gnawed away at the lining of her womb.

Oh God, am I dying? Even if she were, Anastasia opened the door—at which point, the mysterious flower girl concluded her song. Still, the scent of the pimpernel guided Anastasia forward—until there could be no doubt she stood before the visitor.

For the longest time, the flower girl said nothing. *She must have realised by now that I'm blind, and perhaps my condition embarrasses her.* Desperate for someone to becalm her nerves, Anastasia tapped her foot against the pavement. 'Please do something, flower girl, please,' she whispered. With that, she reached out with her free hand. *Perhaps the flower girl will arrange her hands upon my cheekbones. And in laying on her hands like that, she'll cause the diadem spider to die. Or she'll make it vanish altogether.*

Nothing happened, and the awkward silence persisted. What if the poor flower girl presumed Anastasia to be deranged?

Anastasia cringed. *Words fail me. What am I doing? Maybe I've got to go into therapy after all.*

Now the diadem spider gnawed even more wildly—as if determined to make the lining of her womb bleed. The anguish came to feel like a whole clutter of diadem spiders tunnelling up toward the surface of her skin.

She wrapped her hand around the Huguenot cross.

As she did, the scent of pimpernel grew stronger—as if the flower girl had drawn a little bit closer. 'Are you feeling discomfited?' she asked. 'Quite so, eh? Regardless, you must not let yourself get foxed. No, my friend. I'll help you. Do you remember your address? If so, I could take you back to your door.'

Anastasia remained silent. Until that moment, she had wanted to believe that the flower girl must be an angel—someone more than capable of exorcising the presence inside her.

Ungracefully, the flower girl cleared her throat. 'You look puzzled. Maybe even a little bit crestfallen. What's wrong?'

Anastasia tapped the end of her support cane against the pavement and poked the tip of her tongue against the inside of her cheek. *The beautiful flower girl, she's just got to be an angel. With over-bright eyes shining. And she's just got to lay her hands upon me. And in that moment, an all-engrossing heat will awaken all throughout my eyes. 'What're you doing?' I'll ask then. And then I'll drop my walking stick to the pavement. And then I'll wrap my hands around the flower girl's taut forearms and . . .*

Her tongue grew stiff and weary. The whole of her body atremble, Anastasia broke into a tepid prickling sweat. *No.* She lowered her blind eyes and sought to envision the diadem spider slipping from her womb, the insidious creature falling very slowly down her leg and landing at her feet.

As sardonic as the fox ever was, the diadem spider will probably speak up and say something insolent. If nothing else, the diadem spider will enter into an ironic performance and deliver an impression of me. Or will the creature fall silent? If so, the spider will probably go on and destroy me then and there. And then spirit away my remains. Later, even if Scotland Yard were to effect an arrest, the magistrate will have no choice but to offer the monstrous thing a plea deal of some kind. How else to cajole the deviant into revealing the location of my shallow grave? And what if the negotiations fail? There will be no one to give my body the last rites.

The flower girl tapped Anastasia's wrist. 'Hello? Are you deaf, too? *Please.* If you've got the power to hear me, let me help you.'

Anastasia dropped her free hand from the cross to the pendant dove. 'Yes, I hear,' she answered, her voice very nearly drowned out by the unrelenting traffic.

'Good,' the flower girl said. 'So, are you feeling strong? I ask only because I know how trying things must be for you.'

No matter how helpful and kind the flower girl sounded, Anastasia required so much more than an everyday favour. With a sigh, she sought to explain. The whole idea proved to be impossible, though. Given the tormenting notion that some hideous beast were tearing its way out from her womb, she could not bring herself to say much of anything. Before long, she felt hopelessly alone. 'Hello, are you there?'

No one answered. The flower girl had, in fact, abandoned her.

For several minutes, Anastasia tapped the end of the support cane against the pavement and sought to remember how many hesitant, unsteady, faltering steps she had taken to arrive at this place. *How do I get back to Fiona's place?* Anastasia tapped a section of the support cane against her hip. She longed to cry out but did no such thing. Given the ongoing traffic, there was no reason to think anyone might hear.

Several sets of footsteps came along, but not one of the passersby stopped to check on her. One of the passersby paused to blow his or her nose, but that person said nothing and soon continued along.

The summer breeze all around, she let herself sway. As she did, she imagined the peculiar youth watching her. *But he's no one to fear.* She stood very still and reached out her hand. 'Jack, are you here? Let's come to terms. We'll speak of youthful sorrows and all the perils of illusory love. Yes, and I'll tell you all about the Arctic fox. And the diadem spider.'

From somewhere across the street, a set of footsteps hurried toward her. Whoever it was, though, the person continued along—and the sound of the footfalls diminished.

'Jack, if that was you, please come back here,' she called out. When nothing happened, she went back to swaying in the breeze. 'We've got to forgive one another. Then you'll go on and live your life, and maybe you'll find someone to love you. And I'll go on and live my life, and once the diadem spider has gone, if it ever does leave my body, I'll find someone.'

A set of strong, determined footsteps approached. The person proved to be a police constable. He escorted her back to Fiona's door.

Before he could leave, Anastasia felt for his arm and grabbed his wrist. 'Tell me the ghost girl's purpose. Please. Tell me the flower girl's charge, too. And tell me why the dream fox had to change into a diadem spider.'

At first, the police constable remained silent. 'Maybe you ought to go on inside and have yourself a rest,' he finally said. 'The ghost girl, the flower girl, the diadem spider. Why do they assail me the way they do? What do they want from me?'

Even if the police constable should have stayed by Anastasia's side, he removed her hand from his wrist and marched off—the sound of his footfalls firm and strong and unmistakable.

~

London. 23 June 1918.

Early that morning, Anastasia faltered her way outside and sought to find her way to the very same place where she had spoken with the flower girl. When she reached what she believed to be the correct spot, she paused to imagine the diadem spider lying at her feet. Every muscle in her body tense, she lowered herself to the pavement. *What if the gruesome creature really did lie sprawled out here?* The thought repulsed her so much that she would not even permit herself to reach out and feel for its presence.

The noise of Oxford Circus grew deafening—it was a cacophony of motorcars, lorries and horse-drawn carriages. She covered her ears and considered the notion that the spider had metamorphosed back into her old adversary. *If I reach out my hand, I'll find myself touching the Arctic fox. Of course, and his coat and tail, they'll feel moist and warm from the waters of my womb.* With a sigh, she touched her cross and then dropped her trembling hand to the pendant dove. For the first time in her life, she paused to consider how innocent and how beautiful and how unfairly maligned a creature such as a fox was. *Truly, there could be no animal more deserving of love.*

A motorcar's horn blared, and for a moment, the cacophony sounded something like a brass fox-hunting bugle.

She touched her belly and melted into tears.

A set of footsteps approached her side. Could it be the flower girl? Whoever it was, the footfalls ceased.

'Never mind me any,' Anastasia spoke up. 'You can't help me. No one has the power to do that.' Anastasia blinked several times over. *What if it's Jack? What if he's come to make peace with me? Yes, I might as well imagine so.* Anastasia's body posture perked up.

'It must be lonely to be blind,' the stranger spoke up— the voice that of a youth. 'Still, you mustn't despair. Perhaps you ought to speak with an alienist, someone who could help you with your woes. I spoke to one, years ago. Fat lot of good it did me, though. But even so, it might work out well for *you.*' The stranger seemed to kneel beside her. 'Did you drop something? Are you looking for something? What about a button?'

Impulsively, Anastasia fumbled for the ailing fox. Of course, she found nothing there. Still, she longed to believe she could locate him. *How very good it will feel to trace my fingertips over the contours of his spine and ribs. And if the fragile fox rolls back upon his back, I'll press the palm of my hand all so gently against his belly. And then I'll listen to the beat of his heart until I'm overcome with delight.*

The friendly youth snapped his fingers. 'Are you looking for something? Did you drop something onto the pavement there?'

'Oh, yes, the miracle of life,' she answered. With that, she sought to gather the creature up into her arms—but there was no angelic fox spirit anywhere about.

The youth wrapped the warmth of his palm around her wrist. 'Let me help you. I'll take you wherever you wish to go.'

Lost in thoughts of beauteous foxes and hideous diadem spiders, Anastasia grew even more muddled. In her state of confusion, she pictured a graceful fox lying before her now yet transforming back into the gruesome diadem spider. As a shudder moved through her body, she broke loose from the youth's clutches. Then she wrapped her hands around her windpipe. For the longest time, she held her breath.

The youth tapped her knee then. 'What're you doing, love? You're giving me quite a fright. Stop that.'

Anastasia exhaled at last and removed her hands from her throat. 'Have you any idea how trying it is to be blind?'

'I can imagine.'

'At times, I can't help but go lost in terrible thoughts and sinister daydreams and any kind of confounding emotion. What do I do?'

'You've got to improve your *other* senses,' the youth told her. 'What about your sense of smell, or what about your ability to hear things? Once you hone all those other senses, I should think you'll be better able to distinguish between fantasy and actuality. Don't that sound right enough?'

Anastasia's belly ached and throbbed and pulsated violently. *I ask you.* For a time, she listened to the sounds of the city—the roar of the traffic, the summer breeze in the boughs of the plane trees. 'Are you still here?' she said.

No answer came, for the youth had departed. Or had he ever even stood there, and had he spoken a word?

Once more, Anastasia groped for the fox spirit. *How good it will feel to poke his ribs. His body will feel dry. Unreal, too, like a stuffed toy.* With a clenched smile, she pictured the desperate, heartrending expression sure to be etched into the creature's face and glazed glassy eyes. Laying a hand over her left breast, she pictured the pitiful entity's body dissolving into a heap of warm whistling dust. *How could anybody think to kill something so beautiful? And so innocent.*

The steady sound of footfalls approached, and a friendly gentleman helped her to her feet. Afterward, the do-gooder placed her support cane into her hand. After a brief conversation, he helped her back to Fiona's door.

Anastasia found her way inside, and with unsteady steps, made her way up the staircase and advanced down the familiar corridor. *Time for a much-needed nap. I'll dream of the future, better times. That's what I'll do.*

When she awoke, she did not quite know where she was. A part of her longed to believe she had travelled back in space and time—as if the deity had presented her with another chance to attend the gala out at Konstantinovsky Palace. *Oh yes, that's right. A great, wondrous miracle has happened. I'm back home in Saint Petersburg.* Trembling all over, she finally climbed out of bed and found her way over to the armoire— and as she opened the door, a salvo as of a splendid fireworks display rang out.

The noise repeated several more times until she recognised the din as nothing more than the backfire of some undependable motorcar. *Yes, that's all.* She forgot all about getting dressed, closed the armoire door and felt her way over to the window. There, for a fleeting moment, she thought she discerned the aroma of traditional Russian oven-baked apples. *Oh, the fine taste of cinnamon.* She bounced from foot to foot for a while and then stood still. *I'm in London now.*

One last time, the loud noise of the motorcar's backfire resounded. Then the motorcar's transmission slipped into gear, and the driver continued along on his way.

In the evening, she climbed back into bed. Still, every now and then, she woke up shrieking. Each time, she winced. *What if I wake Fiona? She'll be cross and rightly so. Any scholar reading for a business degree will require a great deal of sleep.*

Down the hallway, Fiona's clock struck nine o'clock—but the chime sounded all wrong, something like a dying cuckoo.

Three hours to midnight. Anastasia rolled onto her side. For a moment, she wondered if she felt a spider moving along her ankle. When the creature seemed to have vanished, she felt for the bedchamber wall. *It's so oily.* She placed her palm flush against a section of peeling paint and breathed in. *If only I had someone to talk to.*

She imagined the flower girl standing alongside the footboard. 'Tell me what's what,' Anastasia implored her. 'Why did the fox transform himself into a diadem spider, and why did the fox do it without any fanfare? What do you think?'

The imaginary flower girl caressed Anastasia's foot. 'I think the fox did what he did to affright you. Put another way, I think your unconscious means to put you through one last battle. A test to force you to make one last push.'

Anastasia removed her hand from the wall and stared with her blind eyes in the direction of the footboard. 'But why?' she said.

'Maybe your unconsciousness has great plans for you. Deep within your mystical psyche, your beautiful Huguenot mind, a part of you wishes to inspire . . . greatness.'

Anastasia sat up, crawled to the footboard and gripped the cracked wood. 'So, have I got some remarkable purpose to my life?'

'Maybe you do.' The imaginary flower girl traced a fingertip over Anastasia's hands, her knuckles. 'There must be a reason why your unconscious mind has always tormented you. Could it be your true self has always longed to make you suffer so that someday you'll learn the way to redemption?'

~

London. 27 June 1918.

After a long hard day teaching herself the Moon alphabet for the blind, Anastasia set her papers to the side and fell asleep. But then she awoke. Had she heard something? She caressed her neck awhile, wondering why her throat burned.

When she drifted back to sleep, she slept as soundly as she ever had—until a voice cried out as loudly as the flower girl did.

Once more, Anastasia awoke and opened her blind eyes. *Who could be responsible for all that commotion?* At first, she wondered if the tumult might have been some local drunkard out in the street. She stumbled over to the window and listened. *No.* Her throat burned, as if she herself had cried out. Perhaps she had, and maybe she had been doing so all night long. *Yes, I think so.* She pressed her fingers to her lips and felt her way back into bed.

Downstairs, the front door opened, and the noise of footfalls—it sounded like two people—proceeded into the foyer. The visitors climbed the stairway, their footsteps resounding as they continued down the hall and up to her door.

Has Fiona brought Jack over for a visit? As a soft summer breeze stirred the beaded tassels dangling from the ornamental wreath upon the wall, Anastasia sat up. 'Fiona?'

'Don't be alarmed,' Fiona told her.

'Where did you go?' Anastasia asked. 'Have I been crying out in my sleep?'

'*Yes.* That's why I went off to find someone to come have a look at you. Anyway, I've got me a visiting nurse. Her name's Miss Entwistle. From Edmund Arrowsmith House.'

'Never heard of it.'

'Yes, well, it's a good, well-provided Catholic shelter not far from Marble Arch. Sorry, but I couldn't find a right proper Huguenot caregiver. Not at this ungodly hour.'

Miss Entwistle approached the bed, and when the woman dropped something onto the floor, Anastasia imagined it was the nurse's specialist bag.

Miss Entwistle checked Anastasia's pulse. 'What's all the trouble?' The woman's tone seemed full of despair, yet her voice contained a faint giggle. 'Have you any idea just what ails you? Describe the symptoms in your own words.'

Anastasia drew a deep breath. As calmly as possible, she rubbed her palms together and related the whole of her story. When she concluded the tale, she rested her neck against the crest rail of her bed. 'I don't suppose an everyday nurse could help me any. Some kind of seer, that's what I require.'

At first, Miss Entwistle said nothing. Neither did she move. Had the harrowing story dumbfounded her?

Anastasia placed her hands upon her lap, wondering if someday she ought to consult a professor of psychology. She imagined herself waiting in his quiet anteroom. *Quite soon, the scholar will come along and bring me into his office. Then he'll sit down at his rolltop desk. And then he'll tell me all about his qualifications.* Gradually, Anastasia's thoughts drifted back to the matter at hand. 'What are you thinking?' she asked, hiding her hands beneath her blanket.

By the sound of it, Miss Entwistle fussed with her

specialist bag. Then the nurse grew quiet. Gently, she tapped Anastasia's shoulder. 'I think I might be able to help you. As a matter of fact, a long time ago, I rather fancied myself something of a seer.'

'Oh? Does the Papacy permit such things? Take care the Roman Pontiff doesn't accuse you of heresy.'

Miss Entwistle did not reply. Instead, by the sound of it, she wandered over to the window. 'Listen, please. A long time ago, when I was your age or thereabouts, I longed to join the Sisterhood. Yes, it's true. And you'll never believe the name of the nunnery where I studied.'

Anastasia removed her hands from beneath her blanket. 'I'll probably believe anything you say.'

'It was a fine Italian abbey built by a family from the Duchy of Milan. Anyway, they called it *Chapel Sant'Anastasia*.'

'Oh?' Anastasia's bottom lip trembled. 'So, did anything happen there? By any chance, did you meet someone like . . . *me?*'

'*Yes!*' Miss Entwistle answered. 'One day, a peasant girl from Genoa stole into the tomato garden and collapsed at my feet. And then the peasant girl muttered something about a terrible creature that once took refuge in her soul. A powerful, maddening spirit.'

'What kind of spirit?' Anastasia asked, lifting her head from the crest rail.

'*Una volpe rossa*,' the nurse answered. 'A red fox. A lecherous ghostlike one.'

'Oh?' The summer breeze stirring the wreath anew, Anastasia climbed out of bed and felt her way over to the window. 'Please tell me more. How could it be that a fox might take refuge inside a girl like that? Could it be that the poor Genovese girl had suffered great trauma in her childhood? Perhaps she once experienced some nighttime terror-tantrum, or a waking dream, or a waking nightmare. Or maybe someone, a mischievous little girl, had played a terrible trick on her. What happened?'

'The poor girl didn't tell us too much more. She mentioned an exorcist who had laid hands upon her. Yes, and the peasant girl told us that afterward she had experienced the most unbearable ache in the bones of her face. From what I could gather, she intuited the fact that the exorcist had not simply contented himself to destroy the entity. In addition, the exorcist planted deep inside her body the seeds of a remarkable transformation. As if he hoped to transfigure her into something boasting great prophetic powers.'

Anastasia rested her brow against the casing and breathed in to find the nighttime breeze smelled of toffee apples and perhaps even a trace of ginger root.

Miss Entwistle ambled back toward the bed. 'I'm sorry that I ever mentioned the peasant girl. I fear that I've confounded you. If so, I didn't mean to do so. On the contrary, I only hoped to . . .'

Gradually, the scent of summer flowers and spice plants and fresh ginger root came to dominate the toffee apples.

Anastasia lifted her brow from the casing and licked her lips. *What a delight, the fragrance of ginger root.* Anastasia tapped her pendant dove. 'Maybe there's a divine reason why you should be the one to come visit me tonight. Maybe the Good Lord preordained our meeting.' She dropped her hands to her sides and fixed her blind eyes on the ceiling. 'Please tell me more about the blind peasant girl. What happened to her?'

'No, I've said enough already. Now then, let me take your temperature.'

'No,' Anastasia said. 'You've already helped me more than you will ever know. If nothing else, you've confirmed my calling. The King of Glory must've chosen me for some divine purpose.' She lurched back toward the bed and groped for the woman. Then, feeling like an irate parent trying to discipline some unruly child, she wrapped her hand around the nurse's forearm. 'Tell me everything you know.'

When Miss Entwistle failed to say anything, Anastasia squeezed—until the nurse cried out.

Fiona snapped her fingers. 'What're you doing?' she said. 'Do you mean to assail your own visiting nurse? You ought to be heartily ashamed.'

Anastasia reached for Miss Entwistle's chest—at which point her fingertips brushed across what seemed to be a cameo pendant dangling from a little chain around the nurse's neck. *Oh.* Anastasia held her hand flush against the nurse's chest and pressed down, the contours of the cameo pendant digging into her palm. 'What became of the peasant girl?' she asked. 'Go on. Tell me already.'

'According to all the rumours, the peasant girl could not accept the notion that some great miracle had happened. She believed that a powerful enchantress had placed the red fox inside her for life. And the peasant girl swore the red fox meant to infect her with the blue sickness. As odd as it seems, the peasant girl *disbelieved* she could ever triumph over the creature. So, in a temper, she killed herself.'

'She did *what*?'

'You heard me right,' Miss Entwistle answered. 'Please don't ask me how she did it, though. I'd prefer to spare you the lurid details.'

Anastasia dropped her hand from the nurse's chest. Her bladder burning as if filled with lye, she fumbled for her support cane. *Hurry now.* Her free hand reaching out this way and that, she made her way into the hallway and down to the water closet.

By the time she found her way back to her room, the nurse had departed—and Fiona had gone downstairs. Anastasia pretended that the nurse stood not far from the armoire. 'Does it vex you that a Huguenot girl like me ought to have such a great destiny?'

'No,' the imaginary nurse said. 'I despise no one. If you were born to be some kind of prophetess, why should I be the least bit jealous?'

Her body tense, Anastasia groped her way back to the window. She breathed in, only to find that no pleasant scent remained in the air—neither the scent of ginger root nor the scent of toffee apples. *Oh God, how I miss the toffee apples.* She tested her palm: already, the contours of the cameo pendant had faded. The absence made her hunger for transcendent hope such as she never had before, so she lifted her blind eyes to the ceiling. 'Ave Maria.'

XVIII.

The North of England. 8 July 1918.

Late that night, just after midnight, Jack lay in bed, marvelling at the sweet taste that had only just awoken at the back of his mouth. *What's that?* As the taste seemed to spread to the very tip of his tongue, he wondered if the effect followed from faint traces of fresh clover honey in the summer breeze. *Who knows?* He smacked his lips, and when he swallowed, the treacly taste in his mouth made him think of sugarcane growing wild upon some forgotten Greek island. Little by little, a feeling of elation came upon him. From down the hallway, the wind harps resounded—and the arresting melody made him close his eyes.

The nighttime breeze kicked up, and as the music of the wind harps adopted a faster time signature, the current made some of his sheet music tumble off the tallboy.

At the same time, the hypnotic hum of a motorcar's engine drew closer and closer—as if the driver must be pulling up to the nursing home's back door. Sure enough, a motorcar stopped to idle beneath Jack's window.

He opened his eyes and sat up, for how soothing the rumble of the motorcar's engine was; moreover, the glow of the headlamps shone through the window frame—and in so doing, the fine gleam created a symmetrically perfect pattern of light extending from the north wall across the better part of the ceiling.

Down below, one of the motorcar's doors opened and then slammed shut—and Jack heard what sounded like someone opening the boot.

'Why don't you take your shoulder bag and your lute as well?' a stern, fatherly voice said. 'Don't trouble yourself with the rest. The attendant should be willing to take the wardrobe trunk.'

Jack's chest burned. He leapt off the bed. By the time he reached the window, however, both the newcomer and the attendant had already continued inside. The motorcar, a black, manual-transmission Phoenix, pulled away slowly.

The return to darkness and quietude made Jack shiver. Given how hypnotic the hum of the engine had sounded and given how pleasing all those erstwhile patterns of light had been, his room seemed all so lifeless now. *If only the bloody motorcar had idled below me window all through the night. That would've been grand.* He rubbed the nape of his neck, and then he looked up and cocked his ear.

Two pairs of footsteps approached from the direction of the stairwell. Had the hospital director chosen to house the newcomer in the empty room across the hall? There could be no doubt about it, for the footsteps stopped just outside Jack's door.

A moment or two passed by. 'I think my lamp's gone out,' a young lady's voice announced, her accent vaguely Greek as much as anything.

301

Impulsively, Jack smoothed out his nightshirt and checked his hair. *The newcomer; it's a bird.* His chest burning even more, he inched over to the door. *Why don't I open it a crack and have a look at the girl?* He reached the door, placed his hand on the brass knob, and gripped it tightly. *Open the door.* Before long, he did so—but just a crack. *Hello.*

The young lady stood quite tall, her skin pale and immaculate. Most miraculous of all, the gods had blessed her every feature with seemingly perfect symmetry. Even her long silky sable hair looked as if not a strand had ever once fallen out of place.

Like any other vain youth, he considered her style of dress. *Look at that.* Her pearl-white gown seemed to be bereft of a solitary wrinkle. *A gown fit for Omphale.* All tension left his body, but then he shook all over as he wondered if the young lady might be a Greek witch. Even if the young lady were not a sorceress, nevertheless, she had to be less than healthful. *Why else would she be here? For all I know, she's a bloody murderous siren.* Holding his breath, he sought to close the door.

Just in time, she turned in his direction. 'I'm Miss Moonfleet. Dorian Moonfleet.'

He flashed a crooked smile and opened his door wide. Scratching at a little bump upon his scalp, he stepped forward. 'I'm Jack,' he said, breathing faster and faster.

'What do you think of this madhouse?' she asked with a nervous twitch.

'It's not so bad. Sometimes it gets a wee bit lonely around here, that's all.'

'I don't mind loneliness. I've always got my lute. It's a genuine *bazouki.* Hey, do you know if the kitchen ever serves Greek spinach pie?'

Before Jack could answer, the attendant marched back from the end of the hall and handed a light bulb to Miss Moonfleet. 'There you are.'

'Thank you kindly.' Having left her shoulder bag and lute in the corridor, Miss Moonfleet entered her darkened room. A light soon shone, but then the room went dark again—as if she had switched off the lamp.

Despite the oddity of it all, Jack helped the attendant to bring Miss Moonfleet's things inside.

She pulled up the sash. As if mesmerised, she gazed out toward the ruins of a priory standing some two hundred yards away. Then, her nervous twitch growing worse, she kicked at the east wall's skirting board. What to make of her tragic affectations? Could it be she presently suffered a mild epileptic event, or could it be her parents had forced her to undergo electroshock at some point in her past? A method of treatment like that could have accounted for recurring spasms.

The attendant grabbed hold of Jack's arm, guided him back into the hallway and then closed Miss Moonfleet's door. 'Go to sleep,' the attendant told him.

The rest of the night passed by uneventfully enough, and when morning came, Jack accompanied Miss Moonfleet to the dining hall. There, they sat down at a table that wobbled.

Twice, she twitched. Then she flashed an expression that seemed to indicate perplexion.

He wondered if he might confide in her some of his troubles. After giving her a quick glance, he picked at his creamy haddock omelette. 'Do you wish to know what I'm doing in this here brand of Bedlam?'

'No. Don't tell me.'

'Right.' Sitting back, he breathed in the aroma of gooseberries presently spreading through the crowded dining hall—and now his mouth filled with the same sweet taste he had registered the night before. *Treacle. Bloody treacle.* He shifted in his chair.

As he did, Miss Moonfleet tapped upon the table with a marmalade spoon. 'On second thought, *yes*, go on and tell me why you're here.'

He continued to pick at his omelette. *How to explain me habit of losing meself in the madness of illusory love? If I tell her all that, she'll think of me as something shameful. Even worse, she'll fear me. And then maybe she'll never speak to me again.*

A woman wearing a felt bowler sat down two tables over. Her expression inscrutable, she reached the tip of her index finger up beneath the brim of her hat and gazed out across the dining hall.

As Jack watched, she seemed to apply increasing pressure to her temple. He intuited all, and he had to blush. *That bloody peculiar woman, she's attempting to send someone a series of telepathic messages. Blast.* As a dozen beads of sweat broke out on his brow, he wondered who the woman's intended target might be. Mostly, he thought back to his own sordid past—until his hands shook.

Thankfully, Miss Moonfleet concentrated on her poached eggs—apparently not noticing his torment.

He drew a deep breath. 'Do you see that woman in the bowler?' he said. 'She's another patient here. Anyway, I think she's madly in love with one of the other patients. Yes, and she's attempting to send him a telepathic message.'

'Does that trouble you?' Dorian said.

'Yes. Someone ought to tell that mad woman in the bowler to put a bung in it. A healthful person does not content himself to believe in telepathy. Isn't it better to talk to the object of one's affections? That's what I do.' Jack finished his omelette, certain his comments had proven him to be a proper gentleman—someone worthy of love.

Midmorning, he received a telegram from home; in the dispatch, his father hinted at his wish to bring him back to Bloomsbury in a few weeks' time.

Pushing the telegram into his pocket, Jack wandered into the day room and sat at the cabinet upright. Twice, he tapped the key corresponding to D double flat. *How to leave Miss Moonfleet? I'd better stay the hell away from that skirt lest I fall for her.* Two more times, he tapped D double flat. And there he sat, brooding until late afternoon—when the scent of clover honey came drifting throughout the nursing home.

Finally, the pleasing scent enticed him to step outside. As he did, the back of his mouth filled with that same sweet taste from before—ancient Greek sugarcane. *Maybe it's a sign from the gods themselves. Maybe they've sent Dorian to me . . . to be me bride.*

A mute swan approached the adjacent marsh and let out a hoarse whistle that echoed across the hospital grounds, and as the summer breeze rattled the boughs of the Indian-bean tree, a fleet of moorhens came fluttering this way and that.

A windborne fragment of horseweed drifted by, entangling itself in Jack's long brown hair. He removed the telegram from his trouser pocket and reread everything. *Bloody hell, I'm going home. London Town.* Jack shook his head. What if his going home were to preclude him from growing close to this Miss Dorian Moonfleet, and what if he never encountered anyone like her ever again? He stuffed the telegram back into his trousers, and then he studied the windmill standing atop the hill. As a tattered cloth sail snapped in the summer breeze, he realised the door stood ajar. *Hello. That's odd.* He climbed the footpath through the Queen Anne's lace. When he reached the windmill, he discovered Miss Moonfleet standing just inside the doorway. 'How'd you get in?' he asked, crossing the threshold.

'The attendant gave me the key.' She held it up and then sat with her back against the door frame.

A strong breeze awoke the blades of the windmill, and as they creaked and rasped, he sat beside the brake wheel.

Miss Moonfleet struggled with her nervous twitch for a while, her right eye blinking repeatedly.

With a twitch of his own, he traced a few patterns in the dusty floorboards—until the tip of his finger shone black.

She pointed at the doodles. 'They look like little black truffles. Just like the ones our kitchen maid serves alongside her old-fashioned shrimp Mykonos.'

He traced a few more truffles. 'Why'd your parents send you away here?'

As if to take the weight off her backbone, Miss Moonfleet repositioned herself. Then she grinned. 'I'm just like you. And I know because I asked the attendant, and he told me all about you.'

He looked to the wind shaft, then the spindle, then back at her. As the sweet taste at the back of his mouth gradually spread to the tip of his tongue, he grew still.

Miss Moonfleet looked deep into his eyes. 'I have a soothing effect on you.'

'Yes, I think so.' He licked his lips. Until that moment, he had believed nothing more nor less than Dr Allcock's hypnosis techniques and therapeutic affirmations would be strong enough to counterpoise both his long-standing sorrows and natural diffidence. *But no, no. A lady friend, that's all I require. Yes. Someone to take Anastasia's place.*

In the evening, Jack accompanied Miss Moonfleet to the

dining hall. As crowded as it happened to be that night, they had to sit at a table situated below a flush-mounted ceiling fixture that shone down a harsh glare. As he sat there, he could not help but think of the moon shining down her blinding light. *And why? For no other reason than to beguile Endymion.* The sweet sensation of sugarcane lingering in his mouth, Jack downed some of his steamed pudding. No matter the heat of the ceiling fixture beating down upon his brow, he ate his supper. When he was done, he sat back. 'Do me a favour. Cut me hair.'

'Why? Are you feeling better? More social?'

'Yes, already you've changed me. At least I think so.'

Together, he and Miss Moonfleet walked up through the stairwell and down the length of the dimly lit corridor. When they reached his room, she sat him on the edge of his bed and then darted off to find her shears. As soon as she returned, she did away with his long unruly mop of hair. She gave him a classic side part and then retired for the night.

~

The North of England. Jack's Last Night at Plumbland, 18 July 1918.

Just after midnight, Jack lay down in bed. *Come the morning light, I'm gone. Father means to collect me, and that'll be that.* He thought back a few days. *That was the very last time I spoke with Miss Dorian Moonfleet. Will I ever speak to her again?* For the past few days and nights, he had avoided her. *Soon, I'll be back in London. And then I'll probably forget about her.* In time, he fell asleep—and Pegasus invaded his dreams. *The mythical horse brings him to Syntagma Square, landing* beside that glorious marble statue of Ptolemy. 'Heed this sacred message,' Pegasus announces. 'I command you to plant a kiss on Miss Moonfleet's lips this very night. If you do, I shall bless you. Indeed, I shall help you publish your music. And you will be the most celebrated composer since Orpheus.'

And now Jack cannot help but laugh. 'I should be so lucky,' he says, thinking of his onetime make-believe friend, Mr Sylvius. 'Tell me something. What's happened to the old footman?'

'I trampled him to death,' Pegasus answers. 'Mr Sylvius, he'll never trouble you again.'

Jack awoke from the vision with a jerk. He studied the darkness awhile. The taste of ancient Greek sugarcane growing at the very back of his mouth, he tossed and turned a few times. He wondered if Pegasus had brought about the sensation to entice him into heeding his commands. *Sleep.* He could not manage to, though. Even if his own psyche had conjured the dream, he could not deny the urge to obey. *If I fail to do so, I'll feel hexed.* Yawning, he checked his timepiece and realised that the midnight hour had come and gone. By now, Miss Moonfleet would be asleep. Despite this, he climbed out of bed. *I'll wake the girl. No matter how daunting it might be to talk to a bird, it'd be good to have someone to love.* He slipped into his robe and dragged himself out into the corridor.

Across the dimly lit hall, Miss Moonfleet's door stood ajar—and her darkened room emitted an inexplicable glow, just like a picture show in which the director had not wholly understood concepts such as realism and source lighting.

When he peeked inside, Jack realised she was gone. *Where could she be at this hour?* He studied the view through her window—the derelict priory some two hundred yards off, the structure all aglow with a blaze of creamy-yellow light.

What's all this?

A figure in silhouette appeared, outlined against the light within one of the windows.

Could that be her? As he mulled things over, the taste of the sugarcane spread from the back of his mouth to the tip of his tongue. *That must be Pegasus again, hoping to enthral me and get me all excited about Dorian and . . .*

From the west, a herd of wild horses happened along— and as one of them stopped to nibble at a little patch of clover, a terrific ray of moonlight shone across the creature's point of shoulder. Suddenly, the fine beast shone the colour of silver—from the horse's forelock and mane down to its hip and croup.

King of Glory. Look there. No matter how foolish the passing fancy, Jack interpreted the powerful animal's presence as a sign that he ought to trust in Miss Dorian Moonfleet. Even if the affectionate friendship with her had developed all so quickly, there was no danger in that. *As fast as wild horses, we've grown together. But so what?* With an alert gaze and furrowed brow, he marched downstairs to the grand vestibule and ran outside.

Spooked, the horses galloped off. As Jack watched, the light in the priory window shone brighter. Had the mysterious Miss Dorian Moonfleet lit a few more candles?

The cool breeze whipping through his nightshirt, he shuffled his feet. *Does me hair look right? Probably not.* He footslogged forward like a soldier, and when he reached the priory door, he called out her name. Even though she failed to answer, he stumbled into the darkness of the antechamber and ascended the stairway to the brightly lit room. 'Enjoying your summer?'

She did not answer. Nor did she greet him. She lifted

the hem of her long flowing skirt and took hold of her lute, settling herself in a feather-back chair. Once she had adjusted the tuning keys, she played a simple étude in D minor. What beauty the way her much-too-long fingers danced as she plucked the horsehair strings.

Though he had heard her play, he never appreciated just how effortless her talent was until this moment. Grinning like a fool, he wondered if the gods must have created her for no other purpose than to play music. *How do I kiss someone so bloody magnificent?* He thumbed his ear, wondering if he even looked presentable in his nightshirt. *I'm a minger.*

A low powerful rumble rolled through the walls. Was the ancient priory crumbling apart? Only when the disturbance grew slow and steady did he realise what the noise was: the wild horses had returned at full gallop. *It was nothing. Nothing more than hoofbeats.*

Her lips parting, Miss Moonfleet ceased to play. 'Are you going home tomorrow?' she asked.

'I'm afraid so. I think me old man found an alienist willing to see me, and he probably charges reasonable rates.'

'Someday I'll join you down there in London. Won't that be splendid? *London.* That's the heart and soul of the English life.'

'Yes, of course.' He nodded like a simpleton trying to look clever.

'We'll cobble together a concert band, and we'll light the Thames on fire,' Miss Moonfleet said. 'Maybe someday we'll play Royal Albert Hall.' She tapped upon the lute's tailpiece a few times. 'Not long ago, I heard a rumour the Parlophone Company Limited means to expand its operations. If so, we ought to ask them to press our records. Let's do a version of this one here.' In a soft, honey-coated voice, she sang:

Pease porridge hot, pease porridge cold,
Pease porridge in the pot, nine days old;
Some like it hot, some like it cold,
Some like it in the pot, nine days old.

He studied the cracks in the walls. 'Hardly worth a listen, a song like that.' He shoved his hands into his robe's pockets. *How to trust such a mercurial character?* Slowly, he creaked over to the window. *I've got to trust her.*

Outside, the horse from before still shone an otherworldly silver. And now the beast looked off into the distance and snorted, as if the animal had only just espied a rival.

Jack imagined the rival to be a ridgling, no less, trifling with some splendid buckskin mare.

Plainly anxious, the aggrieved horse kicked at the earth. On and on, too, the creature snorted.

Miss Moonfleet tapped upon the lute's tailpiece again. 'I wish you trusted me,' she said, twitching again. 'Whether it's true love or not, an everlasting bond begins with *trust.*'

A throbbing awoke below his ribcage. *Does* she *intend to seduce* me? Now he trembled like a condemned captive, so he held fast to the sill and prayed he might soon detect some kind of faint fluctuation—a hint the priory did indeed teeter on the brink of collapse. *If so, I'll have to run for dear life. Wouldn't want to be crushed to death here on a night like this. No, no.*

Miss Moonfleet sat back. 'Maybe I've got it all wrong,' she said. 'Maybe love's a game as much as anything. And if the gallant aims to prevail, he's got to be clever. Most needful of all, he's got to be *insolent.* That's the way a lad proves himself to be stout-hearted.'

Frowning, Jack glanced at Miss Moonfleet and debated

whether he ought to criticise her way of speaking. Though he did not know why, he found her tone a bit cheeky and unbecoming of a comely girl like her.

'And a chap must be right self-assured,' she continued, 'or else he'll never have enough nerve to gather some fine damsel into his arms and kiss her.'

Jack smiled, but his heart pounded. 'Why the flippant tone? A girl like you ought to talk gracefully.' The sweet taste in his mouth growing stronger, he wondered if this might be the perfect time to kiss her.

She twitched. When she regained her composure, she stood and performed what looked to be a traditional Greek sidestep. *Does she want me to dance? Yes, obviously.* Careful to avoid eye contact, he turned back and traced the tip of his finger along the length of the windowsill.

Down below, the silvery horse beat a hasty retreat. And now its adversary came into view. The rival proved to be a silver stallion glowing brightly against the night.

Below Jack's ribcage, the throbbing grew worse—so much so that he pressed his lips together to keep from groaning. *Take your quarrel somewhere else. Please.*

The two stalwarts stood upon their hind legs and smote one another with their forearms and hooves.

Miss Moonfleet must have heard all the commotion. When she joined him at the window, she looked down and gasped. 'It never fails,' she announced in a cheeky tone. 'There's always some bubbly jock scheming to claim your mare.'

He could have kissed Miss Moonfleet just then, but how to know if she truly wanted him to do such a thing? He closed his eyes, and he thought of Anastasia—the telepathic bond that he once believed to have existed between them. *What a pity that love cannot work that way. Like magic.*

In the morning, Jack introduced Dorian to his father. Then an attendant followed the three of them into town, and no one spoke—until Jack stopped beside a wayfaring tree. 'I want all of ye to know I've reached me turning point. Ye got no reason to doubt me none.' A gnarled piece of twistwood lying at his feet, Jack looked into his father's eyes. 'As the summer days and nights pass by, I'll be growing stronger. You got me pledge.' Jack kicked the piece of twistwood into the brush. Then he took Miss Moonfleet's hand and looked deep into her eyes. 'Someday soon, all the agony of me loneliness will no longer be strong enough to conjure the madness of illusory love. And we'll be proper friends and talk everything through.'

Miss Moonfleet grinned and nodded. She picked at some of the wayfaring tree, and then she looked at the sky. 'Please, whatever you do, don't forget me. When I come to London, we'll write songs together.' A piece of tree litter fell onto the neckline of her summer gown, but she didn't even seem to notice. 'Together, you and me, we'll be proper buskers,' she said.

'Of course,' he told her. 'Maybe we'll get ourselves a gig at the Bessarabia Ballroom and places like that where the people welcome experimental music and all. Or maybe we could rent some big picture house and have ourselves a concert right there.' The attendant marched along, so Jack collected his bags and followed the rest of the party past a few hedgerows and country houses and tall English oaks.

Down at the railway station, as the attendant spoke to Jack's father about the war and a certain battle unfolding yet in the Champagne region of France, Dorian drew close to Jack and twitched. 'We've got to look after one another,' she told him.

'That's right,' Jack said. 'Maybe if we talk things through, we'll not be ashamed of nothing neither. You and me, we'll preserve one another's honour.'

'Yes, that's right,' Miss Moonfleet said. 'When we reunite, we'll heal each other, and we'll get along quite well.' With a look of calm in her eyes, she presented Jack with a tortoiseshell plectrum and closed his palm around the finely wrought implement.

The conductor opened the train's doors and welcomed any and all passengers.

Along with his father, Jack boarded the train. Once he had taken his place beside the window, Jack opened his palm and stared at the plectrum. The little curio made him imagine he heard music—perhaps a beautiful young lady sitting right behind him and humming the tune to his composition, *Anastasia's Midnight Song*. He went lost in thought and pretended Anastasia herself must be the one sitting behind him. 'So, are your eyes still coopered?' he asked over his shoulder in a whisper. 'You mustn't let yourself get to feeling all of a doodah, eh? Still, I guess it's got to be right trying to buzz about purblindly the way you do with your eyes having grown knackered.'

Jack's father sat down beside him. 'It's times like these I wish I'd paid for First Class,' he muttered. 'No train line ever gives the Standard Class enough legroom.'

Jack ignored him and went back to thinking about Anastasia. Perhaps by now the fleeting apparition had just begun to dematerialise. 'Goodbye,' he whispered over his shoulder. When the train pulled out, he turned to the window and waved to Miss Moonfleet, where she stood near the mechanical platform display. 'Orchids to you, dear! Orchids to you!'

XIX.

London. 29 August 1918.

In the darkness before dawn, Anastasia rolled over and spoke up. 'I've got to be hopeful,' she said, talking in her sleep. 'I've got to achieve redemption. I've got to find some kind of art to perform. Something to bring me bittersweet satisfaction, a new direction.'

An hour later, when she awoke, she could no longer accept the fact she had lost the power of sight. *Have I gone irreversibly blind? No.* Breathless, she sat up and blinked. *God willing, my vision should restore itself soon enough.*

Much to her chagrin, the all-encompassing shroud of darkness remained—her blindness as gentle and as merciless and as indomitable as ever. Straining her sightless eyes, she studied the blackness. And now she gasped, for she found the stubborn nonappearance of things all so *mythical*—as if the absence of light persisted for no other reason than to teach her something esoteric and profound regarding the presence of evil. She fingered her Huguenot cross and pendant dove. 'Where does the idea of evil come from?' she asked, poking her belly.

'Why must you ask me such things? I'm but a lowly diadem spider. Could it be you don't feel sated? Perhaps you yearn for the sense of fulfillment that comes with having learned some great lesson. Maybe you think the epiphany ought to grant you a purpose in life.'

She threw the blanket to the side and dropped her feet to the floor. 'This unforgiving incurable blindness, it's unbearable. The darkness imprisons me. That's right, it proscribes my doing anything with my life.'

The diadem spider remained silent, and she found its restraint confounding. 'Tell me the origins of evil. Teach me, why don't you? Where do all the malevolent things like violence and perniciousness come from?'

Again, the diadem spider remained silent—as if the creature had no intention of teaching her anything.

'Tell me something. Have you no inclination other than to prey upon me? Just what might be your great purpose in life?' She flexed her fingers, expecting the nightmarish creature to launch into a frenzied sermon. 'Please say something. Maybe you suppose the presence of evil follows from something in nature. What about the predator instinct, or the ways of the hunter and the hunted? Do you know anything about the art of thinning the herd, the preservation of nature's delicate balance?'

The insidious diadem spider said nothing, the only sound the whistle of the morning breeze sailing into the room.

A moment later, Anastasia heard Fiona's footfalls going down the staircase. Anastasia smoothed her nightdress. *Shall I ask Fiona about the origins of evil? No, she'll content herself with some dodgy liberal theory. She'll insist all those oligarchs with all their riches must be the oppressors and all those poor*

souls out in the rookery only ever commit crimes of desperation.
Anastasia never thought that way, however, for how could
leftist theory ever explain away the honest-minded poor?
For that matter, how could leftist theory and socialism
reconcile the fact plenty of moneyed people choose to live as
philanthropists and never oppress anyone? Given the obvious
limits of political radicalism, there had to be some proper
intellectual explanation for the origins of evil.

Anastasia kicked her feet awhile, revisited the phenomenon
of the predator instinct in nature and then patted her belly.
'The idea of evil—could it be nothing more than a biproduct
of hominid evolution?'

The diadem spider hissed. 'Let me sleep.'

From somewhere out across Oxford Circus, the peal
of church bells resounded—and what a stark, solemn
hymn. Then, no sooner had the bells fallen silent than the
most unsettling clamour commenced—what sounded
like gunshots.

In time, she convinced herself it was nothing more
than a motorcar with a failing exhaust muffler. Her fingers
trembling, she reached her hand into the dark space that
surrounded her on all sides. *I'm all alone here.* She crawled
over to the footboard and curled into a ball. '*Dieu aide moi,*'
she whispered. '*Oui. Á present.*'

If only some deity had answered her childlike prayer. Nothing
happened, though, and the warm summer morn dragged on.

She sat by her bedchamber window and prayed anew. A
thousand times over, she pleaded for some divine force to
grant her true purpose to her life.

At one o'clock, Fiona sought to alleviate her nerves
by bringing her a slice of fresh butter pie. 'Why must you
sit there with a dreamy expression? Do you aim to starve

yourself? Have a bite.'

'No, I doubt a treat like this should do me any good,' Anastasia told her, sniffing at the savoury dish.

'What about some lemon-curd tarts?' Fiona asked. 'Or I could make you some shortbread biscuits.'

Anastasia placed the dish on the windowsill. 'Where does evil come from? Do you think it might be nothing more than an accident of physiology? Maybe some people suffer from rather low blood-sugar levels, and that's why they commit terrible crimes. Or maybe some people can't help but develop a brain lesion, and that's why they snap and do something awful. What do you think?'

'I know,' Fiona said. 'I learned this back at Saint Paul's Girls' School. *Hubris*. Arrogance against the gods. That's Man's one great flaw. Yes, I'm quite sure of it. We're all of us haunted by the very worst kind of insolence.'

'You're not serious, are you? Besides, no one could ever be more arrogant toward the gods than the kind who attend public universities like the London School of Economics.'

Fiona laughed at that, as if unfazed. 'Yes, of course, what could be more prideful than an academic? Still, I think you ought to get yourself an education. Or at least a proper tutor. If you want, I could find a girl to come around and help you with your Moon-script lessons.'

'*Yes*,' Anastasia agreed. 'Someday it would be good to go back to reading books, but even so, just now, I've got to settle my affairs. And I've got to find some kind of purpose to my existence.'

'Maybe someday you'll found a Moon-type newspaper. Wouldn't that be good? There's so much happening all over the world. The Great War, for one. Yes, and the Russian Civil War, too, all the executions and such.'

Anastasia turned toward the window and let the breeze blow through her fringe. Not one week earlier, Fiona had told her what had happened to the House of Romanov. Three days later, Fiona had read the evening edition of the *Daily Express* out loud—reciting every last word of an especially grim article describing the recent North Russia Intervention. Even now, the thought of famished British soldiers billeted in Arkhangelsk had Anastasia consumed with fear.

Her belly throbbed, meanwhile, as if the diadem spider wished to challenge her to try to expel it from her womb.

Her thoughts drifted back to the miscarriage—and the memory of the whole trauma made her think of Captain Holywell. Her blind eyes glazing over, she pictured the handsome officer wandering the jungles of India. *What time of day would it be in a place like that? Does he ever intend to see me again? No, he never loved me.* Gently, the breeze made a section of the curtain lace glide across her cheekbone—and the sensation made her laugh sensually.

Down below, the distinctive scent of fresh flowers passed by the window. Still, there was no way to tell if the flower girl was responsible—for she did not sing.

As the breeze continued to play through her fringe, Anastasia revisited the past—the train journey from Saint Petersburg, the box containing the volcanic glass. *I should've asked Svetlana to explain the origins of evil.*

The breeze died down, and Anastasia rubbed her belly and thought of the diadem spider inside her. 'What're you doing down there? Do you mean to drive me into a state of frenzy? Oh, why must I feel this compulsion to believe in you?'

~

Later that Same Day.

Anastasia resolved to seek professional consultation, so she asked Fiona to help her to the stately opulent manor that housed Westminster Spiritualist Society. *If anyone might be able to resolve my predicament, they ought to be the ones.*

When she reached the front door, she fumbled for Fiona's forearm. 'Go now,' Anastasia told her. Once Fiona had departed, Anastasia lifted her blind eyes to the sky. 'Let me taste proper redemption,' she prayed. 'Hope alone should never be enough. Help me *transform.* Yes, help me to be as peaceful and as quiet and as meditative as . . .' She paused now, for she could swear she detected the presence of someone approaching—someone reeking of dust.

'Don't trouble yourself to rap upon the door,' a sultry but monotone woman's voice spoke up. 'I've been to every entranceway, ah, but no one answers.'

Anastasia remained silent. Had she only imagined the voice? Instinctively, she crossed her arms and hunched her shoulders.

The woman drew closer. 'Could you spare me some lolly? You'll get it back on the morrow, and that's the truth of it. I'm no cat on testy dodge. My great uncle, he's dying down there in Strasbourg. That said, he's promised to wire my inheritance any day now. That's why you've got no cause to fret none. I'll recompense you properly. Just as soon as the cable gets here.'

Anastasia fussed with the Huguenot cross dangling from the chain around her neck. 'Who are you? For what reason are you here? Why do you require money?'

'I won't fritter it away on no strong spirits,' the woman said.

'No, I'm perfectly sober. Been a teetotaller for donkey's years.'

Anastasia reached out her hand and groped for the beggarwoman's wrist. 'You're a heathen, a deceiver, a thief. But I'm not here to judge you. I've come to learn if the Lord has chosen me to develop great powers. The ability to perform Christian magic.'

'So, you're not cross with me?'

'*No*. I'm glad you're here just now. You make me realise why *I'm* here. I've come to learn if miracles are true, if miracles are lies.'

'Capital.'

The rush of footfalls approached from inside the manor house, and from the sound of it, the beggarwoman backed away.

The spiritualist society's front door opened then, and as the odour of dust abated, someone smelling like aged beer— could it be an old woman?—continued outside. 'May I help you?' a voice tinted with sarcasm asked.

Anastasia tapped the tip of her support cane against the heel of her shoe. 'Do you work for the spiritualists?'

'Yes. I'm Miss Lambshead.'

'I'm Anastasia T Grace, and I wish to speak with someone here. It's about a spiritual matter. Or maybe a psychological matter. Or maybe the place where spirituality and mental health overlap or something like that.'

Miss Lambshead did not reply at first. By the sound of it, she darted off down the drive—as if searching for someone.

Left alone in front of the door, Anastasia breathed in the fragrances drifting out from the spiritualist society's residence. The scents seemed to be an admixture of Egyptian chamomile, a touch of wild-mountain tea and some kind of medicinal bouquet including wormwood. *The aromas of Sinai.*

Some five minutes later, Miss Lambshead reunited with Anastasia. 'I'm sorry I left you like that. It's just that we've got a lady pauper lurking on the grounds. All day long, she's been here. And when you knocked a moment ago, I thought for sure it must be her. At any rate, tell me more about what brings you here.'

Her knees wobbling, Anastasia very nearly tripped over an object filled with clinking glass bottles—what must have been an empty milk crate. She blinked her blind eyes and tapped the support cane harder and faster. Then she sneezed, as if the lady beggar must have deposited quite a bit of dust into the air before darting off.

Once more, Miss Lambshead ducked down the gravel drive—as if determined to locate the unwanted mendicant. When she came back, she apologised anew in a slightly high-pitched voice and then ushered Anastasia into the cool of the foyer.

From somewhere down the corridor, a crackly recording of an Old English madrigal played.

What a lovely tune. Anastasia groped for Miss Lambshead's hand and followed her into the parlour room. There, in measured terms, Anastasia related her tale. Afterward, she pleaded with Miss Lambshead to help her to make sense of everything.

At first, Miss Lambshead failed to speak. She only tapped her foot. Had the elderly woman gone lost in thought?

Again, Anastasia groped for Miss Lambshead's hand. 'Please say something.'

In the end, Miss Lambshead spoke of her pen friend—Staff Sergeant Rupert T Lux, a troubled soldier presently serving with the New Zealand Expeditionary Force somewhere about the Sinai Peninsula, of all places.

What a character, too. He had always believed an evil spirit possessed his soul—just as Anastasia had always imagined a diabolical entity lived within her womb. At any rate, as a child growing up in New Zealand, he had reasoned the evil spirit that possessed him must be 'one of the Gods Polynesian'. Apparently, all throughout childhood, he had wavered between the notion the entity might be the primordial sky father or else the god of storms or perhaps even the god of volcanoes. Regardless, in his longing to overcome the culprit once and for all, young Rupert had developed the habit of praying to the star god—the great oceanic deity of healing. His prayers achieved nothing, however. As a consequence, by the time the youth had come of age, he had concluded the entity could very well be the transmigrating soul of a notorious tyrant king from Easter Island. Subsequently, the troubled youth came to believe the strong ocean winds must have propelled the malevolent being across the waters—until that fateful day when the spectre came ashore and slipped into his otherwise healthful psyche.

The late-summer breeze blew through the house now, and Anastasia let the current glide across her face. She longed to imagine the wind had travelled all the way from Sinai— and for no other reason than to implore her to come back to the wilderness and to connect with the strange gentleman from New Zealand. *Do we not belong together?* Surely, they would share countless commonalities. If nothing else, all throughout their lives, they had probably experienced the same tormenting fits of agitation.

Sensually, the late-summer breeze continued to play through her blouse—and now she returned to her feet and let the current guide her over to the windowsill. As she stood alongside the casing, she breathed in the odour of dust and gagged. *Could that dodgy lady beggar be hiding outside? Maybe that peculiar mendicant has something to tell me. What if the lady beggar knows all about the secret origins of evil?* Her face tightening, Anastasia chose to disbelieve the whole idea—for how stale and how commonplace the dusty odour was.

Miss Lambshead drew close, and by the sound of it, clicked her heels. 'Shall I bring you a cup of tea?'

Anastasia shook her head. 'It's wisdom I require.'

Miss Lambshead walked away very quietly and then called for Anastasia to rejoin her on the settee. When Anastasia remained where she was, Miss Lambshead snapped her fingers and pleaded with her. 'Why so aloof?'

With a series of stalling gestures, Anastasia stumbled back. 'Tell me more about your pen friend down there in Sinai.'

Miss Lambshead cleared her throat. 'Someday, I'll write Rupert a letter, and I'll tell him all about you. Maybe he'll agree to meet with you somewhere. Who knows? When the war ends, and we lay down arms, perhaps he'll prove to have the power to convince you the diadem spider was never even inside you. And then you'll do the same for him and convince him no wicked spirit dwells inside *his* person.'

Anastasia rubbed her belly. 'Do you mean to burst forth from my womb?' she asked the entity inside her. 'Do you mean to consume me?'

If the diadem spider were still inside her womb, the creature did not respond. Nor did it gnaw at her.

With the whole of her hand, she tapped her belly hard. 'A diadem spider like you has no conscience, no limits, no impulse to penitence. *None.* If Mother were here, she'd probably say an assailant preys on others only because he's got an empty space inside him, the absence of shame, the absence of remorse. And because of that, the evildoer doesn't have the power to counterpoise whatever monstrous compulsions follow from his animal instincts.'

Once again, if the diadem spider were there, the creature said nothing. Neither did it stretch its legs, nor did it make any kind of movement.

The silence and the stillness made Anastasia doubt herself. *Could something as banal as the absence of shame be the origins of evil?* She clasped her hands together and trembled. *Yes, indeed. Evil must be nothing more than the failure to master one's animal instincts.*

Deep inside, the diadem spider finally moved—as if weaving a silk snare.

~

In the Evening.

Back in the parlour room, Anastasia attempted to ring Fiona— but Miss Lambshead grabbed the handset. 'Anastasia will stay the night,' she said—and then she hung up the telephone.

After dessert, Miss Lambshead guided Anastasia to the grand staircase and stopped at her back. 'Go on,' Miss Lambshead told her. 'Three more steps and you'll be standing at the newel post. When you make it upstairs, I'll assign you a room with a good bed. Come tomorrow, we'll ring your flatmate and send for your things.'

'Do you mean—'

'Yes. From this moment on, you'll live here with us. And you'll be happy. It's like living in a convent.'

Anastasia shook out her arms, rolled her shoulders, and curled her toes. Then she inched forward, groped for the newel post, and took hold of the cool banister. 'I do believe I belong here,' she said over her shoulder.

'Yes, we'll make you into a new person. And I'm sure it'll satisfy.'

'I suppose so. Whoever or whatever I become, I'll be free of the diadem spider.'

Upstairs, she entered her bedchamber and gasped. The room seemed much too quiet, the whole expanse as hushed as an ancient Egyptian tomb.

Miss Lambshead drew close, as if she thought Anastasia's sudden quietude constituted an invitation to intimacy. 'What's wrong?' the elderly woman asked. 'You've got no reason to feel even the least bit apprehensive. In time, we'll address your concerns. Maybe tomorrow we'll administer some tests. And the director should be willing to answer all your questions, and someday soon, he'll help you to determine your charge, your purpose, your future.'

'Tell me. Why does the Lord play such maddening games? Why does He send us dreams and repressed memories and delirium and fears? And when a Huguenot girl prays for salvation, why doesn't He answer those prayers? And even if He has some good reason for not doing so, why doesn't He just come out and explain Himself?'

'Because He *can't*.'

The support cane fell from Anastasia's hand. 'Oh, but He commands the power to do *anything*,' she insisted.

'No, God Almighty can't explain anything. He's too clever for His own good. No daily-breader could ever hope to make sense of His wisdom. That's why God Almighty has no choice but to send us mad dreams and visions. Remember, that's His way of translating the esoteric into ideas a mere mortal might fathom. He plants His ideas deep in our stream of unconsciousness. And all the adversity He sends our way, that's got to be little more than His rather cavalier way of preparing us.'

'Preparing us for our charge?'

'Yes, I think so. He prepares each of us for whatever grand purpose or charge He would have us fulfill. Does that make sense?' Miss Lambshead collected the support cane and guided Anastasia into her bed.

She had little trouble nodding off, no matter the early-evening hour. It had been a long day. *I've got to sleep now.*

In time, a waking dream visited her—and she suddenly believed some kind of villain had stolen into the room. Had the intruder climbed the garden trellis outside, only to slip in through the window?

Anastasia took several deep breaths. 'What're you doing in here?' she asked. 'Did you come to take my money?'

If the intruder were there, the person remained silent.

Anastasia debated whether to call for help. Her intuition told her if she did so, the intruder might very well fall upon her. Gently, she rubbed her belly. 'What should I do?' she asked the diadem spider. 'Do you hear me in there? Tell me what to do. Please.'

The intruder crept over to the other side of the room.

By the time the footsteps stopped, Anastasia had already sat up—all of which proved she had in fact awoken and the present goings-on did not constitute a waking dream. *No. I've got a real intruder here.* She breathed in the scent of dust and rasped. *Yes. I wouldn't be surprised if it's the lady beggar from before.*

On the other side of the room, the intruder seemed to move. Then a soft chime rang out, as if the thief had taken some precious art piece from the bookshelf.

Heavens. Anastasia shuddered. *There must be an empty*

space where the art piece ought to be, an empty space, an absence.
The very thought made her recall a lecture Mother had given
her on her eleventh birthday. *What did she say?*

Mother had spoken about young Anastasia's coming
of age and the fact that, at eleven years, she stood on the
very threshold of womanhood. 'Soon, very soon, any
number of evildoers will be ogling you and doing so with
malice aforethought,' Mother had told her. And Mother
had never doubted it, for even if she had always disbelieved
in such things as dream foxes, she had always dreaded the
antisocial type. Furthermore, Mother must have intuitively
understood the visceral kind of reaction Anastasia's beauty
could potentially conjure.

The intruder crept back across the room now, and
Anastasia's thoughts drifted back to the matter at hand.
'Who's there? Might it be the lady beggar from earlier today?
How did you get inside? Have you got a ladder? You probably
ought to go this instant. If Scotland Yard comes around,
there's no telling what they'll do. I'm sure the spiritualist
society will prefer charges.'

By the sound of it, the thief made it all the way back to
the window. Then the intruder seemed to turn back—toward
the bed.

Anastasia pressed her elbows into her sides and willed
herself to shrink. When nothing happened, her breath burst
in and out.

The intruder's footsteps crept back toward the bed.
'Why'd you come here?' a woman's monotone voice asked.
'Do you mean to serve these wicked spiritualists? Don't do
it. They're a band of confidence operators, nothing more.
Bloody fraudsters, that's all they ever was.'

The muscles in Anastasia's face became slack. She sought

to remember how the lady beggar sounded when she spoke. *Could it be her?*

The odour of dust seemed to grow a touch more intense— just for a moment. Had the lady beggar reached out her hand? For all Anastasia knew, the dodgy woman intended to take hold of the Huguenot cross and pendant dove.

How to let someone purloin something so precious? Anastasia wrapped her palm around the family heirloom.

The lady beggar laughed the way malevolent old women sometimes do. 'You fear I mean to purloin your talisman, eh?'

Anastasia did not answer. Instead, she squeezed her cross and pendant dove so hard it made her heart race.

'I know it's only right you should love your Huguenot ancestry,' the lady beggar said, her tone a touch sultry. 'The fact you're an exile, it proves ought to be something very special in the eyes of the Lord. If you weren't an exile, what kind of big story would you even have? All things considered, you probably got yourself a story as remarkable as the Wandering Jew's tale. Maybe the King of Glory has ordained a great purpose for you.'

Anastasia thought of the diadem spider, let go of the cross and pendant dove, and placed her hands over her belly. 'Go away,' she whispered. 'Do you hear me? There's no reason why a terrible spider like you should be living inside my womb. So, go away this instant. Let me live and learn and acquire my purpose, my calling.'

The lady beggar must have heard and must have assumed that Anastasia feared some imaginary creature dwelling within her belly. With the utmost zeal, the lady beggar reached her long, strong, bony fingers down into Anastasia's mouth and onward down her throat.

Anastasia gagged. *What's this terrible woman doing?*

Anastasia could not breathe. Worst of all, each one of the lady beggar's fingers had an overpoweringly salty, chemical taste—a taste as of lithium oxide. At last, Anastasia kicked— until she slammed her left foot into the footboard.

The lady beggar removed her hand and patted Anastasia's thigh. 'You've got nothing to fear. Whatever you think was inside you, now you'll tell yourself I went and took it and popped it into my own body.'

Anastasia gasped for breath. When she placed her hands back upon her belly, she sought to discern whether anything seemed to be inside her yet. *No, it's not there. The diadem spider, it's gone. I'm sure of it.*

The lady beggar placed her hand around Anastasia's ankle. 'I've got to travel on now, if you don't mind. I'll be gone in the dark.' Without another word, she hastened her escape.

Once the odour of dust dissipated, Anastasia sat up again, took a deep breath and let out a shriek.

Someone raced into the room. 'What's happened?' a voice as of Miss Lambshead's said.

'A thief crept into the room,' Anastasia answered. 'Yes, and I think she took something from the bookshelf.' A moment later, as Anastasia wondered what the missing item might have been, she experienced a kind of epiphany. *The diadem spider, it's no longer inside me.* There could only be one explanation: the intruder had exorcised all her compulsion and hysteria and torment. *Yes, I do believe I'm healed. I'm all alone.*

For the longest time, Miss Lambshead made no movement. 'You look different,' she managed to say then. '*Why?* You seem . . . full of wonder.'

Her neck tipping back, Anastasia touched the contours of her face and sought to picture herself—the quality of awe emanating from her blind eyes. *I'm as strong as any Huguenot ever there was. Yes, I'm something strong and modernistic. Strong enough to conquer any would-be oppressor.*

Miss Lambshead drew closer to the bed. 'I'm quite sure you'll be happy staying with us here. What could be more fun than living with a spiritualist society?' The elderly woman tapped Anastasia's leg. 'Living here, you'll meet others with troubles similar to your own. And before you know it, you'll have plenty of friends. Telepaths, empaths, clairvoyants, too. And I'm sure you'll grow into the greatest one of all. I doubt anyone will feel jealous of you either. I doubt anyone will resent you. No, you'll never be lonely.'

'*Lonely,*' Anastasia whispered. For a moment, she thought of Jack. Then she touched her cross, considered God Almighty, and suddenly realised just how lonely *He* must be. Even if He had a handful of believers, each one would have to be a fool—someone bound to be perplexed by the simplest trespass, the simplest waking dream, the simplest parable.

A NOTE FROM THE

AUTHOR

If you enjoyed this book, I would be very grateful if you could write a review and publish it at your point of purchase. Your review, even a brief one, will help other readers to decide whether they'll enjoy my work.

If you want to be notified of new releases from myself and other Alkira Publishing authors, please sign up to the Alkira Publishing email list. In return you'll get a free ebook of short stories and book excerpts by Alkira Publishing authors. You'll find the sign-up button on the right-hand side under the photo at www.alkirapublishing.com. Of course, your information will never be shared, and the publisher won't inundate you with emails, just let you know of new releases.

ACKNOWLEDGEMENTS

A heartfelt note of thanksgiving to everyone at Alkira Publishing and Literallypr!

Oh, and a very special note of thanksgiving to Jonathan Swift for the use of his poem

'A Satirical Elegy on the Death of a Late Famous General'.

OTHER BOOKS

BY THIS AUTHOR

On the Threshold

Obsessed with solving the riddle of the universe, a
Scotsman named Fingal T. Smyth conducts an occult-
science experiment during which he unleashes a projection of
his innate knowledge.

Fingal aimed to interrogate this avatar to learn what it
knows, but unfortunately, he forgot how violent the animal
impulses that reside in the deepest recesses of the unconscious
mind can be. The avatar appears as a burning man who
seeks to manipulate innocent and unsuspecting people into
immolating themselves.

With little hope of returning the fiery figure into his
being, Fingal must capture his nemesis before it destroys
the world.

Available from all major retailers everywhere. ISBN
Paperback: 978-1-922329-58-5